REIGN OF BRAYSHAW

USA TODAY BESTSELLING AUTHOR

MEAGAN BRANDY

- BRAYSHAW, BOOK 3 -

Copyright © 2019 Meagan Brandy

Reign of Brayshaw
Brayshaw Series, Book Three
Release Date: October 3rd, 2019

Edited by: Ellie McLove, My Brother's Editor
Proofread by: Rosa Sharon, iScream Proofreading Services
Cover Designer: Jay Aheer, Simply Defined Art

Dedication

To the weak, to the strong, to the hopeful.
We are the same.

Thank you for being you.

Synopsis

"Trust only those who earn it."
A sentiment I follow without direction but holds more
consequence than ever before.
One decision, five lives, three futures.
This is what's at stake.
One night, one choice, four broken Brayshaws.
That is where we're headed.
Unless I stop it.
I *have* to stop it.
I have to remind him of what he's chosen to forget.
My town. My choice. *My* ending.

Dear Reader,

Reign of Brayshaw is book three in my Brayshaw series. In order to follow and enjoy this story, you must have read book one, Boys of Brayshaw High, and book two, Trouble at Brayshaw High, as this will pick up where the other left off. Thank you so much for reading!

Find book one and two here:
Boys of Brayshaw High (Brayshaw, book one)
Trouble at Brayshaw High (Brayshaw, book two)

Prologue

"Boy," Ms. Maybell calls, patting the seat beside her on the porch. "Come. Sit."

I listen. I always listen when she asks me to do something, if I don't, she might decide she doesn't want to stay here with us and go away like our moms did, like Dad says he has to soon.

She pulls some candy from her sweater pocket, hands me a piece, and lifts a finger to her lips with a grin. "Don't tell your brothers."

I nod, and quietly unwrap the caramel, popping it in my mouth.

When Ms. Maybell's smile slowly goes away, she turns, looking out at the big trees all around our home.

We asked Dad if we could cut them down once so we could see if there were other kids around who might want to play with us, but he said no, that the trees were there for our protection. Like the high walls to a king's castle, they protect us from others.

Nobody ever comes here.

It was us, our dad, Ms. Maybell, and the guy that loves to drive us around.

Maybe after tomorrow, our first day at a real school, that would be different. We could make more friends and ask them to come over. We could swim or teach them how to play basketball.

When Ms. Maybell sighs beside me, I look up at her.

"Boy," she says quietly. "Have you ever heard the tale of the Wolves?"

I shake my head and she glances my way.

She smiles a little. "You want to?"

"Yes."

She stares at me for a few seconds and I almost wonder if I somehow got candy on my face, but then she starts talking.

"Wolves are fast and strong, they hunt and eat creatures three times their size. In their world, they're the predator." Her eyes slide between mine. "And all others, bigger or smaller, are their prey."

"Really?" I ask, turning all the way toward her. "Did you know we're gonna be wolves, Ms. Maybell? When we get to our school, at Brayshaw High, we'll be wolves!"

"You will," she says quietly, lowering her head to mine.

"Wait, Ms. Maybell, if wolves are predators, and if they're faster and stronger than others who are bigger, does that mean people fear them?" I ask. "Will they fear us when we're wolves?"

"Yes, boy." She nods. "They will, but not *all* will fear you."

"Even though we're the strongest?"

"Yes."

"Why?"

"Because wolves? They don't work alone. They have a helper, one who leads them, helps them to their prey."

"Really?!"

She smiles again but brings her finger to her lips and I clamp my hand over my mouth. "Yes."

"Who?!" I shout in a whisper.

"A bird."

My head pulls back, my nose scrunching. "A bird?" I laugh.

But Maybell doesn't laugh. She nods. "A beautiful, black bird."

"A black bird..." I think out loud, snapping my finger when it comes to me. I look back to Maybell.

"A raven."

"Yes," she whispers. "A raven."

"But... why wouldn't a raven be afraid of a wolf?"

"A wolf may be stronger than a raven, but they need each other. The raven will call on the wolves. Where she flies, the wolves will follow. What she can't touch, the wolves can. Where she's too weak, the wolves are strong."

"So... they're a team?"

"They are." Maybell looks to the sky. "Ravens are very special."

"How?"

"Some say they're godlike creatures."

"That's weird."

She laughs, bumping her arm against me. "Maybe to you, child, but you'll understand it one day." She turns to me then. "One thing to remember about a raven, is they only have one mate in life."

"A mate?" My face scrunches up. "Like a husband or a wife?"

"Yes." Ms. Maybell nods. "Just like that. Once they choose, that's it, for the rest of the raven's life. Then, the two pick a territory where they stay and defend, fighting off all those who are seen as a threat to their home."

"Just like Dad says we will defend ours when we're big."

Ms. Maybell's smile is sad. "Yes, boy, just like that."

"I can't wait to tell my brothers. They'll like this story."

"Oh, I bet they will." She pats my knee, turning to look at me again. "But, it's no story. It's fate, just you wait and see."

Chapter 1

MADDOC

MY FATHER'S EYES TURN A SHADE OF DARK I'VE NEVER SEEN.

All these years we have followed his every move, stood tall with his presence in mind and fought for all he taught us to believe in.

Family are the ones we chose.

Loyalty is given where gotten.

Trust only those who earn it.

His words were engraved into our bones before we even understood the meaning, and we've lived and breathed them ever fucking since.

Only one free pass was ever given, and without realization.

To *him*.

Instinctively, fully. With every fucking inch of who we are we believe in the man standing in front of us.

Bad move on us?

As if sensing my thoughts, our father's eyes tighten with his form.

I swear we stare at each other for a solid five minutes before he so much as blinks.

Finally, he speaks.

"No?" he repeats my last word. Slowly. Cautiously.

Good, he's getting it now.

I don't bother responding. He said Raven is the end, and no damn doubt about it, she is.

But she's *my* end.

My everything.

Above all. Before fucking all.

Raven Carver, or shit, Raven Brayshaw will forever be at *my* side. Period.

"I'm afraid this isn't up for negotiation." He eyes us carefully.

"*I'm afraid* you're dead fucking wrong." Royce pushes forward.

Our dad's eyes slide to him, only to move directly back to me.

"You'd go against me, for the girl?" He gives a mask of anger, but we're his sons, so we see the truth. Nothing but distress and uncertainty stares back.

He has no fucking clue. None. And, how could he? He hasn't been here.

"I don't know what you expected to happen." I give a slow shrug, shaking my head. "We feel like you know who we are, you say you do, but if that were true, we wouldn't be having this conversation." I level him with a hard look. "You may not have known what she became to us, I get none of your watchers could break it down for you in a way to make you understand, it's some next level shit you have to witness up close to fully comprehend. Thing is, though, you've been up close, and you *have* seen, Dad. I know you have.

"You've studied, dissected really, our every fucking move with her. You've caught all of Captain's subtle shifts toward her when he senses she needs to feel him. You see how Royce clings to her, how his anger and need for a real connection drives him where she's concerned, helping him to open parts none of us thought we'd see. We don't even need to talk about me. You're just like I am, you know a possessive asshole when you see one.

"All the shit over the last few months, the way we grew as a unit. Stronger, bolder, fucking braver. She did this. *She* came in and reminded us without even speaking why we want this world. Why this town and lifestyle is important to us. We want what we were born for, Dad, what you groomed us for, the life you earned and promised to us, and we will have it."

"We told you." Cap steps forward. "She's not just some girl, never was, and now we know she was never meant to be." He confirms the answer to our dad's initial question – Raven comes first.

"There's a way around this," I say what I'm one hundred fucking percent sure of. "And I'm bettin' it's a lot less messy than the route we'll take." I look to my brothers a moment before turning back to him. "Tell us what you know. If you don't, we'll find the answers ourselves, even if it means walking through you to do it."

"And you think you're ready to hear it, hm?" he edges, and Royce cuts me a quick glance. "What if it's more than you can handle?"

"We can handle anything." I answer.

He nods, his eyes dropping to the floor before slowly returning to ours.

"There is a way." He speaks slow, a hint of resentment laced in his words. His features harden. "But I can promise you this, when I tell you, it will not serve as motivation. It will be a knowledge you wish you never asked for. The thought of it alone will haunt you at night, I swear it."

The conviction in his voice has the three of us pausing, our eyes briefly meeting before resolve is all that's left.

We're ready.

"Raven stays with us," Royce declares. "Now, tell us what we need to do to make sure this happens."

Our dad pushes to his full height and leisurely walks around his desk. He lowers himself into the leather seat, casually leaning back.

His eyes hold a hardened glare, but his hands lift as if to say *simple*. His words that follow are anything but.

"Give them Zoey instead."

Chapter 2

Raven

I groan, rolling over and slowly peel my eyes open.

The sun has finally set and I blink to refocus.

Slapping my hand beside me, I find Victoria is gone and Maddoc has yet to make his way in.

The second I push up on my elbows, my head starts to pound, my stomach both growling and turning at the same time.

Alcohol and being drugged by a dumb bitch doesn't mix.

I lick my dry lips, cringing at the bad taste in my mouth.

"Uh, fuck."

I toss my blankets off and strip my bed bare – I was sweating like crazy. Thank God Maddoc's not in here, I'm fucking disgusting.

Clammy and queasy, probably have puke in my hair.

Clothes in hand, I drag myself into the hall bathroom, locking the door behind me just in case Daddy Bray is still home and for some reason comes back this way.

Why was he in Maddoc's room?

I sigh as the steaming water hits me, but my body is still so heavy, so I quickly wash my hair, leaving the conditioner in it, and plug the tub.

I've never taken a bath before, but this oversized one is calling my name right now.

The water on my feet is too hot when it's pouring like it is, so I turn down the heat, grab some shampoo and pour it against the running water like you would in a bucket for a carwash. Instantly, the bubbles start forming.

A small grin takes over my lips as I watch it fill, and finally, I lower myself into the warm water.

I reach over, grab a towel from the rack and roll it up behind my head like a pillow.

After a few minutes, the tub is full, so I turn off the water and close my eyes.

Wow. This is the shit.

My muscles instantly start to calm, the tautness vomiting created finally soothing out.

It's simple things like this people from my neighborhood will never experience. Not that this tub is any kind of simple, but still.

Bathtubs, in general, aren't something you find in low-grade trailers. We were lucky to have running water, let alone a working water heater.

A few blocks from the trailer park, where the railroad tracks meet the highway, there's a small truck stop with showers.

The city keeps the water running for the sinks and toilets and things, so a cold shower is free, but you can pay extra for heat. A lot of the people from the park go there to clean up and fill jugs for drinking. Wheeling it back is a pain in the fucking ass, but most have shopping carts or beat up strollers stashed behind their places for shit like that. Of course, cans or random shit found along the way that could potentially bring in money was priority over water.

I smile to myself at the thought of Gio making it out of there.

He was good to me, would hang out in the broken train carts until my mom's louder clients would leave. I would never invite him in, though.

He may have only been older than me by a few years, but that didn't stop her from trying to entice him.

I told her he was gay once when she wouldn't let up, kept trying to convince me it was time for me to 'grow up' — she wanted me fucking my friend at eleven years old — but she said his sexual preference didn't matter, that he was still a horny boy who would love the feel of his dick inside a "fresh vagina." Sick bitch.

Wait...

I try and shake off the thought, but it's useless and already growing deeper.

Ever since the day I started my period in fifth grade, my mother would push and push and *push*, constantly hounding me about being a prude.

She'd tell me to "get it over with already" talking about my virginity, said hanging on to it so tight would only cause me problems later.

She failed to see I wasn't holding on to anything — I was simply a fucking kid who wanted no part of the things I hated her for.

I knew what she was doing, saw people fucking on movies and even on picnic tables or in backseats of cars in our lot.

Grown men would walk out of her room naked, not sparing me a glance — if I was lucky — as they'd come fish a beer or what the fuck ever from the mini-fridge, so I'd seen dick before, pussy, too, for that matter.

I was disgusted by it.

The sounds they'd make, the smells. The way they acted as if my mother was a fucking queen while their wives or husbands sat at home probably wondering where the fuck their partners were. Betrayal and disregard for any and everything around.

So, no. Sex wasn't something I wanted.

For a long time I saw sex as a tool for manipulation, and I had no reason to use it. It wasn't until I was desperate to erase what I knew sex to be, dirty and shameful, painful, that I was interested.

Crazy thing about all the shit popping up, my mom trading me for money in her pocket doesn't surprise me in the least. There were tons of times I thought she would, and honestly, if it didn't offend her when her men would make sleazy comments about me, she probably would have.

Or maybe not since I was technically already owned by another – bought by a rich man who posed as a commoner, who used to bring me ice cream and movies to keep me busy while he spent an hour in my mother's room, supposedly talking about me. A man I knew to be good as far as good went in my world, who gave me my knife for protection before he was gone, only to make his way back into my life as my man's dad eleven years later.

How much more twisted can this shit get?

With a sigh, I sit up and reach for the body wash, but the second I pop it open, my senses are assaulted with the overpowering aroma of coconut and something else as equally disgusting.

I quickly shift to my knees, open the shower door, and lean over the toilet.

My stomach is damn near empty, so liquids and dry heaving it is. A chill runs through my body as sweat beads form at the crown of my head.

Fuck!

I hate this. The shit Donley had Vienna inject me with is taking its day-after toll – one of the many reasons I touch nothing harder than the green.

As soon as I wipe my mouth, I submerge myself under-water and run my hands over my hair, using the bubbles in the water to wash my body off – thank hell the shampoo and conditioner were unscented.

I drag myself from the tub and dress as quick as I can without getting sick again, then drop onto the toilet to brush out my wet hair.

I feel like I got hit by a fucking truck. Still, conversations must be had today.

Maddoc

I SWEAR TO GOD YOU CAN HEAR THE HARD HIT OF OUR PULSES echoing against the high ceiling and bouncing back, wrapping around our throats and cutting off our airways.

Give them Zoey instead.

What. The. Fuck.

My chest aches and I can't even fucking force myself to look at my brother, but I do when he stumbles a bit, falling back and dropping to his ass on the leather ottoman.

His hands slide through his blond hair, coming back to drag down his face. His skin is pulled tight, hands still covering half his face as his tortured eyes hit mine.

My lungs fucking fold, not an ounce of oxygen left to feed my body.

Cap isn't breathing either, his face starting to turn colors, and Royce cusses, quickly dropping in front of him.

He shakes his shoulders, but Cap never breaks my stare.

"Breathe, brother," Royce tells him, his head snapping my way, worry in his eyes when Cap refuses.

Doubt he's hearing Royce right now, he may not even be seeing me, even with his gaze locked on mine.

"Cap," I rasp, and unsure if it was loud enough for him to hear, but suddenly his hands fall, his arms flopping to his sides as his chin meets his chest.

He knows.

He *knows*, never in a million years would we turn our backs on our niece, my brother's daughter, for anything.

For anyone?

My chest stings. I'm pretty fucking sure a knife right through it would hurt less than the realization of what's in front of me.

My baby... or his.

I drag my eyes back to my dad, who now sits forward in his chair, eyes taut and face pained.

"I'm sorry, son. I was hoping you were still simply my boys who would take my word as gold and let me make the move, then allow me to be here for you during the aftermath. I never wanted this to hang over your heads. This is not how it was supposed to be."

"But this *is* what you planned when you brought her here."

He hesitates, but only for a second before giving a curt nod.

"So why not take her straight to them?" I ask.

If he had, we wouldn't know her as we do, wouldn't care who she was or the reason behind any of this shit. It wouldn't matter, Zoey wouldn't be at risk. We wouldn't be standing here cracking on the inside, facing decisions we could never make.

Acid lining my tongue as I say, "I wish you never dropped her here."

"Maddoc!" Royce snaps. "The fuck, man?"

I ignore him. "What's the reason behind all this? Why wasn't she with Graven the second you found out she existed?"

"I was waiting, hoping Collins would find someone else and we'd be clear until the next generation came, worry about it then, bring her home without telling her who she was, watch out for her, offer her a place here, but then..." He trails off, looking toward Captain.

I follow his line of sight, finding Cap staring right at him.

"But then Zoey was born," Cap rasps. "The first female Brayshaw in decades, or so they would have thought."

"Yes, son," our dad whispers. "Everything changed in that moment."

"Tell me the fucking truth," Cap speaks, but his words don't match the defeat in his tone. "Did you do this? Did you have a hand in Mallory giving her away, hiding her from me? Are you the reason I almost lost my daughter completely?"

My head snaps toward our dad.

"No, son." He shakes his head slowly. "I knew nothing about her until you hired our men to watch out for her. As soon as I learned, I brought in Maria. I made sure she was the one who would care for her. I knew she was the only person whom I could trust with my granddaughter, if not us or Maybell."

Cap shoots to his feet. "Maria Vega, you know her? She's good? She's... she's safe?"

"You had her checked out, have had her watched. You know this, Captain," he tells him.

Cap slams his palm against his desk, dipping into his face. "I know what I'm told. I don't know the truth. We know better than anyone, anything could happen behind closed doors."

"If you really believed that, son, you never would have put her back in her car."

"Say it," Captain demands.

He relents. "She is safe, loved, and will be very much missed by that woman once we bring her home."

"And when will that be?" Cap pushes.

Our dad winces, his eyes hitting mine briefly and I drop my chin to my chest before meeting Cap's stare.

This is why the decorator thought she'd be preparing the room across from Captain's for Zoey – it would be empty for her.

"Madman," Royce whispers and Cap's eyes tighten.

"No..." he whispers, shaking his head, eyes pleading and completely fucking wrecked.

He loves her like I do. They both do.

I give a small nod, gut twisted and tight. "She can come home when Raven is delivered."

No one speaks for several minutes, but it's the loudest silence we've ever suffered.

Our dad is the first to break it.

"Do you understand now, why she must go? Why I had to bring her here now? Why I could no longer protect her by keeping her away?" our dad asks.

Royce scoffs. "Man, don't start with the protecting her bullshit. If you really cared, you'd have sent someone there to guard her."

"You think I didn't try?" He narrows his eyes. "I sent many people, but Raven trusted *no one*, no matter what role I tried to place them in her life."

"'Cause she's fucking smart," he throws back. "Still could have had someone making sure she was fucking fed, something—"

"She had that Gio guy," Cap interrupts. "I'm bettin' he didn't end up with the Riveras by accident. Why not set him up there, have him pull her in more?"

"I thought about it, though I'm not sure it would have even worked."

16

"Why?" I ask.

"For one, he was her friend, yes, but she still held back. And two, kids like them don't pin against each other when outsiders ask, not even for money. They'll take it, then show their loyalty to each other," he says. "I couldn't afford curiosity from either of them. As far as where he is, no, he didn't. I led Trick Rivera, Oakley's father, to Gio after I saw and decided his character was pure." Our dad looks across us. "The only person we saw Raven grow a liking to outside of him, was her last principal. He would have looked out for her but leaving her there was no longer an option. Collins learned she existed, and he was determined to find her. Our only move left was to bring her here, throw her in with the other girls and hope he didn't figure out who she really was."

My brothers and I share subtle looks. We're not fucking stupid – he's hiding something.

He had to bring her here, fine. He had to protect Zoey, good.

So, why not take her straight to Graven?

"I am not the villain here, boys. I was simply protecting my family. She was never supposed to be expendable. I was saving her for one of you, I planned to bring back the power having someone from the bloodline provided, but I had to make a rash decision and I chose my granddaughter." He shrugs, unapologetically. "Had I explained this to you in the beginning, we wouldn't be having this conversation. She never would have set foot in this home, and she'd be at Collins' side already. You'd have agreed in a heartbeat."

"This is what Collins meant when he kept telling her she didn't belong with us. He knew she was meant to be his," I growl.

"You put her in the Bray house to try and distract them." Captain frowns. "How did they figure out the new girl was Raven?"

"Besides the striking resemblance?" our dad asks, his tone off, softer than normal. "People searched for Ravina, their runaway princess, for years. Many believed she was killed, others thought she was locked in a dungeon somewhere..."

"Someone saw her," Cap offers.

I look to him then back to our dad. "She told Raven she couldn't be in this town long. She knew people would spot her."

He nods. "It was the first time she set foot here in eighteen years."

"Let's back the fuck up a minute," Royce snaps but his shoulders fall. "Raven... what do we do? I mean we can't..." He trails off, licks his lips and looks away.

"We can't tell her," Captain stresses, his eyes hitting mine.

"Cap." I glare. "Don't."

"I'm serious." He steps in front of me, pleading eyes and fucking all. "Maddoc, we can't."

"Cap, we can't keep this shit from her, man." Royce steps closer, but his tone disagrees, and his next words prove it. "I mean, can we?"

"Graven made a move on her," I tell them, filling them in on the bit they missed when Cap went after Perkins. "Donley drugged her, and he got a girl from our fucking group home to do it. He had a doctor waiting, pulled Raven's fucking pants off, and stuck shit inside her, checked her. They could have done worse. She needs to know."

Captain's temple ticks. "If you tell her, she will be gone quicker than you can fucking run."

My head draws back, my jaw locking shut a moment. "She won't run from me," I growl.

He gives a slow, mocking nod, eyes widening. "I know, brother, trust me, I fucking *know* what she'll do. So do you. Don't refuse to accept it."

"Fuck!" Royce shouts and starts pacing, dragging my attention to him. Hands folding over his head, his beaten eyes smash into mine. "She's too fucking loyal, brother," Royce whispers and it hits me. "Too fucking loyal to sit back and do nothing."

My face pales, my eyes slicing to my dad's.

He gives a rueful smile. "She didn't grow up here, yet she embodies who we are. She is Brayshaw by blood, at heart and will. She'll do whatever it takes to save one."

My facial muscles constrict to the point of pain, an instant pounding in my head taking over and dulling my vision.

I swallow, dropping against my dad's desk, fucking struck for the first time I can remember.

"Nothing we say will matter, no move will make a difference. She'll go to them willingly."

Royce turns to our dad. "We need time. Can you make it happen?"

Regret washes over his face, his stare quickly cutting to Cap before returning to Royce. "There is nothing you can do, son."

"Just fucking try to delay!" he yells, his moves growing frantic. "Can you do this for us or not?!"

"It will delay Zoey's homecoming," he says.

We look to Captain who gives a tight, instant nod.

"Delay, not prevent," Cap rasps, looking away. "We have to try. We owe it to Raven."

I keep Cap's eyes on me, masking my face as they shift, reassurance and promise now staring back at me. His eyes beg me to see what he won't say.

What do you know, brother?

Our dad nods. "I'll cancel the meeting I set with the other families, but we can't avoid Donley forever. He wants to collect what his family is owed, and I can't promise they'll stay away. Collins knows she's to be his and he likely won't be quiet about it."

"So it's settled." Captain makes sure to meet and hold our

eyes, our dad's too. "Raven can't know she's promised to Collins."

"Wow."

All our heads whip around to find her in the doorway, arms crossed, glare on me.

Fuck.

Chapter 3

RAVEN

PROMISED TO COLLINS.

What the hell?

As in, what, an arranged marriage?

What is this, the fucking stone ages?

The boys' uncharacteristic silence has unease swimming in my gut, but I refuse to allow Rolland to see it, so I put a foot forward and walk in the room, glancing around the office I've never set foot in before today.

It's everything you'd expect from a rich man's private space, thanks to stereotypical movies and magazines.

Bourbon in the corner, textbooks from the floor to ceiling that have probably never been read, but someone takes the time to dust so it seems they aren't for decoration. Cherry wood and leather all around, a golden cased globe at the edge of the desk and box of cigars on the other.

I could roll my eyes right now it's so unoriginal. Nice and expensive, but unoriginal.

I drop onto the ottoman, cross my legs and lift my hands as to say *lay it out for me* but nobody says a damn word. They stand there frozen.

"So, we're back to keeping secrets now, are we?" I ask, arching a brow.

Rolland sits up. "This is Brayshaw busi—"

I start laughing, cutting him off and Rolland's eyes narrow. Mine follow.

"In that case, why don't you spell it out for me real slow, Rolland, so I can soak it in."

"Just because you—"

"Stop," Royce barks. He shifts, stepping toward him. "You don't get to insult her to save face right now. You fucked up. Own it. It's not her fault who her mother is."

The crease in Rolland's forehead intensifies, and he sits forward, so I do the same.

"Raven," he starts. "You've come to learn pieces of your life you didn't know existed, but you don't know everything yet. Right now, we'll require you to do as asked while we work out some things."

"Like how you plan to get me to agree to jump ships?"

His head tips to the side the slightest bit, the vein in his neck, much like the one in Maddoc's, pulsing against his tan skin as he attempts to read me.

"You're trying to come off authoritative, but I've never been one to listen, so all you're doing is irritating me. Not that you care, but I think you're a lying piece of shit, Rolland. You may not be able to read me, but I can you and it's obvious you're giving half-truths, not the full thing.

"I only caught the tail end of the conversation, but I can tell by the struck look on their faces this is far more than a pass off. Still, I guarantee there're missing pieces and you won't give them until you absolutely have to, when it serves *you* best." I push to my feet and glare down at him. "That's one way of being a shitty leader, allowing your *men* the chance to be taken off guard. Again."

Their eyes are on me, but I completely ignore the boys, who have yet to volunteer any information.

That's okay, though. I'm not mad at them for it, I trust their reason for the silence they're giving me. It doesn't mean I won't find the answers myself, even if I have to be a sneaky bitch to make it happen.

"And you think you're strong enough to give full disclosure where disclosure is needed?" Rolland challenges.

"You think they're too weak to handle it?" I throw right back. "Or maybe your fear comes from the unknown. Maybe, the things you know will shake your world up a little more than you're willing to allow."

"Don't assume to know all there is to know about me."

"Don't assume I'll let you decide a damn thing for me," I spit right back. "Collins Graven can go fuck himself, but careful, asshole, or you'll be right there with him."

With that, I turn and walk out.

And damn if they don't let me.

Maddoc

FUCK!

Royce flashes for the door, but Captain slides in front of him, halting his advance.

Royce whips around to face me, throwing his arms out. "You really not gonna go after her, what if she dips right fucking now?"

"She didn't hear everything."

He gives a humorless laugh. "No, she didn't, other than the fact that she's the future Mrs. Fuckhead Graven! Oh, and we're fucking hiding something from her!"

"It's the only way."

"I fucking know, man! But that doesn't mean she won't leave us because of it! We said no more secrets, no more solo moves. This shit? This is what leads her to go all Raven."

The panic in his eyes causes a cramping to shoot through my chest. Her leaving wouldn't only wreck me, it would fuck us all.

I walk to him and hold his glare with mine, my hands firmly grasping onto his shoulders. "Royce. She will *not* fucking leave us again, not like this, *not* without solid reason and fact. She almost lost us too this last time. She won't risk it again, not without complete fucking assurance."

"She won't even be mad at us," Cap whispers, over-whelmed. "That's not who she is." His glare moves to our dad and mine follows.

Shame washes over his face, tightening his features as he looks to Royce, realizing the distress this is causing him. He looks to Cap next and holds his stare, and I'd swear regret fills his eyes next.

What was that?

Finally, his stare comes back to mine.

"This wasn't a contract I made," he says quietly. "I was just a kid, running deals and trades back then, proving myself. Raven's grandfather is the one that set this up. He only had a son, who married a gold-digging junkie, and the two had Ravina. They both died along the way from drugs and Ravina was left in his care.

"He called up Donley, put Ravina on the table for his top man to take. Donley only wanted it if she was in love with the man, he wanted an amicable marriage – a *real* marriage, not one for show – between the families, so he added the clause that Ravina, on her own and without influence, agree. It was his way of assuring it wasn't a move against his people.

"His boys and ours, Ravina included started going to the same parties and functions. They were allowed at Bray events at the school. Everyone started making friends with everyone and things looked good for the town. Peace among us all."

That explains the photo in the yearbook.

But, wait a fucking minute...

"Top man to take," I repeat, stepping forward. "Are you telling me Felix Graven wasn't Donley's son, that Collins isn't Graven blood?"

Our dad nods. "Felix Graven wasn't Graven at all, he was a runner between families."

"An outsider."

"He chose them?" Royce asks.

"In the end, yes, but I believe it was simply because he's the one she fell in love with. All he had to do at that point was accept the position. Like I said, he was a nomad, stayed out of both the families' ways but thrived in our town. With Graven, he would be the lead. His decision was instant."

"Why were we not told this shit?" Royce shouts, angrily.

"At the end of the day, it's irrelevant. He was Graven, his son Graven, just as you three are Brayshaw. We live by the name, the name is who we are."

"What happened with Ravina and the marriage, did she not want it?" Cap gets us back on track.

"Oh, Ravina wanted the marriage," Dad scoffs. "She wanted to be waited on and showered with gifts and praised for her beauty. She didn't get that at home, she had unlimited income, but was invisible to her grandfather, and our love for her, mine and both your fathers" —he nods toward my brothers— "wasn't enough for her. She didn't believe in our feelings, thought we cared because we were forced to being, we

25

were men of Brayshaw, but that was so far from the case. She wouldn't hear it though.

"Felix Graven, however, was desperate to have her, and he let her know it at every turn. He was a few years older, so he used that appeal to win her over. I said he didn't hesitate to take the offer once he had her heart, and he didn't, even left his *pregnant* fiancée to be with her and without a second thought."

"Collins' mom?"

"Yes. He didn't hesitate to decide, was willing to throw his unborn son away if it meant he got to marry Ravina."

"He was obsessed with her." Royce frowns.

"He was *in love* with her." Our dad's eyes cloud with memories. "She was as captivating as her daughter. People fell at her feet from a simple smile. Only it wasn't just her beauty. She was kind, forgiving. *Good.* Untouched by greed." He looks to me briefly. "Untouched by a man."

A virgin Brayshaw.

He continues. "Ravina had an innocent soul once, very much a contrast of her daughter in that sense. Raven was born jaded, but Ravina, she was turned that way."

"You have to know Raven isn't a virgin."

He nods. "Collins wants her regardless."

"Is that his call? That's not what they were promised."

"A fact Donley doesn't seem concerned with this time around."

"So what happened?" Royce asks, irritated, getting us back on track. "Ravina changed her mind last minute?"

With a deep sigh, he says, "The wedding was planned for her eighteenth birthday. In the time leading up to it, Ravina spent much time with the Graven family, felt she loved Felix deeply, but, as I mentioned, he was a little older, so their schedules would clash. He had Graven business and she had school. Felix hated leaving her behind, so much so he arranged for someone to keep her company. There was only one person in his life who he trusted with his untouched bride, someone who was still a student like her." His eyes move between ours. "A Brayshaw High student."

"Who?"

He stands, sliding his hands in his pocket as he meets our eyes. "His brother."

Raven

I HIT THE LITTLE BUTTON ON CAP'S KEYS TO UNLOCK HIS SUV and quietly slip out the front door, making my way to it. I dig around in the back seat, not finding Perkins' damn business card I took from the limo, but only a second empty envelope identical to the one that was left for me.

That's how they found out, Donley went to them too.

Asshole.

I tiptoe back into the house and up the stairs, going straight for Cap's room.

I rummage through dirty jeans pockets and come up short, but the second I pull open his bedside drawer, I spot the edge of it, sticking out of the side of his notebook.

I freeze.

Cap's been writing in this thing a lot.

Maybe their secret is in there?

I reach for it, but the second my fingertips brush over the cool leather covering, guilt slices through me.

They don't allow people into this home because they can't trust their intentions. This is their safe place, hence the journal sitting right there for anyone to find.

I can't destroy their only place of peace.

I hurry back to my room, only then pausing in thought.

Why would Captain hold onto that card?

He has to know it was dropped there by me, his brothers would have shared their reasoning for having it if it were theirs.

Maybe he plans to ask me about it?

It would be one thing if it were in his discarded pants pockets, like he picked it up to throw it out or something, but secured in his bedside drawer and settled between the pages of what might be his deepest thoughts... or dirtiest desires, who knows. Still. Why?

He's been so on edge lately, and Perkins has been one of the many root causes for it. I mean, shit, he beat on him just yesterday!

Cap knows something, and I'm going to find out what it is.

Chapter 4

Maddoc

She's in bed by the time I make it upstairs, but she isn't sleeping. She's drawing circles with her flashlight against the ceiling, not bothering to look my way when she hears me come in.

As soon as I lock her door, the flashlight clicks again, and suddenly it's pitch black.

My frown is instant – she's closed her curtains.

Her deep inhales and exhales give her away, she's doing all she can to control her fear of the dark.

I kick off my shoes, drop my jeans and shirt, and climb in beside her.

I reach for her flashlight, and she allows it, but says, "Don't turn it on."

"Why not?"

"Because I don't feel like staring at your face while you lie to mine."

Ah, fuck.

I slide my arm under her pillow, tugging her closer to me.

"How about I say nothing then, so I don't have to lie?"

She scoffs. "Man, not even a hint of uncertainty, like you know for sure keeping me in the dark like this is what's best."

"It is."

"For who, Big Man?"

I pause at that and a dejected laugh leaves her.

Her head shakes against the pillow. "Have we not already proven holding out on each other is the worst of options?"

Neither of us speaks for a few minutes, both lost in thought when she starts again.

"You know what I'm realizing about fear?" she asks but doesn't wait for a response. "It holds us back, takes away our power. You, Big Man, you never had a reason to lie to me, and now you do."

I frown into the dark room. "And what's my reason?"

"You're afraid," she says simply and my muscles tense against her. She pulls the flashlight from my hands, tossing it to the floor. "And if there's something big enough to scare *you*... then it must revolve around me."

She looks up, and now that my eyes have adjusted to the darkness, I can make out the shape of her face, spot the worry I sensed in my gut the second I walked in here.

"I told you," she whispers, her fingers coming up to graze across my lips. "I warned you. Love? It makes you weak."

I shake my head, roll over and climb on top of her.

Her legs fall open for me and I settle between them. I bring my lips to hers, running my palm down her thighs, and her knee lifts to rest against my ribcage.

"You've got it all wrong, baby. Loving you doesn't make me weak. It makes me unstoppable." I drop my hips against her, and her hands come around, her fingertips spanning across my shoulder blades as she guides me closer. "*Nothing* and *no one* will ever have the power or strength to step between me and you." I run my nose along her jaw. "No one."

"The fact that those are the words you chose tells me someone will try." She grips my chin bringing my eyes back to hers. "Tell me what to do."

"Give me all you've got, always," I whisper, grinding against her and her head pushes into the pillow. "Think of me first. Come to me first. *Come* for me only. Can you do that?"

Her forehead tightens with concern, but she whispers, "Yes."

I free myself from my boxers and push her thong aside, positioning the head of my dick right against her heated pussy. I push the tip in and her legs pull up, wrapping around me.

Her fingernails dig into my back as I fill her, and make slow, short pumps.

"Maddoc?"

"Hm?" I drop my head beside hers, my lips on her shoulder.

"What if it's not enough?"

"What you give will never be enough, Raven. I'll always want more." I groan as she starts rolling her hips into me, begging me to do what she knows only I can. "Love me, baby, and we'll be unstoppable together."

A moan leaves her, and she pushes on my chest.

I let her roll me over and climb on top, but she doesn't want it like this, she wants to feel all of me.

"Sit up," she demands, keeping me inside her, but moving her legs behind me.

I do as my baby tells me and she slides even farther down my shaft, making my thighs clench. My hands fly to her ass, pushing her into me, squeezing, spreading.

Her head falls back and my mouth drops to her throat, moving when she whips her shirt off and tosses it somewhere behind her.

With her hands on my shoulders, she starts riding, the curve of her back pulling her ass in and out, in perfect forward motions.

I lean forward, sliding my teeth across her nipples and she whimpers, her pussy twitching against me, and I groan, my self-control snapping.

I keep her on me, but scoot so my feet are on the ground, sitting straight up on the bed.

She gives a husky laugh, lifting her head, as one hand slides up to cup the back of my neck.

"My man, never one to give up power for too long."

I lift her little body, moving her how I want to, and her legs wrap behind me, her long black hair falling around her, chest to chest, mouth to mouth.

"You're so fucking sexy, baby. So fucking beautiful."

She gasps when I hit the spot she loves, her grip on me tightening, her lips pushing into mine.

She holds my eyes. "And *so* fucking yours," she moans, her tongue slipping between my lips quickly.

I groan, sliding a hand between her ass cheeks, using my middle finger to apply pressure as I pull her closer.

That wasn't a question, and yeah, it's something I already know – she is mine – but to hear her say it just now, after the few fucking days we've had... I could come right now.

"And that."

I speed up, and she pulls her legs back around so she's on her knees. With my feet on the floor and her knees beside me, our fucking grows wild, hard, and fucking needy, both of us desperate to come while holding off, not ready to let go yet.

Hard, wet, slaps can be heard around the room, probably in the fucking hallway, but I don't give a fuck.

Her moans grow louder, my groans grow deeper and finally her teeth sink into my bottom lip and she starts to shake against me.

I flip her onto her back, drag her pussy to the edge of the bed and slam into her, forcing the orgasm to hit harder and her legs fly to my sides, clamping tight, but I force them open again and her hand moves between her legs.

I let her rub herself, but only so I can watch while I come hard inside her. My grip on her thighs is likely leaving a nice little bruise, but she'd never complain.

She wants all of me like I demanded all of her.

She reaches for me when I finally stop twitching, so I pull out, climb back on the bed and tug her up to the pillows with me.

When our breathing slows, she starts tracing my tattoo.

I know she's curious as to the reason I got it and the meaning behind the four tethered ropes, but she'll have to ask. And she will.

I wrap my arms around her and she exhales.

After a few minutes, her hand stops moving, her breaths even out, and I know she's fallen asleep, in my arms where she belongs.

That's when it starts, the thoughts I shouldn't have and would never give in to, the ones that make me sick to my stomach.

The ones my dad warned us about.

It would be so damn easy.

One call is all it would take... to destroy my brother's world and save mine.

Guilt eats at my conscience, keeping me awake all night in the process.

Chapter 5

RAVEN

"She is debased" the words of the doctor, who laid me out in Donley Graven's limo, have been turning in my mind, over and over again since Rolland's accidental revelation last night.

My mother was from here.

Shit, not just from here, she was Brayshaw.

Before Rolland talked with the boys, he hinted at something, and now it makes more sense. He'd said if I wanted to blame someone, to blame my mother for her inability to keep her legs closed until her wedding night. So, I can only assume she was once standing where I am.

'Course, in true Ravina style she fucked something up along the way.

Did she know a Graven would eventually come asking me questions?

Why the fuck would she care?

I frown at nothing.

Nothing makes fucking sense!

My mom was Brayshaw but ran away. A Graven drugged me, poked and prodded – literally – and then simply let me go like the shit he pulled was normal, like he was untouchable and allowed to do with me as he may.

He's not and he can't.

"Hey."

I glance over my shoulder when Captain speaks, pulling me from my thoughts.

He looks like shit, restless.

"What's up?"

"You and Maddoc talk last night?" he asks.

I set my hoodie on the bed and turn around with a frown. "No, Cap. He didn't suddenly decide to betray your trust by filling me in where I've been left out."

His eyes fall and instantly I feel like shit.

With a heavy sigh, I start, "Sorry, I'm extra cranky being up so early today, my head's still fuzzy, and I haven't had a maple bar in a few days now, think I'm feening," I joke.

His lips tip up and he slowly brings his eyes back to mine.

So much sadness...

Cap pokes his head into the hall, and then steps all the way in, gently closing the door behind him, and my pulse starts kicking.

"Cap."

"You saw the card in my drawer."

Well, shit.

Did I not put it back exactly the way it was?

I nod.

"Do you want to know why I kept it?"

I drop onto my mattress, shaking my head. "Come on, Packman. This is a game me and you play well. You *know* I do, but I'm gonna need you to volunteer the information. You have to want to talk shit out." I shrug.

He sighs and walks over, bending his knees once he's in front of me, bringing us eye level. "You'd ask Maddoc."

"Eh, I like him when he's angry." I laugh and Cap chuckles

with me. "No, but for real. I'd ask Maddoc because that's how he likes it. He wants me to push him, so I do. You though, Cap, I can't ask because while I wish you could share things, you're not ready to yet and I'm sure you have a reason. You're smart, the logical one of the bunch. I trust you."

"You shouldn't," he rushes out instantly, and I pull back. "Raven, don't let me ruin your life."

I draw farther away from him. "What are you talking about?"

A pained expression covers his face and he runs his hands across it, but it doesn't wipe it away.

"I'm trying, so fucking hard, not to betray everyone closest to me, but it's only been hours since I knew how to fix what's broken in my world and already I'm losing control. I feel like I might snap at any moment," he admits, shame and self-hate seeping from every word.

Shit. What the hell is going on? What the fuck am I supposed to say?

I go with the same thing I did Maddoc, in different words. "Tell me what you need from me, Cap."

"Push back. Accept nothing as the final word, fucking fight." Footsteps on the stairs have both of us looking toward the door briefly and then at each other again. "We were born *for* Brayshaw, but you, Raven, you *are* Brayshaw. Use that power if you have to, even if in the end, it's against us."

"I..." *What the hell?* "No."

"Raven," he croaks, stepping in a little. "Please."

"Not happening." I hold strong. "If there's something so serious coming, something that'll pin me against you for real, any of you, I won't be a part of it. I can't."

"You can."

"No." I stand, frowning down at him. "I *can't*. I physically can not. I have never cared about another person in my life, Captain. I don't even really know how, but I'm learning, and the last thing I'd do is turn my back on the first people to mean a damn thing to me. Me or one of you, it's you guys. Always. That's how this works."

"Raven—"

"Stop. You act like you three don't have the same way of thinking. I know what you'd do for me, you need to accept what I'd do for you. I love you, Captain. I love Royce. And Maddoc..." My throat grows suddenly dry, the words settling into my soul. Refusing to be buried any longer, they fight for a way out for the first time.

I love him. Completely.

I swallow, giving him my full truth. "I'd fall in an instant if it meant you guys stood strong."

He jumps to his feet, the angry glare on his face taking me off guard. "That's the point, Raven," he growls, blue eyes cloudy from a clear lack of sleep. "We can't be strong without you, not anymore. You fall or leave, turn your back on us, we're seconds behind. We'll fucking crack, Raven. Stop thinking you're worth less than we are. You're a part of us."

"So... it sounds like one by one we all fall." I pop a shoulder, at a loss when I don't even know the cost or what the hell he's talking about. "Who does that leave standing, Cap?"

His face falls in an instant, like he just realized the outcome to whatever reality is playing out in his mind. "Shit."

He turns toward the door, pausing to look at me over his shoulder. "If I told you to leave this alone, to stay away from Perkins and the Gravens..."

"I'd say something like *kiss my ass.*"

He scoffs a small laugh, making me grin.

Before he can grab the knob, it turns and opens, both Royce and Maddoc standing on the other side.

Maddoc instantly frowns, sensing the tension the same way Royce reads it in our expressions.

Royce snaps his head toward Cap, accusation in his glare, while Maddoc keeps his locked on me.

"What's going on?" he asks.

"Oh, you know. Secret sharing." I can't help but come across a little sour.

It's not that I want them to feel like shit or for them to spill their guts, it's more how I know, if at this point in our relationships, they have to keep something from me it has to be something real shitty. I admit, the thought makes me a little nauseous.

Royce exhales as he stares hard at his brother, he's pissed. Realization sets in, then he looks at me. "He wants you to fight us, doesn't he?"

I look at Maddoc who cuts his stare to Captain.

"Cap?" he snaps.

Captain's eyes squeeze shut a moment. When they open again, he looks at me briefly before focusing on his brothers.

"She was right last night, and we know it. We're missing fucking pieces, and if my intuition is correct, they're big ones. Face it, brother, all she'll have to do is ask the right people and they'll be dying to fill her in on what we do know. We can't not be prepared for her to figure all this out before us, and if she does..." He trails off, looking to me with miserable eyes as he reaches out to capture my hand and squeezes. "Then we need her to battle it out."

My eyes drop to the contact as unease fights its way in.

They're standing here, talking like I'm not right beside them, worry and anger and flat-out fucking uncertainty written in all their eyes.

My mind races.

These boys, they're all about protecting their own, and outside everyone in this room – their dad doesn't count – there's only one other person I'm aware of who would evoke this type of reaction from them.

My stare snaps up to Cap's and my teeth clench. He said *his world.*

Zoey.

The lines on Cap's forehead become more pronounced, his grip grows subtly tighter and I know he knows.

Maddoc's harsh exhale and Royce's whispered "fuck" tells me they do too.

"Is she in danger?" I ask, anger vibrating through every bone in my body. "Tell me now."

Cap starts to shake his head but hesitates a moment, then continues.

"Say it, Captain. Stand here and tell me she's safe."

"She's safe, I swear it."

The way his words trail at the end has my frown intensifying. "But she's at risk?"

His eyes fall, unable to meet mine, his tone sure and steady as he says, "She will never be at risk, Raven. Ever."

I nod, some of the strain in my body easing, but it only grows tighter when Royce then adds, "That's sort of the problem."

My eyes slide to his. "How?"

"We can't allow her to ever be in danger, we have to protect her."

"As you should."

"At all costs." Royce rasps, moving his stare to Maddoc's.

Mine follows.

Pure anger lines his face, sharpening his already sharp edges, hardening his already hard eyes.

A soldier's strength in a king's body.

Maddoc's eyes laser in on mine.

The cost?

Chapter 6

MADDOC

Cap's hand leaves hers the second my body moves forward.

She stands taller, her game face slipping into place, but that shit won't work right now.

I'm in her space in one step, but before a single word leaves my mouth, three fly from hers.

"I love you."

I freeze, my pulse drumming harder in an instant.

She cautiously lifts her fingers, trailing them across the ticking vein in my jaw. "*I love you*, Big Man. I don't know why," she says as if she's honestly confused.

The corner of my mouth tips up and my brothers' low chuckles come from behind me.

"But I do," she continues with a shrug. "You can ask or demand I stay a sitting duck, but I won't even pretend to listen. I wanna puke right now at nothing but the thought of something – or someone – trying to take you from me. You, Maddoc, whatever your middle name is, Brayshaw" —another round of chuckles— "are mine. The only person allowed to take you from me *is* me."

At her words, my chest caves with the pressure of the fucking world.

She has no clue, but that's exactly what it would be, if she found out.

Fuck, who am I kidding, *when* she finds out.

She'll take herself from me, to save my family the way she thinks we need saving, to protect my niece.

Would I let her or betray my brother instead?

Neither option is a fucking option.

I'd never turn my back on my brothers, and I'll never let them have her.

My head starts to pound as I look at her. My dad said Ravina had to accept the marriage, so Raven will have to do the same. She will when she finds out it's her or Zoey.

She'd do anything for us.

So damn selfless. So fucking strong. So mine.

For now?

As if reading my thoughts, her features pull, so I quickly wrap my arm around her waist and tug her closer. I run my lips across hers, but she's feelin' vexed, and bites mine.

"You could try to take yourself from me, but I'll tell you right now it won't fucking work." I shift to squeeze her hips. "And I love you too, baby."

"Yeah, almost as much as I do," Royce throws over my shoulder and a laugh bubbles out of her, her eyes shifting to the ceiling before she steps back.

She studies the three of us, but before anything else can be said, the front door opens and closes, and our dad's voice echoes up the stairs.

"Boys, Raven. I need a few minutes of your time before school!"

Raven's frown is instant, and my brothers look to me.

With a curt nod, Royce turns and leads us out, but Raven grabs my wrist, keeping me back.

Her glare intensifies, but I let her get her look, search for whatever it is she feels the need to find.

She lets go, stepping past me, so I wrap her up by the waist and bury my face in her neck.

"Me and you, baby," I remind her, nipping at the soft skin there.

She drops her head back a split second before pulling away.

We meet my brothers at the landing, our dad a few feet away, balanced on the edge of the couch.

He takes in Royce and Captain's wide feet and squared shoulders and the slight edge forward I have over Raven, who stands beside me, chin held high.

Discontent clouds his eyes but it's gone with a single blink, his focus on Raven in the next second.

"I've had Ravina's old account unlocked and switched over to you. Everything from your grandfather's personal account has been transferred into it, along with fifty-one percent of all Bray earnings from the day I discovered you existed to last month. It's calculated and dispersed monthly, so you'll see a fresh deposit by the fifth of every month." He holds out an envelope and her muscles lock at the sight – same shape, size, and color of the one Donley gave her. "Few papers need signed by you. Your card and some on-hand cash are in here."

She shakes her head. "I don't want your money."

"This is your money. I have my own." He lowers his hand, gauging her.

"I don't want it," she refuses.

He pushes to his feet and all three of us naturally inch closer to her. He doesn't miss the move, and anger tightens his eyes.

He calms himself. "It belongs to you. You *will* take it."

"Yeah, and how do you plan to make me?" She bounds forward, and I quickly slide between her and my dad, blocking him from her view.

She looks up at me, so fucking feisty. Testiness burns in her eyes but the more she stares at mine, the more it eases, and a small smirk finds her lips. She gives a bratty blink, so I step back.

My dad's questioning gaze moves from me to her.

"Look," she starts, calmer this time.

He stands a little taller, thinking he's got her, but he doesn't know Raven.

"I'm not intentionally pushing you at every fucking corner, but you keep throwing stupid shit my way. I need you to chill out a little, especially with this stuff. It's ridiculous. I won't take the money from a man I never knew and who never even knew I existed. It's not right. You knew him. He trusted you enough to hand this all over in the first place, so it's yours."

His brows draw in, but not in anger. "That's not how this works, Raven. It *belongs* to you."

She shrugs, her brows lifting. "Yeah well, I'll sign it over or whatever if you're worried about logistics."

He stares at her, a little in awe, a little in shock, while Cap and Royce wear soft smiles, and me, the organ in my fucking chest beats like crazy.

She's fierce despite her weak mother.

Loyal despite her inability to trust.

Honest even when it hurts her.

She's Brayshaw even though she had no idea what it meant to be one.

With zero guidance or push.

She proves it more and more every day.

Our dad slowly steps closer. "I will not take something I am not owed."

Raven lifts her chin, her long, dark hair brushing against my wrists. "Which is why you paid for me, yeah?"

"I agreed to pay for you because I thought, in giving her money, it would provide a more stable life for you when I knew it wasn't time to bring you home," he snaps. "I didn't know she would blow it all on drugs and more. I have no idea how she could have possibly gone through so much. She not only got money from me, but the state, and, of course, her clients. Yet still, she couldn't keep your house clean, warm, or full of food."

Raven shrugs, but it holds less pop this time. "Tales of an addict, Rolland."

"Right." He nods, his frown matching hers, a hidden something passing between them. "The money is yours, Raven. I know you're running out if you're not out already and the warehouses are not an option for you anymore. There must be things you need or will soon, hygiene products and such. Perhaps you'd like a phone or even a car." He holds out the envelope again, and when she takes another step away, he announces something that has her freezing in her spot. "There's an identification card in there, social as well. Your mother informed me when you started tearing your trailer apart searching for them. They've been in my possession since I found you."

I tense beside her and her eyes fly to mine.

ID card. In her mind, that was all she needed to run, she said herself, without one she couldn't get a real job or function like she wanted. This was all that was holding her back from the normal life she craved, the life she wanted before us.

Why give it to her?

"There are also emancipation papers in there," he says and Raven's eyes narrow. "They've been fast-tracked, were signed by your mother the day Maria picked you up. All you have to do is sign them, and they'll be processed within twenty-four hours. No court needed, it's been handled. Sign them, and you're an adult in the eyes of the law, not that we need to worry about laws much here."

She reaches over, grabbing my hand, and when I look back to my dad, his eyes are locked on our connection.

"I know what you're doing, Rolland, and it won't work," she tells him and ever so slowly he meets her stare. "The money, whatever. I don't even know, maybe that's something you have to do, but the other... giving me something I've been searching for, for years? Offering me the little taste of freedom these things provide, it's your way of trying to mollify me. Make me think I'm in control when in your mind that couldn't be further from the truth.

"You've watched us closely, and decided I won't run, it's the only reason you'd even consider handing me a way out. You want this to act as your confirmation, and you know what, I won't make you wait to witness the answer."

She meets my eyes, then Cap's and Royce's.

"These boys..." A quiet laugh leaves her, and she gives a small jerk of her head, her stare moving back to his. "I could never leave them, so there you go. Now you know for sure, from my own fucking mouth, they come first."

Our dad's jaw clenches, but not in anger, in prospect, so when he steps toward her, I stay planted at her side instead of shifting to guard her.

He nods, his feet fixed an inch from hers. "You are more than I could have imagined, Raven Brayshaw," he admits. "But like you, I only want to protect my family, and while I understand they are now yours, they are still mine." He frowns. "We have the same goals, Raven, I promise you this, but something your young souls have yet to face or understand is with life comes loss. With love, comes sacrifice."

His eyes hit mine, and I can't tell if he's talking of his sacrifice, mine, or hers.

Maybe all three?

He holds the envelope out for me, so I take it, and he turns and walks away, calling over his shoulder, "Make her sign the papers, boys. The alternative isn't something any of us want."

Fuck.

Raven's glare snaps to mine and she yanks her hand away, speaking before I can. "I don't want it, Maddoc. Even I know money brings more problems."

"You want to be able to care for yourself, right?"

She glares. "Yeah, myself. Not like this. This makes me feel like my mother. He gives me money and what, my taking it is me accepting my life is his?"

"Your life is mine."

She can't help it, and she laughs, looking away.

I step closer to her. "Sign the papers, Raven. You don't have to touch the money if you don't want, but it'll be there. Keep whatever cash is in here" — I shake the envelope — "and we pretend it never happened. You have the card, you do what you want with it."

"What if I give it all away?" she challenges.

I shrug. "I don't give a fuck what you do with it. It's yours. Cut the card up, hide it, mail it to your mom to blow on blow, who fucking cares. We have our own money, too, so it's not like you're screwing us. What you decide to do with it is on no one but you."

She glares at the envelope. "It can't be so simple."

"Nothing ever is."

"I don't want anyone to know."

"No one will unless it comes from your mouth."

She huffs. "So, what, do I sign it as a Brayshaw or a Carver?"

I tear it open and pour out the contents on the coffee table. Her ID bounces from it to the ground, bottoms up. She looks from it to me.

"Let's find out," I tell her, bending to pick it up, but she rushes in first.

She flips it over, reading her name aloud. "Raven Carver Brayshaw." She frowns. "My middle name is *Carver*?"

With a deep sigh, she reaches into her backpack for a pen and doesn't bother reading over the forms, but blindly signs on each tallied line. She grabs the rest of the shit from the envelope and heads for the door. "Come on, I still want a coffee."

We let her walk out and I turn to my brothers.

"Was he trying to say if she didn't take it, it would default to the Gravens once she was given to them?" Royce asks.

"She won't be given to them," Cap quips.

"Probably, at least now it'll be in her name and they won't be able to touch it."

"Yeah," Royce scoffs. "If she hits him with a prenup."

"Royce!"

Cap smacks him in the back of the head and his hands lift. "Sorry, fuck I know. I gotta stay pissed or make fuckin' jokes, man. I don't have an in-between. It's either this, I fuck my way through the cheer squad, or choke everyone out with bare hands."

Cap shakes his head. "Let's go, she knows we're talking about her."

"Yeah, meet you out there in one sec." Royce bounds up the steps and the two of us move for the car.

He's back down within a few minutes, tossing Raven her iPod and headphones.

She picks it up, frowning at him, but he just shrugs.

"Keep 'em with you in case you want to drown out everyone. Plug 'em in, turn it on and fuck everyone else, RaeRae."

She nods lightly and does just that.

We head for the donut shop, Raven at my side, happy to go get her dollar fucking coffee and maple bar, not at all affected by how only five minutes ago, she became an instant multi-millionaire.

Chapter 7

RAVEN

"YOU GONNA EAT THAT?"

I tilt my head back to spot Victoria.

She drops onto the grass beside me. "You realize the grass is wet, right?"

"And you just sat on it."

She grins. "Never said it bothered me."

I laugh lightly, offering her the donut I only peeled a small corner of maple off of, but is otherwise untouched.

She shakes her head. "I was kidding. I don't like sweets."

"Well I do, and I'm pissed I can't eat it. My stomach is still turning. I couldn't even finish my coffee."

She gives me a side-eye before shifting her frown to the basketball courts where the guys are jacking around, shooting hoops before the bell rings. Why we all woke up at the asscrack of dawn today, I don't even know. Guess we had too much on our minds to sleep.

"Maybell tossed out all of Vienna's shit last night. Straight into the dumpster, carried it out herself even. Guess she heard what she did?" She looks back to me.

"That woman knows more than any of us could guess, I'm sure. You'd have to being around this family as long as she has. Secrets on secrets on... secrets."

My brows pull in.

Maybell.

"Uh-oh."

I look to Victoria. "What?"

"You have your '*I just figured some shit out*' face on."

I slide my eyes to her. "Since when do you want to know things, I thought your MO was the less you know the better?"

"It is." She glares. "Did I ask you what you figured out? No. I didn't. I just recognized your *I'm gonna make a sneaky move that will piss them off* face."

"I thought it was my *I figured some shit out face*?"

"Yeah. Which means the same damn thing in Raven language." She laughs.

I can't help but laugh with her. "You know, you should rethink your position on the not wanting to know front."

Her smile is suddenly washed away, her frown now focused on nothing. "It's more complicated than that, Rae. Honestly, I shouldn't even be sitting here talking to you, and I sure as hell shouldn't have been with you guys these last several days. The fact that I want to chill with you kind of annoys me."

"You're making me think I shouldn't trust you."

"Maybe you shouldn't." She stares at me dead on. "I'm not gonna lie, there are things you won't like about me, maybe even hate me for. I can also swear I'm not malicious, even though I have things to hide."

"What the fuck am I supposed to do with that, Victoria?"

She gives an unapologetic shrug. "Do what you want with it, but I'm being as honest as I can. I can stay away, no problem, but at the risk of sounding like a weak bitch, I don't hate having someone around who gives fewer fucks than me."

"You do sound like a weak bitch," I joke, still a little on edge from her confession, but damn, I mean, she volunteered that, right? That has to count for something. "But I could use another vagina around sometimes to balance out the dicks a little better."

"What RaeRae means is, to balance *on* the dicks," Royce teases as the guys grow closer. "As in..." He trails off wiggling his eyebrows. "Ain't that right?" He looks to me, a big ass, innocent grin on his far from innocent face.

I glance at Victoria who blinks up at him, her head tilted the slightest bit, and a laugh bubbles out of me. I reach for Maddoc's hand when he extends it, letting him pull me up.

"Nope." I chuckle. "Not at all what I meant, Ponyboy."

"Ah, come on." He wraps his arm around my shoulder. "Don't lie. 'Ponyboy' proves you were thinking about the ride, even though it should be more like massive steed." He grins. "Tell her how good we are, RaeRae. I'm thinking Cap wants to bone her down. Me and him could keep her up through the night, I'd bet."

Victoria smashes her lips to the side as she pushes to her feet and turns to walk away, but not before I spot the slight blush creeping up her neck.

"You do know we're not blood brothers, right?!" he calls out, teasing her further. "We can play with our toys at the same time and it not be weird, just sayin'!"

Cap's glare prompts me to step out of Royce's hold and then he gives him a solid shove.

"You're such a dumbass," Cap grumbles. "I'm going to class. I'll come get you for second period, Raven."

I nod, leaning against Maddoc when he steps against me.

Royce just laughs at his own idiocy and bends to snag my uneaten donut with his mouth. He heads for class.

"Thought you were dying for that thing?" Maddoc kisses my wrist as we follow the other two back into the building.

"I was, but after all the shit last night, Cap earlier and then the bomb from your dad, it's not hittin' the spot."

As soon as we walk in the door, Maddoc stops me, slowly pushing me against the wall, hands on my hips, and glares down at me.

I lift my arms, lazily draping them around his neck and he turns his head, running his lips across my skin, smirking when I shiver.

"You've switched it up on your people, Big Man. They're not used to seeing their king get so openly handsy," I tease.

He steps closer, his hands sliding up my sides, under my sweater, completely ignoring everyone around who has paused to watch with side-eyes. "Don't care," he rasps. "They need to see anyway."

"See what?" I meet his lips with my own.

"What's mine. I want them jealous and understanding that they can't have you and I can. Whenever I want."

I hum against his mouth and he grins but turns serious a second later.

He pulls back a little. "Tell me you know we're not keeping shit from you because you're not a part of us."

"Tell me you understand why I have to try to figure it out on my own."

His glare intensifies. "I won't allow you to try and protect me again."

I let my arms fall from around him and he steps back.

"I told you before, I do what I want."

"So do I. I will lock you in the fucking house if I feel the need to, Raven."

"I don't doubt it for a second, Big Man."

With that, I walk toward Royce who waits for me with tight eyes outside our classroom door.

I glance back at Maddoc, and the stiffness lining his fore-head works as a weight on my shoulders.

Thankfully, Royce senses it and snakes his hand around me. Maddoc tips his head at his brother.

"Chin up, RaeRae," he whispers. "Don't let these assholes read you."

With that, he leads me into the room where we hide our inner issues and pretend we're as solid as they think. Physically, we are, but mentally we're becoming a fucking freak show.

We take our seats and not ten minutes in I'm already getting antsy as fuck.

I look at the clock.

It would take me about five minutes to run to the Bray house to try and catch Maybell. That's ten minutes there and back. Doable.

I was vomiting all day yesterday, so I could get away with playing the upset stomach card. The only issue is getting Maybell to talk and how long it would take to do so.

The boys are like her kids, so her loyalty is to them, but the other day on the porch she was about to tell me something before Maddoc burst outside to make sure I was still there. She must have something she feels the need to say.

I have to try.

I shift in my seat, gripping the edge of the desk when a paper hits my head. I look to Royce.

He glares and shakes his head, knowing damn well what I'm thinking – not even a bathroom break alone is "allowed" at this point.

To further prove my point, the door flies open and Captain ushers a puffed-up Victoria into the room.

She jerks in his hold, her glare flying over her shoulder but he doesn't even spare her a glance.

He looks to Royce, nods his chin, meets my eyes and walks out.

Victoria slams her paper on the teacher's desk and then makes her way to me.

Royce chuckles quietly in his seat and looks past me, motioning for the kid on the other side to slide back a few desks, which he does without question, and Victoria drops into it.

She scowls at me. "You are starting to dictate my world without even speaking."

"Fuck you," I throw back. "What are you talking about?"

"Seems I'm now in all your classes, you know, as an extra set of eyes. Grown ass girl and you need a babysitter?" she bitches.

I can't help but smile at that. "I've always been a problem child."

She scoffs, but it comes out as a laugh and she digs out her notebook, instantly cutting me off and focusing on the teacher.

I glance back at Royce who lifts his hands.

"Precaution, RaeRae."

Precaution, right.

They know by now she won't snitch me out, even if they asked her to. It's not in her nature, like sitting on trouble isn't in mine. I guess they want to be sure I have some sort of backup at all times in case they aren't around, someone to run to them if needed like she did when Collins attacked me in the bathroom.

"Are you my piss partner?" I whisper to her and she cuts an annoyed look my way.

"Apparently, yeah, but not my first day in this class. I can't afford to fail. Hold your fucking fists in for twenty more minutes, and we can worry about whatever shit you're wanting to pull during PE or Study Hall or... something."

I sit back, satisfied, winking at Royce when he glares at our whispering.

She gets me.

Chapter 8

Maddoc

RAVEN IS COVERED, BY EITHER ROYCE OR VICTORIA, AND CAP just now went to class. This gives me a solid thirty minutes to try and get ahead, make some fucking sense of what's to come.

I slide inside, slamming the door, and his head snaps up.

He jumps to his feet with a glare. "What the hell are you doing?"

His words are strong, but his eyes fly over my shoulder, making sure only one of us stepped through – like one isn't fucking enough – before cutting back to me.

He can't go anywhere. He's trapped in here, with me, until I decide to let him out.

"So, you were on track to be Brayshaw, huh?" I study him. "Yet your brother became a Graven."

"I am no Graven," he draws out slowly.

I'd almost swear he says it with conviction, as if the thought disgusts him.

"But Felix *Graven* is your brother—"

"*Was.*"

"Were you jealous of how easily he got to the top?"

He bares his teeth. "I was offered a place beside him, I declined."

"Because you were hoping to be a part of my dad's team."

It works, Perkins' jaw sets tight, his hands making fists against his desk.

"You know nothing," he hisses.

"As soon as she fell for him, and he asked you to protect her, you jumped at the chance, didn't you?" His eyes widen slightly. "Tell me, were you stupid enough to ask for her, his power?"

His jaw clenches. "I never wanted his power."

"No, you wanted his ticket. Donley offered Felix the top, of course he could only have it if the heiress was at his side." I widen my stance. "And she was... until she wasn't."

He knows what I'm getting at.

"Ask what you came to ask."

"Are you Raven's father?"

His eyes grow taut, unmistakable anger and regret. "No. I'm not."

I dart forward, yanking him by his tie until his face is near mine. "Don't fucking lie to me."

"I'm not her—"

I yank tighter and he groans, his hands coming up to pull at the satin material. "She disappeared just over eighteen years ago, Raven will be eighteen soon. The math is fucking simple. You knew your brother was promised her pure, so you made sure she wasn't! And then what, threw her out when you found out she was pregnant? Just wanted to ruin her, but the kid was worth nothing to you, right?!"

He jerks, so I shove him away and his ass slams into the seat.

He jumps right back to his feet. "You know nothing, and you're wrong! I loved her! I wouldn't have fucking cared if she was pregnant with someone else's kid, had I known for sure, because I fucking wanted *her*! Not the title that came with her, the money or the Graven empire, not anything else. Just. *Her*," he growls.

"You trusted her."

I whip around to find Captain standing there.

I hadn't even heard him pull open the door.

He keeps talking. "You begged her to leave, to be with you and walk away from it all, and she agreed, didn't she?"

My eyes slice back to Perkins who glares at Captain, and Royce catches my attention just outside the door. He nods his chin, shifting his stare back to the other two.

"But she betrayed you, in the end," Cap keeps going. "Left your sorry ass behind."

"Don't," Perkins hisses, his eyes begging.

"So you got revenge the only way you felt you could. Slept with someone else, hoping she'd come back and hear all about it, but she never did, did she?" he goads him.

It works.

Perkins' entire body turns to stone, his face paling.

Captain stands to his full height. "Every puzzle has pieces. I found yours. And as for the *document* Collins hid at his cabin, you know the one you flipped out over the thought of Donley finding – my daughter's birth certificate," Captain hisses and Perkins' face tightens. "We stole it weeks ago. How do you think he blackmailed Raven to being by his side?"

"Captain, you can't bring her—"

Cap punches him in the face before anyone sees it coming and he stumbles back, hitting the wall.

"You will never dictate what happens with my daughter again, do you understand me?!"

"I was only trying to protect—"

"Nobody fucking asked you to!"

"I had no choice!" Perkins snaps. "As soon as I realized Mallory was pregnant, I knew I had to get her out of here, hide her until the baby was born. Donley is aware of your relationships, he watches, so when you showed the first sign of possibly caring for a girl, he waited for the slipup. Had he found out about the baby, Mallory would have been pulled under his thumb, and then Zoey taken the second she was born. I couldn't allow that. I've seen what those people create, how they can take an innocent girl and turn her into..."

Ravina.

"You had no fucking right to step in where you weren't wanted," Captain spits.

"That girl would have milked you dry." Perkins glares. "Look what she gave up for money and a secure lifestyle, both of which she knows damn well she could have gotten *from you* if she just stayed, if she had *wanted* to stay."

"None of that concerns you!" Captain shouts. "It was my problem to worry about!"

"The risk was too high to leave it in your hands! Even though you act like you're not, you're still only a kid!"

"Why do you fucking care?!"

"You know why!" Perkins snaps.

Captain shoots up straight, all three of us freezing at Perkins' words. Perkins himself even seems struck that he's said it.

Captain swallows, looks to me, then Royce, and back to Perkins.

"So, it's true," Cap says after a few minutes. "And the paternity test results that I get back today will prove it."

Every move has a purpose.

The lab. That's why he had to make Perkins bleed yesterday.

"Yes," Perkins confirms on a whisper. "Don't bring her home, not yet. Soon she'll be safe, but not—"

"You think we don't know it's her or Raven?" Captain glares.

"You know," Perkins' voice is nothing but a whisper, his desperate fucking eyes coming my way. "Then why's the girl still here?"

"You thought we'd give up one of our own, just like that?" I ask.

Perkins steps back.

"Stay away from Zoey. Stay away from all of us," Captain demands of him.

Perkins stiffens, his tone almost pleading. "She is my blood."

Cap leans in, his voice a deep rumble from within his chest. *"Family runs deeper than blood."*

"No..." Royce finally speaks. "He's ..." He looks to Perkins. *"You're* Zoey's dad?"

"No." Captain glares at the man in front of him. "He's mine."

We're sitting in the truck during what is supposed to be our PE hour. Not one of us has spoken since we left Perkins' office, but I know all our minds are spinning.

"I was going to tell you yesterday," Cap offers.

"When did you suspect, man? Or fuck, how?" Royce asks.

"Only the last week. I found an old hospital record in the paperwork from the shit Raven gave us, one we pushed aside as nothing. The man who we were always told was my biological dad got sick his junior year at Brayshaw, missed half the year."

"Sick?"

"Testicular cancer." He looks to me. "The paper was his op report. Which meant—"

"He couldn't have fucking kids."

Cap nods. "Then everything Raven said about Perkins telling Collins he was protecting his own. It made no sense. The only answer was in the beginning he was trying to hide her not only from us but from them too." Cap looks out the window. "Hiding Zoey didn't protect Graven from anything, it only protected her."

"He was protecting her... for *you*," Royce says, his confusion obvious.

"All this shit over the years, being in our business, stopping us from pulling stupid shit, Dad letting him stay around." Cap looks back at us.

"Dad has known this entire time."

"Yep."

"And he lied to us."

"Why?" Royce hedges.

"Because, at the end of the day, my sperm donor or not, Connor Perkins wasn't Brayshaw." He brings his eyes back to ours. "The second he agreed to protect Ravina for Felix, he became Graven."

Family runs deeper than blood.

Perkins chose his blood, that's who had his loyalty.

Fuck.

"Yo," Royce drags out, sitting forward in his seat. "I know we're talkin' serious shit right now, but uh... we got a couple fugitive females ahead."

Both mine and Cap's eyes flash to the windshield finding Raven and Victoria crouched down, sneaking past the trunks of the cars not two rows up from where we're parked.

Raven's head snaps over her shoulder and she says something to Victoria. Victoria, who flips her off in response, but keeps after her.

Despite the fucked hour we've had, we laugh.

"How far should we let 'em get?" Cap slides the key into the ignition.

I frown, sitting back in the seat. "She's far enough."

He turns it over, firing up the engine, and we laugh as Raven freezes mid crawl, causing Victoria to bump into her ass, then fall back on her own.

Both their eyes slice our way.

Raven drops her head back, glaring at the sky, while Victoria lays out where she's fallen, shaking her head against the asphalt.

"Go on, Cap." Royce pats his shoulder. "Let's get our girls."

I raise a brow at Royce who smirks.

"Ah, come on. Raven said she kinda likes her, I say we keep her, too. I'll even share with Cap so it's fair." He grins, quickly dropping against the seat before Cap can reach around and nail him.

"Let them come to us," Captain says, hitting the unlock button on the doors.

It takes a second, but Raven tugs Victoria off the ground, rolling her eyes at her, and the two make their way over.

"Ah, shit. Look at that face." Royce nods his chin toward Raven.

There's no glare, no bratty ass smirk or sign of sass comin' my way. She gives nothing.

"Looks like she's not the only one in trouble, brother."
Looks fuckin' like it.

Raven

FUCKING WOW.
Wooooow.

I'm not sure how many more private conversations I can take. I'm well a-fucking-ware they don't have to share anything with me. I get that. What annoys me is normally they want to.

How am I not supposed to flip when suddenly this changes? It makes me want to fuck shit up out of spite.

Proving further she gets me on a different level than others, Victoria starts running her mouth, not that I want to hear it.

"So, is this how it's gonna work now, huh?" Victoria mumbles, being sure they can't read her lips as we walk their way. "You play the good little lamb and they do what they want?"

"Shut up."

"Bet they let Daddy start telling you what to do, too."

"I said shut up."

"What do you think will follow, huh? Maybe they trade you beds each—"

I spin around, slamming my forearm into her neck while slipping my left foot behind her. I push, knocking her into the car beside us, setting off its alarm.

I get in her face. "I said shut the fuck *up*, Victoria."

I wait for her to shove back, to attempt to fight me off. She doesn't.

She smirks, causing my eyes to narrow.

Footsteps head our way.

"What the hell are you doing?"

"They need to see you angry. You're Raven fucking Carver, fighter by nature. You do what you want."

"They know this already. Why the fuck do you think we're sneaking out of here right now? Because at the end of the damn day, I make my own decisions."

Her face hardens. "This is about shared information, not decisions. Don't let them keep you in the dark."

I study her. "How do you know they are?"

She holds my eyes a moment. "Make them talk or go to the man himself. They may be his sons, but in the end, Rolland is still in charge."

"Victoria," I growl, pushing harder.

"You know as well as I do, in the dark is where it happens."

In the dark, we lose.

I shove off her right as the boys step up, and their eyes slide between ours in question, but they say nothing.

I glance to Victoria.

She stares at me a moment, relaxing when I lick my lips and look back to the boys, the boys who frown when Victoria pushes off the car, leaning an elbow on my shoulder lazily.

"What was that about?" Royce finally asks.

"Where were you going?" comes from Maddoc.

But it's Captain that steps closer, his eyes searching hers before settling on mine.

"Don't," he whispers. "Let us be the ones."

Victoria's muscles tense, but nobody catches it but me.

I keep my eyes on Cap. "When?"

He looks to his brothers who both glare angrily and frown in contrition.

"Let's go," he says, moving aside for me to step past.

When I do, he slides back in place, standing directly in front of Victoria.

With her shoulders squared, she faces him head-on. Slowly, her eyes move to mine.

"She stays," he says to me, looking at her.

"For now," I add.

She keeps her stare steady on mine a moment before backing up, not looking at him and heading for the school.

The four of us move for the SUV, but when Cap should make a left and head for the house, he doesn't. He makes a right instead.

"Where we going, Cap?" I ask.

His grip tightens on the steering wheel, his eyes meeting mine in the rearview mirror. "To Zoey."

Chapter 9

RAVEN

NOT A SINGLE WORD WAS SPOKEN AFTER CAPTAIN'S announcement as we pulled from the Brayshaw High parking lot, and a half hour drive later, we come to a parallel line of palms, a path just large enough for the SUV to roll down separating them. We turn onto the gravel road lined with painted rocks and bright purple flowers.

Clean cut grass spans out on both sides, at least the size of a few basketball courts. The right side has a home playground set perfectly centered, while the left has a little plastic house with purple windows and the same purple flowers all the way around.

Speaking of basketball courts, once we get a little farther down the road, a mini court with little toy hoops placed on each side comes into view.

My chest tightens when I see the wolf's logo painted in the center of it as if it's the Brayshaw home court.

Like it's her daddy's home court.

I look to Cap in the mirror, finding a small smile on his lips.

I glance at Maddoc.

He sits tight and tense, glaring straight ahead, like he can't bring himself to look around.

I slide my hand in his and his eyes cut to mine, the edges contracting even more.

Cool air hits me then and I look to Royce.

He's rolled his window down, his head practically stuck outside as he takes in every inch he can get his eyes on.

"You been here before, brother?" Royce asks him.

Cap shakes his head. "Pictures and video from our PI." He places the SUV in park, sitting still a moment.

"Is it what you imagined?" I ask him.

He glances around, meeting my eyes again. "Better."

Right then a big burly man in a suit steps from the right side of the wrap-around porch, and a second from the left.

"Security. Nice." Royce nods.

"Guessing they didn't know we were coming?" Maddoc asks.

Captain unbuckles his seat belt. "I will never ask to see my own daughter again."

With that, he pushes open his door and climbs out, but the three of us have the same idea and don't move an inch.

Cap only gets a few steps before the front door flies open and Maria's wide eyes hit his.

She glares and takes a half step forward.

I dart for the door handle, but Maddoc's quick, and his hand covers mine.

I slice my glare to him, but he's not looking at me. His eyes are on the porch.

I look back just in time to see a little hand grip around Maria's thigh. Her eyes shoot wide, her head dropping to the contact.

Maddoc's grip tightens on mine and Royce shifts to the edge of his seat.

Her little head pokes out next, blonde hair as curly as I remember it and sitting high on her head, a purple bow locking it in.

Her head tilts up to Maria first, but when Cap takes another step, it cuts his way.

Instant, full, and the most precious thing I have ever seen — she smiles wide.

Royce lets out a sharp exhale, a soft chuckle following as she wedges her little shoulders between the frame and Maria's body and bounds forward.

She gets so excited she pauses to stomp her little feet, her hands extended as if he's close enough to grab her.

I look to Captain, and of course he gives his baby girl what she wants. He jogs to her, getting to her faster. Not bothering to hit the porch steps at all, he holds his hands out and she doesn't hesitate.

She jumps.

He catches her, lifts her up high for a moment before pulling her to his chest.

"She understands who he is." Maddoc rasps.

My eyes cut to him in question, but he doesn't take his eyes off them. "I wondered, but..."

But he couldn't ask. It makes sense. Zoey didn't get to see Captain much and for someone so young, just shy of three, it could be hard for them to grasp, especially when she goes to bed without him every night. There's no question, though. She knows exactly who her daddy is.

Zoey looks over Cap's shoulders right then and her back shoots straight. She pats Cap's and points to the SUV.

"I think she sees me." Royce whispers like she might hear him.

Cap says something to her that has her nodding, and then

tickles her, and she laughs with her whole body, making the three of us follow suit.

He starts this way and our amusement halts, our bodies going stiff.

My eyes move to the porch where Maria raises a hand as if she's going to stop him, but then her fingers fly to her lips. She takes a step back.

My eyes narrow.

She's nervous.

Maddoc grips his handle and Royce's eyes quickly find his. "Yeah?" he asks a little hopeful, a little nervy.

I grin. "Go."

Royce frowns. "You too."

I shake my head, sitting back in my seat and pulling my hand from Maddoc's. "No. This is your time. Go."

They hesitate a moment, and as if sensing it, Cap pauses a few feet from the hood.

The boys open their doors and exit.

Zoey's head bobs one way to the next, and she clings to Cap's neck more but she's not afraid. A little nervous maybe, but she only drops her chin to her shoulder and watches them.

Both pause right in front of her and she looks to Captain.

I find myself chuckling. I'm pretty damn sure little Zoey is blushing.

Royce steps up to her first and lifts his hand for a high five.

Zoey smiles, but instead of high fiving she puts out her knuckles, making the brothers laugh together.

Zoey kicks against Captain, so he puts her down. Her little lips move and she points toward the dollhouse.

Cap nods and starts walking but Zoey, reaches up and he offers her his hand, but she wants Royce and Maddoc's too. She tries to hold them all but can't figure it out and frowns up at Captain.

He laughs and shrugs his shoulders at her, but Zoey smiles and grabs Royce and Captain's hands, locking them together.

I laugh, scooting closer in my seat, holding my breath as she reaches for Maddoc's hand. She can only grip two of his fingers, her other hand holding tight to her dad and damn if I don't wish I had a phone for the first time. That's a helluva picture right there.

Cap and Royce hold hands while Zoey holds Caps with her left, and Maddoc with her right. One little blonde-haired baby girl, leading all three right where she wants them.

Captain's eyes cut back to the SUV and I still. His stare a moment and I know what he's wondering – do I not want to meet her. I hate the moment of doubt it causes him, but when they shift to Maddoc I know, without words, having not even needed to hear it from my mouth, he communicates my reason.

He knows I want this for them, and this isn't me not wanting to meet her, but them needing this moment for themselves – a niece and her uncles.

Movement from the porch catches my eyes.

Maria steps farther out, fishing a phone from her pocket, and I jolt for the door handle, quickly hopping out and rushing straight toward her.

Her head snaps up, eyes wide in shock.

"You."

"Me." I keep forward.

She glances back to her phone before looking to me again.

"Don't do it. I don't want to have to fuck you up while your security watches," I warn, holding out my palm.

It takes her a second, but she hands it over with a not so gentle slap.

"By the way, security for a *social worker*, huh?"

"Security for the little girl I protect day and night."

"When you're not posing as a social worker and dragging

other girls hours away from their homes and dropping them in new ones?"

Her eyes narrow. "Some would say I brought you home, not drug you *from* your home."

Can't quite argue with that. They are my home more than anything else ever was. "Some would be right then, wouldn't they?"

It's on the tip of her tongue to ask me, so I hold eye contact until she can no longer keep it in. "Why would he... why would they bring you here? Why would they allow you near her at all?"

"Isn't it obvious?"

She frowns after them, a deep sigh leaving her. "I worried this would happen. The day I read your file I thought it, but the day I met you..." She trails off, her eyes tightening at the edges. "At the school with the principal who clearly cared for you even though you were a brat, how Ravina spoke to you and how you handled her." I tense at the mention of my mom's name. "Your overall attitude and the look in your eye when you spoke to me. Everything about you was... refreshing. I knew it in my gut. I warned him you'd be everything they never knew. That made you dangerous for them, for this world." She looks to me. "But at the end of the day, we all want something we can't have."

I fight not to frown.

What the fuck does that *mean?*

Her features soften some as she asks, "Which one?"

"Like you don't know."

"I—" she cuts herself off but decides to keep going. "I don't," she admits.

My brows pull in at her abashed tone.

"It was in my contract." She audibly swallows. "In exchange for caring for her, I wasn't allowed to look for or ask anything about them or their world."

"You wanted to care for her?"

"I wouldn't trust anyone else to." She stares at me head-on.

My eyes narrow.

"You can try to read me, but I told you before, I was somewhat like you once. I can hide what I want from who I want."

"Yet here you stand giving more than you realize."

"Who said I don't realize?" she draws.

I scoff. *Right.*

I look to the boys.

Zoey tries to push Royce inside the dollhouse, but he makes himself fall onto the grass and Zoey throws her head back, laughing at him.

She bends and hits his chest with the palm of her hands before climbing across his body and inside, where the other two must already be.

"Who were you about to call?" I ask, assuming she won't answer.

She does. "Rolland."

"In the contract?"

She turns away, moving for the patio set that allows her to hide back, but keep an eye on them all the same, so I follow, dropping into a chair.

"You shouldn't judge what you don't know."

"I judge what I do know, and I know Captain's daughter is here with you instead of at home with him, where she belongs."

A playful growl catches our attention and we look over.

Captain has Zoey on his shoulders as he chases Royce around while Maddoc leans against the little house with a smile. A real smile.

Not a smirk or a grin. Eyes open and loving and on his niece.

As always, he knows when I have him in sight, and his attention shifts to me.

A thought clouds his features, resented anger and dare I say pain seeping through. The smile is washed away instantly, but the corner of his lip tips up the slightest bit.

It's forced.

The same beat-up expression is on Royce's face, but the moment my eyes hit his, he licks his lips and looks away.

Cap offers a reassuring smile, but his attention is quickly caught by the little one now calling on them to follow her, as it should be.

"Hu-mon, hu-mon." She laughs. "I make it, I make it."

My brows pull in.

"What'd you make, Zo?" Cap asks her, tickling her sides.

She runs faster.

"Hu-mon, Daddy!" she says dramatically, making me smile.

She stops and rushes back to him; grabs hold of his fingers and drags him along.

"She learned how to shoot a basket," Maria says sadly.

My eyes slice to hers, but she only continues to smile warmly at Zoey. "She watches his games all the time, we have them all on video. He's her favorite show. Her favorite bedtime story. Favorite everything."

My chest aches, and I can't even look at them as they approach the little court.

"You and everyone involved are fucked up individuals." Her eyes reluctantly meet mine. "You think he or his brothers wouldn't have wanted to be the first to show her that? I bet Captain has laid in bed playing out the entire fucking thing in his head. What he'd say, how he'd explain the use of her wrist in a way for her to understand. How she should stand, what she should focus on. Of all the things, this is one I know he hoped to have for himself. Her first basket."

Maria's tears catch me off guard, but I don't show it. "I know," she rasps. "I tried to avoid it, but she just wanted to be like him. She kept saying she wanted to show him, cried for a ball, so I got her one, but then she cried for the basketball hoop. I couldn't deny her. She's not even three and she saw, just from watching his game film, how he loved the sport. She wanted to play too."

My ribs ache, but I push it away.

"You're not keeping her," I say.

To my surprise, she lets those tears fall freely, but here they mean nothing to me.

"It doesn't matter how bad you want her, and I can tell you do, she's not yours. They're bringing her home."

Maria swallows. "Yeah," she whispers. "I heard." Her eyes come back to mine. "But it seems something is standing in the way of her homecoming."

From sorrow to disrespect so quickly?

"I'm aware," I say, lying through my teeth.

"Then stop giving them hope they can keep you both," she hisses. "*Everyone* here serves a purpose of some kind. There are no coincidences, no accidents. You're delaying the inevitable, and in turn, Zoey goes to sleep every night telling a picture of her daddy that she loves him instead of him himself."

Wha...

I am delaying she said, not they are delaying. And keep *us* both?

Us who? Me and Zoey?

No. No, no no.

Fuck, I'm gonna be sick. My stomach turns, heat spreading across my body and creating beads of sweat across the back of my neck. My entire body flushes.

Holy shit.

I take a second, turning away and closing my eyes. I take a deep breath and when I open them and look back one of the security guards is heading for me.

My muscles tighten but relax when he holds out a cold-water bottle for me to take.

"Ms. Brayshaw." He nods his head.

He catches me off guard, but slowly I take it from him.

He walks away, and I take a few small sips to settle myself.

"They're Rolland's men," I say, doing my best to play off what she just said when I'm flipping the fuck out in my head having no idea what it truly means.

"They're Brayshaw men," she corrects with an inquisitive tone. "*Your* men."

I scoff. "You knew all along, didn't you?"

"I did, but I'm not sure I fully believed it until we went to get your things."

I could tell when she mentioned my mom, she knew her. "When you saw her for yourself."

Maria nods. "Yeah," she whispers, regretful. "The woman I saw was not the Ravina I knew." I don't ask because I don't fucking care, but her next words catch me by surprise. "She was my best friend once."

I can't hide it, my eyes widen. Her best friend? "You're from here."

She scoffs. "You'd never know it. My existence was erased a long time ago." Her eyes move to mine. "I was never strong enough for this world. I wasn't like you. I was too weak, emotionally and physically. Too naïve. I didn't see the knife, only felt it in my back."

I eye her, finding no reason for her to talk out her ass.

She gives a small smile. "I knew you didn't know yet."

I glare.

"There is no way you'd be sitting here if you had." She looks to the four Brayshaws, so I finally give in and do the same. "I may not know you well, but there is a freedom that surrounds you that the people here aren't used to. You can't be controlled, you rebel, you push, you *question*. Your mind works a little different than those we know. I think it's why Rolland fears your influence."

"Rolland has bigger issues than me."

"I wouldn't be so sure," she breathes.

The boys pretend to guard Zoey and she widens her little legs, lifting one and then the next as she leans from side to side, an adorable effort at juking before running completely around Royce, tossing it into the little hoop that is just slightly taller than her reach. She gets so excited when she makes it and almost falls over, but Maddoc is right there to catch her before she can.

"She'll never have a scraped knee again if those three have anything to say about it…" Her voice trails off and I look to her.

She stares at Maddoc and Zoey, and her lips smash together, a deep crease forming on her forehead.

Wait.

She knows I'm watching, and slowly her eyes come back to mine. She holds back nothing, showing her pain and loss and… longing.

Something hits my foot and my eyes snap down to find the little basketball at my feet.

Steps echo across the cement and I freeze, unable to look up for some reason, but then tattooed knuckles come down on the ball and my eyes lift.

Cap reaches up, touching my cheek, his blue-green eyes on me. "Stop," he whispers, then moves his mouth to my ear so Maria can't hear. "It's okay. I was scared at first, too. There *will* be a next time, Raven."

I squeeze his wrist only letting go when I have to, and he walks back to his family.

My eyes slide right, and I spot Zoey, her big eyes are locked on me. She pushes her blonde hair from her face as she stares at me. Her little hand lifts, and she almost looks shy as she waves her tiny fingers at me.

My stomach muscles tighten and my teeth clench as pressure begins to knock behind my eyes. Somehow through that, I manage to raise my hand and wave back.

Her smile is instant and huge and I bite my tongue.

She spins around and throws herself in Royce's arms.

"That way!" She points down the back of the house, where I can't see, and they disappear.

"She has a little train back there, it's tiny, goes in a circle around a tree, but she loves it."

Me too, kid.

I push to my feet and head back for the truck.

"Raven," Maria calls.

I don't turn back but stop walking.

"Just because you didn't know love as a child doesn't mean you won't know how to love one."

Doesn't it?

Chapter 10

RAVEN

IT'S NOT UNTIL THE SUN HAS STARTED TO GO DOWN THAT footsteps float through the cracked window. I sit up to find Maria has made her way back to the front door, and it's only Captain who walks Zoey up.

She hesitates a moment but then offers him inside.

The three disappear, closing the door behind them.

Maddoc and Royce move over to the security guards, likely grilling them on processes.

I look from them to the house, to the basketball court and anger fills my veins.

Maria's words were clear, the boys hint without hinting about protecting Zoey at all cost was crystal.

Me or Zoey.

I pull my knife from my waistband, glaring at the inscription.

Family runs deeper than blood, but Zoey *is* their blood.

They love her with all they have. I'm the outsider. How dare they leave me in this position.

How dare they let their feelings for me cloud their judgment.

There is no risk, no fucking sacrifice too big in this instance.

They're delaying the inevitable.

It's become clear, this place is bigger than a power ran high school and its rival, though that's been their world the last four years. This is bigger than the team they built there, and the plans they have for once they graduate.

This town and its secrets had the power to make a man of power, Rolland Brayshaw, choose to stay in prison instead of running free. It kept a money-hungry whore away, living in a rundown trailer with the kid she didn't want instead of living lavishly in a mansion. It kept me hidden, kept Zoey hidden, ran Maria away. The reasoning may be unclear, but the result the same. If this place can do all those things, taking me is kid's work.

The secret Brayshaw returns, not by accident, but intentionally. Give one to save the other.

The boys start back for the car and with each step taken, their feet drag a little longer, shoulders lose a little height, and heads hang a little further.

This kills them.

And as if this sight alone wasn't fucked up enough, the front door is tugged open and a tear-streaked face and messy blonde curls bounds out.

She cries, calling after her daddy and the three-stop dead in their tracks.

Captain whips around, dropping to his knees right as Zoey reaches him, her little arms wrapping around his neck, cutting my air off.

My eyes move to Maddoc, but he doesn't look at the little

girl desperate to keep her dad with her. His eyes are on the SUV, temples taut, lips smashed in a firm line.

His hand lifts to his face, and he runs his fingers across his jaw, pausing once his entire mouth is covered. He squeezes his jaw, his eyes falling.

I lay across the seat, staring at the ceiling.

I'm pretty sure this trip backfired. We came out here so Cap could share his world with us, to hold him and them over until they could make it out here next. To convince them this was the right move, trying to keep us both, delaying.

There's always a sacrifice to be made.

A few minutes pass and the three finally slide in the vehicle, a heaviness with them, threatening to crush me whole, but anger is enough to keep me together.

The car ride home is a silent one.

Once we get to the house, the four of us climb from the SUV and head straight up the stairs. Royce and Captain disappear into their own rooms and Maddoc pauses by mine.

He grips my chin, his eyes bouncing between mine, suspicious. Knowing. "We're sleeping in my room tonight," he says, leaving me to follow.

He turns on his shower, so I start stripping from my clothes, tossing them to the floor, and make my way to him.

We step inside, and he moves me into the spray with a soft grip to my shoulders. He smooths his hands over my hair as the water soaks it, running his fingers down my spine until he reaches the curve of my ass. He trails to my hips and turns me away from him.

His head dips into my neck, and he kisses there a moment before a small sting from his teeth pierces my skin. His lips hit my ear, but his words never come.

I spin in his arms, stepping backward until my shoulder blades hit the cool tile, bringing him against me.

He falls into me, his eyes hitting mine and I know.

He knows.

This is it.

The broody rich boy was never supposed to fall for the project problem child anyway, and the problem child never should have allowed herself to believe her world could be more than settling and survival.

I run my tongue along my teeth, lifting my chin to grip his bottom lip between them. I clamp down until he growls lightly.

"My baby." His eyes close. "She doesn't bare her teeth in vain," he whispers, running his tongue along the wound. "She *bites.*"

His lips hit mine and he kisses me rough, demanding, but then it shifts. His muscles fall, his hands sliding into my hair with a gentleness he's fighting to control. He savors every swipe of his tongue, every move of his mouth against mine.

He takes his time knowing we have no more.

Tomorrow, it all changes.

Maddoc

CAPTAIN STEPS FROM HIS ROOM AROUND FOUR IN THE MORNING, pausing in his tracks when he spots me sitting against the wall of mine.

He walks over, eyeing me carefully.

I nod my chin, and he drops down opposite of me. He taps his knuckle twice against the wall behind him and not five seconds later Royce steps out, half asleep.

He frowns at the sight of us, but slowly drops beside Cap.

I look from Captain to Royce.

"She knows."

Royce looks to my door. "What does this mean?"

My stare meets his, and realization hits him.

He closes his eyes, dropping his head against the wall. "We take her or she runs on her own."

Captain's chest rises with a deep inhale, and he looks down the hall.

"Captain."

He licks his lips, like words are lodged there and need help out. "I have an idea." He lets out a tortured chuckle. "I have no fucking clue if it'll work, but I do know you'll hate it."

"Fuck, man," Royce rasps, pinching the bridge of his nose.

"Does it keep her from them?"

"Sort of." Captain's eyes hit mine. "But not only them."

My vision blurs, so I close my eyes. My airway starts to close, so I swallow past the grating in my throat and force out the only fucking thing I'm one hundred percent sure of at this moment.

"I trust you."

Chapter 11

RAVEN

"Do you have questions for me?" Rolland asks quietly.

I scoff, looking out the window. "None I would trust you to answer honestly."

"That's fair."

My eyes slice to his. "Fair?" I repeat. "*Fair?*" I shift in the seat to face him fully. "Are you for real right now?" I gape at him.

"I simply meant I can understand why you wouldn't trust me. I haven't given you much reason to."

A humorless laugh leaves me. "You're seriously sitting there talking like we're headed to a fucking basketball game and this is the small talk on the way."

He moves his eyes to his phone, typing away. "I'm sorry you feel that—"

I slap the phone from his hands and his glare flies to mine.

My eyes narrow. "I'm not sure you know your boys at all if you think this isn't gonna go ass fucking backward to whatever you've cooked up in your head. I know them, each fucking one. They would *never* agree to stay away for this. I can promise you this will not be as cut and dry as you want."

His forehead tightens and he settles more against his seat. "What do you think they'll do?"

"I don't know, but I suggest you think back into that vault of a mind you seem to have and figure it out, that or stand there with wide eyes and tense muscles letting them know what a great leader you are, can't even keep your own sons in order." I tilt my head. "How ever will you control an entire town, dear Brayshaw?"

"You sound like you want me to govern them in."

"As if you could if you tried," I force past clenched teeth. "What I want is for you to understand and accept the shift you refuse to see."

He eyes me a moment. "And what shift would that be, Raven?"

The car slows to a stop, the locks on the door popping up.

"What was once yours no longer is. This is their town, best if you figure it out now, Rolland. I'd hate for you to be embarrassed when you give an order and all eyes shift to them for confirmation." I push my door open and walk straight for the man blocking the entrance across from where we're parked, not acknowledging the gun sticking from his pants.

He pulls out a metal detector, his eyes locked on me as he moves it across my front, pausing when it beeps at the waist of my jeans.

He eyes me. "No weapons allowed."

"Are you telling me the men inside, the men who run entire towns and meet in an abandoned warehouse on a dirt lot, have not a single form of protection on them?"

The man's eyes narrow.

"Sergio, please meet Raven Brayshaw." Rolland steps up behind me.

Sergio's eyes snap back to me and he dips his head, moving to the side with another breath.

I scoff, squeezing through the iron door that's slowly started to roll open.

We're met with two more security, but they don't look either of us in the eye.

Again, they dip their heads and move aside.

A few feet in and the walls change. From rusted old iron to black drapes, just like the one at the end of the hall.

It's pushed open for us and we step into a small cubed space. A curtain is pulled closed behind us, and the one in front is slid open.

My pulse begins to race.

I don't realize my leg is bouncing until Rolland leans closer to whisper, "Settle yourself, Raven. You must be sure for this to be accepted. They will smell your fear or hesitance."

"Fuck you," I whisper back, and take a deep breath. "I'm not fearful, or hesitant."

An empty chair comes into view, and then the farther the curtain rolls, the more chairs are revealed, only these ones aren't empty. In each one sits a different man, and behind each man is another.

"Ready?" Rolland asks and extends his elbow for me to take.

I push forward without him.

I don't miss the twitch to the man at the end's lips. I glare at him first.

The soft chuckle behind him has my eyes snapping over his shoulder.

Alec Daniels.

He winks, and my muscles settle slightly.

Again, my stare finds the man in the chair in front of him. Tan skin, tattoos creeping up his neck – the only one in jeans and a t-shirt.

This must be Gio's boss – Trick Rivera, the Riverside family.

Movement to my right catches my attention and I spot security spacing out every inch of the room, one every three to five feet, none making direct eye contact, all wide-eyed and aware.

"Ah." A grating voice wraps around my shoulder blades and I spin for the entrance right as Donley and Collins walk through with their heads held high.

Donley holds his hands up. "The princess has arrived." He gives a nasty smile. "And so punctual."

I look to Collins, who, much to my surprise, only nods his chin.

"Rae."

"Collins." I eye him as he and Donley move toward the men in their seats, shaking hands with each of them, both eyes focusing on the empty chair for a moment longer than necessary.

Mine tighten, cutting across the room once more.

Five families, five chairs, only four taken by the men before me.

My stare slides to Rolland and his pinches in warning.

A laugh leaves me before I can help it and suddenly all eyes are on me.

One of the men in a suit sits forward, his elbows on his knees.

"You look much like your mother."

"I take offense to that," I reply instantly.

I think I catch him off guard as he laughs lightly.

"I see you're much more outspoken than her."

"Let's not with the unnecessary banter. I'm here for a reason."

"Indeed, you are." The man grins, his eyes moving to Rolland. "I assume she's aware of all she needs to be?"

Rolland opens his mouth to speak but I step forward.

"You people may like to pretend women are weak and have no voices, but I'm not and I say what I want. I can speak for myself." I stare the man right in the eye, enjoying the way his tighten in surprise.

"I see." He sits back, looking to the others a moment before moving back to me. "Ms. Brayshaw, I'm Calvin Greyson."

I blink at him.

He fights a grin. He can't be more than twenty-five, if that. "We're simply here as witnesses. Your town is your town, your issues with the Graven family are your issues. That being said, a town divided cannot sit on the council with us. That is the purpose of the union that was promised before your time. In order for us to be a strong unit, we need to be just that, a unit. A town divided is weak. It was agreed upon that should Brayshaw openly accept the marriage to Graven, the Gravens would see it as a move of good faith, and the Brayshaws would take final lead." He turns to Donley. "This is correct, Donley?"

"It is." He moves his eyes to mine. Nothing but victory swimming in them. "She marries in, unites our families once and for all, we no longer push for power in lead as our strength will come in time."

"Raven."

My eyes slide back to the tattooed guy.

He confirms who he is in his introduction. "I'm Trick Rivera. You understand what they're saying, right?" He eyes me. "You must *accept* the marriage."

Donley scoffs beside me and Trick's eyes darken as they slide his way, a fierce expression in place.

"I promise you, I only *ever* do what I want," I tell him. "Something Collins is well aware of, so maybe it's he who should *accept* me, the bitch of a bride he'll be getting."

Small chuckles float across the room.

"In a heartbeat, Rae." Collins pushes his chest out, not bothering to look my way.

I bite into my cheek.

"Actually," Donley draws out, his smirk as revolting as his presence. "I threw that little clause in a long time ago, and it earned me a runaway bride. I don't wish to extend this to Raven, especially since Collins will already be marrying an impure bride when we were promised a virgin. Contract says she's mine regardless, though..." He trails off, his eyes meeting mine, knowing. "I don't imagine we'll be forcing anyone's hands today."

Piece of shit.

The man who looks the eldest of them all, studies me curiously. "Ms. Brayshaw, I'm Romero Hacienda of Hacienda Heights. Welcome home."

I nod, having no words for the stranger.

"Regardless of Donley's show of power he does not have," the man remarks. "If you would, please make the announcement you gathered us here for today, so we can be on our way."

"Be sure to state your name first," Trick offers with a small nod.

"I'm Raven Brayshaw," I say with zero hesitation, a numb body, and shattering heart. "And I acknowledge the union between families."

"You wish to marry Collins Graven?"

I look to Collins who stares at me with open, honest eyes. An apology shines in them, regret and hope all rolled into one.

He truly wants this?

"I'll be good to you, I swear it," he says directly, in front of everyone as if it's just the two of us standing here.

Brave of the bastard.

I face forward. "Yes."

Not a second after Donley's single clap, the air shifts.

I don't have to look to know who is coming, my boys' footsteps vibrate the floor beneath us.

My eyes slice to Rolland's, witnessing the strain that takes over in an instant.

"This will be tough, Raven," he whispers quickly. "I'm so sorry."

With a deep breath, I spin, my heart dropping to my feet at the sight of the boys.

I fight the urge to go to them, to swallow the anger radiating off every inch of Maddoc, to burn the unknown swimming in his eyes, in all their eyes.

"You're late to the party, boys, but no worry, you'll receive the invitation to the real celebration in the mail." Donley smiles as he steps forward.

He pushes Collins to my side, and my eyes slice back to Maddoc's, but he masks his mien well.

"I want you to stay away from her," Collins dares to say. "Raven belongs—"

"To a Graven," Captain cuts him off, his voice strong and determined, his head held high, brass knuckles on and gleaming against the light. "I'm here to ask for that spot." He steps beside me and the entire room stills. "Raven should be mine."

What.

The.

Fuck.

Chapter 12

RAVEN

My breath lodges in my throat, a numbness shoots from my neck to my toes.

Four words that, while I don't understand their meaning, should bring me relief, but dread is what locks me in place instead.

I believe Maddoc would go toe to toe with his dad, this town, these people if he could. He'd do anything in his power to keep me at his side, fight neck to neck if push came to shove and reason was thrown out the window, if Zoey wasn't at risk.

But Captain?

Two brothers who love each other soul deep having something standing between them, threatening to shred what is supposed to be an unbreakable bond?

Having *me* stand between them?

"No," I whisper, shaking my head, and a strain of other rejections follow – not one from Maddoc.

"Stop," Captain demands of everyone. "Ravina Brayshaw

was promised to the top Graven." His eyes hit Donley. "That doesn't mean her daughter defaults to his son."

"She has to marry a Graven," Collins adds, stepping forward.

"You're right, *cousin*."

I grow nauseous.

Cousin.

"Cap..." I think I say out loud.

"Donley." The man who addressed me second stands.

Donley frowns at Captain, but after a moment, anger paints his face red. "What is this?"

"I have the paternity test—"

"There is no need. Raven has accepted the marriage; your daughter is irrelevant to us now."

"I know," he says, nice and calm. Too calm.

"Then why—"

Captain shoves an envelope into Collins' chest. "Open it."

"What is it?" he asks hesitantly, his eyes finding mine a moment.

Captain says nothing and a few of the others stand as Collins tears open the envelope. His eyes skim over the folded paperwork a moment, a deep crease forming over his forehead.

"This is... this can't be true," Collins says, looking to Donley when he snags it from him.

Captain addresses the rest of the room, avoiding his dad's eyes. "As you know, I am not of Brayshaw blood."

Donley fumes, tossing the papers to the floor. "Family runs deeper than blood," he mocks.

"I'm aware. I claim nothing you are, represent nothing you've been," Cap says strongly. "But my real father was brought into Graven as my adoptive father is Brayshaw. Does that not give me the right to ask for this?"

"Cap," I rasp, my hand moving to my throat as my breathing becomes increasingly louder.

He continues, "My choice was stolen from me. I'm here to ask for it back."

Finally, Captain turns to me, grief, pain, and prospect clouding his light eyes. My body wrenches forward from the force in which his pain hits me. His stare tightens even more as he says, "A Brayshaw and a Graven is what is needed, yes?" His eyes are glued to me as he says it, but his words are for them. "This will give Brayshaw power." He looks to Donley. "But what about the Gravens, they only gain a queen?"

Collins jerks forward, but Royce is quick to step in front of him.

Donley walks around them and closer to Captain, Rolland moving closer to his son as the enemy creeps in.

He eyes Captain a moment, and he can't help himself. He asks, "What are you offering, *son*?"

"A game changer." Captain lifts his chin. "Raven will be mine, I hers, and together, the head of an empire. No one surrenders anything. A new era begins. Both Graven and Brayshaw under Graven and Brayshaw."

"What makes you think we can't do this without you?" Donley asks.

"It doesn't matter what I think, it's what I know. I'm stronger than Collins. I have an influence he never will, respect he could only wish for, and Raven's love, which I can promise you he will never gain. You wanted Ravina to love her husband, it's why you chose Felix. With me, you will get that."

"And what is it you want in return for this?" Donley asks.

"You mean besides knowing Raven is cared for, safe and away from your grasp?" Captain glares. "My daughter's safety. Your word in writing, right here right now and in front of everyone, that she becomes untouchable, irrelevant to you and anyone else who may believe she's anything other than mine to care for and protect, only. Always."

My head starts to spin, and I fight for air.

Donley frowns, but it's clear he's swaying. "You'll have your own name's best interest."

"*We* will have this town's best interest, the town my daughter will grow up in, as it should be. This isn't about a powerful family. This is about a bulletproof empire. She deserves the strongest Graven has to offer. That's not Collins."

"You'll take the Graven name, give it to Zoey?" Donley asks slowly.

His acknowledging he knows her name has all the boys inching forward, and Cap's hands ball into fists at his side, but he swallows, holding his head high. "Yes."

"This is bullshit!" Collins shouts.

Donley shuts him up with a simple hand raised. He gauges me. "How about you, princess?"

Suddenly all eyes are on me, and I want nothing more than to tear his out.

Donley looks over my shoulder and I know it's Maddoc he's focused on. "You'll have to give him up. Completely." His foul stare comes back to mine. "This would have to be an honorable marriage, a new beginning."

"Why?" I snap. "Five minutes ago you were prepared to force my hand, now you wanna talk honor?"

He continues like I never spoke. "I won't allow you to marry one, and secretly keep the other. Maddoc will be expected to find his own bride. Will you accept this, accept Captain's offer?"

I swallow past the bile that makes its way up, forcing my features blank for the bastards before me. My gut tightens to the point of pain.

Captain turns to me, but I force my feet to shift.

I look to Maddoc.

He stares back, blank face, dead eyes – the boy I met on my very first day in this twisted city.

The boy I love, who loves me back. The one who would do anything for his family, for those he loves. No sacrifice too big.

I love him, I love all of them.

I look back to Captain.

My decision to marry Collins saves Zoey. I marry Collins, she's safe. She goes home where she'll be cared for and protected to no end, with her true family.

The boys would have her and each other, as they were meant to.

They would be okay and I would be in the arms of the asshole who touched me without permission, who attacked me to the point of loss of consciousness, who wants me so he can feel like he's worthy in Donley's eyes.

I agreed to marry Collins, but Cap is offering me his hand. Someone I trust and care for.

Marrying him, Zoey would still be safe to come home, but with the trade of grooms, Captain becomes everything he hates. The boys lose their brother, sort of. Maddoc would be forced to watch me at Captain's side.

Forever?

I lick my lips and look to the ground.

No sacrifice too big.

"No."

Cap's face falls and Collins smirks.

"No?" Donley repeats, almost as if he doesn't like my answer.

"I don't want him." I step away from Captain, moving toward Collins.

"No," Cap says.

"Raven," Royce starts.

"I said no!" I shout, looking to my boys, but it's too much, so I break the contact just as quick.

"Brayshaw stays on top. Brayshaw keeps control and Collins gets his wife. Me." I look to Donley, the others still struck by my decision. "It's what you wanted walking in here. I will be everything expected of me, I swear, but only for him."

At my words, Maddoc snaps, the indifference he tried to put off for the others in here gone.

He rushes me before anyone can stop him. Gripping my shoulders, he tugs me close.

"Stop it," he growls, eyes wrecked.

"No," I whisper, attempting to tear away from his touch.

"Baby," he breathes, so low I almost miss it. His grip tightens, his hands shaking against me though nobody else could spot it. "Don't."

"You knew why I was coming here."

"And now there's a better choice."

"If it's not you, it doesn't matter."

"Yes. It does," he growls. "Marry Captain." His brows meet in the center, deep creases buried in his forehead.

"I can't."

"May my family have a moment alone outside?" Rolland asks.

Before an answer is given, Maddoc yanks me down the hall and out the front. He pulls me around the corner, telling the security standing there to leave.

He turns to me.

"You love him," he rushes out, desperation screaming behind his green eyes. "You could love him more."

"I don't want to."

"He's *saving* you."

"By breaking *you*."

He steps against me, his hands sliding up both sides of my face.

I lift my chin, and his palms slide farther, tangling into my hair, his thumbs on my cheekbones.

"Nobody can break me but you, snow," he whispers. "And

you will, you will fucking shred me if you marry Collins when you could have Captain instead."

"No. We both win or we both lose."

"That's fucking stupid!" he hisses. "Why when you can have more, be safe?"

"I won't destroy your family so I can sleep easier at night."

"You think we'll be functional knowing you gave your life for us? We won't."

"Maddoc please…"

His lips push against mine, but they don't move. They don't demand, and they don't take as they should. They plead.

He pulls back, eyes sloped at the edges. "Let me go, give me peace of mind. Cap will love you, he will protect you."

"And you?"

He looks to the ground. "I'll never replace you, but if you don't accept him, I'll hate you."

"I'm okay with that."

"I'll wreck your world."

"It's already wrecked!"

He glares, jerking away from me, tearing my heart a little more in the process. "I will leave them."

I freeze, my eyes bouncing between his.

Abandon his family?

"I'll leave this place, right fucking now and everyone in it, never looking back."

"Maddoc—"

"Don't test me, Raven." His eyes turn to stone, freezing me out in a moment's notice.

My eyes start to water without permission, so I look to the sky, denying their escape.

Damned if I do, damned if I don't.

"You're backing me into a corner, Big Man."

"Where I can protect you."

I look back to him, giving a slow shake of my head. "I won't be yours to protect."

I swear his eyes haze over, but he blinks the pain away. "You will *always* be mine where it matters."

"Don't make me do this."

"Don't make him wait."

With that, he turns and walks back inside, and I'm left standing there, a dozen men waiting only feet away for me to seal my fate.

I squeeze my eyes shut, wipe my face with my sleeves, and take a deep breath.

I know I look busted and weak, everything a girl in their world is likely known to be, but I go back in with my head held high.

I step forward, into the room full of men I don't know, men I do, and the only people in the world I trust.

The ones I trust, who are asking me to deny one, give up the other, and take another.

Everyone knew I'd give myself for them, it's why the boys were fearful, and how the Gravens were so sure. Dangle Zoey and I'd save her, for them. It's what Perkins meant when he said I would make the decision once I learned the alternative. It's why Collins helped hide Zoey from his dear leader as long as he could – holding out for me.

He wanted my trust, but they earned it first, a fact Rolland didn't fully think through.

He wanted me to grow to tolerate, if not care for, his boys. He knew if I did, I'd do right by them as time went on and I was in my new role as a Graven trophy, but he underestimated the bond he hoped to create. He wasn't aware the boys were missing something they desperately craved – free, untainted love, something they stole from me without my permission, that I'd willingly give them now.

We all had broken tethers before each other, lost pieces we couldn't place and refused to acknowledge.

Nobody could predict or prepare for the strength behind four fused souls.

Captain let the world in on a secret nobody ever had to learn tonight, all in hopes it would give him the power to claim me over Collins, the girl no one cared to defend before this place.

Cap's hand isn't being forced. He's the reasonable one of the three, the deep thinker and over processor, the calm. He's the packman, protecting his own as he can, and here I am turning him down for someone he hates when he just stood in front of his dad and brothers, looked in the eyes of a man he hates and gave up his future for mine.

For ours?

I slide my clammy hand into Captain's.

I wait for Rolland to look me dead in the eye, drop my guard and show him all he's done.

One night, one choice.

Four broken Brayshaws.

"You win."

The slope of his eyes conveys what it should, a self-directed question that I hope crushes him from the inside out.

Did he?

Chapter 13

RAVEN

TWO WORDS CHANGED EVERYTHING IN IN THE BLINK OF AN EYE.

The boys were asked to leave as were the other families while Cap and I had to sit at a round table with Rolland and Donley, where they laid it all out.

Our wedding is planned, honeymoon scheduled and paid for before we're even allowed to leave. Donley adjusted the contract to reflect my "situation." Since I wouldn't produce bloody sheets the morning after, a video will be required. A fucking porno, for lack of better words, of me and my *husband* consummating our marriage. Only after that, will Donley let go of the idea of Zoey – he wants me, not her, but he won't dare say the words aloud. He needs the threat to hang over our heads.

I'll be eighteen in two months.

My wedding is scheduled for the first Saturday that follows, and on neutral ground – the cabins. I assume Donley has no idea I'm technically already a legal adult.

I bet this was all part of Rolland's plan, having me ready to go at a moment's notice.

Asshole.

Donley tried to demand Maddoc be forced from his home until after the marriage, when we'd be expected to live on the Graven Estate, but I refused to allow that and agreed we'd stay away. Donley was pleased, so now we're on our way to a hotel suite, where we're to live until the party pad is gutted and prepared for us, unless the wedding comes first.

I'm almost relieved. I can't imagine facing Maddoc right now and having to pretend we were able to wash away all we are with a simple signature.

A bitter laugh leaves me.

Relieved.

I must be sick to be feeling anything of the sort right now.

I should be flipping the fuck out, breaking windows and shattering the chilled champagne in here against the doors. I should be plotting Donley's slow and painful death or maybe taking it out on Captain for making this happen.

I roll my eyes at myself.

Again, I'm pathetic. I can't even find it in me to hate him right now, like a normal person in my shoes would.

He stole my choice, defending me when I didn't want him to.

Didn't I do the same?

I went off, offered me for his daughter like he offered himself for me?

But those are his brothers. His loyalty should have been with them over me, no matter fucking what.

A sad chuckle leaves him, and my eyes reluctantly slide his way.

"Come on, Raven. You know them better than that." His eyes slowly meet mine. "If they knew I had a way to protect you and didn't, regardless of where it left them, they'd hate me for it."

"Who says I won't hate you for this?"

His brows pull in and he lets out a deep exhale.

"You might," he whispers, pausing a minute before he says, "But you'll forgive me with time. They wouldn't."

"Is that why you did it, Cap? So they wouldn't hate you?" It's a good enough reason.

"No, Raven," he murmurs. "I did it because you deserve more than this place has given you."

I shake my head against the seat, looking away.

He's wrong. This place gave me everything I never had, a family, people to care for. A purpose.

Am I pissed right now? Fuck, yeah, but at the world, not him. How could I be? He only did what his brothers would, what he felt was right, but that doesn't mean this will be easy in any way, and I can't promise I won't ruin everything.

"I could never love you more than him," I say, watching the trees fly by outside my window. "And I'll never stop wanting him."

"I know," he rasps. "I can live with that."

I shake my head. "You shouldn't have to, Captain, that's my point. You're worth way more than what you're getting in me. A thousand times more."

"I lost nothing today, Raven. I've loved someone before, or I think I have. She fucked me over. You won't. I can make you happy. I know who you are, and I know I can love you like you deserve. It won't be the same for you, but you will feel it. You will smile and laugh, and sometimes you'll even feel guilty for it just like I will. All that's okay and expected. I didn't stand there and ask for your life for sport. It might be a slow start, but it will be a strong finish."

The weak in me comes back in the form of moisture stricken eyes and his hand slides into mine.

He squeezes. "Trust me."

That's the thing. My world is fucked, I was more or less pushed into this when I thought the day would end much differently. He was sneaky and knew, in the end, only one answer would do. Still... I trust him with my life, and it seems that's the entire point. It's his now.

I nod. "I do."

The rest of the drive goes by in silence.

"You can stop pretending to be asleep now," Cap says quietly as the car rolls to a stop. "We're here."

I open my eyes and step from the car when the door is pulled open for me. I glare at the smirky bastard and move up the steps, Captain falling in line beside me.

A man meets us at the desk, handing us a room key without a word, and the two of us head for the private elevator.

Of course, it's an over the top suite with gold shit everywhere.

Captain picks up the note from the entrance table. He shakes his head, tossing it to the floor. "Food will be up in fifteen minutes, and they had clothes and shit put in the drawers and closet."

I nod, moving to grab something so I can shower.

Escape a minute.

I tug open the drawer, an instant frown taking over.

For fuck's sake.

Lace after lace. I pull open the closet. Dresses, glittery, long ones.

"Are they shitting me?" I tug them from their hangers, dropping them to the floor.

Captain steps up behind me and I let my hand fall, shaking my head.

He reaches over, pulling a shirt meant for him down and holds it out for me to take. "Ignore them, they're all a part of the mind game he's trying to play."

I spin around, looking up at him. "He can't really think I'll be a voiceless statue of perfection."

Cap's eyes shift between mine. "If he does, we'll set him straight quickly."

I keep my eyes on his for a long moment before he steps back and holds a hand out toward the bathroom.

"I'll let you know if the food gets here and you're still in there." He turns around, moving for the balcony doors.

"Cap."

He looks over his shoulder.

"Thank you. I know you don't agree, but you didn't have to do this."

He gives a sad smile. "You're right, I don't agree."

A light laugh leaves me, and I move for the bathroom, pause at the door. When I glance over my shoulder, my mouth clamps shut when I find he's already staring at me, shaking his phone in the air.

"I'm calling him now," he says softly. "Take a shower, I'll fill you in when you're done."

I don't respond but head straight for the bathroom. I close and lock the door, setting my knife and iPod on the counter, then turn on the water and step in with my clothes on, cold water and all.

This is fucking insane.

Arranged marriages and decades-old moves of alliance. It's bullshit. All because a dead man made a promise he couldn't keep.

I strip my soaked clothes off and toss them over the glass. I'm not sure how long I stand under the spray before there's a light knock on the door.

I ignore it at first, but then it gets louder and louder and I freeze.

And then they knock again, but it's not a hand against wood – it's metal.

I don't shut off the spray, but slowly step out and wrap a towel around me.

The knock gets louder, harder, to the point that the wood shakes against the frame.

I flip open my knife and slowly wrap my fingers around the knob.

Knife still in hand, I gradually turn the lock.

The banging starts again, and I get ready to push it open.

"Get away from that door!" Captain's sudden voice shouts. "What the fuck do you think you're doing?!"

"I need—" another voice answers but is cut off.

"You need to back the fuck up," Cap demands.

"Tell her to open the door."

"Stay inside, Raven."

My lip twitches.

"I need to confirm she's in there... alone."

My mouth drops open and Captain laughs mockingly.

I quickly dry off and slip on my underwear and the shirt Captain gave me.

"You think, after all the shit today, she'd already be locked in there with him?" Cap draws out slowly.

"I'm—"

"Leaving. You're fucking leaving."

I yank the door open and glare at the goon in front of me.

His eyes find me a moment before he quickly moves them over my shoulder.

So, no respect from Graven security. Good to know.

"Ms. Brayshaw."

"Fuck off, do your little inspection and get the fuck out." I push past him, snag a throw blanket from the little chair, and walk out onto the balcony.

"He's not here," Cap tells him. "Now go back to your boss and report it. Be sure to let him know you'll be the first to be fired."

A few moments pass and then a door slams.

Captain steps onto the balcony only seconds later, a pair of boxer briefs in his hand for me.

I take them, slipping them on quickly, and tossing the stupid blanket to the ground. "I guess this is what we have to look forward to, right?"

"Wrong," he says. "I'll fix this."

I nod, looking away. I know he will.

There's a light knock on the door, and Cap looks over his shoulder briefly before glancing back at me. "You know what, I'm not hungry."

"Me either."

I follow him inside, standing to the side while he opens the door and tells the staff to take the food back to the kitchen.

When he closes the door and turns to me, my eyes slide to the sofa sleeper he apparently prepared for himself while I was in the shower.

I frown. "You don't have to sleep there."

"I do."

"You wouldn't have before today."

He nods, looking from his makeshift bed to me. "You're right. Lots happened today though, Raven. I think you need at least a night in bed alone with your thoughts."

"Yeah, and what do you need, Cap?" I ask him.

He licks his lips, knowing it's a fair question. "I need to convince myself I didn't betray my brother in the worst way, and I can't do that lying next to you on night one."

A deep ache forms beneath my ribs and I look away, moving for the bed and climbing under the covers. "If he feels betrayed, he hates himself for it."

"Yeah." Captain slips under his blanket, staring up at the ceiling. "That might be the worst part."

Yeah.

"Are we going to school tomorrow?"

"We said we would, but I'm thinking we don't."

"Same." I glare at the wall. "We also said we'd let Collins back in without busting his chops, can we agree not to do that either?"

"He won't step out of line."

"I don't know, he lost a lot today in his eyes. He'll either flip the fuck out or he won't."

"He lost the life he thought he deserved, like we warned would happen. If he causes problems, he won't get the chance to find another one."

We're both quiet for a long moment before I tell him, "You know, through all the shady shit, I gained some respect for your dad today."

Cap looks my way, a light crease in his forehead.

"He had us both in his hands for years. He could have set this up when we were little, but he didn't." I shrug. "Having all he thought he wanted wasn't worth losing you."

"And now he might have lost us all."

I nod. "He has to be realizing you three are more than he could have ever been, bet that's all he ever wanted. Coming home though, being thrown back into a world he hasn't seen this close in so long, it messed with his mind. Maybe he needs time to work out all the changes."

"Time isn't something we'll be giving him anymore. He'll answer when asked."

"Spoken like a king."

Despite the shittiness, Cap lets out a small chuckle and rolls over, facing away from me.

"You can turn the light off, Cap."

"Nah, let's leave it on."

A small smile finds my lips, but it's gone just as quick. The night's closing and reality comes crashing down.

He promised no one could take me from him, that it was me and him, no matter what.

You lied, Big Man.

Chapter 14

MADDOC

My head rolls against the... the fuck is it?

"Dirt or grass maybe?"

"What was he doing when you found him?"

Royce.

"Busting out the windows in the shed. With his fists."

Victoria.

"Having Maybell call me was the right move."

"Where's Raven?" she asks.

"Ha!" I shout, rolling onto my knees and forearms. "Fuckin' ha!" I push off the ground, but my legs aren't working, and I face plant.

Yeah, it's fucking dirt.

My eyes peel open when a hand tugs at my shoulder.

Floppy fucking hair and a neck tattoo is in my face.

"Brother."

"Yeah, man," Royce mumbles under his breath. "Help me out, yeah? Put your fucking foot on the ground."

I do and he tugs me up.

A little body slides under my other arm and my head rolls that way, nothing but blonde hair getting in my face. She looks up with a glare. "Move your feet."

I push toward her and she pulls her head back but stays under my arm.

"Bishop!" Royce yells but I don't look away from Victoria. "Bring my truck over here, now!"

"I should take you like he took her."

"Shut the fuck up, Maddoc," Royce growls.

Victoria's eyes slice to him. "What is he talking about?"

"Nothing."

I scoff, my head falling back. "Yeah, nothing. Fucking everything."

The dark sky mocks me. It's empty, like my bed will be.

Not his though.

"Let me." My head snaps left meeting gelled-back hair and a metal fucking mouth.

I should rip that lip ring right off this fucker.

Bishop shakes his head. "What, Raven disobey again?"

I tug away, throwing a punch at him but he dodges it, and I trip forward into a crate.

"Fuck," Royce spits. "Shut the fuck up, Bishop, or I'll lay your ass out! Help me get him the fuck in the car."

My body is jostled as I'm tossed on a seat.

I open my eyes. Pretty sure this is my ride.

I slightly register Maybell walking toward Victoria who's standing a few feet away.

"It's over, Maybell. Bet you knew that already though. Can't trust nobody. Only my brothers. And her."

"What the fuck happened?" Bishop asks.

"Not now," Royce growls and goes to slam the door, but I block it with my foot.

"Bishop," I slur. "Be at the house in the morning. I need to switch your positions."

Bishop frowns, his eyes sliding to Royce. "Why? Profits are up, I have a new fighter every couple weeks, we haven't had an incident in—"

"Shut the fuck up," I manage to get out. "You're a hands man. This is a promotion. I need you on security," I slur.

Royce cusses and slams the door.

My eyes close, nothing but long black hair and grey eyes in sight.

She disappears.

ROYCE SLAPS A HAND ON MY BACK AND MY EYES PEEL OPEN.

"Get up, Bishop's here," he spits.

"Fuck him."

"Man, fuck you. You asked his ass to come here. You're lucky I let him in. Get the fuck up."

That's right. Security.

"I need something for my head, it's fucking pounding."

"Good, maybe it'll knock some sense into you." He tosses me the water bottle from my dresser. "Get your own fucking pain meds, asshole, or better yet, don't." He slams the door against the wall on his way out.

I push myself to my feet, stumbling, still drunk on last night's shit.

I take a quick shower, dress and meet them downstairs.

Royce and Bass are playing a silent game of pool, but put down the cues when I walk in.

"I want you on security," I get right to it.

"For you?" Bass narrows his eyes. When I don't respond, he guesses again. "Raven."

Royce drops his eyes to the floor when I look his way.

"What will I be doing?"

"Following her everywhere she goes, no matter who she's with. You'll live with her, check in on her every night and morning."

Bass looks to Royce then back to me. "Is she moving or are you telling me I'm moving in here?"

Royce's eyes cut to mine. "You sure you get to make that decision?"

"Who's gonna stop me?" I push.

He shakes his head with a glare.

Bishop studies the two of us. "What if I decline this *promotion*?"

"You're fired."

He nods, glancing around. "And Raven, does she know about this yet?"

"No."

"Are you planning to okay it with her?"

"No."

"Bishop, go," Royce forces past clenched teeth. "I need to talk to my brother."

"No need for secrecy. Everyone'll find out soon."

"Maddoc," he snaps.

"Raven is marrying Captain. Captain can't always be home. She'll need someone with her when he's gone. Someone we can depend on; someone she should be able to trust. It will be you."

Bishop's face goes slack, his eyes moving from Royce to me. Slowly, he pushes to his feet, moving closer to me. "What happened?"

"We don't pay you to ask questions. You taking the job or not?" I cross my arms.

His jaw clenches and he jerks his chin, before storming past me and out the door.

The second it closes, Royce shoves me from the side,

making me stumble.

He gets in my face. "You better fucking watch it, brother. You helped make this happen. You knew what it meant when we left there. I won't let you act a fucking fool. I know this is ugly, I know this shit hurts, but—"

"Hurts?!" I boom. "I fucking wish it hurt. I want it to hurt, Royce! I want it to fucking burn me up, eat me alive, tear me fucking apart!" I shout, shoving him into the bar.

Bottles tumble over, shatter and spill around us.

Royce comes back and lays one across my jaw, and I lose my footing.

He rushes me, and my hip slams against the edge of the pool table, knocking the wind out of me. With a grip on my collar, he headbutts me, blood instantly pouring down his brow as he pulls me closer, teeth bared.

"Do it again, brother," I wheeze. "Harder. Do it."

His face goes slack before his forehead falls to mine. "Fuck, Madman," he breathes, squeezes me tighter before pushing away completely with a shake of his head.

He takes a step away but turns back with barren eyes. "I know your entire fucking world is shattering, but so is mine. Shit, so is all of ours."

"You sure about that?"

"You don't get to do this. *You* made the final decision." His jaw clenches as his lip curls, but the defeat in his eyes is what kicks me in the ribs. "At least he gave you the choice." He takes a few more steps away, and with each one, more life drains from his eyes. "I had just as much to lose, and I didn't get one."

He picks up a barstool, smashing it against the wall on his way out, slamming the door with his exit.

With a cough, I push to my feet, taking a look around the room.

My eyes fall on my dad standing at the end of the hall,

hiding away and watching like a coward, with his hands in his pockets, a frown on his face.

"You fuckin' happy?" I spit, blindly throwing a pool ball at the trophy case, the shattering of the glass and the toppling of bronze and gold worthless accomplishments mocking me with every hit against the grain. "The Gravens got what they wanted, you're still standing, and all it took was the fall of your own sons." I shake my head. "We should have denied you, accepted the scholarships we were offered for basketball, taken her with us. We wouldn't have needed a fucking thing from you or this place. We'd have lives, real lives, away from fake laws and faker people. Captain wanted time to focus on his daughter after graduation, now he has to run an empire that will take time from her, just like it took your time from us, like it took time from Ravina when her grandfather was in charge, and you saw what happened there. A girl, desperate for love, so desperate she agreed to an arranged fucking marriage from the first person to make her feel wanted." I shake my head.

"Royce has connection issues; did you know that?" I don't let him answer. "But with Raven here, he was getting better, she moved him in a way we couldn't, loved him in a way he needed and never had. Bet that's been blown to shit. And me?" I shrug, looking away. "All I ever had was my brothers and strength, it grew with her. Now I'm standing here, by my fucking self, having never felt so weak in my damn life." My eyes hit his once more. "Guess that means I'm useless to you now, too, huh?"

I force my steps steady as I make my way to my room, but my feet carry me to hers instead.

I drop down, my ass on the floor, back against the bed.

Hours must go by as I sit there alone.

I take my time, replay every moment from the first glare to the last kiss, and I gulp when I'd swear my fucking chest plate is cracking open.

I'm so fucking sorry, baby.

Footsteps shuffle in, and after a moment a shoulder hits mine.

My eyes peel open, sliding sideways.

Royce glares as he passes a fresh cracked bottle of Crown. He looks away once I grab it. We take turns, passing it between us in silence until our hands are no longer steady and the bottle drops to the floor.

Both our heads fall to the mattress behind us and stay there until the sun is gone and rises again.

It's futile, the time spent.

With the new light only comes more darkness.

Chapter 15

RAVEN

"FUCK SCHOOL," I WHINE, GLARING AT THE CLOCK. "I FEEL like crap."

"I feel you." Captain fishes clothes from the drawer, glancing at me over his shoulder. "But Maybell said the boys didn't go yesterday either, and Victoria told her Collins was there. We can't abandon the school. Our people don't feel safe when Graven is around and we're not."

"We are Graven."

"Not yet, we're not." He shuts the drawer and spins, leaning against it with a frown. "We need them to see while things are changing, we aren't, and they can still trust us to do what's right there."

With a huff, I push off the bed and move for the closet. I glare at the pile of shit I let fall to the floor the first night.

"I'm not wearing any of this garbage."

The same time I say it, there's a knock on the door.

I glance at Cap as he rubs a towel over his wet hair. He winks and disappears into the bathroom again, so I move to open the door.

My eyes widen in surprise, then close in relief when Victoria tosses a bag into my chest.

"I don't have much, but I brought you a couple days' worth of shit," she says.

"Fuck yes." I drag her inside, shutting the door behind her.

She slides her hands in her back pockets, looking around the room. "Fancy."

I scoff, pouring out the bag and picking up the faded black jeans and long sleeve shirt covered in mini cheeseburgers. "Yeah, check out the freakin' buffet, breakfast for two they said." I roll my eyes.

She walks over to the expensive golden trimmed table, running her fingers across it.

I push the boxers down and tug on the pants. I grab one of the ridiculous bras from the drawer, sliding it under my sweater to clasp it.

I toss the shirt over my head, and right as I'm sliding my arms into it, Cap's voice peeks out the bathroom.

"You changing?"

My eyes happen to hit Victoria's right as he speaks, and a grape freezes at her lips. She frowns, slowly setting it down.

"I'm done." I frown right back.

Captain steps out and she shoots up straight.

He nods at her, then moves for the closet for his shoes.

Her eyes bounce around the room, then lock on the bathroom door before the balcony and it hits me.

"No one else is here."

Her eyes fly to mine. She wants to ask, and she might if Captain wasn't here. She'll have to work on that if she wants to make it in this place, and I need her to, so she'll have to find her voice on her own.

I drop beside Cap on the bed.

"You ready?" he asks.

For day one in our new roles.

"Do we need a plan? I mean are we walking up in there announcing or are we letting them connect the dots."

"We'll help 'em out a bit, but I'm sure Collins will make sure word spreads." He eyes me a minute. "You good with that?"

I nod.

"Are you sure?"

"Don't ask me that, Captain. I'm here." I glare. "I'm sure."

His eyes snap over my shoulder and hold, so I look and Victoria's staring at us.

She takes the hint, silently stepping onto the balcony.

I turn back to Captain.

His eyes soften. "I don't wanna push you. Everything may have changed as far as the next steps, but nothing has changed apart from that yet, if it ever even does. I need you to tell me when it's too much."

"I wouldn't hesitate," I admit. "So, you shouldn't either if it's ever not enough. This world is fast-paced, and we have to keep up."

"I agree." His eyes move to the balcony.

"Why did she seem like she expected Maddoc to walk out of the bathroom?"

"Because I asked Maybell to send her here with clothes for you." He shrugs. "She had no reason to assume different."

Right.

He looks to the food. "You didn't eat."

"I have no appetite."

"You need to eat."

"So do you."

With a shake of his head, he stands. "We should head out."

He grabs the keys, pulling his phone to his ear right as the door clicks shut after him.

I stand and look to Victoria.

Her eyes cut from the bed to me. "Where's Maddoc?"

"I don't know. On his way to school?" My eyes harden.

Come on, Vee. Don't be weak.

She frowns, her lips thinning a moment, but she starts past me.

My shoulders fall, but then she whips around and finally asks what she wants to know.

"Why are you two here alone?"

I step up to her. "Don't make me be *that girl* and do the whole *shoulder to cry on* shit. You want answers, then I need you to ask me for them."

She glares a minute, but it fades the longer I stare.

"All right," she agrees.

I jerk my head. "Come on, I'll tell you everything on the way."

VICTORIA DIDN'T SAY MUCH WHEN I BROKE DOWN WHAT I could on the way to school, but she's deep in her thoughts now.

She confirms it when she says, point blank, "You wouldn't agree to this. Captain, yes, but not you."

My eyes slice to Captain.

He doesn't take his from the road, but his hands wrap tighter around the wheel.

"There is no fucking way." She's adamant. "I know you well enough to know that."

"I said no, at first," I admit.

She doesn't say anything, so I meet her stare with mine.

Victoria's only narrow farther, irritation and revelation seeping through. "You let him force you into this."

"*What the fuck!*" Captain shouts. "I would never force anything on her! On any fucking girl!"

"I'm not talking about you," she tells him with her eyes on me. Victoria doesn't back down. She twists in her seat and demands, like I asked her to. "I don't know how you got to be the way you are, but you are not the *watch out for yourself* type, Raven. You would *never* do something you thought would hurt them, especially Maddoc. Tell me right now he didn't threaten you with something."

"Don't answer that, Raven," Captain snaps.

"*Why?*" she sasses back. "Can't handle the truth?"

"You stop talking." He flicks a quick glare her way and speeds up, whipping into the parking lot and killing the engine. He glances back at the two of us before stepping out and moving toward the hood to wait.

I look back to Victoria. "He said he'd leave them. I won't allow it."

Her brows jump, and she simply stares. After a few seconds though her face contorts, her brows meeting in the center as her eyes flick between mine. She gives something between a head shake and a nod. "You can say no, you can run. This isn't the fucking eighteen hundreds."

"You're right, it's not," I tell her, eyes still on Cap. "Nowadays there're guns and greed. Better locks and stronger walls. I could go, say no, but if I leave, they make their life hell and likely find a way to take me regardless. I get locked away and only serve purpose at night. They get themselves killed trying to save me from somewhere I never had to be. Besides all that, Maddoc will leave if I do anything other than this. It's his way of guaranteeing I'm safe, knowing I won't allow them to hurt at my hand."

I say no or leave they lose each other, Zoey loses her dad. This town loses its hope and the Gravens win.

No.

123

"He's extorting you."

I look to Victoria. "How could I deny him?"

Her eyes move to the front windshield. She whispers, "This is big of you."

"No." I look to Captain just the same. "This is big of *him*." Slowly, my eyes meet hers. "You like him, don't you?"

"You're marrying him, *aren't you?*"

Tou-fucking-ché.

We're both quiet a minute, then we step out together, meeting him at the front of the SUV.

Cap slips his phone in his pocket, his frown focused on the school. "Royce is running late. Maddoc isn't coming today."

And the separation begins.

"No point in delaying," I manage to say through the anger and pain bubbling in my stomach, threatening to spew the water sloshing around in there.

I push forward but jerk to a stop when Victoria grips my elbow and spins me around.

I yank from her grasp and she frowns.

"You need to hold his hand," she says, and I keep in my glare, but she knows it and lets hers form. "It'll look different than the arm around the shoulder thing they sometimes do. If this is for real, if you expect everyone here to believe it—"

"I don't give a fuck what people believe."

"Well, you should." She steps closer, so others can't overhear. "You agreed to more than a marriage, you agreed to take over this town. They'll learn of it soon. You think Graven can't change their mind before it's all said and done if they decide it's not in their interest? They get rid of the things that don't serve a purpose. If they think people won't buy into you two..."

"For a girl who shouldn't know much, you sound like you know a lot." Captain crosses his arms.

She ignores him, but her features grow taut. "You know I'm right," she says to me.

After a second, I look to Cap, and he holds a hand out for me.

I take it, and together, the three of us walk into the school.

Chapter 16

RAVEN

I LEAN AGAINST THE SUV, LOOKING OUT OVER THE PARKING lot, my annoyance growing more and more with each passing second.

It's only been three damn days since we agreed to this and everything is continuously getting worse.

Royce won't look me in the eye, Captain can't meet my eye without sorrow creeping over his face, and Victoria glares everywhere but me.

The whispers started the second Captain and I walked in holding hands, grew louder when he kissed my knuckles before gym the next day, and the dirty looks came out to play when his hands hesitantly found my hips this morning.

People have restarted with their insults, girls are batting their lashes again, and the guys are suddenly braver.

Captain keeps quietly handling things while Royce has taken pleasure in letting his fists fly every chance he gets, and me? I've kept my knife in my jeans and my hands at my side.

My mouth has stayed shut but I've cataloged every word with every face and when I snap, they'll be the ones who feel it.

To make it all worse, still no Maddoc. Not a word from him, not a word about him.

Royce and Captain have to realize the only reason these assholes are acting this way is because we're missing a link. Maddoc being MIA makes it seem like there's a crack in our armor.

I'm fucking over it. They want to run their mouths, I'll give them something good to talk about.

They decide to push after that? We'll shove harder.

I jolt off the bumper and move quicker than the others can follow, stopping beside Collins' car, where he stands... with Leo.

Another disgrace let back in as a condition to our contract, a hand for Collins bitch ass to hold.

Both their heads snap my way, then toward the others I left with gaping mouths, deep frowns and clenched fists.

"Rae... whatcha doing?" Collins draws out, suspicious.

"Getting to know my future..." I make a show of pretending to trail off in thought. "What will it make us when I marry your cousin?"

Leo chokes on his drink, his wide eyes flying between the two of us.

That's what I fucking thought.

If Collins hasn't even confirmed to *him,* the only guy who can stand him here, then nobody else has heard. Their game must be the aftershock that'll come with the knowledge, the storm it would create amongst the students here if they get left out.

Well, too fucking bad.

Collins licks his lips. "I guess it makes you a bit of a whore, hm?" He glares, a nice bite to his words.

There we go.

"Guess it does, huh?" I tilt my head. "How's it feel to know you couldn't even get the whore?"

His jaw clenches. "Guess I dodged a bullet then."

"Guess you did." I look to Leo, knowing he'll never be able to keep his mouth shut. He'll share what he's learned, what half the damn school is likely already thinking. "I tested them all out, Captain won in the end. I'm sure Collins would love to have you as the plus one to the wedding."

Leo is a weak bitch and can't hold in his shock – he'd be a useless hands man.

When Collins body shifts toward me, movement over his shoulder catches my eye.

Bass moves from behind a tree, takes a step forward only to pause a moment later.

"Raven." Captain's steady voice hits my ears.

With a masked face, I turn to him. "Baby."

His eyes slide between mine, a blank slate for the others to see – concern clear as day to me.

I'm tired of that, too.

I'm sick of the concern, the worry, the eggshells that seem to have been scattered around me the last few days. I've been treated as the weak doll, and then to my own horror, I slightly filled that mold. I fell into a brand new type of fuck-it mode, let the jaded me fall away and allowed these people to run their mouths while I brushed it off, because fuck them, right?

Wrong.

This is my home now, was supposed to be all along, and now it's more confirmed than ever before it forever will be.

I made a choice and we have to live with it. There's no room for unnecessary emotions in a place like this. I gave away one Brayshaw while gaining another. I can't sit here and claim I lost. It could be worse.

The Gravens, they wanted a Brayshaw, but in the end, gained two.

We'll show them what that means.

These people, they fell into a comfort they shouldn't have, privileged assholes who forget – this is only high school and once it's over? They'll be nothing but the rich of this town. *Our* town.

I push against Captain and silence surrounds us.

His brows drop low as he studies me, and slowly his hand slides around me. He pulls my body into his, moving us back a few spaces, his mouth hitting my ear.

"What are you doing?" he asks.

"We're losing respect by the second. Collins is back, Leo too. Maddoc isn't here and in their eyes, I've traded more times than I can count now."

"What do you want me to do?"

"Show them we aren't falling apart, make them think we're stronger than ever."

Cap pulls back and looks at me.

"We should be. That's the point of this right, join the families? Create a power couple?" I whisper, my gaze flicking between his. "A couple in general."

A sharp pain shoots up my spine at the words, but I welcome it.

His fingers tighten against me, his expression not changing. "You can't even say it, can you?"

"Why should I have to, Cap?" I shake my head.

At that, his brows wrinkle and he moves his lips back to my ear to hide it. "You don't know this side of me, how I am with a girl who's mine, so I'll fill you in on one thing now." There's a slight rumble in his voice. "Words, Raven. I need them."

"I'm standing here, already yours, right? So, what's the point?"

"Wrong and that in itself is the point." His words come out sharper this time. "You're not mine, Raven. Despite the promise we made, you're not." He hesitates before adding, "Not yet."

Not ever.

That's what we're both thinking but don't say aloud.

A moment later, the silence surrounding us is quickly overtaken.

First, it's music, then the screech of tires. Gasps follow, then low whistles and laughs. Heads snap my way then the other and both mine and Cap's follow.

A black SUV, identical to the one I drove here in pulls up beside Captain's. Royce and Victoria both stare at me with tight eyes, but mine are locked on the passenger seat of Maddoc's ride as it opens and a girl with sleek straight, blonde hair chopped at the collarbone steps out. I've seen her before, though the hair is new.

Graven Preps queen bee.

She steps around the hood, Maddoc meeting her there and the two walk over to Royce and Victoria like it's any other day and she belongs.

It's not and she sure as fuck doesn't.

I embed my fingers into the skin of Captain's chest, and apparently subconsciously attempt to move past him, but he grips me tighter, forcing my feet to stay planted where they are.

He holds firm, his way of trying to steady me on the inside, but my body is numb, my face blank, my mind void.

And somehow my chest still stings with the prick of a thousand needles.

I want to rip her head off and stick it back in the Barbie box it came out of.

The girl holds her hand out to Victoria but gets a bored blink in return. Royce and Maddoc exchange a fist bump and then the two shift toward us.

His eyes are hidden behind dark lenses, his face smooth, mouth closed in a tired, lazy line.

So much effort to look so careless.

"You're shaking." Cap's words waft across my skin and I drag my eyes to his.

My throat starts to close, heat spreading across my face as I attempt to squash the sudden anger boiling. An emptiness forms at the base of my ribs, and I almost bend to erase it.

Captain's eyes move between mine.

More worry.

No.

"Do it," I rasp, swallowing past the clog in my throat, trying for air that won't come.

He keeps staring.

"You wanted words, Captain." I scowl. "Everyone is around, everyone is watching. We can confirm this right now."

"Raven—"

"I said do it."

Captain tugs me closer. He's mad. "You don't want this. You're doing this because you're pissed off and hurt and it's the first time you've laid eyes on him since he asked you to walk away from him, since you did."

I jerk against his hold, but his tight grip makes it unnoticeable to the prying eyes.

Maddoc spots it though, his brows disappearing under his frames.

I move my eyes back to Cap. "I was asking you to kiss me before he got here. Don't I have the right? I'll be your wife in three months, forever fucking you in four. I should have your mouth on mine anytime I want."

"If I kiss you right now, he will never be able to erase it. He'll lie awake at night, like I'm bettin' he has the last several nights, and play out every move he anticipates we'll make. He'll think about the ways you touched him and how you'll touch me. He'll think about the things you liked him to do and how I'll learn of the same. You make me kiss you right now,

Raven, and those fucked up fears become his fucked-up reality. They won't only keep him up at night, but they'll follow him with every step."

"That's the thing, Cap," I whisper, forcing my arms around his neck.

His forehead tightens, and in my peripheral, I notice Royce drops his eyes to the gravel.

"This is our reality now, and he knows it." I push to my tippy toes and align my lips with his. "You know your brother, acknowledge what he's doing. He took a few days to process and now he's back. He brought her here. He's being strong." I swallow, then whisper, "Show him you can be, too."

Captain's palm slides up my back, his fingers sprawling out across my spine. His eyes are heavy with guilt, his jaw set in anger. He slides his lips across my cheek to my ear as his other hand comes up to sink in my hair.

"No," he whispers. "Not yet, and not here. Our touching, eye contact, and private conversation is enough for now, but if you have to hold me tighter when you see him or if you need a connection when you feel you've lost one, you take what you want from me and I'll give in return, ten fucking fold. But *only* for you." He strokes my hair, kissing my temple. "Not for the sake of anyone else."

His words hit hard, and shame follows.

His concern is me, and I'm not giving him the same. This is hard for him too. He's admitted to feeling like he fucked his brother, more and more with every day that passes and every move he makes and I'm over here forcing his hand.

So, I do as he said, laugh it off and move back a step. I force myself to grab his hand and the others take it as their cue to move toward us.

The six of us walk for the entrance with our heads held high knowing every eye around is locked on us.

The six of us come to a screeching fucking halt when we spot Donley, Rolland, and Perkins waiting just inside the hall.

Victoria spins on her heels and heads right back outside, while the girl walking a step behind Maddoc slows. We keep forward.

Maddoc steps toward the three men. "The fuck is this?" he demands.

"Donley showed up, asking for a tour of the school," Perkins announces as he glances around, then quietly adds, "And unlimited access to the surveillance, so I called your father." His eyes slice toward Captain when he says it. "Seems I'm missing something."

"Suddenly you're on our side now?" Royce spits.

"There are no sides." Donley grins, holding out his hands as he moves his smirk to me. "We're all on the same team now. I'm simply... looking out for my... investment." His eyes drop to our hands, and a gleam fills them. His smirk grows into a smile and he nods. "Safe to assume Collins isn't causing too much trouble?"

"We'd handle it how we wanted if he was," Royce spits.

"The surveillance," Perkins attempts to get them back on track.

"Ah, yes." Donley claps. "Perhaps you were left in the dark, where you belong, Connor, but your blood has agreed to become mine."

Perkins' eyes move to Captain, but Donley keeps speaking.

"He will take the name you were offered with your brother but couldn't honor. Captain will become Graven, and Raven will be his bride."

Perkins' eyes slice to mine, then Maddoc's and back to Captain. "Why would you agree to this? Everything was handled, your life wouldn't have been affected."

"What do you care about my life?"

"I've spent eighteen years protecting it!"

"You didn't protect shit. You got in the way, stepped in where you were never and will never be wanted." Captain steps toward his biological father. "You thought you could tip them off that Raven existed, they'd take her, Zoey'd come home and everything would go away?"

"It should have been that simple, yes."

"Except you weren't bold enough to get the job done, and we grew close to Raven while you sat back and waited for someone else to do the dirty work. You may know no loyalty, but we do, and she has ours. Always." Captain gestures in his face. "Just so you know, I didn't agree to anything, I *asked* for this, and I'd have begged for her, on my hands and fucking knees if I had to because that's what she deserves."

My eyes zero in on the tight fists at Maddoc's sides.

When I look to him though, you'd never know he was staring at me, his glasses are directed at Donley, but I feel him.

Tortured, angry, ready to burst.

Me too, Big Man.

"Right, well, I have places to be." Donley smooths his blazer down. "Perkins, if you will, email me the links and passwords to the cameras."

"No."

All eyes fly to me when I speak.

"No?" Donley tilts his head. "I'm afraid that isn't your call, little girl."

"I'm afraid this isn't your school, Donley." I push forward. "It's ours, as will be this town in a matter of days. Get used to it."

I wanted him to get angry, but the bastard smiles, seemingly proud. "Oh, I am more than ready for you to hold the Graven name, until then I need to make sure the bargain is being held. Call it a protection plan."

"She said no." Captain steps forward. "Terms were set

when we left, this wasn't in it. These are our people; we handle what needs handling. That's not changing."

Donley eyes him and after a few moments a deep, satisfied sigh leaves him. He turns to Rolland who wears no expression at all and pats his back. "This is the start of a beautiful thing; I can feel it in my bones." With that, he walks away.

With a strange frown, Perkins follows after him.

Rolland steps up to Maddoc, but Maddoc says nothing, shouldering past him, past us all and takes off down the hall.

I bite my tongue to stop myself from screaming, dig my toes into my shoes to keep from running, and glance at Cap, whose face grows tighter with Maddoc's every step taken.

Royce steps up, his tone angry but his eyes soft. He whispers, "the girl was dad's idea. She's nothing, RaeRae."

I nod, swallow, and plug my earbuds in as an excuse to ignore everyone around me, but the music isn't enough.

Nothing will ever be enough.

Chapter 17

Maddoc

I HAVE NO FUCKING CLUE HOW I ENDED UP HERE, OR HOW I GOT in for that matter, but I'm standing just inside the entryway, my back against the door.

I glance around, making sure no one is near, then push off the wall.

I'm sloppy on my feet – a half dozen shots will do that to you – so I stumble a few times, catching myself on the back of the sofa as I pass it.

My eyes cut across the darkened room, finding no one coming to check out the sound.

The staff must be off duty, guards who the hell knows where.

Not here.

I keep down the hall, gripping my bat tighter when the smell of a fresh cut Cuban hits my nostrils.

I blink hard, pulling in my focus as much as possible and straighten to my full height.

My footsteps are silent, my pulse screaming in my ears as I enter Donley's office.

His chair is turned, only the silver of his hair to be seen over the edge of the seat. The smoke of his cigar fanning out over his head.

The piece of shit claiming what's not his, threatening what's ours, taking what's mine.

My lip curls, my fingers twisting against the rubber grip.

I take a single step right, raise the barrel, and with every ounce of strength the alcohol allows, I swing.

A loud growl leaves me, the snap of a bone against metal following.

He falls from his chair, shrieking like a little bitch and I walk around.

My eyes narrowing when I find a random fucking face, bloodied at my feet.

In the same second, a hard object smacks against my spine, my shoulders bowing as I fall to the floor with a groan.

My head snaps around, finding Donley standing there with a glare, a security guard at each of his sides.

Guess I wasn't as quiet as I thought.

When one of them raises a baton, I lift my hands to block it, but my movement is too slow, and in the next second everything goes black.

Raven

THE LOUD SCREECH OF TIRES HAS ME SHIFTING IN MY SEAT.

Headlights shine through the trees, and I glance back at the line of cars parked.

Rolland's, Maddoc's, and Royce's, all accounted for.

I slowly push my door open and step out right as the brakes squeal with a purposeful, last second stop.

Captain and Royce burst out the front, Rolland behind them and my head snaps back to the town car as the rear door is thrown open.

Maddoc's body slams against the gravel.

I gasp and dart forward, but suddenly, Royce's hands are around my elbows, Captain already at Maddoc's side.

I let out a breath when he pushes to his ass, his head wobbling as he does, only for my anger to flare instantly when I spot the blood covering his temple.

My jaw tightens and I slice my eyes to Donley.

"Keep a better eye on your boy, Rolland." He buttons his suit jacket. "Or we won't bring him back next time."

"Fuck you," Maddoc spits, allowing Captain to drag him to his feet, only to yank away from him.

He doesn't look at any of us, but storms into the house, Rolland on his heels.

"Get the fuck out, Donley. You're not welcome on these grounds," Royce forces past clenched teeth, letting me go and rushing into the house.

Captain walks backward toward me, and Donley's eyes shift between ours a moment.

I step forward, my body shaking.

"Raven," Captain speaks under his breath. "Don't."

My feet don't stop until I'm inches from Donley.

"Ah." He studies me. "Princess, fancy seeing you here, since I do believe you said you would not be."

"You better watch yourself, Graven."

"Watch myself..." He trails off. "The boy attacked me. Or, he tried to." He smirks.

I clench my teeth. "I don't care if he rams a pipe up your ass. Touch him and I will fuck you over in every way."

His eyes narrow and he hesitates a minute. "Should I be concerned over your loyalty?"

"You should be concerned if you expected anything different."

His frown tightens, hardening before me and he nods. "I'll assume you're here to gather some things, perhaps what I had prepared for you wasn't enough. I will note this as your one and *only* trip home needed."

My hands ball into fists at my sides, and I stand there, unwavering, until he finally gets in the car. The second his tail-lights are gone, I spin, rushing for the porch only for Royce to block my way.

"Move."

His brows crease. "You don't wanna go in there."

"I don't want to kick you in the nuts, either, but I will, Royce. *Move.*"

He doesn't, but allows me to push past him, following closely behind.

Captain stands off to the side, his entire fucking face crest-fallen, at a damn loss.

Maddoc, drunk and sloppy as hell, bleeding, has Rolland by the throat and shoved against the wall.

Rolland stands still as a statue, allowing it, his expression just as tragic as Cap's.

Maddoc continues to pull him close, only to slam him back, over and over again.

"Stop," Royce shouts, hard put as ever.

"You," Maddoc growls at his dad, ignoring his brother. "This is on you," he tells him, going in for a headbutt that has me wincing.

Rolland blinks but still, he doesn't fight his son.

"Does it hurt?" Maddoc screams in his face. "Does it?" He punches his ribs. "Do you even know what hurt feels like? Have you ever cared about a damn thing enough to feel pain from inside your fucking body?" He headbutts him a second time, stumbling a little from his own force. "From under your skin?!" he shouts.

Turmoil blankets Rolland's face, low groans leaving him, but I have a feeling it has nothing to do with the power of Maddoc's hits.

"Maddoc, fucking stop, man," Royce tries again, but he doesn't.

He lifts his fist, but before he can swing, I take a mini step forward.

"Maddoc," I call him quietly, and he freezes.

Every muscle in his body locks, his arms slowly falling to his sides as his dad's body slumps against the wall.

Everyone stays quiet.

Sluggishly, he turns to me and his face falls with his shoulder. Murky green eyes, lost and desperate, give up right before me.

Baby...

He stumbles toward me, so I take a quick step forward, ready to hold any of the weight he needs me to.

The pads of his fingers come up to skim across my cheek and I pull my lips between my teeth, my nostrils flaring.

Slowly, his eyes slide between mine and he nods almost imperceptibly.

He shifts closer. "I tried, baby," he whispers, and a silent sob shakes my chest. "I tried."

He jerks away suddenly, rushing down the hall with my heart in his hands, leaving his to bleed out at my feet.

Hopeless, that's what we are.

Chapter 18

Raven

I've been standing on the balcony for hours, looking over what was supposed to be their city, fully and completely in just a few short months when graduation rolls around – the day they were supposed to take unlimited control.

I can't help but think they'll look at this place and hate it now. Hate the power hidden in the ground, hate the air that suffocates them, the hands that force them. The rules they lived to enforce and the future they couldn't wait to start.

Everything changed.

Now Maddoc and Royce will be the second to Captain. Captain who won't be Brayshaw but Graven.

And then there's me, the reason for it all.

Cap steps up beside me, folding his hands and looking out just the same.

I take a deep breath. "I never wanted to love or trust anyone. Never." I frown at the sun. "I *knew* only bad would come from both those things and I knew it would be at my own hand." I look to Captain. "I warned him, Cap. I told him it would be me fucking him over later. Why didn't he listen? Why didn't he just... leave me alone?"

"It wasn't an option. He never wanted to love or trust outside us either, Raven. You took that choice from him."

"And now I've taken more. His future, his town, his brother."

"His heart."

I swallow. "How do I live with that?"

"You don't have to."

A sad laugh leaves me, and I give him a side-eye.

Captain turns serious and shifts his body toward me. "Today was tough, Raven. For all of us, but I need you to know I'm not forcing you into something you don't want."

"That is *not* what this is, Cap."

He steps toward me, tips my chin up, eyes tight and full of sorrow. "Raven." His voice is a low whisper as his stare slides between mine, deep creases forming between his brows. "Ask me to take you somewhere, anywhere you want, right now and I will. I won't question you, I won't be mad at you. I won't even tell my brothers where I took you. You can walk away from all of this, we'll get your money from the bank and you can start over without this weight. They'll look for you, our family and the Gravens, but I won't let them find you." His thumb strokes my chin and my head starts to pound. "Your life, your choice, but I have to ask you to make it right now, before this goes any further."

My eyes squeeze shut, and I lift my hand to grip his forearm.

Sweet Captain.

I should take him up on his offer, go and put this place behind me. Let them heal together instead of hurt apart.

It's what I intended to do all along, but things are different than they were when I got here. To leave here wouldn't only be abandoning them, it would also be turning my back on the home I never knew I had. This is where I am supposed to be, in this town with these people. With them.

With him?

Could be. Had Perkins taken his son when Captain's mother was killed, Graven would have two princes for the pawn to choose between, Collins or Captain.

Maybe everything played out backward. Maybe it was never supposed to be Maddoc but Captain all along.

The secret Brayshaw and the secret Graven.

I shake my head at myself.

Pretending to believe that, even for a second, is wrong on every level.

My loving Maddoc wasn't by mistake.

It was inevitable.

We were inevitable.

Still, none of this changes where we are right now.

I open my eyes and Captain's drop but I squeeze, and they slide right back to mine.

"You've never lied to your brothers, Cap, you won't be starting now, and definitely not because of me."

"Raven—"

I shake my head, cutting him off. "I'm not leaving. I don't *want* to," I assure him. "Shit, even if I did, I couldn't."

"We're doing to you what your mom did your whole life. Treating you like a damn throwaway."

"Not even close. My mom never sacrificed a damn thing for me. She's selfish, self-centered and as greedy as they come. You three are so opposite of all those things it's not even funny. Just look at you, Cap. Look where you are right now, ready to give up everything you ever wanted just to make my life a little easier."

"We would do anything for you, always."

"I know." I nod. "And even if you didn't offer yourself up to them, if Maddoc refused to accept it or if Royce demanded a different outcome, I'd have stayed, married Collins just so I could be in the same place as you guys."

I offer a small smile, continuing, "It is exactly why Donley still wanted me after he found out I wasn't a virgin. It's why your dad brought me to you guys first instead of giving me to them directly. Maybe their reasons came from different places, but they both came to the same conclusion."

"What conclusion?"

"That I'd walk through fire if it kept you guys from getting burnt. Your dad wanted me to grow close to you guys so when I was passed over, someone on the Donley side would be looking out for you three. Donley wanted me because, for the first time, he felt he was taking something of value from Brayshaw.

"In his eyes, having me meant he had power over all of you, over this town and the Brayshaw name. I mean, think about it, Cap. He wanted my mom as a virgin bride who loved her future husband, yet he was willing to take me used *and* force me to marry Collins if he had to?" I shake my head. "He only wanted me because he knew, if he dangled any of you in front of me, I could be played as his puppet, do whatever he asked when asked. Be his little doll."

Captain steps closer. "You won't be a doll, or trophy, or side fixture. You will be treated with nothing but respect from every person in every room everywhere no matter where we find ourselves through this, I promise you."

"You don't even have to say it, Cap. I know, and I trust you."

Captain moves his hands to my biceps. "I don't... what do we do about..."

Maddoc.

Pressure builds behind my eyes, an ache taking form in my chest, so I give a small shrug.

Captain's face contorts, pain and affliction laced through every inch of him.

I'm sure his loss hurts as much as mine, maybe even worse if such a thing exists.

My mind won't stop racing, and what it keeps leading me to both settles and stings in some way.

There's no longer such a thing as a good move, only an easier one, and what I'm thinking *is* easier, but not for me.

For him. For Royce.

I drop my eyes to the concrete beneath me. "I've been thinking. I know we can't do anything about what happens later, how we feel or react in situations, but ... I think we can save us all from a lot of unnecessary grief." I meet his stare.

He studies me, and after a minute, agrees. "I think you're right." He hesitates a moment before saying, "I know someone who can help."

"Now?"

His forehead tightens, but he nods.

"Make the call, Cap."

I DIDN'T SLEEP, BUT WHEN THE SUN REFUSES TO BE IGNORED ANY longer, I open my eyes, meeting Captain's sleepy ones beside me.

He gives a small smile, tension lining his brow.

"Stop," I whisper, reaching up to wipe it away.

He grips my hand, squeezing, unease taking over his eyes more and more by the second. "Are you okay?"

I nod, dropping mine to his chest.

With a heavy sigh, he slides from the bed, quietly disappearing into the bathroom.

And the first tear falls, followed by another, and before I know it, I'm covering my face with a pillow to muffle my own cries.

Pathetic.

My tears are pointless, if I didn't hear myself and if the heat from each one falling didn't warm my cheeks, I wouldn't even know I was crying. I feel nothing, felt nothing last night. Not even regret, which might be the worst part.

A heaviness forms against my chest and I gasp, searching for air I can't find. I rush over to the little sink, quickly splashing water on my face, and rubbing it across my neck.

I tie my hair back, pausing to stare at myself a moment.

Of course, Captain steps from the bathroom right then, frowning when he sees me.

After a moment he walks toward the bed and grabs my sleep shorts from the floor, bringing them to me.

He spins around so I can slip them on under my long shirt, then turns back reaching for my hand. I allow him to lead me to the balcony, but we don't step out, instead sitting on the edge of a little chair.

"Raven—"

"Don't, Cap. I'm fine, I promise." I pull myself to my feet, turning to look him in the eyes.

He holds mine a minute before dropping his to the carpet at our feet.

With a heavy exhale, I tug his hand so he's standing and move us into the sunlight more. I step into him, and he wraps his arms around me in a hug.

"We need to get dressed so we aren't late." Cap pulls back, tipping my chin up to look at him. "Or we can ditch?"

With a deep breath, I shake my head. "There's no point. We only have a few months left. Finish strong, right?"

He gives a light chuckle, but it falls off. "All right, come on."

We're dressed and heading out the door within twenty minutes, and not ten after that, we're pulling into the Brayshaw High parking lot.

Chapter 19

RAVEN

"IS THAT YOUR DAD'S TOWN CAR?"

Cap leans over to look. "Yeah."

"Did he tell you he'd be here today?" I frown.

"Nope." Cap's expression mirrors mine.

I'm about to ask what he thinks it means when I spot Chloe perched against her car chatting with a few of her friends, so I tell Cap to stop.

"When I first got here, Chloe said she could make me go away with one phone call. What did she mean by that?" I turn to him.

His eyes narrow. "Her dad is our head of security, has been since we were kids. She thought she could get him to send you packing for fucking with her. She was wrong. He didn't tell her who you were right away, that's why she acted the way she did with you. She never would have dared had she known beforehand."

"You trust this man, her dad?"

"We do. He checks in on Zoey every day, calls me every night. We get daily reports of everything going on in this town. He's a good man, strong and always dependable."

"Yet his daughter is a bullying bitch, treats people weaker than her as just that." I shake my head. "She should be the opposite of what she is. She should be standing up for the quiet girls in the hall who get pushed around, not doing the pushing."

"Only a true leader stands for, with, and against others when they sense it's needed."

"Like you guys do."

"Like you did before you even knew us."

I look back to Captain, and after a minute I push my door open.

"You're getting out here?" He raises a brow.

"Yeah." I sigh, looking to Chloe. "I need a minute with her. Meet me in the middle, and we'll wait for the others, then find Rolland together?"

He frowns but agrees, so I hop out.

Her eyes are already on me as I do and she pushes to her full height, dismissing her fan club.

She crosses her arms, tilting her head like an asshole. "*Rae.*"

"The boys trust your dad." I get straight to the point.

That has her shifting on her feet, her head lifting some. "More than their own dad, I would guess."

"You might think it sucks, not having influence over him, but it's actually a really good thing. It means he's honorable, dedicated to them and what they stand for."

"What do you want, Raven?" She eyes me.

"You've steered clear of Leo since he got back. Why?"

"Why do you care?" she snaps.

"It's because he showed his true colors, isn't it?"

She rolls her eyes, but shrugs. "He may look pretty, but loyalty can't be shifted around here."

"That's what I thought." I nod. "Look, I don't trust you, but I know you're aware of what's going on on the inside of things. You're at least sneaky if not purposely informed."

"If you're referring to how you change guys as often as I change handbags, news flash, Rae, you've made it disgustingly obvious so no snooping would be necessary," she sasses, but when I only stare, she rolls her eyes and looks away. "I found out about the contract the day you and Captain signed it. I didn't know about the Captain and Principal Perkins thing though. Sucks for you I guess," she says and damn if it's not half sincere. "You really going through with it?" She studies me, an expression I can't quite read, but has me wondering if she knows even more than she should.

I ignore her question. "I need your help."

Her eyes narrow. "With what?"

"I need you to be who you are already. Stand up for people, show them they can trust those who trust Brayshaw. There's been too many shifts in the last few months, you have power. Use it."

"This is about that Graven Prep bitch being on Maddoc's jock, isn't it?" she crosses her arms.

"No," I tell her honestly. "It's not, but it is about Graven. We can't let them come in and think they can take over where they don't belong. This is still Brayshaw grounds, and they need to remember it." I get in her face. "You considered this your school before I got here, right?"

She glares but can tell I'm not being a pompous ass about it.

"I don't need the school, Chloe. I have the town. You can have a part in it, too, if you can prove it's your people you care about more than yourself. Keep the fear you, no doubt, worked hard to create but direct it toward the right people."

"Why are you standing here saying this shit?" She studies me.

"Because, before I got here, your entire world was different. In your eyes, I came in and took from you. All you wanted was one of them on your arm. I know what it's like to have someone take what you think belongs to you from right under your fingers and not being able to stop it. It's fucked up."

Her eyes fall to the blacktop but raise back to mine just as quick.

"What the girls here don't seem to realize?" My brows lift, and I give a slow shake of my head. "You don't need a *Brayshaw*... to become one. All you have to do is earn it."

As if she's never thought of it, her face goes slack.

I leave her with the thought, turning to meet Captain a few feet away.

Royce steps up with Victoria right as I do.

"What'd you say to her?" Victoria asks.

I glance over my shoulder, finding Chloe smirking after me. "Nothin'."

I look back to Captain, who side-eyes his brother, before moving his stare back to me only to ask Royce a question a moment later.

"Where's Maddoc?" Captain frowns.

"Not here, brother. Not fucking here."

Fuck.

Royce takes a few backward steps, saying nothing else on the matter. "Let's go see what dear old dad wants from us this time. Maybe our fucking souls, huh?"

With that he spins on his heels, not waiting for us to reach his sides as he steps through the doors.

Something has me looking over my shoulder, but when no one stands there, I push through.

Mac meets us just inside, letting us know Rolland is in Perkins' office again, so we rush straight there.

Both their heads jolt as we step inside, and Perkins even attempts to hit the back button on his screen, but Royce reaches across and knocks the keyboard off the desk before he can.

Rolland glares at Perkins, then looks to the boys.

"You fucking kidding me?" Royce spits angrily. "Hiding shit, again?"

Rolland stands straight. "If I were hiding, I wouldn't be here in plain sight. Why Connor panicked, I don't know, but I had every intention of coming to you all after." He looks across the three of us and frowns. "Where's your brother?"

"Probably still drunk and in bed," Royce bites.

I scowl but say nothing.

Captain turns the screen, and we all freeze.

A picture of Zoey sitting on her porch, Maria at her side reading her a story fills the screen.

It's a side angle, so taken from somewhere on the property, not from the outside gate.

"What the fuck is this?" Captain's voice rumbles with rage and he whips his phone from his pocket, dialing. He brings it to his ear.

"This was sent to me this morning, addressed to you," Perkins tells him, tension lining his face.

"And you called our dad instead of Captain?" Royce shouts.

"Maria," Cap says into the line in the next second. "Where's Zoey?"

I grip Royce's wrist as we wait for another word.

"Show me," he growls.

A second later, a small tap fills the room and then her little gasp sounds.

"Daddy!" She laughs. "Hi!"

My muscles relax, and I look to Royce when his hand covers mine.

155

He nods, tugging me under his arm.

Cap steps from the room for some privacy and I look back to Perkins.

"Who sent this to you?"

Right then, Rolland's phone rings. He glares from the screen to us. "It's him."

"Donley had this taken?" I jerk forward.

Rolland nods then goes to answer the line, but Royce snatches it from his hand, puts it on speaker and sets it on the desk.

Donley's chuckle grates every nerve in my body. "I see you're at the school, old friend, guessing you got word of my email, just as I had predicted?"

"What the hell do you think you're doing?" I snap.

"Ah, princess." His smile is evident through the line. "Lovely to hear your voice."

"How did you get the picture?"

"Which one?" he jokes and my eyes fly to Perkins.

He holds up his hands – four pictures.

"Donley!" I shout, slamming my hand on the desk.

"Found a guy with a great, long distance camera. All he had to do was climb a small fence. He was in and out in seconds. No harm done," he says.

"Are you trying to fuck yourself?"

"On the contrary, princess. I'm protecting myself. The girl is fine, safe and sound. Even sent her a new little bear from Grandpa Donley."

I clench my teeth. "Stay away from her."

"Oh, I plan to. Soon as you're mine, or his rather, but I see it as one in the same, hm?"

"She'll never be yours!" Royce shouts.

Donley only chuckles louder. "You all have yourself a nice day."

He hangs up right as Cap steps back inside with a glare. "She's fine."

"Cap." I turn to him with tight eyes. "Maybe—"

"He's trying to intimidate us," Cap rushes out, giving a subtle shake of his head.

Not yet.

"He won't touch her." Cap looks to his dad. "I want a guard every fifteen feet, rotating every hour."

"Done," Rolland agrees.

Perkins slowly stands. "If I can help in any—"

"Never," Cap growls before rushing from the room.

I turn back to Perkins. "Give Rolland the password to this account, and don't touch it again."

"This is my contact for here at the school."

"*Was* your contact. Find a new one."

Royce and I step out, looking around for Captain, but he's already out of sight.

The two of us head to class, finding Victoria already sitting there waiting.

"Everything okay?" she whispers.

Not even a little bit.

Chapter 20

RAVEN

MADDOC SHOWED UP THE DAY AFTER DONLEY SENT THE EMAIL, but he's yet to show his face since. It's been two weeks now, three since everything went down and now break is here. That's ten more days I know I won't lay eyes on him.

It's bullshit.

My eyes snap to Victoria when she kicks me with her boot.

She frowns. "Stop staring at the TV like you wanna murder it and fast forward the commercials already."

I toss the remote to the floor and drop back on the carpet, frowning at the ceiling.

With a heavy sigh, Victoria drops beside me.

"Wanna get high?" she asks.

"Not really."

"Drink?"

"Nope."

She sits up, looking down at me. "Wanna go sit by the pool

and do absolutely nothing like we are now, but with a better view?"

I start to say no when she adds, "There's a train track behind the property. You can see it from the upper deck. You're a rich girl now, you can get us up there."

I turn my head to look at her, a small smile on my lips.

She pushes to her feet, so I let her pull me up, and the two of us do just that.

We don't even have to say a word to anyone, and the rope leading to the top deck is held open for us.

We find a seat closest to the large glass window that allows us to look over the ledge, and not two minutes after we're seated, fresh ice waters and a tray full of grapes, weird little slices of meat, and cheese is set before us.

The man says nothing, sets them down and walks away.

"It's no wonder rich people stay rich." Victoria pops a piece of funky colored cheese in her mouth, only to drop it into her palm with a small gag, making me laugh. "They get tons of shit for free."

I play it safe and pick up what looks like salami only lighter. "They probably give it to you, then charge your room for it later."

She chuckles, wiping her hands.

A train starts by right then and we shift to look at it.

"Where'd the boys go again?"

To visit Zoey, but I can't say that to her, so I give a look that says *don't ask so I don't have to lie.*

She changes the subject easy enough and we spend the rest of the day swapping stories about the funny shit we've seen and anything else we can think of that's worth a solid laugh.

It's a less than shitty day.

Maddoc

THIS IS THE WORST DAY I'VE HAD SINCE I FORCED MYSELF TO walk back into Brayshaw high, all twisted and fucked and wrong in every way.

Raven at Cap's side, the Graven bitch at mine. Not that I bother talking to her, looking at her, or acknowledging her presence at all. She couldn't care less, though. All she wanted in return for her few days spent was for word to get back to Graven Prep of how she sat comfortably at the Brayshaw table. Doubt she was any kind of comfortable, but it didn't matter, it was all for show.

Shit, my entire life, my brothers, and my girls, is nothing but a fucking show right now. One I was done playing a role in, so I stopped fucking going. Again.

Now, here I am, wanting to enjoy my niece like my brothers are, but finding every excuse I can to walk away.

First it was to check the electrical fence, next to walk the property line and make sure there were no signs of forced entry or prep for it. After that, I went inside and checked all the windows, reset the alarm system and looked in the attic.

I couldn't fucking think of anything else, so now my face is in my phone, but only for a second before little feet land in front of mine, big blue eyes looking up at me.

"Cheese!" she says, smiling, staring at my phone.

A laugh leaves me, and I take a small step back and take her picture like she wanted.

"I wanna see!" She reaches for it, so I bend down and turn the screen toward her.

She laughs at herself, pulls the phone from my hand, and then drops onto my bent knee.

I quickly adjust my balance so we don't fall back, and her

feet start to swing in front of me. She pushes a bunch of buttons, but when nothing happens, she hands it back and stands.

"Hu-mon!" she says, waving over her shoulder as she makes her way back to Captain and Royce, both who stare at me from only feet away.

I take a step forward, only to freeze the second Cap bends down to pick her up and hugs her close.

My mind places Raven at his side, his smile on her, and Zoey's hand connected to them both.

I turn, get in my SUV and go.

This is why I drove myself today.

After a quick stop at the house, I pull up in front of the large gate of the warehouses and wait for it to be pushed open. I slowly back in, stopping when the head of my vehicle is right at the line. This way, neither Cap or Royce's can fit behind me. Not that they'll be coming.

Mac steps up, nodding his head with a frown so I push my door open, pulling the bottles from the passenger seat and waving them at him.

With a small chuckle, he shakes his head moving aside so I can step out.

I hit the button on my key fob and the back opens.

We both drop down, and I waste no time popping it open and take a few shots straight from the bottle.

I pass it to Mac as he says, "Guessing you being here without your brothers means they don't know you're here?"

"Nope." I look out over the crowd.

They're prepping for the fights, placing bets, and getting fucked up while doing it.

I look to the building at the edge of the property. "Get someone in there, gut the fucking thing and deck it out. Make it a place we can kick back, but out of sight. Put a room in there, too."

Mac nods, pulling his phone out. "On it."

I take another drink, shaking my head out when this one burns on its way down. "Who you got making the cards tonight?"

"Bass has it all handled. We send him names; he sends us the setup. Signs off on everything."

I glare at the people partying, having fucking fun.

Bishop should be focused on one thing and one thing only, keeping his eyes glued to Raven.

I take another shot, wiping my mouth with the back of my hand. "Fight of the night, change it. I want in."

My head snaps to Mac when he doesn't say anything.

He eyes me a second but nods and walks off.

Every few minutes, more and more people file through the gates and soon the place is packed, security locked down and the music is cranked up. The alcohol has kicked in and my blood is running warm.

The crowd begins to gather in the back as the first few fights start, so I kick off the bumper and pull my shirt over my head. My hand subconsciously rubs across my tattoo, but the second I realize it I rip it away.

Fuck.

I run my hand down my face. I'm fucked up, and it's having the opposite effect I want.

I need a blank fucking mind; I want my head and the organ in my chest to numb like my body. How is it I feel no physical pain, but on the inside it's like someone's taking a razor to me, slowly, methodically slicing across every fucking inch, leaving not a centimeter untouched, unmarked, unfucking punished.

That's what this is, the sting in my gut.

My bitter and cruel reward.

Give away all you got, die with a beating heart.
Keep it, live with a heavy one.

I gave her away, and now I'm a walking fucking zombie.

Mac comes back, ready to tape my knuckles, but I shake him off, take one last shot for fuck-its sake, and move for the edge of the largest ring.

I stand there, swaying on my feet a bit, not moving from the front post as the fight ends with a quick knock out, and the next begins.

The smaller cards around us are over now, too, so the crowd here grows, wider and wider, deeper. Louder.

And me, I grow drunker, my body heavier, but I feel light as a fucking feather.

Dante, our crowd feeder, puts his megaphone at his side, and steps over to me. He slaps me on the back, his eyes on the two in the center, dancing around each other.

"What's good, Brayshaw?"

I shake my head. "Shit," I slur. "Ready to get in there."

He nods. "Guy wants to know if he's got a pass tonight or what you need from him?"

"I'll never come in here looking for a fucking ego boost, D. Don't need one. Tell him to go hard." I look to him. "Tell him not to stop."

Dante's head pulls back slightly, but he nods, hits my back again, then swivels around the circle again, yelling into his megaphone for the two in the center to stop playing footsy or take it to the church.

Not sure how long their fight takes, or when I stepped to the center of the ring, but shouts echo in my ears and then a fist in my face.

I stumble back, a smile finding my lips and I right myself.

I throw my hands out, taunting the guy with my fingers.

Closer, bitch.

Another hit to my head, but I manage to shuffle my feet to stay steady. I give a hard blink, and the gorilla motherfucker comes into view, so I swing, hitting him in the ribs, only to catch a knee to mine.

I laugh, spitting what must be blood from my mouth and go in again, but suddenly I'm staring at the fucking sky, flat on my back and weight drops on top of me.

My body jolts with each hit, but I keep grinning.

When I laugh, the dude's head comes down on mine.

In the same second, his body is gone and mine is being drug across the dirt.

I yank from the hands, and push to my feet, using the rope to guide me outside of it.

I stumble against the crowd, each body serving as leverage until I'm in the clearing, but before I fall onto my ass, a shoulder hits my side, taking my weight while another finds the other.

"When did he get here?"

"I can fucking hear you, you punk bitch."

Bishop scoffs, shoving me into the open trunk of my SUV.

Suddenly the seats fold and my body falls flat against them.

"Fuck are you here for anyway, you should be—"

"Where you should be?" he throws back. "And I was, but Captain is there, Royce, too. Think she's fine for at least an hour."

There goes my fucking chest again.

I lift and slam my head back. It's pointless, there's no pain.

"I need to go make sure everyone gets paid," Mac says before footsteps crunch against the ground.

I peel my eyes open, finding what looks a lot like a three-headed Bass fucking Bishop.

"I can barely fucking handle one of you, asshole," I slur, my eyes closing again.

He scoffs, then a water bottle hits me in the shoulder.

I don't reach for it. I'll take the fucking hangover tomorrow. Wish for it.

"She's lookin' thinner, paler. I've tried to track when she's eating, which is close to never when she's in sight, but maybe she is behind closed doors."

Behind closed doors with my brother.

"I didn't ask for a report."

"Nah, but you need one. You're acting like a little bitch," he says.

I jolt up, but the Macallan in me won't allow it and my muscles give out.

Bishop sighs, then my legs are being pushed aside and a door slams.

After a few minutes my car starts rolling, and a few minutes after that, alcohol wins out.

I stay this way, fucked up, and delirious for the rest of break.

Fuck everybody.

Chapter 21

RAVEN

"Where the fuck is he?" Captain snaps when Royce steps from the SUV without Maddoc. "I thought he agreed to be here?"

"He did. And he is." Royce gives an emotionless stare.

"Where?" Cap asks.

Royce shrugs. "Truck. Fell asleep on the way here."

"It's a two-minute drive," I say.

"Yeah, well." Royce starts walking away. "Not like he's getting any sleep at night."

Cap glares, shaking his head. "That's fucked up, man."

Royce only shrugs, though. "Lots of shit's fucked up."

He pushes ahead, not bothering to wait for me, so we can walk into class together like normal.

Victoria steps in behind him, giving a nod over her shoulder before disappearing, too.

Cap looks to me, but I shake my head. "Go, I'm good."

He doesn't believe me, but he leaves anyway, glancing back once before he turns the corner.

I close my eyes and slide my headphones in, pushing

myself against the door frame. I hit the little button without looking, skipping song after song until a more fitting one comes on, then I turn it up as loud as it can go.

"Hear Me Now" by Bad Wolves blares through my ears and I soak up every word, wishing I could fall into the world of the song. Wishing the world around me could be simpler.

It's not.

It won't be.

Five weeks. It's been five weeks and the toll it's taken on me weighs like five years. My body is sore for no reason, my head a constant war zone, and my drive is nonexistent.

It's not right for me to act—

My thoughts are cut off when a familiar warmth grows closer, causing me to squeeze my eyes shut tighter. My breathing speeds up, coming and going in choppy spurts, broken gasps.

The back of a knuckle slides up my jaw, a fire trail following, both burning and soothing all at once. When he reaches my right earbud, he tugs, forcing it to fall out.

I bite into my tongue, my hands planting themselves against the wall behind me as he grows closer. I can feel him all around me now.

His fingertips brush my collarbone as he grips the wire, and I know he's lifted it to his own ear to listen.

As the song comes to an end, he speaks.

"No, baby." His words fan across my face. "I can't hear you... not anymore."

I let my head fall, and he tugs the other earbud from my ear, pulling on the string until the entire iPod slips from my pocket.

"I can't do this," he rasps, the sound so broken my throat closes in on me. "I don't *want* to do this."

My body grows cold as his disappears.

I slip, not bothering to try and lessen the blow as my ass hits the floor.

I stay there until Royce finally loses his cool, poking his head out and collecting me from the floor.

He says nothing, but his hug before he drags me in is more than enough.

Snagging the glasses from his collar, he slips them over my eyes, and we shuffle into the room.

My plan is not to speak to anyone the rest of the day, and it works for a while, but then it's lunchtime.

I step around the corner, headed toward our usual table when my lack of self-control snaps, and right back where it belongs.

The Graven girl is back. She drops into what was my seat beside Maddoc. He doesn't even look her way, but she smiles wide and puts off a sense of belonging that irks my fucking nerves.

Captain steps up alongside me, and Maddoc's head jerks this way, eyes covered with those damn glasses I forgot how much I hated until recently.

"What's wrong?" Cap asks.

When I don't respond right away, Captain's stare slides to the table, then back to me. "He doesn't want her, Raven."

I can't help it, a laugh bubbles out of me.

Man, this is some fucked up shit – my new future telling me his brother doesn't want the girl who has taken the seat I gave up without a fight.

What choice did I have, though, really?

Donley has sent a text straight to Captain's cell every couple days where he makes sure to mention Zoey. Sometimes it's in a roundabout way, like how she enjoys ice cream, and then Cap will call Maria and sure enough, Zoey had a cone earlier that day.

I tried to convince him to go get her, to say fuck you to everyone around. We're doing our part he deserves his daughter and needs to feel her safety, but Captain refuses. He says he doesn't want to uproot her yet when she'd be forced to leave all she's known and move into a hotel where she doesn't even have her own space. He wants to bring her home, but when he has a home ready for her, so the transition is smooth and doesn't confuse her.

We both know Donley is only doing this to make sure we keep up as agreed, and there's been no true threat as far as harm or danger to her. That would be a completely different story.

Regardless, we're doing what was asked.

Zoey is safe.

Maddoc is here, where he belongs.

"Raven," Cap tries again.

I turn to him.

"I know things feel fucked right now, and I won't stand here and pretend they're not, but you were meant for this."

"Stop doing that." I glare.

His brows jump in confusion. "Doing what?"

"Stop acting like you didn't give up your life for mine," I force past clenched teeth. "Something I *never* would have asked you to do. Stop acting like I won't fuck this up. *Stop* telling me I was meant for this. I'm a fucked-up stoner with two chips on her shoulder. I'm a fucking shit storm waiting to happen."

"You can do this."

"I will crack. I will hurt you, and I will hate myself."

Captain steps up to me, his palms finding my cheeks as he holds my head up, forcing my eyes to his.

He opens his mouth, but he doesn't get to speak.

Shouting starts behind us and Royce calls for him in a panic.

I spin just in time to see Maddoc throw his fist across Leo's face, then quickly slam a chair into Collins' back.

"Fuck," rushes from Captain as he runs for the mess, but he doesn't have to stop him.

The second Captain's hand hits Maddoc's shoulder he yanks free; drops the second chair he's picked up and storms for the exit... the one I'm standing in the middle of.

He stops right in front of me, his heavy breathing fanning across my face.

A deep divot takes form between his brows, the vein in his jaw ticking hard against the skin.

Show me those eyes, Big Man.

He does.

He yanks the glasses from his face and everything inside me crumbles, bone after bone shatters and I have no idea how I'm still standing.

He senses it, and the strain in his eyes mirrors mine.

Pain.

Need.

Inability to have it.

Our new reality.

He pushes past, but not before giving a quick whisper that stings harder than any cut.

"I changed my mind."

Changed his mind...

"He can't have you."

I... oh God.

No...

"I'll fix this, baby, just hold on."

And then he's gone.

My vision grows foggy, my muscles giving way, but before I can fall, an arm is through mine, holding me up.

"Stand up straight," Victoria hisses, slowly turning and leading me into the hall.

"What the hell did I do?"

She pushes me against the wall to steady me, her eyes

roaming over my face with a tight frown. "What do you mean?"

When I squeeze my eyes shut, shaking my head, she hits my shoulders against the wall, and they fly open.

"Are you okay?" She eyes me.

My body grows even heavier, and I look away. "What's that even mean anymore?"

"Raven," she snaps.

"I'm fine, Vee," I answer, rubbing my temples. "Just... a headache."

Royce and Captain join us in the next second, deep frowns on both their faces.

Royce slides my way, wrapping an arm around my waist. He's nonchalant about it but takes my weight as he intended. He leans over to whisper, "I told you, the chick is only for show."

"Fuck her."

"What happened just now?" Captain asks quietly.

Royce gives his brother a blank stare. "Fuck you think happened, man? He wigged out. You touched her, comforted her from pain he thinks he's caused. The one girl he'd never fucking hurt."

Captain's eyes harden. "And I will keep doing it. She'll never hurt alone. Ever."

Royce gives a sad smile, his arm on me tightening. "I know, brother. So, does he. Kinda makes it even harder to swallow."

I hate this.

I look up at Royce. "Walk me to class?"

"Yeah, RaeRae," he rasps. "I gotcha."

The four of us leave the cafeteria, early for class for the first fucking time ever.

Chapter 22

RAVEN

"GOOD AFTERNOON, WOLVES. HOPE YOU ENJOYED YOUR LUNCH hour."

My head snaps up as the intercom turns on, Collins Graven's voice echoing throughout the school hallway.

Our school.

"I know I did." He pauses for a moment. "It was particularly fantastic, in fact, with the return of Maddoc Brayshaw."

My feet jolt, and I slowly push from the floor.

Royce's eyes slice to the door, his brows snapping together when he spots me in a panic.

"See, I've been holding something in for some time now, but finally, the gang's all here and I can share the news, but let's backtrack, shall we?" His arrogant chuckle muffles the speakers. "See, there's this event coming up... a *big* event, the grandest this town has seen in some time, one I'm sure you'll all go home today to find the invitations sitting in your mailboxes for."

"Oh fuck," I croak, and Royce pops from his seat, but I dash for the door and down the hall.

No, no, no...

I run as fast as I can.

"Raven Carver, who is really Raven Brayshaw, is supposed to be getting married soon. Now, I know some of you have heard, but in case you were left out of the loop, I'll fill you in. She's not marrying who you think, but none other than Captain Brayshaw, who, in an interesting twist, can technically claim Graven. So yes, folks..."

I skid down the entry, blowing past Captain when he suddenly jolts around the corner.

"Raven!" he shouts, but I keep going.

"Raven Brayshaw, your very own princess, is marrying Captain, as a Graven. I thought it would never happen, that we'd all get together and they wouldn't show, but it seems... they were so eager to move forward, the two took it upon themselves to speed things along."

I throw open his classroom door, freezing in my spot when I find Maddoc has his eyes closed, my earbuds in.

My shoulders fall, but like always, he senses my presence. His eyes snap open and he flies to his feet, worry tightening his features.

"...the two married in secret, and have been hiding it for weeks now..."

Maddoc tugs the wires from his ears, his stare quickly snapping around the room before landing back on me.

"...so if you see the newlyweds in the hall, be sure to offer them your belated congratulations ..."

A slow frown forms on Maddoc's face, his eyes moving between mine.

One last time, Collins' voice echoes above us, "So, congratulations on your private wedding, Raven and Captain, I hope you get *everything* you deserve."

Silence.

Maddoc stares, not saying a word. Not moving an inch.

And no one around us does either, fearful of his wrath should they even breathe, everyone remains stuck where they stand.

In the next second, I'm jolted forward as a chest runs right into my back.

I don't have to look to know it's Captain, and with the worst possible fucking timing.

His hand shoots out, wrapping around my stomach to keep me from stumbling.

When he rights me, he freezes, slowly pulling his arms away.

Maddoc starts to shake, his head ticking to the side, like he can't control it.

But it's Royce who storms up, pissed off about being lied to, and wraps his brother by the neck, dragging him back into the hall.

I gasp, spinning around to look at them, but quickly whip back to Maddoc.

I walk right up to him, open my mouth to speak, but he jerks his chin, his eyes dulling before me.

"Guess I'm too little too late, huh, Snow," he breathes, a numbness to his words that has my chest caving.

My heart breaks even more when his eye contact does, and he steps around me.

I lash around, following him into the hallway.

He walks straight and tall right past his brothers who wrestle around on the ground, not sparing them a glance.

"Maddoc, wait!" I shout, but my feet are stuck to the floor. Fucking frozen in the spot as betrayal burns from my feet to fingertips.

Victoria steps beside me, looking over at the two who have finally realized their brother is walking away.

They both jump to their feet, neither able to look at me.

I glance to Victoria who shrugs, unsure of what to do.

"Bitch," comes from behind me.

I spin around ready to fire the fuck off at anyone and everyone, but Chloe slips in, her back to me, face to the girl.

"Jealousy is as ugly as your last season Prada." Chloe's chin lifts slightly. "Watch how you talk to a Brayshaw, Camile. I won't remind you again."

Chloe doesn't acknowledge me but spins on her heels and keeps down the hall. "Nothing to see here people, go the fuck away!"

I come out of my stupor and run for the front of the school, the boys' heavy feet pounding behind me, but it's too late.

He's gone.

I drop my head back, looking up at the sky.

Fuck!

Royce shoulders past Captain and starts jogging toward the house.

After a few minutes, Cap ushers me to his SUV.

We drive back to the hotel in silence, both knowing how fucked up this seems, but I can't find it in me to regret it.

We did this for them, so they wouldn't have to watch, so Maddoc wouldn't drive himself mad on our wedding night, playing out what happens after. We planned to tell him, saying it's over and done and he wouldn't have to stand beside his brother while he married me.

It was supposed to make things easier.

Now, thanks to Collins, he found out in front of the entire school.

"I changed my mind."

Fuck.

My chest pulls tight.

What the hell did we do?

He changed his mind, meaning fuck the world, it's me and him no matter what, just like he promised me?

I let out a shuddered breath.

Fuck!

Captain opens our room door, and we step in, but we only get through the landing before Cap suggests we leave again.

"I think we should take off for a while," he whispers, almost unconvinced of his own words.

"Leave?"

He nods, moving toward the balcony doors. He turns to face me again. "Just a week, maybe two."

"It's been weeks, he hasn't been around. He just had an extra ten days."

Cap nods. "I think he needs it, both of them at this point."

In other words, we fucked them hard today.

I grind my teeth together, shaking my head. "What about Zoey, your visits?"

He swallows with a nod. "I can ask Maria to distract her, take her to Disneyland. We can FaceTime."

"Miss her first Disney trip, Cap?" I drop my shoulders. "Come on now."

His eyes hit mine, and the self-prejudiced flaring about knocks me on my ass. "I'm serious. And it's okay, I can take her again. She'll have way more fun with me anyway."

"Where would we even go?" I ask.

He shrugs. "Mountains, city. Anywhere. We can pay someone to do our work from school, not lose credits. Please just... please."

It's been almost six weeks since we got married in secret.

Six weeks of lying to everyone around us, by omission, but still. One plus one is still two. And one secret from two Brayshaws is three lies told.

I look around this stupid fucking hotel room, our little jail cell, and then move onto the balcony.

177

I grip the edges, looking out.

Graven orchestrated everything so far. We deserve a say in some things.

I look over my shoulder at Cap who now stands off to the side behind me. "A honeymoon of our choice?"

It's an awful joke, but a scoffed laugh leaves him, and he nods.

I shift, leaning against the railing and reach for his hand, pulling him closer.

He wraps his arm around me, breathing into my hair.

We both know how much we hurt the boys today, and it's a bitter bitch to swallow.

"I'll never forget the look on his face today," I whisper.

"I'm sorry, Raven. So fucking sor—"

A loud boom vibrates in my ears, causing me to tense as Captain's body clenches around me, his arms tightening before slowly losing their grip.

I pull back slightly, looking up at him, and his eyes fill with water, his lips parting some. "Captain."

He stumbles back, hits the patio table and falls to the ground.

I gasp, my eyes darting to the movement inside the room only to fly back to Captain and the blood spilling from his side.

"Holy shit!" I drop to my knees, touching his face, his side, his arms. Tears spill down my cheeks, clouding my vision and my eyes move back to the gun hanging at her side.

What the hell?!

Chapter 23

RAVEN

"What the fuck did you do?!" I scream, pushing to my feet and running for the hotel phone. "Why are you here?!" I cry. "What did you do?!"

She rips the phone from my grasp, yanking it from the wall. In the same second, I snatch the base from the stand, whip around and hit her over the head with it.

I grip her by the throat and rush her backward until she hits the wall.

"What the fuck are you doing?!" I scream, slamming her against the frame. It shatters behind her, crashing at our feet. I slam her again, but this time she pulls the gun up and hits me over the head with it, but only with enough force to push me back a few steps.

She rushes forward, gripping me by the neck, so I move my foot behind her, and shove, both of us falling to the floor.

"Stop!" I yell, elbowing her while trying to push her hands down, but she's strong.

Her knee comes up and she kicks me between the legs, making me fall forward. She uses that to wrap her arms around me and rams the gun into my kidneys.

I groan, rolling off her and she climbs on top.

She hits me across the face with the butt of the pistol and my vision goes black a minute.

"I'm helping you, you ungrateful bitch!" she screams at me.

Her body is trembling against mine.

I blink several times and move my eyes back to her.

Now that I can get a good look, it's clear she's wrung the fuck out. Dark circles, streaked makeup, overgrown roots, and bruising across her cheeks and arms.

"I need to call for help." I shift beneath her and she pushes the barrel of the gun into my sternum.

She opens her mouth to speak but suddenly is shoved off.

My eyes dart to the side, and I take Cap's extended hand but don't allow him to pull my weight.

He drops against the mattress, slipping and falling to his ass with a groan. He's pale, blood covers his side and pours out more by the second. He holds a hand against himself but it's fruitless.

"Captain," I shriek when his eyes start to close.

His head bobs as he tries to focus on me.

"Your phone! Where is it?!"

He hits his pocket, so I try to fish it out, but he suddenly shoves me away not a second before a lamp comes around and slams against him.

It doesn't shatter, but he's already weak, so it causes him to slouch over even more.

I crawl across the floor, scrambling for the gun, but she spins, catching me off guard and kicks me in the head. I fall back, allowing her to grab it once again.

She points the gun at Captain again, pushing the barrel against his head.

His eyes meet mine a moment before they roll closed.

"Don't!" I scream, rushing to my feet, but my head is pounding, and I fall back to my knees.

"I warned them," she says monotone. She cocks the gun back with both hands. Moving her finger to the trigger.

She braces herself, and only seconds before she shoots, does my blade pierce her gut, the move causing the bullet to only graze across Captain's shoulder.

He flops, his head hanging lifeless against his chest, hand falling from his wound as he goes unconscious.

She crumbles too, and with me standing at her back, the sudden weight of her loose body takes me down with her.

I tumble to my ass while she falls on top of me.

My knife still in her side, she shifts in my lap, her watery eyes wide and on me. "I told them they'd never get another piece of me." She coughs, blood now spilling from her mouth. She spits in my face, but I don't even flinch as her mucus and blood splashes against my skin. "I should have shot you instead," she realizes.

Sensing her next move, I grip the handle of my knife right as she swings the gun around, pushing it into my throat just beneath my jaw.

She grunts, her legs stretching out as her forehead tightens. Her breaths are coming quicker, shorter, now. "I have to."

I push against the cool metal, my body shaking, unwelcome moisture building to the surface. "I dare you."

She blinks once.

"Raven." She states my name rather than saying it as she tries to smirk through the blood, a vile look in her eye. "It's an interesting name... isn't it? So much hidden meaning and only one letter short." Her entire body jolts with her coughs, and she groans. "You... you ruined... everything."

I don't speak.

"Still, he doesn't get to have you." She cocks the gun, her

eyes hardening through her tears, but the tears aren't for me, they're for herself.

The door is kicked open, but I don't dare look.

She does though, and it's just long enough to distract her.

I smash my lips together and with a loud, angry grunt, I twist the blade, driving it deeper into her flesh.

She tries to swallow but chokes, her hand clawing at my arm.

Her nose turns red as her nostrils flare. Her eyes slice to mine, the first and only time I have ever seen regret or remorse from her. Her fingernails scratch across my stomach. "This is the only thing that will save you now." Her body jolts as she fights for air. "Ha—" she croaks. "Happy birthday, daughter. I hate you."

My nose tingles, but I bite into my cheek to hold onto myself. "Don't worry, Mom. I know."

A broken gasp leaves her. Her eyes squeeze one second, her body going limp in the next.

A pair of black boots come into view, and slowly I pull my gaze up.

Bass Bishop.

My mother dies in my arms.

At my hand.

WHAT FEELS LIKE AN ETERNITY LATER, MUST ONLY BE SECONDS as Bass is only now quietly pushing the door closed behind him. He props a chair against it to keep it from falling open since he busted the lock from the frame.

He rushes to Captain and feels for a pulse while looking me over.

"It's not mine," I tell him when he glares at the blood covering my shirt and lap.

He glowers harder at my head and the blood falling from it, and then pulls out his phone.

"Don't call them."

His eyes cut to mine as he slowly lifts his cell to his ear. He frowns. "Yeah... hi. I found a man bleeding in room 109 at Vermont, he was shot and he's out cold." He raises his finger to his lips, listening before he says, "There's a woman, too." He ends the call.

Bass stands, walking over, and crouches to his knees in front of me.

I don't realize what he's doing until his hand covers mine.

Mine drops at the contact.

"Let go of the knife, Raven."

My fingers fly open, but he has to pull my hand back.

He gently reaches up and turns my head toward him. The sloshy sound of the blade being ripped from flesh fills the air and I double over, vomiting across his shoes and my right leg.

"Come on." He grips me under my arms, pulling me up and my mom's body falls to the floor with a thud.

Bass sets me on the bed and quickly runs into the bathroom, coming back with two wet towels. One he uses to wipe across my chin, the other he gently places around my neck.

He pulls me to my feet and rushes us toward the door, but I yank away, falling against the wall.

"What... what are you doing?" I shake my head.

"We're leaving."

"Like hell."

Bass gets in my face. "Get the fuck out of this room, Raven. Now," he growls, but worry swims in his eyes.

"I say what goes on here!" I shout, making a mockery of myself. A wetness coats my cheeks – blood or tears, I don't fucking know. "Not you!"

"You're right. Still, we need to leave."

"I won't leave him here."

"There is a man shot and a woman dead. We have to get you *out* before someone comes knocking."

"That is Captain bleeding out on the fucking floor! I leave, and he dies?!" I bark, ignoring the throbbing it creates at my temples. "Alone beside that piece of shit?! Fuck you!" I shove at him. "I'm going to the hospital with him!"

Bass curses and before I know what he's doing he has me spun around, my back to his front, my arms and stomach smashed against the wall. He covers my mouth and plugs my nose, suffocating me.

"Stop fidgeting, it'll hurt your wounds," he says, tightening his hold.

I'm weak, but I claw at his arms.

His chest expands against my back. "I have to get you out of here, Raven. *You* are priority. Don't worry," he whispers softly as my body starts to sway. "They're coming for him."

They – he didn't call the ambulance.

He called his brothers.

Fuck!

Everything goes black.

Chapter 24

RAVEN

My eyes open, my vision blurry at first, but it only takes a second for it to clear.

Bass Bishop comes into view.

The tautness of his features tells me he's unsure of his next move.

Good.

"Captain," I rasp.

"In surgery." He eyes me, and I don't have to ask. "Royce is on his way to get you."

Not Maddoc.

I close my eyes again, giving a small nod.

This is all my fault. A little girl almost lost her dad today because of me. Everyone will have questions. They'll ask me why she was there, what she said, and what followed. Questions that will lead to more questions, most of those being ones I have no answers for.

She spoke in riddles that were lost on me, acted like she was doing me a favor by walking in there with a gun and attempting to take a life, then following up with trying to take mine.

I could have stolen the gun from her hands when Bass distracted her, but she doesn't like to fail, especially if it's against me. She'd have tried again, and again, like the pathetic woman she was, she'd have caught me when my back was turned.

Things were too far gone at that point – my move was the only one I could afford. I have a lot to process, but one thing was crystal clear – she thought he was Graven, a true Graven, and wanted him dead.

Why?

I look back to Bass. "Tell Royce you'll bring me."

"I don't think—"

"You're not here to think, Bass." I glare.

His eyes narrow, but he doesn't argue, only looks away with a nod. "You should wash your face, might cause a riot looking like that."

Shit.

I drag myself to a sitting position, wincing as the pounding hits harder.

Bass points to a bottle of Tylenol and cup of water sitting beside me, so I take it and drag myself into the bathroom.

He somehow got me to another hotel, got Captain to a hospital, and, I have no doubt, got my mom's body off the floor.

I stare at myself in the mirror.

There's blood matted in my hair, my face is fucked and bruised, the corner of my eye swollen, a blood vessel seemed to have popped, but I can see fine and I feel nothing.

I strip and step into the shower, letting the water wash away what it can. I gingerly massage my hair, staring at the rosy water as it spins into the drain. The hotel provided soap is hardly enough to get rid of the grime, but it works good enough. All signs of my mother are now running down the sewer where it belongs.

When I step from the shower, I pull the shirt and sweats that magically appeared on the counter over me and look in the mirror again.

You killed your own mother.

Shouldn't you cry, or hurt, or mourn?

Shouldn't you feel anything other than the sour taste of relief?

I killed my mother.

Bass walks in, patting the countertop, so I turn and lean against it.

With a frown, he pours peroxide on a cotton ball and taps it against my face. When I don't react, he presses a little harder, moving to the next, wider cut.

"Does it sting?"

"Not enough."

He freezes, dropping his hand as he glares at me. "You saved him."

"*You* saved him."

Bass shakes his head and moves back to working on me. "All I did was walk in, and too late. I should have been there to stop her from getting that close. You were with them, so I stepped into a room to take a call." He shakes his head. "You were all gone when I stepped out."

I stare at him, my voice more of a whisper than I intended. "When did he ask you to start watching me?"

"The night he came home without you."

Fuck.

"He trusts Captain to keep you safe, but he needed to know someone had your back if Cap could only have your front."

There's a hard knock on the room door and my eyes narrow.

"Told him what you said." He shrugs, tossing the cotton ball in the sink as he backs out. "Told me to fuck off."

'Course he did.

The second the door clicks, it's slammed against the wall and heavy footsteps bound my way.

A mess of dark hair and wild dark eyes hit mine. His shoulders drop and he rushes for me, his hands planting gently on my face, getting a good look. I keep my muscles loose so he can move me as he needs.

He tilts my head to the side and down, softly brushing against my hair to see the damage the gun made beneath it.

"You keep getting this pretty little head beat on, and you might forget us altogether, RaeRae," he teases, bringing my eyes back to his. "On second thought, I could get down with that, maybe win you over first the second time around."

My lips press together, a small laugh leaving me. I grip his wrist, bringing my forehead to his. "Yeah, Ponyboy. I'm good." I catch his eyes again. "I promise."

With a deep inhale he nods, and then steps back, glancing across my body. "She get you anywhere else?"

"My ribs are a little tight, chest is heavy." I look away. "Not sure what's causing it, though."

He grabs my hand and tugs me to him, wrapping his arms around me loosely.

"Imma need you to stop gettin' your ass kicked, RaeRae. Let me take the hits for you."

"I needed the pain today," I mumble against him.

He jerks back, glaring at me, but he can only hold my eyes for a few seconds now that we're back to the reality of the day.

They found out I married their brother, and without them. I know that's what hurts Royce the most.

He was left out. He doesn't know how to handle being in the dark.

"We didn't want to force you guys to watch."

"We wanted to be there. Silent strength, RaeRae, that's what we could have given you, and him."

I swallow, but it burns. "Is he okay?"

"Let's go." He ignores me. "Someone needs to be there when he gets out of surgery."

He starts walking when I ask, "Maddoc isn't there yet?"

Royce freezes. He turns his head, but not all the way – a slight glance over the shoulder. "Nah..." He starts walking again. "Not yet."

"I..." My brows snap together. Never. He would never not be there or here in a moment like this, no matter fucking what led to it. I dart forward. "*Royce.*"

He pauses again, shaking his head. He looks to Bass who spins on his heels and steps out the door.

I walk around, planting my feet right in front of Royce.

"I can't find him," he whispers regretfully.

"Call him."

"I tried."

"Try *again*," I snap, panic flaring.

He digs in his pocket, flopping Maddoc's phone into my hand.

My eyes reluctantly pull from it to him. "Royce..."

"Had Mac track it when he didn't answer. Found it with his GPS in the alley behind the donut store." He doesn't meet my eye. "He ripped it straight from the dash. We can talk about this later. Right now, Captain needs his family."

He waits for me to nod and together the two of us make our way to his SUV.

The drive to the hospital is a silent one.

When we get there, we pull around the back.

As we step out, another door sounds, and I turn. Bass is ten steps behind me.

He gives a subtle nod, so I nod back.

Royce stops, glancing around and in the next second, what

189

looks like a glass window, becomes a sliding door and we step inside what is apparently a private elevator. It starts to close but I throw my arm in front of it, not looking Royce's way when his head slices toward me.

Bass steps inside with us.

The ride up, I'm sure is a quick one, but with each floor higher, my distress levels double. "There's no way he knows Captain's hurt. He'd be here if he did..." I look to Royce who again glances away. "Right? He'd be here?"

Royce's forehead contorts. "Any other day, I'd say yeah in a heartbeat, laugh at you for questioning it, but..."

But he found out I married his brother today, and at the same time and in front of the entire fucking school.

Big Man...

My mouth opens but I close it just as quick. "He told me to do this, then left when I listened."

Royce glares at Bass a moment so he slips the headphones forever around his neck on, turning away.

Royce shifts toward me.

"Maybe he didn't want you to listen. Usually you suck at it." Royce glares.

"The stakes were too high."

Royce steps closer to me. "And you're too strong to take orders from any-fucking-body," he growls, real anger in his dark eyes. "You need to realize this now before it's too fucking late. Look around you, soak up the power they, that we all, are and have given you without even realizing. The fate of this town lies in a single decision of an eighteen-year-old girl?" His brows jump. "Must be a helluva girl, yeah?"

I close my eyes but don't get a second longer to think, the door behind us opens, a security guard blocking the entryway.

He meets each of our eyes and takes a single step back. He lets us by, but his baton flings forward before Bass can step off.

Bass drops his head back lazily, his hands sliding in his pockets.

"Step back inside," the man tells him.

"Let him through." Anger flares.

The guy's eyes find mine. "I have orders-——"

"Orders that you'll forget about as of right now." I glance at Royce who tips his chin the slightest bit. I step forward, head high. "All your orders will come from me now. The only people allowed to step through that door and off on this floor is the three of us, Maddoc, and Victoria."

Royce leans over me, holding his phone out for the man to look at the screen. "This is Victoria. I'll send you the photo."

The man's frown is deep. "Mr. Brayshaw will be arriving—"

"And you will send him away. He can enter when and if I say."

"You clear, Fernando?" Royce stands tall at my back.

When I look to Bass he winks.

"Yes, sir." He turns to me, dropping his chin to his chest. "Ms. Brayshaw, I wish Captain quick healing."

"Thanks," I rasp, moving my feet when Royce grips my hand and takes off down the hall.

Right when we get to the end – to an open room with hanging TVs, a small kitchen area, and stocked bar – a short, pudgy man walks from the double doors.

"Doc?" Royce's grip on my hand tightens to the point I'd worry he'd break a knuckle, but I don't dare react. I doubt he even knows he's doing it.

"Almost out of surgery, they're sewing him up now."

"He's okay?" My free hand shoots out, gripping Royce's forearm.

"He will be. I've collected the bullet." His eyes shift toward Royce. "Should you need it for any reason."

His meaning is clear – in case we need to figure out who the shooter was.

Royce's response confirms we already know, but the man doesn't dare ask. Royce takes it, and nods, calling over one of the security guards.

He hands him the bullet. "Melt it down, reshape it and give it back to me," he orders.

"Yes, sir." The man asks no questions and walks away.

The doctor starts to turn, but his eyes linger on me.

"Hey, Doc," Royce calls, noticing as well. "If you need anything, for Captain, you'll need to speak to Raven." Royce looks to me, apology and understanding. "His wife."

"Yes, sir." The doctor doesn't bat an eyelash and takes the announcement as his okay to approach me directly. He reaches for my hand.

Hesitantly I slip it into his, frowning when cool metal meets my palm.

"My sorrow is yours, Mrs. Graven." My body locks at the name as does Royce's beside me. "We will protect him as we can, get him well."

"When you look at him, I need you to see a Brayshaw. When you speak to me, speak to one." I tug my hand free of Royce's and close it over his on mine. "There are no Gravens here."

"Yes, ma'am. Go, rest." He looks between us both, motioning to the couches behind us. "We will come get you the moment he's in his room. Not much longer now. His wallet, brass knuckles, and phone have been bagged. The nurse will place them in his room as she prepares it."

"Thanks, Doc."

With that, he walks away, and I open my palm to find a ring sitting in it, an item he chose not to place with the rest of Captain's belongings.

It's small, the band black, the front the shape of a crown with tiny pinkish-purple diamonds at the three tips.

I look to Royce who frowns at the jewelry, a curious expression on his face.

"What?"

He licks his lips and looks away. "Nothing. It's perfect for you."

When I stand there frozen, staring at it, Bass steps over to me. He tips his head to the side a little, so he can meet my eyes better.

He grabs the ring from my palm, seizes my hand, and slips it on... my middle finger.

"Fuck everyone, Raven. This is your crown. Wear it."

I nod, then move to the couch near Royce.

Bass lingers a few feet away, his eyes roaming around every few seconds.

I take a deep breath and sit back with my eyes closed.

Cap will be okay.

My mom is dead.

Maddoc is gone.

And me, I might just fucking crack.

One thing is for sure, though. If I do, everyone will fucking feel it.

Everyone.

"There you go, baby girl," Royce whispers. "Get angry. Get loud."

My eyes open and hit his.

"Get revenge."

Chapter 25

Raven

"Raven," Bass calls, nodding toward the hall.

I spot a wide-eyed Victoria down the long walkway. Her eyes find mine the second I stand.

She slows so I meet her. "Mac picked me up, or more demanded I get in or he'd tie me up and put me in the trunk." She looks around. "I didn't even know this was here."

"Me either."

"What happened?" she asks. "All he'd say is he was bringing me to you."

"Captain was shot, he's almost out of surgery."

"Shot!" Her eyes widen, her forehead creasing. "He's okay, though... yeah?"

I look to Royce and her head snaps his way.

"They said he will be," he tells her.

She nods, glancing back down the hall a second. "Rolland was pulling up right as I was shoved through the glass door."

My eyes fly to Royce again.

"I trust you." His dark gaze holds mine strong.

I nod, glancing to Bass and he kicks off the wall.

"Sit with Royce. I'll be right back."

I get halfway down there when the shouting reaches me.

"Get the hell out of my way! You're lucky I don't put a bullet between your eyes," Rolland is yelling.

"Step back on the elevator before I place you inside it." Fernando is firm, calm.

The corner of my mouth lifts.

When I step around, I see he's backed by three more security guards, all who stand taller when I'm spotted.

Rolland's eyes slice my way and his shoulders drop. He shakes his head. "Thank God! Raven, get Royce and Maddoc! These assholes—"

"Are doing as they were told."

His head snaps back. "No, they aren't. I gave them specific instructions." His eyes cut to Bass and narrow before moving back to mine.

"Instructions I overrode."

He tenses where he stands. "Excuse me?"

"You aren't welcome here, not yet."

That gets him angry. He shifts closer and is met with a wall of men, but I push past them, stepping in front of him.

"Not welcome," he drags out, his eyes moving over my shoulder. His words are calm but hold a heavy power. "I'd bury you for less."

"Don't threaten my men."

His brows jump. "Your men?" When I say nothing he starts to break. It takes him a minute, but then his eyes lose their peril, sloping at the edges as concern seeps through. "Raven," he pauses. "I need to be here for him."

"Not yet."

He shakes his head, not angry but unsure. "You have no right."

"I have *every* right."

"That is my *son*!"

"That is *my* husband!"

He jerks back like he's been slapped, stumbling a bit even before he finds his footing.

I look to Bass.

Without a word spoken, he ushers the security a few feet away, but he makes sure he's within his idea of a safe distance.

"When?" he breathes, eyes on mine.

"Six weeks ago. We wanted it to be easier for everyone. It backfired."

His shoulders fall. "Maddoc... he heard, didn't he?" His eyes move between mine. "That's why I can't reach him. He's gone?"

I open my mouth to speak, but he surprises me.

"This is my fault. All of it." He steps back, propping himself against the side of the elevator door. "He has no idea what's happened, does he?"

"He'd be here if he did." My eyes travel his face. "How did you hear?"

"My men." He gives a sad laugh. "*Our*, your, I don't even know anymore, but I was contacted the moment he was wheeled in. Gunshot they said?"

I consider not answering but, in the end, I do. "Two, but only one broke the skin. We're waiting for him to be moved into a room." I swallow. "Rolland, I can't let you in here."

"As much as it saddens me to say, I understand, Raven, and I respect the strength in your decision. I'd do the same."

"Raven!"

Victoria shouts and I look over my shoulder.

"He's in his room, we can go in!" Her eyes are tight, smile tighter.

I nod, turning back to Rolland.

His chin falls to his chest.

I almost give in, almost crack, but at this point, I have no idea what's going on.

Everyone is suspect, and he has yet to earn my trust if he ever does.

"Get into the elevator, Rolland. Make this easier for everyone. If you don't, Royce will walk out here, and I don't want to put him in the position to choose."

"He'd choose you, Raven."

I look to him, finding nothing but sincerity and certainty staring back.

"They all would," he whispers, a proud smile on his lips, hurt in his eyes. "I underestimated you."

"Everyone does."

"They won't anymore, not at the end of this. No one will."

"You sound so sure."

His weighty gaze holds mine. "I recognize the fight in your eyes. You want answers, and you'll stop at nothing until you get them." He pushes the button behind him without looking, stepping back into the elevator when the door pings open. His shoulders square and he stands tall. "Go. Be with them."

I don't respond, but wait until the doors close between us, then turn and jog down the hall.

Royce grabs my hand and together we walk through the double doors at the back of the room, Vee and Bass behind us.

My palm freezes on the door we're told Captain is behind, my eyes flying to Royce.

His hand comes up to cup my cheek, the vein in his hitting against his tan skin. "You're not weak. His being behind this door is proof of that. You're the bravest fucking person I have ever met, RaeRae, believe that." He kisses my temple, pulling back to look at me. "Go. I'm right behind ya."

I push through the door, my heart pounding harder against my chest with every step taken, but when Royce's grip finds mine from behind, my hand tightens, my eyes flying to him over my shoulder.

I'm hit with an overwhelming sense of obligation. I don't only need to be stronger for him right now, but I want to be. This is his brother lying here helpless – something they aren't accustomed to being. And it's just him.

What once was three is now one, at least that's how it must seem in his eyes.

One decision from me took both his brothers from him, temporary or not, it's what happened. He hates being alone, can't handle being left out, has no clue how to trust or believe in something better.

My eyes move back to his.

His features are soft but rugged. The tattoos from his neck to his knuckles scream bad boy, unapproachable, but he's so much more. He wants, more needs, someone to dare to look further, reach deeper. Look the angry in the eye and bear the burden willingly.

I'd do it in a heartbeat, but I wouldn't be enough. He needs someone's all, not the pieces I have to share with him.

"I'm good, RaeRae," he whispers for only me to hear. "Keep those feet moving."

We push farther into the room, the bleeps of the machines as irking as the sterile smell burning my nostrils.

"Hello." A soft, warm welcome from the nurse at his side. "I'm Carmen, I'll be here until he's ready to stroll away on his own."

Nobody says a word as she quietly walks out.

I force my eyes to Captain, and to my surprise, relief wafts over me. Royce steps behind me, so I drop my head against his chest allowing him to shuffle us to his bedside.

There are already three chairs placed directly beside it, so Royce and I lower ourselves into them.

The third chair mocks me, and guilt crashes hard, serving as a heavy weight on my body and mind.

I lean forward, laying my forehead on his lifeless hand.

Royce's finds my lower back, and then his head joins mine.

My eyes close, my favorite shade of green flashing behind them before everything fades away and all that's left is an empty pit of darkness, the universe's sick way of saying *not even in your dreams can you have him.*

I crash.

THE EARLY MORNING SUN SHINES THROUGH THE WINDOW WHEN my eyes open and I push myself straight in my chair.

Royce's hand grips my thigh and I look to him.

"He hasn't woken up yet, but they think he will soon," he tells me.

I glance behind me to find Victoria sitting on the little couch, staring right at me, while Bass stands at the edge of the door, just in case.

From there, the days are repeated. One turns to two, then six, and before we know, fourteen days pass and we're still here.

They removed the ventilator on the second day, and Captain started to stir on the third, but he's yet to stay awake longer than five minutes. He looks around, groans here and there. The nurse was able to get the doctor in quick enough for him to do his doctor shit once, flash some lights in his eyes and check his pupils, told him how long he'd been here, but Captain fell back asleep before he was able to talk to him about his injuries.

Maddoc is still nowhere to be found despite the army the Brayshaws have out looking, and no one has said a word regarding the whereabouts of my mother's rotting corpse. Rolland calls Royce several times a day, and Mac says Collins has been sniffing around in our absence.

I turn back to Captain right as the nurse steps in with a small bow.

"He's still so pale," I rasp, running my fingers along the stark white sheets, pausing before my hand meets his. "Why?"

"He lost a lot of blood, had to have a transfusion, and his body is still recovering, rebuilding strength and coming down from the shock," she says quietly as she pushes buttons on the screen beside him. "His color will come back soon, more and more each time he wakes." She offers a small smile when I glance to her. "Your husband is strong." I tense but she doesn't catch it. "He was fighting to wake before surgery began. It took a lot to put him under, that's why it's taking him longer to come to fully."

"He has a lot to live for."

She gives a small wink. "More than he realizes."

I frown but then a thought hits. "Wait... his blood type." My brows lower. "He's mentioned it was rare."

"Very," she agrees, grabbing her clipboard and turning to me. "Luckily, everything on this floor is designated for Brayshaw and whom they, whom *you*, allow. We have all five of your blood types in stock, just in case."

Five.

My eyes slice to Royce who jerks his chin in a nod. They know about Zoey here, but...

"Where did mine come from?"

She gives a tight smile, her age showing around her eyes when she does. "I drew every blood bag we have in our storage myself. Every bag but yours. Yours were delivered, and then tested for security reasons. They were cleared and stored following the result."

"Delivered by who?"

"Estella Graven."

"Collins' mom," I whisper, cutting a quick glance from Royce to Bass.

Makes sense I guess, she's their maid, likely runs in circles doing whatever the hell they need, but wait. "When, exactly, did the blood bags get delivered?"

She pauses to think, then turns to her rolling computer. "Let's see," she muses, pushing some buttons. "Almost two months ago."

Right when we signed away our lives.

"Go," Royce tells her.

She nods and walks out as I bury my face in my hands trying to process.

"Raven," Royce edges.

"He went to her." I whisper.

"Raven."

My eyes hit his.

"Donley went to her, or he had someone do it."

"Maybe it's an age-old thing, something all the families do?" Royce suggests, but tension lines his brows.

I push to my feet, shaking my head. "But... he'd have to know where to find her to get it." My eyes find his.

Did he know where she was all along?

Royce shifts to the edge of the couch not following.

I lick my lips looking between the three of them. My mother's glossy grey eyes flash before mine. I give a hard blink to erase it. "She said she wouldn't let them have another piece of her."

"What... you?" Royce whispers.

I shrug, but it takes effort, my muscles are tense, my stomach queasy. I swallow past the bile fighting its way up.

"But they didn't have her." His brows drop low, eyes coming back to mine. "Right?"

Sweat builds across my upper lip and I blow air across it, fanning myself in an attempt to cool my body temperature.

I vaguely register Bass asking someone for a cool rag before the chilled item touches my skin.

I open my eyes, finding his narrowed on me. "Breathe through your nose."

"Back the fuck up, man!" Royce shoves at him, taking his place. "I fucking got her." He glowers.

Bass doesn't fight him on it and moves for his place at the door.

Royce turns back to me with a rundown expression. "Are you okay?"

My eyes move between his, and I force a whisper he won't want to hear pass my lips. "I need to go."

His eyes harden. "I'm coming with you."

I shake my head and he jerks away from me.

"You go, I fucking go, Raven," he growls, but fear burns in his eyes.

"You can't," I breathe. "He'll wake up again soon. He can't be alone when he does."

"He needs *you* here just as much, maybe more. You're his *wife*," he spits the word with a nasty edge. "Or are you running with this new information that might not mean shit, so you can pretend the last few days never fucking happened if it does?"

Bass's footsteps sound behind me and Royce's head shoots up, his lip curling. "I fucking dare you, bitch." His chest rumbles with his words.

"Wait in the hall. Both of you," I say, not taking my eyes off Royce who won't take his off Bass.

As soon as the door swings open and closed, I reach out, gripping Royce's face, forcing his eyes to mine.

His harsh exhales grow deeper. He's hurting, angry. I deserve so much worse than a few heated words he'll feel like shit over later.

"If he wakes up, tell him I'll be back." My eyes bounce between his. "I will be back, Royce. I'm not leaving you."

"And if you find answers that change things, then what?" he spits. "You pretend nothing ever happened?"

My face must say it all, because in the next second his falls, his features screaming his honest truth – he wanted me to say yes, that it would all change, go back to how it was, but Captain is in this bed because I asked him to join me in mine, and sooner than we promised to.

How could I possibly turn my back on him when he so quickly gave his for mine?

I couldn't.

"How am I supposed to let you walk out of here not knowing what you're walking into? My brother would fucking kill me." His chest caves as mine does, and he cuts a quick glance away. "Both of them. Not that they'd have to. I'd fuck my own self up."

I swallow. "Bass will help me."

"Fuck him," he spits, angrily. "I *hate* him. I hate him near you, I fucking hate him around and I plan to make sure it's mutual. I'm gonna fuck him over, one way or another for good measure." He glares. "He's not me. He can't protect you like I can. He wouldn't die for you like I would."

I give a tight smile. "I know." I step against him, pulling his head down to mine. "I *know*, but I need you to stay with him. Be here for him while I can't be, while Maddoc isn't. I need you, ponyboy, but he needs you more right now. Please."

Royce's facial muscles constrict, and he drops his forehead to mine. A sad scoffed laugh leaves him, his hands finding my hips. "Problem child's sayin' please?" he teases, closing his eyes.

A small laugh escapes. "Guess I am."

His jaw clamps shut, but he leans in, kissing the corner of my mouth before pulling back, his dark lashes low. "He's gone if you come back with so much as an added scratch. Make sure that's clear."

I agree, moving for the door.

"I hate this," he says on a shuttered whisper.

"I know." I pause to look at Captain then meet Royce's eyes again. "I'll be back."

"You better be." He frowns. "Or we all die today."

Chapter 26

RAVEN

The elevator doors open, and I step onto the cement, my eyes finding Bass a few feet out, Victoria at his side. He slips a cigarette between his lips, nodding his chin as he brings his lighter up.

I glance the way he's motioned and jerk to an immediate stop.

Rolland sits against the side wall, tie undone, head in his hands. Not one of his security around, his driver not perched near waiting.

It's just him.

I walk over, stopping right in front of him, kicking his shoe when he doesn't move a single muscle.

He jolts, glare flying to mine, only for panic to flare the second he sees me. He jumps to his feet. "Is he okay?"

I bite into my cheek, glaring at him. "Not yet, he's not."

His heavy inhale causes my chest to ache, even more so when his eyes morph into the ones I used to know, concern laced through them. For me. "Where are you going, Raven?"

"To make a point. To let them know I'll fuck their world harder than they've fucked mine and without hesitation."

His lips pinch and I know he wants to argue, but he keeps them locked tight, as he should.

"Go up."

Rolland's eyes slice to mine.

"Be there for your sons, especially the one on the verge of flipping out, he's up there and feeling more alone than ever. Be a fucking dad and nothing else, for once. Stare at Captain and replay all the wrong decisions you made, but first I need something from you."

"Anything," he relents.

"I need to get in touch with the Riveras."

"Gio?" he guesses, but I don't bother confirming.

With his forehead drawn tight, he pulls a random card from his wallet and a pen from his dress shirt pocket, quickly scribbling a number on the back of it.

I stare at the number, then meet his eyes.

"He'll come home, Raven. It might take time, but he will." His tone is more hopeful than confident.

"What makes you say that?"

"He knows nothing else."

"You're wrong." I shake my head, looking off. "He knows pain." I force my eyes back to his. "And that's enough to keep anyone away."

I tilt my head, glancing up at the glass building, knowing eyes are on me even though I can't see them. I give a nod, and then step back and Rolland grabs his suit jacket off the ground, moving toward the elevator as it begins to slide open.

"You can trust the others, too," he says. "Trick, Alec, they're good people. Honest, noble."

"Trust only those who earn it," I repeat the words of a Brayshaw.

I'd swear his lip twitches. "Smart girl." With a deep inhale, he says, "You're looking for answers." My eyes move to his as he steps into the elevator. "Start with her."

Rolland looks over my shoulder right as the door clicks shut, and then there I stand, staring at a reflection of myself, but movement behind me has my eyes lifting.

My hands fall to my sides as I slowly turn around.

Victoria.

Everyone here serves a purpose of some kind...

Her brown eyes intensify, flying between mine.

No...

"Raven..." Her voice echoes around me, bouncing off the wall, creating a deep ringing in my ears.

I step toward her.

She doesn't cower.

"Raven." Her hands lift.

Bass looks between us, his spine shooting straight.

He flicks his cigarette and takes quick steps toward her. Gripping her arm, he turns her to face him. "What'd you do?" he demands.

I reach them in the same second, my hand shooting out to clasp her throat and her head snaps my way, her fingers coming up to latch against my wrists. I squeeze, but she doesn't fight me. She nods, accepting, which makes my breaths come in shorter spurts.

Fight me.

"I told you, you might hate me," she gasps, her throat bobbing against my palm.

I blink rapidly to keep myself in check.

Maddoc is gone, Captain is hurt, my mother is dead.

Maddoc is gone.

I'm crumbling.

Bass lets her go and I get in her face, closing my fist as much as I can until not a sound can squeeze past her lips. "You. Are going. To fucking talk," I force past clenched teeth, fighting the tremble threatening to take over every inch of me.

She tries to nod, eyes pleading, but not for me to release her, for me to believe in her.

I shove her away, and she starts coughing, her hand shooting up to rub her reddened skin, but I don't give her the space to calm, I push her again, until her back slams against a parked car.

"Captain was shot," I tell her. "That's why he's here, and by my own fucking mom. My mom who planted more seeds than I have time to grow. I'm out of time and out of choices."

Alarm fills her eyes, but she blinks it away. "What did she tell you?"

"Not enough before she stopped breathing."

She freezes, her eyes sliding between mine and Bass'.

"Talk."

A tortured sigh leaves her. "I don't want to tell you."

"I don't care. Talk."

She glances at Bass as if she wants him to walk away, but he only leans back against a random van, crossing his arms and one leg over the other.

With a shake of her head, her stare moves back to me.

"I was a tool," she starts after a minute of silence. "My role was always the same – the naïve little girl with stars in her eyes for the target of the night. A shoulder for them to boost themselves up on, not attached to their worlds, or so they thought. After a few drinks, they loved to tell me how brave they were, who they screwed over, and how easily it worked."

"Dirty laundry."

"At its filthiest," she mumbles, her eyes focused over my shoulder. "Since alcohol was what we used to get them loose-lipped, Mero, that was his name, refused to touch it, but after a few years with me, he grew comfortable, less careful. He started having a few here and there." Her eyes slide back to mine. "I had to play extra nice to get what I was looking for, but it worked. He practically sang when I stopped playing dead in his bed and pretended to be the girl he bargained for."

Mero...

My mind spins trying to place the name.

She nods like she can read my mind. "Mero." She repeats the name.

"Who is he?"

"The man this town erased – the fourth man in the year-book photo." Her eyes bounce between mine. "The man who gave a secret in exchange for me. The man your mom tracked down five years ago with a shoebox full of unopened envelopes."

No...

"Envelopes full of what?" I rasp.

"Cash," she whispers. "With a Brayshaw stamp sealing each one."

My stomach muscles tighten. "Five years ago..."

She holds my eyes. "It's how I found them, the house."

Five years ago... in the dark...

"It's how I found out about you. Who you were and what you were worth. Clearly, much more than me since the knowledge of your existence is what earned him his rag doll. Me."

"Vee..." I croak, my hand flying to my stomach.

"I sat in the front seat of his car, parked outside your trailer the night he came for you." Her eyes grow cloudy, her scowl never breaking. "I watched your mother walk out, saw the light go off. I listened to you scream, and I was glad, for once, it was someone else instead of me."

"Enough," Bass snaps, trying to step between us, but I hold my hand up, keeping him away.

"Mero Malcari," she says.

Malcari.

I shake my head.

"Rolland's biological brother, Maddoc's biological uncle. Remember the story I told you, about how the night their dads died, one man died on the scene? That's how Rolland remembers it, when really his brother was the one he chose to leave behind, assuming he wouldn't make it, and tried to save Captain and Royce's dads instead, who died anyway."

I groan, my body jolting forward.

"I said enough!" Bass screams, his hand coming down on my back, a strain taking over the corners of his eyes as he stares at me.

She keeps going. "The man who wanted revenge on Brayshaw and Graven and used us both to get it. The man your mother paid to rape you, to ruin you so Rolland couldn't trade you, and so a Graven wouldn't come for you themselves."

My knees give, my body falling into Bass'.

Leave it to Ravina to do the most twisted thing imaginable to her own daughter in her own fucked up way of revenge. The sickest part, I'd bet she was convinced she was somehow saving me, while also reminding herself I didn't deserve it.

But revenge for what exactly?

"Get the fuck out of here—"

I cut Bass off with a shake of my head.

He growls but snaps his mouth shut.

There's no time to stop and think on this right now, but one thing is clear with her words. My mom wanted to fuck Graven over, and I need to find out why.

I take a deep breath to steady myself then walk straight toward her.

She stands tall.

"What else did he tell you?"

"Not enough before he stopped breathing." She gives my words back to me.

Her tone, words, and everything in the middle should be

cause for concern, yet looking at her, for some reason I have none.

She cuts a quick glance to Bass. "Raven..." She trails off. "I've never had anyone, ever," she admits quietly, her next words even more hesitant, embarrassed even. "I don't wanna lose this."

My airway constricts, my glare growing stronger.

Her eyes fall. "I told you not to trust me," she says.

I lick my lips and look away. "Well, I do."

Her head snaps up.

"Come with me." I frown.

She presses her lips together a moment before asking, "Where?"

"If you have to ask, you don't know me as well as I think you do."

Her forehead tightens. "Without them?"

"I don't have much of a choice right now."

She gives a curt nod and takes off toward Bass's car, ahead of me.

"You sure this is a good idea?" Bass steps beside me

"No, which makes it no different than anything else I've done here."

He scoffs a small laugh.

My eyes constrict. "I want my sides back, Bass."

He's quiet a moment, then moves to stand in front of me. He crosses his arms, regarding me with a meaningful glare. "You want it back?"

"I want them all back. I want *it* all back."

He shrugs. "So, take it."

Not having expected his response, an instant frown hits.

Bass stretches to his full height and steps closer. "You're Brayshaw, Raven." He pushes a finger in my chest and I glare at him. "*You*. Not Rolland, not the boys. Nobody... but you. Your mom is dead. You're all that's left. You're strong, make them see. They think they can control you, decide for you, show them they can't." He gets in my face. "You want this world? You take it."

A chill runs down my body, and I step into his space as he stepped into mine.

"You got my back?"

"I got your all. My life belongs to Brayshaw," he promises. "You say jump. I fucking fly."

Not a hint of uncertainty.

He's all in.

"Give me your phone."

He hands it over without a second thought, moving closer to me so he can see the screen.

I type out a text to the number Rolland gave me.

ME: THIS IS RAVEN CARVER

I FROWN AT THE SCREEN, DELETING CARVER. MY FINGERS ARE slow as I re-type the message, this time hitting send.

ME: THIS IS RAVEN BRAYSHAW. I NEED GIO.

ME: NOW.

IT RINGS WITHIN SECONDS, BUT WHEN THE PERSON ON THE other end isn't Gio but Trick himself. I hang up.

Bass gives a slow nod.

"He'll have him call."

I'm done getting less than I ask for. Trick owes me nothing, but he's a smart man. I'd bet if he asked someone for something and got less than, he'd do the same.

We stand there for a few minutes, waiting, and finally the phone rings again.

I answer, speaking not a word as I bring it to my ear.

"What's wrong?"

Gio.

My shoulders relax. "I need your help. Now, today."

"You gotta give me more than that, Raven. I can come now, no doubt, but if you need me for who I am today, you have to lay it out. I have a man to stand behind, too, girl. Clearance is mandatory."

I lick my lips, nodding, my eyes follow Bass as he cases the area around us to make sure nobody is standing near, listening. "Is he with you?"

"He is."

"You can put me on speaker."

There's some ruffling on the other end, and then his voice comes back on the line. "Talk to me, Rae."

"He underestimated me. They all did," I whisper, a deep ache forming between my ribs. "I'm gonna show them... my family is *mine*. Mine to hurt, mine to heal. Not theirs."

"Someone is hurt." Trick's voice hits my ear.

I knew he was smart.

"And someone is dead."

"Who died?" flies from Gio. "Raven, who is hurt?"

"Son," is a sharp whisper on the other end of the line.

"This town is mine to take. Help me." It's honest and to the point, it's all I have.

It's quiet a minute before Gio speaks again. "What happened?"

I turn, looking up at the tall glass building, knowing Royce's eyes must be on me.

Please don't feel like you're alone.

. . .

I drop my stare to my shoes, grinding my toe into the gravel. "I'll do it without you if I have to, but I'm standing here asking you to see these people for what they are. Help me, help my town before it's too late."

"Give us an hour. Fifteen to have a jet fueled, thirty to land, fifteen to reach you."

"I'll tell you where to go."

"I know where to go, Raven." Trick's deep voice is both soothing and chilling.

"Then you understand."

"I've waited for this. The point of our existence is to protect those who can't protect themselves, provide safety to our people, and trust in an untrustworthy world. They've failed you and your people. We'll remind them that is not allowed."

I nod even though he can't see me and turn to Bass.

"Can your phone be tracked?"

He pulls it from my hand and tosses it under the nearest car.

A hint of a smirk ghosts my lips before it's gone.

"I have a key to the Brayshaw mansion. We can go there while we wait."

I shake my head. "No. We're going to the school. I need to talk to Perkins."

Without another word spoken, we make our way to his car.

Donley made a mistake demanding me.

Rolland made a mistake leaving me behind.

I'll show them all, I'm more than they can handle.

Bass puts the car in reverse but pauses before his foot hits the gas. He gives a half glance at Victoria in the backseat before lifting his hips in his seat.

I hold my breath as he pulls my knife from his pocket and flips it open, not a speck of red to be found.

With a nod, I reach out and close my fist around it.

My eyes hit his.

"Ready, Bishop?"

"Ready, Carver."

"Let's make them regret this."

I sit back in my seat, a calmness settling over me.

They want an obedient wife.

They're getting a defiant queen.

Chapter 27

Raven

School is just getting out when we pull up.

Students pour from the building, their steps slowing when they spot me, Bass, and Victoria right behind me.

Wide eyes scan the bruising on my face, but I simply give small nods to the people I pass.

I don't want to fight with them. Before, I'd get angry when they made remarks or stared and assumed, but it's only natural. They've been left in the dark which is wrong when they're expected to stay in an order set by my name.

These are my people, and they need to feel comfortable enough to speak to me whenever they want.

Mac must have heard we were here because he suddenly pops around a corner. He holds a hand up, so we slow to a stop, allowing him to catch up.

"Everything okay?" he asks. "I didn't know you were coming."

"I didn't tell anyone."

Mac nods, looking behind him then back to me. "Perkins?"

"Where is he?"

"The gym, signing off on some new equipment that came in, but the baseball team is in there conditioning."

"I need him alone."

"I can help."

Our heads snap left to find Chloe stepping up, her arms crossed over her binder. She stops right next to me.

"Go into the hall outside the gym, not the one that leads outside, but the one Maddoc tricked you into when he made everyone think you were prostituting here." When my eyes narrow, she keeps going. "It's the only one that has doors on each side. Mac or her" —her eyes snap to Victoria and back— "can stand behind one, Bishop behind the other in case you need someone close. I don't think you plan on doing anything crazy, you'd have waited to get him at home if you had, but just in case, that's where you want to be."

"Why?"

"It's the only place in the school out of sight, the camera position is off. There's a three-foot, two-inch gap from the gym door down. I marked the focal point with a photo last year. You're in sight if you're past the frame."

"Why is the camera off?"

"Because sometimes this place calls for moves others can't see."

"It was purposeful?"

"My father makes no mistakes."

I nod.

"Go. I'll have him there in five minutes." She spins on her spikey heels.

"Chloe," I call.

She turns back to me.

"Thanks."

"I don't know what's happening, but something is wrong, I

can sense it here and at home. I have a suspicion only you can fix it." She tucks her long hair behind her ear. "The Brayshaws are more than three guys to us. We follow because we believe in them and what we know they can do for this town. We may be young, but we've seen what our parents and generations before us did to their own. We want more than that."

"You'll have more than that."

Her lips twitch. "Prove it, *Brayshaw*."

She walks away and I turn back to the others.

Victoria glares after Chloe while Bass and Mac stare at me with raised brows.

"Royce asked me to—"

I cut Mac off. "Do whatever he wants, we're good."

"You sure?"

"Go."

With that, we part ways, the three of us heading for the back end of the gym.

"What are we doing here exactly?" Victoria asks.

"Talking."

She scoffs. "Right."

"Perkins has given us nothing from his own mouth, yet he turned his back on his brother for my mom. Helped watch over the boys while Rolland was away, protected—" I cut myself off."

Zoey.

"He did all that as he stood back as the bad guy, acted as if he hated them while they legit hated him."

"He did what you did," Bass says, his eyes sliding my way. "You went to Collins to protect them, let them think you were the bad guy, allowed them to believe you betrayed them. Let the entire school think they let their guard slip."

I glare straight ahead. "I never should have done it."

"No, you shouldn't have, but that's not the point. You did and without thoughts of self-preservation."

"Is this your way of saying I should trust Perkins? Freely, without him having to earn it?"

"No. This is me pointing out you're capable of even more than these grown-ass men are and without reason."

"I love them. That's reason enough."

"But that's pure, Raven. Not mixed with hatred, or jealousy, or greed. You love them, so you protected them. Period. Everyone else around here has a deeper motivation than you."

I whip around, shoving him in his chest, but he doesn't even budge.

He glares.

"Say what you wanna say, Bishop!"

"You don't owe him anything, Raven." He gets in my face. "If he deserved to know what happened, he would already."

I go to look away, but he moves with me, staying in my face.

"I know you want answers, and you deserve them, but you do *not* have to go in there and tell him what's happened to Captain, or your mom. He didn't earn this from you, and Captain wouldn't give him a damn word. He's the one who told Collins about you. He may have had Ravina's best interest in mind at one point, but you became nothing but collateral damage."

"He knows more than he's saying."

"And he's a piece of shit for not volunteering the information to you."

"That's why I'm here, Bass. This is his chance to tell me what he's hiding."

"One minute," Victoria reminds us.

"And if he doesn't?" Bass lifts his brow, mockingly.

I push forward, tugging the door open and stepping into the hall.

"Make sure the area is empty." They nod and make quick

work of disappearing behind the boy's and girl's locker room doors.

I slide into the nook that holds a water fountain and wait.

Not five seconds later, Chloe's voice is within range.

"My concern is the article doesn't depict the proper tone we strive for." The door opens.

"What would you have me do, Ms. Carpo?"

Chloe's heels clink against the flooring until she stops right where I'm hidden. She doesn't look for me, doesn't blink, but spins to face him, dropping her binder in front of her, standing as straight as a statue. "I'd have you castrated for abandoning a Brayshaw, trying to hurt one, and helping hide another. In my home, there is no room for dishonesty. You lie, you pay. You hurt ours, we crush yours. You should know this already though, Connor. It was your world once, too."

"What the hell is this?" He speaks slowly.

I step out, my eyes hitting his before I turn my body to face him completely.

"Raven," he edges, subconsciously taking a step backward, his eyes flying to the door behind me when Chloe lets it slam with her exit. "What is this?" He takes in my fresh bruising. "What happened? Why are you here alone? Where are the boys? Did—"

"Are you done?" I ask and his shoulders fall some. He closes his mouth. "Good." I nod. "I have questions."

"I can't—"

"But you will because you're smart enough to recognize a give and get when you see one."

"You've already married him, Raven."

"I'm not looking for a way out of this."

"Then what?"

"My mom had me raped when I was twelve," I tell him, not blinking when he stumbles back a step. "By a man you used to know."

His brows knit at the center.

"She paid this man. It makes no sense." I shake my head. "People, her people, from our neighborhood would have done it gladly and free. Men have asked for me over the years, but she'd act jealous and make them leave. I think she used the man she did, a man who had ties to this world, hoping it would get back to Donley. Why would she do that if he didn't know I existed?"

"I..." Perkins shakes his head, looking off. "I don't know."

"What *do* you know, Connor?" I ask him.

He looks to the floor. "What she told me. That she was leaving him, that she didn't need the money or the town. That her and I could go somewhere and be together, away from it all. I believed her. She *wanted* to be with me, I know it."

"What happened?"

"She was supposed to meet me but didn't show, so I went to the Graven Estate, ready to go in and get her, but my brother met me at the gates instead. He was smiling in a way I'd never seen, and I knew the woman we both loved gave him what she promised to keep for me."

"Her virginity."

He gives a curt nod, looking away. "I went out, preyed on someone who was hurting more than I was that night."

"Captain's mom."

"She was crying, devastated. She had no family, was a foster kid who found someone to love. All she wanted was to have a child and show them a love she never knew, and she knew the life she was about to marry into meant no children of her own."

"There are plenty of ways to be a parent that doesn't include a fertile fucking husband."

He gives a small nod before continuing. "I comforted her, knowing she'd break." His sad eyes hit mine. "She was in my arms and then my bed within an hour, but she couldn't stay long. She was getting married that night."

Jesus Christ.

"Ravina was gone four months later but not before she got a note to me. She said she was sorry, and she had a secret she couldn't hide if she were here."

"A belly," I croak.

He nods. "That was my first thought. I never understood why she'd take off. If she chose him, fine. I stayed out of her face, never stepped foot in that house again after he told me she gave him her. Her leaving made no sense to me. It really made no sense when Felix broke down months later." Perkins eyes me.

My chest muscles constrict.

"Ravina seduced Felix that night. He said he found her stepping out of the shower, and instantly she came on stronger than she ever had. He said he tried to stop before things went further, wait for the wedding night, but she wouldn't let up," he whispers. "He said he couldn't deny her, not that he truly wanted to anyway. Only after, he said she cried and asked for a few minutes alone, so he left to get some air." Perkins meets my eyes. "That's when he saw me outside and grew suspicious, so he masked his confusion and made sure I knew they'd slept together."

"He slept with her that night."

"He did, and every night that followed from there until she was gone."

"I don't understand." I run a hand over my forehead, taking a few steps away. "Was he my father or not?"

Perkins gives a regretful shrug. "I don't know, Raven. I wish I did."

"You said she left four months after, what happened in that four months?"

"Ravina and Felix spent every minute together, looking

225

every bit the happily engaged couple that they were supposed to be."

"And when she left?"

"It was abrupt, caused a storm in the town. That's when Donley called the strike on the Brays as revenge. He believed they stole her back, hid her somewhere because they changed their minds which wasn't allowed."

"How did he get to them?"

"They thought they were coming to hear news on where she might be but were ambushed. Everyone but Rolland died."

Holy shit.

"Their dads... that was because my mom left?"

Because I existed?

I'm the reason they lost their parents?

Wait. So Perkins doesn't know Rolland's brother escaped either.

I swallow. "Did you look for her?"

"For years."

"When did you learn about me?"

"When Rolland went to prison, which he only did because he thought it would keep you and her hidden. Felix had no idea who he was accused of raping. Your mother's name was sealed, some back end deal made with the DA, so Felix blindly played the role asked of him by Donley, having no idea he was so close to discovering where Ravina was."

"Did you go to her then?"

He shakes his head. "Rolland wouldn't tell me where she was when he was sentenced, but he told me it wasn't only her. I did the math, too, Raven."

"She shot him," I tell him and his head jars back. "Captain. She found out about the engagement, and she came back. She shot him, twice."

He rushes toward me and Bass dashes from behind the

other door, gripping his elbow and spinning him, throwing him against the wall with one smooth move.

"I wasn't... I'm not gonna hurt her." He fights to meet my eyes. "He's alive?"

"He's alive. She's... not."

His body locks and he stops moving, all the fight leaving him as the color drains from his face. He goes slack, so Bass releases him and he falls to the floor.

"I never meant for any of this to happen. I never should have told Collins about you, but he... he found the birth certificate, and I had to lie. Pretend I was hiding her, and that I needed him, but he knew about the agreement and wanted what he felt he was owed. I had to tell him you existed to protect Zoey."

"And for that, I'll let you keep breathing, but you need to get out of this town. He doesn't want you around, so you can't be. Leave, Perkins, and don't come back unless *he* calls and says you can."

Victoria steps out then, and Perkins eyes move from her to me.

"This is my home."

"Not anymore."

Chapter 28

RAVEN

"THAT'S THEM," I SAY AS AN OLD PICK-UP TRUCK ROLLS TO A stop at the light ahead of us.

Bass parked just after the bridge where the Graven side of town begins.

I've stayed in Collins' house, but I've never actually seen the Graven Estate that is apparently the entire back half of this end of the city.

"He's looking right at you."

I nod, right as Gio looks away, their vehicle passing right by us.

"Okay, let's go."

"Shouldn't we talk to them, make a plan or something?" Victoria sits forward in her seat.

"No. They know how to do their jobs better than anyone, I'm not gonna sit here and tell them how to do it. Drive, Bishop."

He gets back on the road, making the right onto the street and following it down about two miles.

"There it is."

We pull up to the iron gate, three times as tall as me, large, curled spikes at the tips. The street literally dead ends at their property entryway.

"How do we open it?" I ask.

"Where did the others go?" Victoria asks.

I shrug, frowning as the gate opens before us. "Bass..."

"I know." He rolls forward and the second the tail of the car is past the metal strip on the ground, the gate closes us in, a man stepping from behind a shrub with a gun at his hip, a wire hanging from his ear.

I unbuckle my seatbelt, and Bass follows, dipping his hands into his ashtray before we step out.

He stays at my back as I keep advancing. "Get out of my way."

A small smile plays on the man's lips. "Don't work like that."

"I'll ask one more time before I make you."

The man glares this time, reaching for his earpiece, but not before Bass quickly darts forward. He tosses the ashes in his face, dips in and rips the gun from his jeans while tearing the piece from his ear.

The man rushes back a step as he swipes at his eyes, blinking rapidly. "What do you think you're doing?"

"I said move."

The man scoffs, his lip curling. "You're not in charge here."

Bass shoots him in the foot and the man howls.

Victoria steps from the car, tossing him a roll of duct tape – must be a Bray staple, keeping duct tape on you – and places it over his mouth. The two drag him behind the shrub, wrapping his hands and feet together.

I crouch down beside him while they move back for the car.

"You might wanna try hobbling out the gate. Don't be a hero. Heroes die."

He glares but then gives a curt nod, dropping his eyes from mine.

I don't step back in the car when they slide inside it, I walk the hundred yards down the driveway with them on my tail.

The men on the porch glare, stepping closer to me, their hands on their waists but when I keep toward them, something shifts in their demeanor. They hesitate, then stand taller.

They fall aside.

"Ms. Brayshaw." The one closest to the door drops his head while reaching for the handle.

I glance back at Bass and Victoria, who have just opened their doors and stepped out.

Bass lifts his arms, propping his elbow on the hood. "Your call."

"Flip the car around and wait."

"I'm coming with you," Victoria shouts but her feet don't move.

"No, you're not."

I turn back and step through the entryway.

Voices float from the left, so I slowly follow the sounds.

Two women smile at each other, laundry in both their hands, crisp white bedding stacked perfectly in front of them. The flooring alerts them of my presence and both their gazes snap to mine. Their smiles fade instantly, their laughter disappearing with it.

The women quickly drop what's in their hands, duck their heads and begin to walk away.

"Wait, stop." I quickly slide over, blocking their escape.

They gasp, their muscles tensing. "We're sorry, Ms. Brayshaw. We—"

"Did nothing to be sorry about." I frown, glancing between the two.

After a moment, one of the women meets my eyes, and I've got to give it to her. Not once does she look to the bruising surrounding it.

"Tell me where I can find Donley."

Curious, she tilts her head, but still answers. "He spends his evenings in the study."

"And where is that?"

"The way you came, to the right of the entrance, then follow the hall."

I nod, taking a few backward steps. "Get out of the house," I tell them before turning and doing as they said.

I only make it a few feet into the hall when the sweet scent of a cigar leads me past a staircase and to a tall, wide-open archway.

The second my feet pass the threshold his head pops up, and his pen falls from his hand.

He shakes off his surprise and uncertainty with his next breath, but the extra wrinkles lining his eyes give him away.

"Raven."

"Donley."

"I must say, this is unexpected."

"Yeah, you're telling me." I step farther into the room.

His eyes rake over my face and he frowns. "I'm afraid, if you're here to ask to change our deal, I can not accommodate you. If the boy is handsy and you weren't aware of this before, you'll need to find a way to live with it. That, or give it time. You'll learn what he will and won't allow, how he'll react, and you'll mold into what he needs of you."

A scoffed laugh leaves me before I can stop it and he glares.

"Man, you are seriously a piece of work, aren't you?"

Donley pushes to his feet, smoothing his suit jacket down.

"Captain would never harm me in any way. Ever. You should know that, you've been watching them all their lives."

"A man is different with a woman behind closed doors."

"Was Felix?"

Donley's eyes narrow. "Pardon?"

"Felix. Was he different with my mom behind closed doors?"

Donley fixes his tie. "How did you get in here, Raven?"

"I walked through the front door," I tell him.

"My staff didn't notify me of any visitors."

"I'm no visitor."

He leans against the shelving behind him, slowly folding his arms over his chest. "Is that so."

"It is." I look around. "This is my house now, remember?"

His head jerks back, brows knitting before a deep belly laugh escapes him. "Now don't go getting ahead of yourself there, little girl. Not until after the marriage, it's not."

My brows snap together.

He doesn't know? Collins found out, told the entire fucking school, but the news didn't make it back to his stand-in grandfather?

I slowly lift my left hand, dropping all my fingers but the middle one, flipping him off, crown side up. "It fits me better here."

Donley swiftly moves around the desk while I keep my feet planted where they are, my head held high, finger up.

"When?" he asks almost wistfully.

"Eight weeks ago."

Donley smiles wide, but traces of a scowl line his eyes. "Yet you're here, and with bruises. Am I right, is he rougher than you expected in bed?"

Piece of shit.

"Do you have the video I requested?"

I hold in my glare. "Not on me, but yes."

His hands lift, coming together in one solid clap. "I must admit, I wasn't sure I'd ever see the day."

"You won't see the night if you don't get out of my house."

He freezes where he stands. "I'm sorry?"

"In the contract, it says the Graven Estate becomes ours after the marriage. It's after the marriage, Donley." I step aside, holding an arm out.

He eyes me a moment before glancing at the empty doorway behind me. "Where *is* your new husband, Raven?"

"Wouldn't you like to know."

Donley gives a dark chuckle, nodding his head as he steps closer to me. "Okay, *Mrs. Graven*. I'll tell you, I'm quite happy you're so eager, but you do not call the shots, nor will you ever. That is what you have a husband for. Once I have the video, I will gladly have my things moved to another property, and not a second sooner."

"Suit yourself." I shrug, turning to leave.

Donley reaches out, gripping my arms between his fingers and I whip around to face him.

"What are you playing at, Raven?"

"You're missing pieces, Donley." I jerk free. "How'd you get the blood bags, hm? Did you draw it from her arm yourself, or did the good old doc do it for you?"

He shoots straight. "How do you know about the blood bags?"

"Are you gonna stand there and pretend you didn't know she'd show up here? Isn't that why you went to her, to let her know how even all these years later, Graven still wins?"

"What do you mean *still* wins?" His anger is starting to show. "We lost, if you remember correctly. Ravina abandoned her responsibilities and Graven was forced to pick up the pieces after she destroyed our future leader with her betrayal."

"Right." I eye him. "So, no answers from you today, hm?"

I take backward steps away from him, but he keeps toward me.

"Where is Captain?"

The shatter of glass echoes from down the hall and Donley's head snaps right.

Another follows.

His glare slices to me. "What the hell is going on?"

He stalks into the hall, glancing around.

"I told you to go."

The Riverside family walk around the corner just then, minus the wife.

"Trick," Donley draws out. "What are you doing here?"

Trick glares at him, but says nothing, walks straight past us all while Alec and Gio stop beside me.

"Twelve minutes."

"What the hell is going on here?" Donley shouts.

Alec spins, getting in his face. "Wanna live? Leave."

With that, he glances to me, so I turn for the entrance.

Donley shoves past us, and out the front door.

My eyes fly across the grounds as staff rushes for the head of the property line, most piling onto matching golf carts.

Donley glares at Bass and then Victoria, his eyes lingering on her for a long moment before his car pulls around the grounds.

He steps down, pausing to eye me once more before he slips into the car and pulls away.

"We need to sweep one more time, make sure they're all out," Gio says.

Bass nods while Victoria calls me to her.

"We need to get you out of here."

"I'll help."

"I don't think—"

My eyes fly to Gio. "I will help."

He throws his hands up and rushes back inside.

I start with where I saw the maids, but they're already gone, so I throw open each door I can find, but all the rooms are already empty.

"We already went through and evacuated, but it's protocol to sweep twice." Gio steps beside me. He looks at a little tablet looking thing with bright orange and red colors moving across the screen. "I think there's still someone on the south end." He pushes a little button on his watch, speaking into it. "Alec, you on the grounds?" he asks.

"East exit. Opened up the horse pens," comes back through the watch.

Gio stalks off. "Shit, someone's still here. You should head out now to be safe!" he shouts as he starts jogging.

With one last, quick glance I head back the way I came. I pass a large, open window overlooking a garden and skid to a stop. I knock on the glass, but the woman outside doesn't turn around.

"Shit."

I follow the wall, finding no door, so I keep down the opposite hall, finally coming to a sitting room of sorts with a large sliding window. I push it open and rush out into the yard.

Bright pink and purple flowers line the edges of the walkways, perfectly lined rocks and exotic trees strategically placed here and there.

"Hey!" I shout at the woman, but she makes no move.

I approach the cement bench she's perched on, walking a little forward to get a look at her face.

Estella, Collins' mom.

"You need to get out of here."

"I can't," she whispers, a sad smile on her face. "I can't leave him here, alone."

I frown, my eyes following hers.

White flowers sit in an over clustered line. I step closer.

A long, rectangular line...

"People here, they don't die by mistake. There's a purpose for everyone and everything. A risk and a reward. Here, liabilities are not welcome."

My eyes fly to hers.

"He learned the truth," she whispers.

"Who?"

"Felix," she breathes.

My jaw clenches. "Truth about what?"

This time, the sorrow in her smile reaches her eyes as she reluctantly moves them to mine. "You."

I don't break the contact, but she can't keep hers on me for long.

She looks back to the seven-foot-long, almost three-foot-wide bed of flowers.

"He searched for your mother, for years. He thought she was hurt somewhere."

My eyes widen, and I look from the tulips to her. "Felix did?"

She blinks away tears, nodding lightly as she takes a deep breath. "He loved me when we were together, but Ravina..." Her voice trails off. "She had his heart. Completely."

I move in front of her and her eyes snap to mine.

"He was a good man, noble. Far too noble for this place. He should have waited for Brayshaw to see it, and they would have, I have no doubt, but the minute she was on the line, his last chance to have her, he was all in. I know what Rolland thinks of him, but I wasn't pregnant with Collins yet when he left me." She looks to her hands. "It was hard, but he wasn't a monster leaving his unborn son for a woman." She lets out a small, sad laugh. "Who am I kidding, he was never a monster to me. Not even when he almost left me, us by then, a second time."

"You got back together, after everything?"

"Sort of," she admits. "When Ravina left, he was a shell of himself. Donley came to me and asked me to go to his room and take his mind off the loss. I did. For several weeks, after nightfall, I'd go to him."

"And you ended up pregnant."

She nods. "Donley moved me in shortly after that, to the

maid's quarters, of course." She scoffs, a tear falling, but she doesn't wipe it away. "We didn't stop sleeping together. Almost every night since the night I was moved in, I slept in his bed, until one day, he came home from a week-long business trip. I was excited to see him, Collins was excited. I remember the night well. The chef had made prime rib. We served it with a glass of aged Merlot. Felix was so happy," she whispers. "He smiled wider than I'd seen in so long, played basketball with Collins that evening without the trouble in his eyes he normally had when he looked at his son. I was over the moon. I'd thought, he's back," she cries. "Finally, after ten years of being a ghost of the man I knew, he was back."

I swallow, looking across the yard when a small flame appears out of nowhere.

"After dinner was cleaned up and Collins was in bed, so was he. I assumed he was waiting for me, but when I went to his room, I found his door locked, and I knew. It all clicked in a single second."

"Knew what?"

"He'd found her, the love of his life."

My head jolts back. "Found her? My mom?"

She nods. "Suddenly, every weekend, sometimes weeks at a time, he had business meetings and events that kept him away." She looks up. "I'd never seen him so alive as he was during those months. Unfortunately, I wasn't the only one to notice."

"Donley."

"Yes. One weekend, several months later, Donley told me to get in the car. His driver knew right where to go. I'll never forget the feeling of seeing them together, with you. He was weightless. Free and smiling." She swallows. "When Felix got home that Sunday night, Donley was waiting with a nasty ulti-matum. I thank heavens every day that he at least loved his son enough to give her up."

"What do you mean?"

"It was either Collins died, or Felix made Ravina believe he was as sick as the man who ruined her. It took a couple weeks of watching him deteriorate before our eyes, but it was done." Her tears fall freely now. "My son was allowed to live, Ravina's hate was back, and Felix's soul ... it was gone."

She's quiet a moment before she says, "Donley knew what he was doing. What Felix would do next. Felix didn't make it twenty-four hours after that. I found him myself. Buried him here." She takes a deep breath. "His memory was erased the night that followed, his son forbidden to so much as whisper his own father's name."

Smoke fills the air, seeping into my lungs, but my feet won't move.

"He was prepared to leave us, to leave this place and be with her, be with *you*."

"I don't understand." I shake my head.

She eyes me. My confusion must be plastered across my face as she tilts her head.

"Do you not know?"

"Know *what*?"

"The man who came to your mother, the one who allowed you to see a different side of her, a side that maybe you could have loved. That was him."

My brows pull in in thought, my eyes falling to the grass beneath my feet.

I think back to the story I told Maddoc.

"I hate my mother."

He doesn't say anything, so I look his way again. "But that's no surprise, right?"

His brows lower.

"She's always been a piece of shit, my whole life, as far as I can remember anyway. But there was one time where everything sucked the teeniest bit less. Wanna know why?" A wry grin slips. "A client stuck."

"Since he knew about her job of choice, she didn't have to lie about

who she was and what she did. Used and abused and all, he accepted her. Me too. He even claimed to have kids, but I never met them." I focus on the sky.

"She got better with him, wasn't clean, but functioned like a human instead of a toy with dying batteries – still turned tricks, but he never seemed to mind.

"For the first time ever, I had a dinnertime. Every night, when the sensor lights on the trailers started popping on – there were no streetlamps in my neighborhood – I'd run back. Excited for a stupid dinner that was never anything more than macaroni and cheese with hotdogs or rice and sauce. Dumb shit, but it was the first time she'd ever seemed to care if I ate since I was big enough to make my own cereal, so I thought it was cool. Lasted about a year."

"What happened?"

"I ruined it."

"How?"

With a deep inhale, I look to Maddoc. "Puberty."

His features morph in an instant, flashing with incomprehensible anger. "Raven."

"He started paying more attention to me, 'neglecting her,' she'd say. She beat my ass; told me I wasn't allowed around him if I couldn't keep my mouth shut." I remember how angry she'd get. "Kinda hard when my room was the two feet between the table and the couch, that was also my bed."

Holy shit.

"He made her think he was attracted to me, a child, on purpose, to ruin things between them?"

She nods. "He couldn't simply leave; she'd know something was wrong and possibly come back. Donley couldn't risk it."

Both our heads jerk to the side when a loud crack sounds. Flames climb up the edges of the pool house, engulfing it in seconds.

I look back to Estella. "What do you mean by make her think he's as sick as the person who ruined her? And you said he saw me, if that's true why would he not bring me here then? He could have prevented all of this."

"*A female is of no use to me.*" Her eyes slide over the landscape. "That's what Donley told a young maid as he fired her, the day her sonogram came back."

"I..." My hands fly to my hair, trying to make sense of it when the fire shoots across the yard in a perfect line, hitting the right end of the house.

"Raven!" My eyes fly to the slider door. "We gotta go, now!"

I nod, then reach for Estella but she shrugs away from me.

"Come on, we have to get out of here."

"Go."

"I'm blowing this fucking place to the ground."

She smiles sadly at the tulips, reaching out to run her fingers across the soft petals. She drops to her knees in front of them.

"I died in this home long ago," she whispers. "It's only right my body goes with it."

"Estella—"

"Raven, now!" Gio shouts again and suddenly Bass is behind him.

I glare at Estella, dropping beside her. "You'll leave him with no one," I growl.

She reaches out, placing her calloused hands on my face. "The fact that you care enough to say those words, after all he's done to you, tells me he'll be just fine," she breathes, her heart breaking for what must be the dozenth time right in front of me. "He's a good boy, you'd have liked him."

I clench my jaw, admitting for the first time, "I don't hate him, just the things he's done."

Her tears roll through her smile. "I know. I could tell."

Tears fill my eyes despite myself. "I have to go."

"Go."

Bass is there gripping my arm, but I hold my feet firm. "I'm sorry," I rush out. "I'm sorry Felix didn't love you enough."

"I'm not."

"Bishop, fucking now!" Alec and Gio both rush for us.

"Everything happens for a reason, and I think the reason was you. This town needs you. I was simply a casualty in the war that had to happen."

"I can protect you."

"Go, Raven."

The boys lift me off the floor, and I kick against them.

"Grab her, make her leave!" I shout.

"We can't force her," Gio says quietly.

A thought hits me and I scream. "Wait! Wait!" I kick as hard as I can, jerking my elbows around. It's enough to get them to pause a second. "You said the woman's sonogram, she was pregnant. Are you saying Donley has a daughter?"

Her eyes jerk to mine, a desolate smile on her lips. "I'm saying he has two."

Chapter 29

RAVEN

I turn in my seat, my eyes traveling from one end of the Graven Estate to the other. The flames shoot straight up the walls in perfect sync with the ones surrounding it. The pool house is already gone, the stables too, but the house is still standing, but not for long.

I jerk when simultaneously, every window in sight blows, the fire rolling over into the second and third story of the mansion.

The Graven Estate is incinerated, and Estella Graven goes with it.

I spin in my seat, facing forward.

Collins will need to be told of her decision, but not today.

I close my eyes, not opening them until we reach the hospital. I blindly climb from the car and silently, the three of us, plus Gio step into the elevator. I don't speak to anyone, only hug Royce when he flies from his seat and meets me in the entryway.

He holds me tight, breathing me in. "You're back. Thank fuck."

I lean closer, squeezing his biceps, and his arms around me tighten even more. "He woke up, asked about Zoey. He remembered talking to the doc, so that was good."

"How long was he awake?"

"'Bout an hour," he tells me, excitedly. "We didn't get to talk 'cause the nurse came in and did her nurse thing, but he did have a couple crackers, some water, and then went right back under."

I nod, a deep exhale leaving me and Royce steps back. "Longer and longer every time, that's good."

He gives a small smile, gently pushing me toward Cap.

I ignore Rolland's presence and make my way to Captain's bedside, dropping in the seat beside him.

Gio, Bass, and Victoria quietly step inside a few minutes later, each finding a chair around the room.

We sit there without a word, without a damn sound other than the steady beeping of the machines. The nurse comes in twice, but still, no one speaks.

Eventually the sun rises, and when the nurse comes back for her morning round, the others finally drag themselves to their feet. They stretch where they stand and instantly, the weight of every eye lands on me but I don't look.

I have no strength, no drive.

I feel sick to my stomach, but I don't show it. My head is pounding, but I ignore it. My world fucked, my mind mush, my thoughts muddled.

I can't figure out what I'm supposed to do. The right move versus the wrong.

My eyes lift to Captain again.

I did this.

I got him shot, I drove Maddoc away, I left Royce feeling abandoned.

I killed my mother, and inadvertently Collins', too.

Donley will come after us now, for answers if not for more. He—

"Stop it," is whispered in my ear and my head snaps left.

Victoria stares up at me, distress in her brown eyes. "This isn't your fault."

"Isn't it?" I say back, not bothering to whisper. "She was my mother, she showed up because of me, left because of me, hated this world because of me. I did this. My existence brought all this on. I never should have made it out of the womb. Go, Vee. Get some sleep."

Her eyes narrow. "You need sleep, and you need to eat."

"Why should I eat when he doesn't get to?"

"Because he'd want you to. And he'd be angry if he knew you hadn't. They all would."

I shake my head looking away, but she grips my chin forcing it back.

I glare at her.

"I'm getting you something, and you're eating it. If you don't, I'll make sure they tie your ass down, shove a feeding tube down your throat and make you."

I can't help it, a small scoffed laugh leaves me, but my stupid eyes fill with moisture. I clench my jaw, nodding.

Her shoulders visibly fall with her sigh and she rushes from the room.

"Mrs. Brayshaw."

I look over my shoulder to find Fernando at the door.

Royce hops to his feet, moving toward him, but he keeps his eyes on me.

"Ms. Maybell is downstairs. She's staring up at the window."

I look to Royce right as his head snaps to mine. He gives a small nod, so I say, "Let her up."

I never should have made it out of the womb, I said.

Females were no good to him.

Holy shit.

I jolt from my chair, my eyes flying to Royce before I storm out to find the nurse.

"Carmen!" I shout right before she disappears behind a door.

Her worried eyes hit mine and she rushes my way but keeps moving past. "What happened?"

"No, wait!"

She spins on her heels, frowning at me.

"He's fine." I shake my head, thinking better of my words. "Or nothing has changed. This is about something else."

The woman's brows pull in and she steps closer to me. "What is it?"

"Blood," I say, and she tilts her head. "When someone donates blood, it has to be clean, right?"

"Clean?"

"No diseases, no drugs. Clean."

She nods. "Yes, that's right."

"Do you test the blood or take the person's word for it?"

"Everything is tested before being marked clear for transfusion." The edges of her eyes tighten. "I can promise you the blood used for Captain was squeaky clean."

"What about mine?"

Her head draws back.

"Raven..." Royce draws out slowly, but I ignore him.

"The blood you have in stock for me, the blood delivered by Estella Graven. Was it tested yet and found clean?"

"Of course. It was tested the day it arrived. Things may be run a little unorthodox in this wing, but I promise you we still practice good medicine."

"So, there were no drugs found in the blood given to you for me?"

"None."

My shoulders fall and I stumble back slightly until my ass

hits the wall. I use it to hold me up, tipping my head back for a deep breath when nausea fights its way in, but it's no use.

I gag but swallow it down, only to gag again.

I slap my hand over my mouth and dash for the bathroom, just barely making it to the garbage in there before I can no longer hold it.

My stomach, already empty, releases more. Yellow and green acids fight their way out, and I dry heave, coughing and gagging every few seconds.

Once it stops for even a moment, I shift toward the sink and splash water on my face, before dropping my ass to the tile floor. I rest my head in my hands.

In the same second, the door slowly swings open, a water set in front of me.

I shake my head not bothering to look. "You've known all along, haven't you?"

"Yes, child."

"Rolland said he didn't know. Did he lie?"

When she doesn't respond, I drop my hands, my head falling back against the wall.

"Did he know?" I say louder this time.

Maybell shakes her head solemnly. "No, he hadn't a clue."

"Why didn't you say anything? You could have protected this family. You *should* have protected this family. You could have prevented all of this!" I shout.

With a solemn expression, she lowers herself beside me. She reaches for my hand, but I draw away. It doesn't deter her, she moves in again, capturing my fingers. "Don't you see, baby girl," she whispers, shifting even closer. "That's what I've been doing all along."

I eye her, not understanding.

"This family, the Brayshaw family. Your mother. You."

When my brows pull in, she gives a slight nod.

"I was brought here, for her," she tells me. "I raised your

mother from the cradle to the contract, like I helped raise Rolland and his brother. I begged Ravina's grandfather, your great grandfather, not to offer her like a prize, but I was only the nanny then. I had no voice, but I never left her. When she started staying at the Graven Estate, so did I. I watched her fall in love with Felix, then I watched her heart grow for his brother.

"I spent every moment with her in sight, other than when she was at school. When she was with both Felix and Conner, I was only yards away. Always near. Except the night things changed."

My eyes slide between hers, but she looks to the water bottle sternly, so I lift it and take a few small drinks. Instantly, the cool liquid leaves a trail of freshness through my body. It swirls in my empty stomach, settling and upsetting it all at once.

"Donley had asked me to escort a young woman from the grounds, he'd fired her."

"Let me guess, a maid."

Maybell grows curious, but she nods. "Yes, a maid. A pregnant maid who he'd just fired. He told me to take her to the edge of town and discard her there with the money he allowed her to take and the clothes on her back." She frowns. "I took her to Rolland instead."

"Why?"

"Rolland is a good man, Raven, even at eighteen years of age. He was just starting to take on more responsibilities. Your grandfather trusted him to make decisions on his own, and with good reason. I had no doubt he would do what was right."

I glance away, unsure if I'd agree or not.

Maybell pulls a small, wrapped cookie from her pocket and tears it open. She holds it out for me, eyes intently keeping mine.

"Seriously?"

She only pushes it closer.

With jerky movements, I reach forward, break a small piece off and stick it in my mouth. After I chew it up and swallow, I stick my tongue out to be an asshole.

A hint of a smile covers Maybell's lips. "When I went back to the Graven Estate, I found your mother on the floor of the shower. She was curled in a small ball, crying. She kept saying she'd betrayed him, she betrayed him, and at first, I thought she meant Felix. Maybe she was with Connor and the guilt ate her up after, but then Conner all but disappeared from her world. Things shifted that night, her and Felix grew even closer, and four months later your mother was gone, but she left something behind, hidden somewhere only I'd ever find." She tugs a coin purse from her bag and unzips it. She reaches in, pulling out a small, crinkled paper folded into a perfect square.

She hands it over.

Cautiously, I open it – a sonogram photo, the words "it's a girl" typed along the blackened edges of the printout.

What gets me though is the purple heart encircling the fuzzy image, handwritten and outlined, the words "my baby girl" scribbled beneath it.

She loved me, if even only for a moment.

It happens quicker than I can stop it, a long-broken gasp followed by a full body shudder. Tears pour from my eyes as I fall apart on the bathroom floor.

The door bursts open and Royce rushes in.

"Fuck," he croaks. He drops beside me, tugging me onto his lap, instantly rocking me back and forth in his arms. The louder I get, the more they tighten. His lips find my hair, his hand brushing against it over and over again, whispering, "It's okay, RaeRae. Everything will be good."

But will it?

I was a little girl no one wanted. A little girl that forced another one from her home. From the only place she ever knew and into a world of poverty and drugs, prostitution.

My mother's body was used, then decided her body was all she was worth and let people pay her to use it.

She came here to save me, in her own fucked up way, and I killed her for it.

I took her life, and then I *took* her life.

I don't know how long we sit on the floor of the bathroom before Royce whispers, "You need to escape? I can send someone for your iPod, some weed, anything."

My heart clenches, his crestfallen eyes flashing before mine.

"It's gone," I whisper, pieces of me I didn't know existed splitting beneath the skin. "He took it."

Royce tenses against me, then slowly draws back to meet my stare. "What?"

"Maddoc, he took it."

Royce's face morphs and he gently shifts back a few inches to see me better. "Maddoc has your iPod?"

I nod.

He sets me on the floor as he climbs to his feet, then pulls me up. He grips my face between his hands. "Come on, RaeRae. You need to sleep."

I don't fight him but let him pull me from the room and lead me into Captain's.

"I'm gonna step outside the door and talk to Bass," Royce tells me, glaring over at Bass before exiting the room.

I move closer to Captain, ignoring Rolland when his chair scuffs slightly across the floor and he exits, taking Victoria and Maybell with him.

Thankfully, Captain's bed is wider than a standard hospital bed, so I only have to move a few wires to crawl in beside him.

I close my eyes.

Chapter 30

RAVEN

Soft, slow hands run across my arm and my eyes peel open.

The room is dark, the sun gone, but the moon offers a hint of sight.

When the hand brushes once again, my head snaps up, and I gasp.

"Cap."

"Hey," Captain rasps.

"You're awake." I look into his tired eyes.

He nods. "Been for a while, didn't wanna wake you though. Royce told me you haven't been sleeping." His eyes move between mine. "You okay?"

I can't help it, I laugh, burying my face back into the crook of his arm again. "Ugh, am *I* okay?" My head pops back up.

Cap doesn't grin though, instead growing more concerned.

"Captain, you were shot, twice. By my mom. Are *you* okay?"

"Raven," he whispers, his hand coming up to cup my face. "Stop it." His light eyes roam my face, pausing at my hairline. He moves his fingers up my cheekbone to my forehead and pushes my hair back gently. His features squeeze before coming back to mine. "You saved me," he whispers.

"You saved me, too."

Captain stretches his neck, bringing his lips closer. His stare hits mine, a rawness I've never seen in them, one that exposes my own in the same second. My eyes move between his a moment, and then the world around us becomes too much, we lean in.

So much pain and sadness wraps around my heart with this single move, and I can sense his just the same. There's no movement, not exploring, only the firm contact of my lips and his.

He pulls away but keeps the connection between our mouths close. "We could have lost you."

"I don't wanna talk about that."

He nods. "Is she..."

"I'd say she won't cause us any more trouble but knowing her she still might." Her watery eyes flash before me. "Even without a beating heart."

He pulls me close, so I drop my head back beside him and he continues to run his hand across my arm.

Several minutes pass when I finally start talking again.

"She thought you were Graven," I admit. "That's why she came. That's why she shot you before she realized shooting me would be easier."

"She sold you to my dad. Why freak out about it now?"

"Royce asked the same question." I tilt my head up to look at him. "Maybe your dad never planned to give me to them. Maybe he had good intentions, and his way of letting me know was giving me my knife, but things changed, and he had to use what he could to protect his family." I give a small smile and

Cap's eyes drop from mine. "I wasn't family yet, Zoey was. It's what anyone would have done."

He's quiet a long moment before he says, "I was so sure Mallory got pregnant on purpose, try to lock herself in, you know? But then it didn't make sense because she got pregnant and left. She didn't even want her, didn't try to trade her to me. Nothing."

"Maybe she did trick you, planning to go to Collins all along but Perkins found out first and made her a deal she couldn't walk away from."

"I don't know."

I look up at him. "Only one way to find out."

He eyes me. "He's not my father, Raven."

"I know, and he's gone, just so you know. I made him leave, told him he could only come back if you asked him to directly, so Packman, yet again it's on your shoulders to open up the conversation."

His hand comes up and he runs his thumb across my cheek. "Always pushing me to be stronger."

"Not stronger," I whisper. "Certain. I want you to want to share who you are and what's going on in your head. You sit back, you study, you discover, but you don't volunteer anything past the eye."

"Neither do you."

"I'm different. I don't have to say it. What you see is what you get."

He shakes his head. "Nobody could ever look at you and see all you are. How could they when you don't see it in yourself?"

I look away, but he draws my eyes back to his.

"I need you to do something for me."

"Anything."

"Go see Zoey."

My face goes slack, and I start to shake my head but stop when he begs.

"Please. It's been weeks since I've seen her. I can't Face-Time her, not until these fucking tubes are out and I can put a real shirt on at least. She might only be shy of three, but she's intuitive."

"Like her daddy," I whisper.

His grip tightens. "Please do this."

"She doesn't even know me, Cap."

"She will. I need her to feel wanted. She will if you show up wanting to play with her. Please."

Not wanting to disappoint him, I start to agree when Royce suddenly appears.

"I want to do it."

Our heads snap toward him, and a small smile takes over my lips.

His eyes are sloped at the edges as he stares at his brother.

"Hey, man," Cap says.

Royce nods, smashing his lips to the side as he steps closer. "Oh, we're bright-eyed today huh, fucker?" he teases. "And still as pretty as a Ken doll, brother. Even in the fucked up looking rag they've got on ya." He grins.

Cap starts to chuckle, but it cuts off on a hiss. He picks up a little button thing at his side and presses it.

"What is that?" I ask him.

"Nurse said it releases medicine when I push it, but it won't allow me to overdo it."

I nod, looking to the IV drip beside him.

Royce leans over, kissing my forehead, then pushes his fore-head against Captain's before he stands.

"You need something?" Royce asks him.

Cap nods, the corner of his lips lifting.

"Let me go see Zoey," Royce says. "She met me already. I

can play ball with her, show her some pics of you on my phone or something."

"Royce hasn't left since you got here," I tell Captain.

"I could use the fresh air, and I'm pretty sure I'm her new favorite anyway."

Captain shakes his head goodheartedly, then reaches out to grip his hand. "She'd love that. Maybe Maddoc will go with you?"

When Royce's glare shifts over Cap's head, Cap looks to me wearily.

"What?" he draws out slowly.

"We haven't seen him since he walked out of the school that day. We can't find him."

Captain's stare flies to Royce who avoids my eyes.

He licks his lips, running his hand down his mouth quickly. "Yeah, we uh, everyone's looking for him."

Captain's head drops back against the pillow and he nods.

His blinks get slower, longer, and I know he's about to knock out again, so I hit the nurse's call switch.

She enters right as the grip of Cap's fingers lessens, his hand falling to my side.

I gently shift to stand, my eyes narrowing on Royce who scratches the back of his head as he steps back.

"Royce."

"If I go, you need to make sure you stay here. We can't both leave him here."

"*Royce.*"

"And here." He continues to ignore me, pulling a phone from his pocket, pushing it into my chest. "I'm tired of not being able to call you when I need to."

"I don't want to be reachable at all times."

This time his eyes slice to mine. "Too fucking bad, *Raven,*" he growls in my face. "You wanna run off, handle shit without

255

me, with Bass fucking Bishop, fucking fine. Do your thing, but you'll do it where I can at least breathe while you're gone."

My heartstrings tighten. "Royce." I step closer, placing my hand on his chest.

His eyes soften.

"I don't wanna do anything without you, but I needed you here with Captain. He needed you more than I did."

"Why is that?" Royce whispers. "How come you don't need me like you need them?" His dark eyes turn somber. "Do I not make you feel the same way they do?"

My chest compresses. "Why would you say that?"

"You left me here, baby girl." He tucks my hair behind my ears. "Went off on your own, trusted someone else to have your back. I'd die for you, Raven, without a second thought."

"Exactly," I whisper, and his brows pull in. "I took Maddoc from this family, thought I took Cap. How could I live with myself if I took you, too? You were all that was left standing, and I needed you to stay that way. I needed to know if I came back to find Maddoc gone forever, Cap never waking up, I'd still have you." I swallow. "You think you can't live without me? Well, I would refuse to without you."

Deep creases take over Royce's forehead and he gives a curt nod before tugging me against him. After a moment, his chest inflates with a deep inhale, his warm exhale helping my muscles relax.

I squeeze him tighter.

"I love you, RaeRae."

"I know, and I love you too." I pull back, looking up at him.

He slips the phone in my palm, closing my fingers around it. "You need to set a password, do it soon. It's got a ton of apps, enough to keep you busy trying to learn it while I'm gone."

"It's two in the morning, Royce. She's sleeping."

He looks away. "I'll be there to cook Zoey pancakes."

"Does she like pancakes?"

He looks to the floor. "I don't know. Maybe I'll stop, get a chocolate sprinkle donut and maple bar, huh? She can pick which she likes better?" He gives a small smile.

I nod. "I got twenty dollars on the maple bar."

He gives a small chuckle, looks to Captain then spins for the door.

"Don't tell him about my mom," I rush out.

Royce's entire body tenses, his hand freezing on the door.

Tears fill my eyes, but I don't blink, forcing them to dry where they sit.

After a minute his head drops, and he gives a regretful nod.

He found him.

As soon as he exits, I let out a harsh breath, my hands flying to my temples.

"You should be careful."

I whip around at the nurse's soft words, my eyes narrowing.

Fuck, I'd forgotten she was in here.

"What the fuck did you say?"

Her face drains of its color.

"I wasn't... I'm so sorry I didn't mean to—"

"To threaten me?"

Her eyes widen. "That's not what I was doing, I swear Mrs. Brayshaw. I only meant the anxiety. You have a lot going on, more than I'm aware of, I'm sure. High levels of stress can cause many problems."

With a roll of my eyes, I look away, heading for the door. "Trust me, this is nothing new."

"Raven," she calls before I can exit fully.

I glance over my shoulder.

"This wing was built on Bray donations. This is essentially yours, as are the staff within it. We are very good with discretion." She offers a small smile.

"It's Rae, and I have no idea what the fuck you're talking about, lady."

I push past the door, spotting Victoria the second I round the corner.

She pops from her seat, meeting me halfway. "Hey."

"He woke up again, I think he was awake for a while before I even realized."

A sharp exhale leaves her. "That's awesome."

"I don't think he'll go in and out so much anymore. Pretty sure it was the pain meds that knocked this time."

She eyes me, nodding lightly. "Royce said he'd be back later."

I nod, dropping onto the sofa she was on, and she moves to sit beside me again. "He knows where Maddoc is."

Her eyes widen. "And you're sitting here?"

"He didn't tell me, I guessed."

"And still... you're sitting here?" she draws out.

"What am I supposed to do?" My eyes slide to hers. "Go find him, beg him to come home, yell at him for lying to me and saying if I married his brother, he wouldn't leave them only to leave the same fucking day he found out I did what he said he wanted, what he *begged* me to do?"

"That's exactly what you do," she snaps.

I shake my head, dropping it back on the couch. "Then what, Vee? He comes home and is forced to watch everything that follows?"

She's quiet a minute before she slowly shifts on the seat, twisting her body to face me. "What do you mean, everything that follows?"

My brows pull in and I look to her.

"Raven..." She shakes her head. "You just burned the Graven Estate to the ground. You took control. You found out things you never knew, things that could change—"

"Change what, Victoria?" I glare at her. "And what things

did I find out, huh? Because I haven't shared a fucking word yet, have I?"

Victoria's jaw ticks.

"What is it you know that *you* aren't sharing?"

"I told you," she forces past clenched teeth. "I existed to uncover the secrets of a man."

"Yeah, and what did you find out?" I push. "Because as far as I can tell, you're useless on the info front," I goad her.

She jumps from the couch. "That's not fair."

Bass pushes off the wall, moving closer.

"Isn't it?" I eye her. "What happened to the loose-lipped girl I sucker-punched at the Bray house?"

"Stop it," she snaps.

"You've been here the longest." I push to my feet. "You don't like to ask, don't wanna seem too interested because then people might have a reason to question you, and you don't want that."

"Shut up, Raven."

"So, like Cap, you use your eyes and your ears. When I first met you, you tried to act like you were different. You wanted me to think you were just another gossip girl when I know now that's the farthest damn thing from who you are."

"That means nothing."

"It means everything. You had a purpose."

She shakes her head, her blonde hair falling from her messy ponytail.

"You led me to that binder. You told me about the boys' backstory on purpose because you wanted me to take it."

"It didn't belong in that house where anyone could find it and—" She cuts herself off.

"And... what? Use it against them?" I nod. "'Cause I agree. You wanted it to be safe, where it belonged, and you trusted me to make it happen."

"1 didn't trust you," she spits, but looks away. "But I wasn't blind either."

"You knew I'd give it to them."

She rubs her lips together, giving an almost unnoticeable nod. She sighs. "Everyone has said it, Raven. You're not like the others here." She glares, taking a second before deciding to share more. Her guilty swallow has me confused. "I knew immediately they'd want you. You got on their radar on your own, but I still nudged a little to be sure."

"The Graven party you insisted I come to, all part of the plan, right?"

She frowns. "I didn't do this for them. None of it was for their benefit, I was just helping push things along faster."

"I know. You being loyal to Graven wasn't even a question in my mind. At all."

"I would never," she rushes out. "Ever."

I nod. "I know, but I was there on purpose, right?"

"Yes." She eyes me a moment before continuing. "I got you to the party knowing Collins would spot you. I knew he needed to see you, speak to you for his obsession to fully take over."

"The boys showing up?"

"I tipped them off, made it known a Graven was snooping that night."

"How'd you get the Graven girl to their party?"

"The guy I was 'dating?' He worked for them. He was only a mouse in a lion's den compared, but still. I casually let it slip that the Brays had a new girl they were locked on and how they were showing her off at their party. I knew they'd send someone. The last thing Collins expected was for you to walk in his house that night. He was sidetracked, pretending not to watch you when his eyes never left you, and forgot to call the girl off. Then the boys showed up."

"And I made a scene."

"No." She shakes her head with a frown. "You paved your

way. You showed loyalty to them without hesitation, without knowing they were yours." She sits again, shifting forward, eyes strong. "You stood for who you saw as the weaker in that moment because you felt it was right. You showed everyone before anyone even knew who you were that you'd stand for people who couldn't stand for themselves. I hated you before that night, but I hated you even more after it."

My brows lower. "Why?"

"Because it finally all made sense. Why you were worth more, why your life was different than mine. I knew then I could never be more than you are, and that night you made me realize, for the first time, that I wanted to be." She looks down. "That that was the real reason I came here, unbeknownst to me. I wanted the safety this world didn't show me when it should have, but I was here for two years and they never saw me."

"How could they when you hid yourself from them?" I ask her, and her eyes come back to mine. "They see you now, we all do. You're as strong as I am, Vee. You have the scars to prove it."

"You know *nothing* about my scars," she snaps.

"I don't need to know how they got there to know they aren't just on the outside of your body."

She glares.

"Stop acting like you're less than I am." I glower. "I'm just a fucking girl trying to save people she loves anyway she can. You can help me."

"Maybe I don't want to!" She jumps up again.

"Bullshit you don't." I jump with her, shoving her into the small table. "I get it, you lied to me, acted like you didn't know I was Brayshaw when I told you I was. I don't care. Wanna know why?" My brows raise. "Because you brought me to them the night I was jumped, helped me in the bathroom when Collins attacked me. You were there with me when I broke down after Donley and the doctor fucked with me. You can handle my boys, you push me, fight me, demand from me—"

"Who cares!"

"I do!" I yell back. "Fuck everything before now. I don't care what you've hidden."

"That's because you don't know the half of it," she snaps.

"You're clearly mad enough at yourself, what right do I have to be mad at you, too? You owe me *nothing*, Victoria, nothing." My shoulders fall. "But I'm asking you to be my fucking friend anyway. Stand with me. Take this fucking town with me. I need you in my corner."

Her eyes fly to mine, tension and unease filling hers. "You'll regret this."

"Then that's on me."

With a shake of her head, she shoulders past, and down the hall.

"Where you going?"

"I need some fucking air."

"And I need you, Vee."

She pauses a moment before glancing at me over her shoulder. "You're gonna need me more than you realize, Raven."

I turn to Bass after she rounds the corner.

"What do you think she means by that?"

"I have no fucking idea."

A few hours pass before Bass plants his ass beside me.

He frowns. "What's your plan, Raven?"

"That's just it, Bishop. I don't have one. I have no plan, no fucking idea what happens from here. Nothing. I never do. That's what nobody understands. You all think I can rock this shit out, but I literally fly by my fucking pants. I think, I do, and deal with what happens after."

"And it works for you."

"Yeah, and for how long, huh?" My brows jump mockingly. "And how well did it work this last time?"

He eyes me. "What did Donley say to you?"

I scoff, looking away. "Nothing, but the maid had a lot to say—" I cut myself off, my brows drawing in as my eyes snap back to Bishop.

"What?" he drags out.

"The maid."

"She didn't come out, but I have a feeling the Daniels guy didn't let her body burn. We'd have smelt it. Think after the smoke took her, so did they."

"Really?"

He nods.

I shake my head, not having realized that. "I... no, I know she didn't come out, but I'm not talking about her."

He tilts his head.

I face forward, thinking aloud. "Someone who was there when my mom was, someone who would have had to of been around her age."

I push to my feet.

Holy. Shit.

I rush down the hall only to have Rolland block my way at the end, and Bass to grip my wrist tugging me around.

"What's going on?" Rolland asks, fresh coffee in his hand.

"I'll be back."

"No, no, no," Bishop says.

I yank my hand from him. "You can't stop me."

He steps closer, lifting a dark brow. "Oh, you think not?"

"She has ten security guards lining this floor, all with weapons," Rolland reminds him. "If she wants out, she's getting out."

I purse my lips like an asshole.

Bass glares. "Royce has only been gone hours; he won't be

back until this afternoon. You'll be leaving him alone all that time."

I force myself not to swallow. "I have a phone now, Royce can call me, Rolland can call me, and besides, he won't be alone. Victoria is here somewhere." I lick my lips and look to Rolland. "And he has his dad. Maybe it'll do some good for you two, bet you could use a private chat?"

"Wait." Rolland steps forward. "He's awake again?"

I shake my head. "He was, but the nurse said he won't be knocking out so much now. Small naps here and there maybe, but that's all."

"May I." He motions past me, a hopeful smile on his face.

"Go."

He takes off down the hall.

I turn to Bass. "Your job is to stay with me, not fight me. Follow through, Bishop, with anything I ask until the dust settles and whatever roles we're meant for come down on us. I promise it'll be worth it for you if you do."

"I'm not going anywhere, Raven, but I don't want you to regret anything later either."

"This is different. This isn't a death wish mission. Promise."

He grips my shoulders with a frown and spins me around, pushing me toward the elevator. He pushes the button and it slides open, the both of us stepping through. "I hope you're right, Rae, because if you're not, it'll only fuck things further."

"Trust me." I close my eyes. "It will regardless."

Chapter 31

RAVEN

"RAVEN." SHE OPENS THE DOOR, PULLING HER ROBE TIGHTER and the breeze blows through the door. She glances behind me, spotting only Bass and her worried eyes move back to me and the bruising on my face. "Are you okay?"

"It was you, wasn't it?"

Her eyes pull in, as her head tilts slightly.

"The maid, the one he forced away. It was you."

Her eyes widen before unmistakable sadness washes over her entire body.

A broken smile finds her lips. "I told you someone rescued me once."

I swallow. "What did Rolland do with you?"

"He gave me a new home. Hid me away for the remainder of my pregnancy."

When my brows pull in, she steps outside, moving to the patio chairs.

"What happened?"

"I went into preterm labor when no one was around. I had to call an ambulance." She looks away. "When we got to the hospital, the nurse said the baby was in distress, so they had to put me under, emergency cesarean." She licks her lips looking back to me. "When I woke up, the crib beside me was empty, but the chair across the room, it wasn't."

Graven.

"Walk away, and she got to live. Stay and she died."

"You went back to the Bray house after anyway."

She nods, tears in her eyes. "I hoped maybe I'd see her out, that I could steal her back, but it was like she didn't exist. I knew Donley had her locked away somewhere. I started to crumble." She takes a deep breath. "And then Rolland allowed me to move into his home, instead of the front houses."

My eyes pull in. "The boys."

She swallows audibly, unable to meet my stare. "They were only months old, so precious. Maybell was there to care for them all day while Ravina was in school, then every second of every day once Ravina was gone, but I always managed to convince her to let me help, but only when Rolland was away."

"You tried to replace her with them."

"With him," she whispers, regretfully admitting.

Captain.

"There was something about him that made me feel a little more whole," she admits sorrowfully. "He'd look at me with his big eyes, some days blue, some days green, and put his little hands up. Slowly, he came to only want me when he was tired or hungry. Rolland noticed, and I thought he'd be upset, but he wasn't. He was grateful at least one of his sons felt the love of a mother..." She trails off and suspicion grows in my stomach.

"It wasn't enough for you," I guess. "What did you do?"

She takes a deep breath, her eyes hitting mine. "I took him," she whispers.

Anger twists in my gut, but for some reason, it's not for her.

"He called me mama, and never once did I whisper the word to him, and still" —tears fall from her eyes— "that's what he called me." She sniffles. "We only made it about a month before Rolland showed up at my doorstep. I thought he'd kill me, but he was overcome with emotion by the sight of his son, safe and warm. He showed me mercy. He paid for a year's worth of therapy where they treated me for postpartum depression, but he made it clear, to come back was to leave in a casket. So, I stayed away, and the little boy who lost his mom, lost another. Because I was selfish."

"The girl," I rasp, my heart pounding. "Your daughter..."

Her lips tremble, her shuddered inhale cracking. "Alive."

"Where?"

Her wretched eyes find mine. "You know," she breathes.

I swallow, looking away as I slowly push to my feet, moving for Bass's car.

"Raven." The hesitant tone she uses to call my name has tension wrapping around my shoulders.

I look, but don't turn around.

"Don't tell."

Slowly, I turn to face her.

"You want me to keep a secret *for you*?"

"Please." Her eyes fly between mine. "I don't deserve anything from you, but please."

"You're right." My jaw locks tight as I shake my head. "You don't deserve anything from me, Maria."

With that, I spin on my heels and rush for the car. I slide in the front seat, closing my eyes.

It makes sense now why Rolland said he'd only trust Maria with Zoey, because Maria loved her father like a son. He knew she'd love his daughter just as much.

When Bass sighs a few minutes down the road, I open my eyes.

He looks at me suspiciously.

"What?" I snap.

He runs his tongue across his lips, squinting as he looks away. "I'm trying to figure out what just happened."

"Don't."

"Fine," he huffs. "But you know as well as I do, the last thing this town needs is more secrets—"

"Bass, look out!" I scream, but it's too late.

A car slams into the side of us, and everything goes black.

THE BLARE OF A NEVER-ENDING HORN HAS MY EYES PEELING open.

The road is still dark, but lights shine from somewhere.

I start coughing, but the jolt causes an ache in my side, so I clamp my teeth together, clearing my throat the best I can.

"Bass," I rasp, reaching to the side to feel for him, but I can't turn my head.

My hand makes contact with his shoulder, so I shake him lightly.

"Bishop, wake up," I say louder this time, shaking him harder, and finally he groans.

"Wha... fuck, Raven," he hisses, shifting around in his seat. "My fucking seatbelt's stuck. You okay?"

"My side and my ribs." I squeeze my eyes shut.

After a moment, he says, "Not seeing any blood, that's good."

The crunch of glass against pavement has both of us going silent.

"Raven," he whispers. "Can you open the glove box?"

I reach forward, under the airbag, feeling for a handle and tug but it doesn't open.

"Shit," Bass hisses, the footsteps growing closer. "Your knife?"

I hold in a groan as I slap my hand against my left pocket.

Bass reaches over, tugging on my jeans until the knife slides up. "Got it," he says. "Close your eyes."

My heart is pounding in my chest as I do as he asked, and not a second later, a shadow blocks the light that was creeping through my window, another set of footsteps joining.

"She alive?"

"She's breathing."

"Get her out."

My muscles lock.

Are they fucking kidding me?

I keep my eyes closed, allowing them to pull open my door, push aside the airbag and cut through my seatbelt.

The second my ass and back are laid against the ground, I jerk my head up, nailing him in the forehead.

Leo groans, stumbling back.

Vienna darts in, wrapping her hands around my throat as she straddles me, but she was always a weak bitch.

I lift my knee, hitting her in the ass as she jerks forward, releasing me to catch herself before she flies over me.

Her wide eyes hit mine as her hands slam against the glass-covered road.

I jab her in the lungs and she gasps, falling over.

I shove her off right as Leo rushes back in but he's laid on his ass when suddenly Bass is out of the car and putting him in a headlock, my knife pressed against his cheek.

I push my foot into Vienna's chest.

"Please!" she shouts. "I'm sorry."

"Sounding like a broken record, Vienna." I use my weight to apply pressure as my strength is suddenly gone again. "I told you to get the fuck out of here."

"I was leaving, I swear, but Leo found me at the bus station." Her eyes fly to his.

He jerks in Bass' hold.

"He said if we helped Graven, that we'd be taken care of." She starts to cry.

"Did Donley ask you to do this?"

"Leo said if we got to you and took you to them, we'd be rewarded." Her eyes fly between mine. "You kicked me out with nothing. I... I needed the money."

I look to Leo who glares at me. I shake my head, and spots cloud my vision, but I ignore it, speaking to Vienna while staring at him. "He lied to you, Vienna. I already gave myself over to Graven, married the new head of their household. What's theirs is now mine." I drop my eyes to her wide ones. "What do you think will happen to you now?"

Tears pour from her eyes as she shakes her head. She says nothing.

I walk toward Leo, each step causing my vision to blur more. "I don't understand you. Why? What do you gain here? I took nothing from you, like I took nothing from Mac. He understood things for what they were when I got here. Why'd you turn your back on them?"

Leo's nostrils flare but he refuses to speak.

I nod, but when I go to open my mouth, nothing comes out. I grow dizzy and have to catch myself on the hood of the smashed-up car. "Bass..." I rasp, my eyes refusing to stay open any longer, fighting to meet his only for everything to grow dark. "Something's wrong."

I slip, my hip slamming against the side, causing the ache that had begun to dull to come back with a vengeance. "Mmm," I cry out, my hand slipping against the sleek vehicle.

There's a soft grunt followed by a crash at my feet and suddenly I'm falling to the ground, but a pair of strong arms break my fall just as my ass scrapes the gravel. I'm lifted, cradled.

The sounds surrounding me continue to pierce my ears, but I have no strength to open my eyes or mouth.

"Where the fuck have you been?!" Bass shouts. "How could you—"

"Not the time, Bishop," Royce growls. "Just get in the fucking car!"

"What about these two?" he shouts. "They could come after her again."

"Leo's out cold, the girl can find her own fucking way back. We'll deal with them later."

My body bounces slightly with each step before it stops, so the arms around me tighten, pulling me closer.

Rough facial hair scratches against my cheek before warm air hits my ear. "I've got you."

My entire body breaks out in goosebumps.

Maddoc.

"You can hear me, can't you, baby?" He keeps going and even though my eyes won't open, the tremble of my lips serves as his answer. "I'm so sorry. I promise you; I will *never* leave you again." His thumb slides across it.

His words and the way in which they find my skin, both warm and laced with a hint of last night's whiskey, don't settle me as they should. A heavy pressure builds against my chest, forcing the air from my lungs.

"She's... she's not breathing," he panics. "She's not fucking breathing!"

I try to inhale, but nothing comes of it.

"Fuck it, I'm calling an ambulance!" Royce says.

In the next moment, the voices join my sight and I pass out completely.

Chapter 32

Maddoc

I DROP MY HEAD AGAINST THE WALL, DIRECTLY ACROSS FROM the door they wheeled her through.

The paramedic cut her top off, and there was bruising, both fresh and fading, but there was no damage they could see, so as soon as we got her here, got her up to the Bray Wing this time around, they took her straight back for some testing.

"I never should have fucking left her here today." Royce kicks the wall with the heel of his shoe, knocking his head against it with a hard thud. His eyes slice to mine, straight fuckin' anger for me, but his worry for her is what has my throat closing.

"Why do we keep finding ourselves here, brother?" He swallows. "What if she cracks? What if she flips the fuck out, crying and breaking shit?" He licks his lips, bending on his knees in front of me.

"She won't."

"How do you know?" His tone begins to shift, rage boiling

to the surface. "You don't know what's happened and you've got Bishop tailing her like a little bitch, doubt his ass would fill us in on anything fucking extra."

"He wouldn't."

Royce scoffs, looking away.

"Bass is more like her than we are. We know her better, yeah, but he understands her in a different way." I admit what I hate most about him. "He'll be whatever she needs him to be. He'll read her mood and say what she needs to hear."

"You trust him to lead her?"

"I trust him to allow *her* to lead *him*." I look away. "I would have cut his nuts off weeks ago if I didn't."

"Yeah, well, try being the one she left behind while he walked fucking beside her. He's gonna pay for it, even if it was demanded of him by you." Royce kicks off the wall, banging on the damn door in the next second. "I want to see her."

"Royce, stop."

"Man, fuck you!" He spins around, shoving me in the chest. "Fuck. You! You haven't been here; you don't know the half of the shit she's been through since the day you ran off!" he shouts at the top of his lungs.

The nurse ducks from what Royce said was Captain's room, disappearing through a door at the other end of the hall while Victoria and Bishop appear at the end of it, both not bothering to hide the fact that they're watching, probably enjoying this shit.

Royce is too hopped up to notice. "She was fucked. I mean straight the fuck up, all-around *fucked*," he snaps. "I'd have sworn after all the shit the last few weeks, it couldn't possibly get any worse. Wrong."

"What happened?"

"Man, fuck you! I'm not gonna make this shit easy on you. You left, and not just her, you left us all. Captain almost fucking died, he could have, they both fucking could have and who knows, maybe I'd have never fucking found you! You wouldn't even know!"

"I wouldn't have stayed gone forever."

"No, just after the funerals and after this place fucking fell apart. If Raven hadn't flipped out and I hadn't asked if she needed her music, I never would have known you had the iPod to even think to use the Find Me app on it." He scowls. "You didn't have to see Captain's fucking face when he woke up after being out of it for over two fucking weeks and we had to tell him his brother abandoned his family like a weak little *bitch*!"

"I was weak!" I shout back, throwing my hands out.

"Yeah, you fucking were!" Royce booms. "Did you even stop to think how he fucking felt? You know Captain, Maddoc. You *know* every second he was with her he felt guilt in his fucking bones. He was doing something you agreed to, helping us all, helping her, and he felt guilt for that. You leaving only made it worse. You confirmed, in his mind he had a reason to feel like he betrayed you, something he would die before doing, you pathetic piece of shit!"

"I am pathetic," I agree with him which only pisses him off more. "I had never in my life felt so damn pathetic, fucking helpless as I did the day I left. Days before that if you really wanna know."

I step closer to him, but he shoves at me, sending my back flying against the wall.

"You felt helpless?!" he barks, getting in my face. "You fucking felt helpless?" A scoffed laugh breaks through his fury. "Try actually being helpless, motherfucker. Try watching her knees buckle from under her, her body going limp as she breaks down harder than she probably ever fucking has! Try being the one to hold her through that, wishing you could settle her while knowing there's only one fucking person she truly wanted in that moment! Someone who I'm not even sure deserves her now!"

275

A knife to the fucking gut.

What the hell happened here while I was gone?

"You abandoned her," he growls in my face, his body shaking with his rage.

"I gave her away, Royce." A deep ache forms in my chest. "I *gave* her away because someone told me I had to." My eyes narrow. "Never, ever have I allowed someone to come in and take what was mine, never have I not fought with all I fucking had to keep or protect what belonged to me, and I just ..." I trail off, my jaw clenching. "I *gave* her away, and I will *never* forgive myself for that. Ever. And I'd never fucking ask you or her or Cap to forgive me for it either."

Royce punches a hole through the wall beside my head before stepping back, glaring.

"Wanna know what's fucking worse?"

Reluctantly, his eyes snap back to mine, his body still facing away.

"I want to go to her, make her forget for a little while, make her feel good the only way I know how. And I want to do it now, while my brother is lying there with bullet holes in his body."

Deep creases form on Royce's forehead.

"Fucked up, yeah?" I look away.

He doesn't say anything.

"I want her, brother. Now, tomorrow, always." I let out a humorless laugh, closing my eyes when it all becomes too fucking much. "I didn't think on it when it happened, didn't have time or didn't let myself, fuck if I know. All I knew was she was good in that moment. Safe and away from Collins." I meet Royce's eyes. "She wasn't gonna accept it. She told me no, like she told him no. She was dead fucking set on marrying Collins, said she would never come between us like that."

Royce groans, shaking his head. "The fuck you do, brother?"

"Told her I'd leave you guys if she didn't."

He takes a deep breath, looking to his bloodied knuckles. "Fucked up."

I nod.

"And you left anyway."

"I tried, but I couldn't fucking do it," I admit. "Standing around, seeing them together. Imagine me sitting back when his mouth touches hers, knowing what goes down at night when they're alone. Then later, playin' family with Zoey?" My jaw flexes. "I'd have fucking cracked. I'd have taken her from him, fucking everyone over in the process. Leaving was the only option."

He glares a minute before he starts talking again.

"I don't feel for you," he says quietly. "I can't, not after everything she's been through recently. I tried to be there for her, to make her feel safe, to hold her, and she let me. It helped some, I know it did, but not efuckingnough. It will never be enough." He swallows, his eyes trailing the blood drops at his feet. "We could never be enough for her."

"You could be."

"We aren't." He shrugs. "She trusts us, but it's not the same thing. She loves us, but it's different."

I let out a deep breath. "I never should have allowed this to happen. I never should have let them take what was mine to have." I look to Royce.

His brows meet in the center, a defeated look taking over, and he sighs. "You were saving your niece, man."

"Yeah," I rasp. "By ripping out my beating fucking heart."

"You—"

"Stop, Royce." My shoulders sag. "Don't make excuses for me."

I lick my lips, my chin hitting my chest a moment.

I look up, meeting my brother's eyes. "Tell me something."

His eyes pinch.

"Would we ever allow that little girl to be taken from us, hurt or harmed in any way?"

"Never."

Instant.

"Exactly." My brows jump into my hairline and I take a step closer. "Why did we not weed out everyone who tried to deny us? Who threatened to take from us?"

"I don't know, man, it was a lot to take in."

"So, we're too weak to handle it, like Dad said we would be?"

"That's not what I fucking said," Royce spits through clenched teeth.

I push forward. "You heard the other families in that room. This is our fucking feud; they have no place in it. They *want* us to settle it. Us or them, they don't get to say, and they don't give a fuck. They're only waiting for the end result, a tight, strong council they can depend on when push comes to shove."

Royce's body slowly morphs, the tension in his shoulders fading as his fists open at his sides. He stands taller, his chin lifting subconsciously as a calm settles over him.

"Madman..."

I nod.

Yes, brother.

"Say it," Royce demands.

"We made a mistake."

Royce plants his feet directly in front of mine. He lifts his palm, so I lock my hand in his, letting him pull my chest closer.

Deserved anger and resentment radiates off every inch of him, but even pissed at me, we're family first. "We didn't spend the last few years rebuilding this fucking town, growing our team, for nothing. We aren't placeholders. These old fucks don't get to step back in and tell us what our next move is supposed to be. *We* were the next move before Dad got home and Donley slid back into light, and everyone knew it. Let's remind them, Madman."

I nod, fucking ready. "We go to the Graven Estate."

Royce scoffs, stepping back, but a hint of a smirk tips his lip, humor finding its way in his eyes.

"What?"

He licks his lips. "Graven Estate is nothing but ash, brother."

My mind races.

"She went in like a boss, burnt it to the ground."

My eyes fly to Victoria when she speaks.

She glares at me, pushes off the wall and then disappears into Captain's room.

The fuck?

Royce's hard slap to my back has my eyes flying to him.

"Told you, crazy shit, bro. Wait 'til you hear the rest of it."

My eyes slim. "You gonna fuckin' tell me or not?"

He lets me go, pausing at Captain's door. His eyes hit mine, hardening. "Nope."

He goes inside, but my feet freeze in place, my eyes sliding sideways when movement catches my attention.

Bishop stares at me.

"What?"

He shrugs against the wall, pushing off just the same. "Surprised is all."

"Yeah, you were probably hoping I'd never fucking be back, huh?"

Bishop stares blankly. "Nah, man." He shakes his head, moving his earphones into place. "I'm surprised you ever left. Didn't expect that. Not from you. Not when it came to her." He grabs his side and limps back into the waiting area.

I'm about to drop against the wall when Captain's door pushes open again and Victoria sticks her head out. "He's asleep right now, but I thought you'd want to know... when she's done back there?" Her eyes slide between mine, and I'd swear pity is hiding behind her shield. "They're bringing her in here. It's a double room so..."

My chest stiffens, but I manage a tight nod.

She pokes her head back in and out again, this time concern is marked. "Don't leave, Maddoc." she whispers before she disappears.

As soon as she's gone, I allow myself to fall against the wall.

Fuck, man.

I take a deep breath, attempting to settle myself.

I was only gone for a few weeks, how much could have really happened in that time?

Does she hate me?

Even as I think it, I laugh at myself.

Yeah fucking right, that'd be too easy.

My baby, she'll forgive me.

Or worse, she won't even be mad. It'd be easier if she was.

I have no fucking clue what happens now. All I know is we're done listening to others, we're done taking orders. They promised this town to my brother and Raven, we'll fucking show them how strong they are. We'll stand at their sides – a king and queen and their knights.

They did what was asked of them, and they were hurt after.

No fucking more.

With us or against us, period.

Our town.

Our people.

Captain's girl?

My back slides against the wall, my ass hitting the floor.

Fuck.

Chapter 33

RAVEN

I GROAN, MY HAND LIFTING TO MY HAIR, BUT SOMETHING KEEPS it from extending. I blink several times, trying to focus and slowly, the white walls come into view.

My eyes jerk down, finding I'm in a fucking hospital bed, tubes in my arms.

My jaw clenches and I slam my head against the pillow, grinding my teeth when it causes a slight pain in my shoulders.

I close my eyes, replaying what I last remember in my head – the maid, the girl, the crash. Leo and Vienna.

Maddoc.

I gasp, shooting up in the bed.

My eyes scan over every inch of the room but only Victoria is here, sleeping on a little couch in the corner.

Maddoc.

Maybe I imagined his voice, his hands.

I bite into my cheek, shaking my head.

Angry and confused, feeling like a weak and lonely bitch, I

tear the tape from my skin and tug the stupid ass IV from my arm, pushing the tape back down as best it'll hold. I bend my elbow to help stop the bleeding and I throw the blanket off me, finding my body is fine. Bruises, but at this point, I might as well get 'em tattooed on.

I reach over, turning off the monitor beside me and remove the blood pressure cuff, peel the little stickers stuck to my chest, and tug the one free from the dressing around my ribs.

I swing my legs over the edge of the bed, giving myself a second to take a breath, and then slowly stand.

Once I'm sure my feet are steady enough, I take the four steps to Cap's bed.

His eyes open when I pull at his blanket. They fly to mine, worry followed by sadness clouding the color in them. He lifts his arms so I can climb in, covering myself with the blanket.

"Are you okay?" he whispers.

"Stop asking me that, Cap. I'm always good," I rasp. "This isn't new to me, the trouble. This is what my life has always been, one problem after another. It's different, but not new."

"That's a shitty way to live, Raven."

I nod. "Yeah, but I'm alive, right?" My chest tightens. "Captain, so many people have been hurt because of me. All I had to do was be born, keep breathing and it ruined so many people's lives."

"You were important, worth the risk even if they didn't know you."

"And that's some bullshit, no?" I pick at the blanket covering us. "Brayshaw demands loyalty, earns trust and respect, yet I was a fucked-up kid, being a dick and running around the streets getting high, putting myself in danger I never even balked at, while these people who require so much from others, gave so much for a girl who didn't know they existed. A girl who wouldn't have fucking cared if she did."

"You were Brayshaw."

I shake my head, squeezing my eyes closed. *"Raven... interesting name, isn't it? Only one letter short..."*

Cap tenses beside me, his fingers finding my chin after a few seconds. He brings my eyes to his. "Raven?" he broaches, eyes tight.

"That's what my mother said to me before she died. One letter short." I swallow. "How could I be so blind? How could we not have put it together?"

"Raven..."

"Graven." My nostrils flare as I fight to keep control I don't possess. "She named me after them. She hated me, Cap."

"No—"

I lift my hand, giving a small smile. "No, don't. Don't say things you don't know. She honest to God, if there is one, did. Why would she run away, leave them, and then name me after them?"

He stares at me, not quite following.

"She wouldn't, Cap. There is no fucking way she ran."

"We'll find out," he promises. "But we need to get out of here. They'll let me leave soon, couple more days at the latest."

"You're still on an IV."

"It's a precaution, fluids and in case they need to run some antibiotics or something."

"So, you're better?"

"I'm good. Sore, little weak still, but good," he stresses. "Raven, I need you to stay out of trouble, stay here, at least that long. Let me help you with all this."

"Me too."

I jolt up when his voice slams into me like a fucking brick to the chest.

My eyes hit his and I can't keep it in. My lip starts to tremble, so bad I don't realize my nails are digging into my leg, until Captain tugs them free.

I run my tongue across my teeth, wishing to come off stronger.

Maddoc walks in, fighting for a blank stare, but he can't manage it.

His entire face morphs, unconcealed agony and regret right at the surface for both of us to witness.

Tears tremble at the edge of my eyes as he takes in our position.

Before, this wouldn't be an issue. He wouldn't even blink, he'd appreciate one of his own comforting me and vice versa.

But before, I wasn't married to the man beneath me, holding onto me... and I gave up the one staring in my eyes in doing it.

I swear the corner of his eyes grow red, glossy.

He wants to so bad, but he can't look away.

He stares, his mind convincing him he's staring at a girl loving on her new husband who she almost lost.

Come on, Big Man... as if I could replace you so quick. Ever.

Cap senses it, the pull between his brother and me. The magnet calling me to him, but I'm frozen. Captain tries to gently nudge me off, but I lock my muscles, begging, so his hand relaxes against me, his grip growing firmer, his way of supporting me in this moment.

Maddoc finally moves his eyes to his brother, and his shoulders fall. "Cap..."

"I'm sorry," Captain says.

Maddoc glares. "Don't."

"I'm sorry, Maddoc. I..." Captain's eyes shift to me, but I still can't tear my eyes from the dark-haired, green-eyed, guy in front of me.

My heart is breaking for real. I thought it hurt when he left, yeah right.

If I didn't know any better, I'd swear my chest was being cut open right here and now.

Maddoc doesn't say anything but torturously slow, slides his eyes back to mine.

"Hey," he whispers and it's no use from there.

Warm, wet, tears roll down my cheeks. I couldn't stop them if I tried.

"Hey..."

His nostrils flare, his jaw flexing and he spins around, giving us his back as he drops his chin to his chest, clearing his throat. "I'll get the nurse."

And he's gone again.

My face falls in my hands and I shake my head.

"I'm sorry, Cap." I quickly pull myself from his grip, and he tries to snatch me back, but I dash to the side, and he can't reach farther. He's still stuck to his machines. I force my eyes to his.

"Do not apologize to me again." He glares. "This isn't easy, Raven, and you're human, even if you act like Wonder Woman."

"More like Harley Quinn."

Through his anger and the tension, he chuckles, dropping his head back against the pillow. A small grin forms on his lips, and though his eyes are still sad, it makes me smile back.

I move back to my own bed, finding Victoria's blank stare on me. Slowly she shifts hers to Cap and then looks back down at her blanket before meeting mine again. She lifts her brows, smirking, going for playful but her concern is there.

"Always in the line of fire."

"Eh." I nod my head back and forth. "I mean, this time I was in the line of a busted ass pick-up truck, but tomato tomatoe, yeah?"

She chuckles, pushing to her feet and coming over to my bed. She drops on the end of it, staring at me.

"What?"

She glances at Captain, bringing her eyes back to me. Strain finds her forehead.

"Vee?"

She opens her mouth, closing it just as quick when the nurse walks in. The nurse who almost gets knocked to her ass when Royce rushes past her, and skids to a stop next to me.

His eyes fly over my face, and he grins, planting his arms on his hips. "Goddamn you, RaeRae."

I give a single shoulder shrug. "I told you. Trouble finds me."

He scoffs, leaning forward to grip my head gently, and kiss my hair. "You ain't lying, girl."

Rolland walks in next, concern etched in his brows, but he doesn't speak, and Bass follows, staying posted half in and half out the door.

"I'm gonna need near her, to check her," the nurse teases warmly, slipping between Royce and me. She gives a sad smile. "Hi."

My eyes narrow when with each passing second, her features grow more tense.

She looks to my arms, then the screen, then the cords dangling off the bed. "You've unplugged. We need to get the IV back—"

"That's not happening. I'm fine. No broken bones, some scrapes, no big deal."

The woman gives a small nod. "Those things may be true, but that's not why you're in here. You passed out from exhaustion and dehydration, the crash only added to your weakened state."

"I said I'm fine."

"Are you formally refusing treatment, at least as of right now?" she asks gently. "I'll need to document if you are, good practice, remember?"

I shrug, nodding, avoiding the frowns directed at me.

"Can I ask everyone to step out a moment, I need to go over a few things with Mrs. Brayshaw privately."

I wince at the name, dropping my eyes to my lap, but then I realize what she's asked and my head snaps up. "No, they can stay."

Her eyes widen. "Are you... sure? I'd advise they wait—"

"Stop questioning me." My eyes shooting to Rolland as he quietly removes himself from the room on his own.

He's learning.

Victoria scoots closer to me, her hand covering mine. "Raven," she says quietly. "Make them leave or better yet, you walk out with her, since it seems you can. Just you and her." Her eyes widen, and she nods.

"Why?"

"Just do it."

"Girl, you are out of line," Royce snaps, glaring from her to me.

I look to the nurse, who gives a subtle shake of her head.

"Help me up, brother."

My eyes move to Captain as he shifts in the bed, dropping his legs to one side.

Both Maddoc and Royce rush to him, standing close as he pushes to his feet and grips the rolling IV machine.

He starts for the door, and reluctantly, they follow.

Victoria stands when they exit, glancing back at me once more before leaving with them.

My eyes move back to the nurse. "There, I'm alone."

She reaches up, turning back on the machine, and then reaches for all the little clips and monitors I took off. "May I put these back on?"

I drop back against the pillow slapping my arms out like an obnoxious asshole. "Whatever."

"Raven—"

"Don't," I hiss, closing my eyes. "No talking, do what you need, give me whatever you want, but no talking."

Maddoc

"I HAVE SOMETHING YOU GUYS NEED TO SEE."

All eyes fly to Bishop.

"Fuck you just say?" Royce creeps toward him.

Bishop doesn't spare him a glance, his eyes moving to Rolland. "Leo and Vienna weren't as naïve as we thought." He pulls a rolled-up paper from his pocket, holding it out to my dad. "I don't know what they hoped to gain in attacking her, if anything, but I assume this" —he shakes the roll— "was intended for blackmail somewhere down the line."

"What is that?" I ask, walking closer.

Our dad unrolls it, reading over the paperwork in his hand.

"Proof," he says.

"Proof of what, exactly?" our dad asks him.

"Ravina Brayshaw didn't run to run." Bishop looks to me. "She ran because she was afraid, of Donley himself."

"Surprised you didn't give it straight to her," Royce spits.

"Almost did." Bishop shrugs. "But don't wanna see her hurt worse."

"How do we even know if this is true?" Royce shouts.

"It has to be," Raven rasps.

Our heads jerk toward the doorway, where she stands, propped against the frame, her face blank, eyes void and focused on nothing. The hospital gown has her looking even thinner than normal, her cheeks a little hollower, but the closer I look, the more I can see it's not the gown at all.

She is skinnier, the circles under her eyes darker, a different shade than the bruising surrounding it.

She's not eating, not sleeping.

"All Donley ever wanted was someone to take over after him. Someone he could guarantee would be strong enough, someone he felt he could control, or gain from," she says.

"He had Felix," our dad reminds her.

"Yeah," she rasps, her hands finding her throat. "He had a man in love with a Brayshaw, who came from Brayshaw High, who wanted to be Bray but earned a place with Graven first."

Dad's head pulls back slowly as if he hadn't thought of that. His eyes move to her and finally she looks up and into his. Hers cut to where Maybell sits near and back to him.

"The maid..." He trails off. "The baby was his. That's why he sent her away... he only wanted a son."

"A female was of no use to him, so what purpose would a pregnant Brayshaw carrying a girl serve him? No wedding had happened yet, so in his eyes, she was still disposable," Raven says numbly, shrugging. Her eyes slide to Victoria who stands frozen in the corner. "Coming in?"

Victoria gives a curt nod, stepping into the room, Raven disappearing behind her.

My eyes stay locked on the door.

"The fuck happened to her?" I whisper.

When no one speaks, I look around the room.

"I fucked up!" I shout. "I know this. I. Fucked. Up, but I love her, man. I fucking *love* her, just like you guys do but harder and with every piece of me. Tell me what happened. What the fuck did I miss? Who hurt her?"

Royce opens his mouth but suddenly Raven appears at the door again, and my chin falls to my chest, my deep breath filling both my cheeks as I try to calm down.

Suddenly her little hand is in view and fuck me if the hesitancy in her touch doesn't sting worse than anything before this moment. I can only manage to lift my eyes, using every muscle in my body to keep my hands at my hips.

I've dreamt of you every night, baby. You and those stormy greys.

Her eyes tighten. "Nobody blames you, not even for a second." Her hand is gone as fast as it came and with it goes my breath, my lungs constricting to the point of pain.

She stops in front of Bass. "Tell them every detail of every minute since you stepped in the hotel room and saved us both."

"I saved no one, Raven."

"Give it up, Bishop," she whispers, and the affection in her tone burns as it should. "You did, and I owe you a solid."

She walks back in the room, and this time a small click sounds after her.

Bass glares at the floor before shifting his eyes across the four of us. "You might wanna get Cap a chair for all this."

Fuck.

Chapter 34

RAVEN

Victoria digs in the bag Maybell brought for each of us when she realized the hospital was our new temporary home. "What can you wear?"

"Just underwear and some long socks from mine, maybe a tank top if there's a clean one, and Royce's long sweatshirt from his. It'll hang close to my knees."

She nods, fishing out what I asked for while I untie my gown, but when I lift my arms over my head for the tie behind my neck, I wince. My chest plate and shoulder blades start to ache.

She walks back to me, tossing the clothes on the bed.

When I don't move, she rolls her eyes. "Come on, Raven. Everybody needs help sometimes."

With a frown, I spin around, and she undoes it for me, handing me my underwear as it starts to fall. I slip them on quickly, and she eases my stretchy tank over my head and half down my ribs, so I can slip my arms into it.

"You gonna be able to get your arms in this sweatshirt?"

"Just pull it over, Vee."

291

With a huff, she does as I ask.

After it's on, I lift my wrist and she tugs my hair tie from around it and gently ties it in a loose ball in the middle of my head.

She drops down on the bed, so I spin to face her.

"You know." She eyes me.

I pick up the plastic cup of ice water, taking a small drink and swallowing the stupid pills the nurse left sitting there for me.

"Raven... I couldn't tell you—"

"Yeah," I cut her off, nodding. "You could have. You absolutely could have."

I finally meet her eyes only for her to break the contact not a second later.

"I get why you didn't though, and it's like I told you before." I drop down in front of her, and her eyes move back to mine. "You owed me nothing. Not your loyalty, or your secrets. Nothing, Vee."

She glares at me, shaking her head, but humor lines her eyes. "You're the strangest fucking person I have ever met."

A light laugh leaves me.

"Are we gonna talk about it?" she asks.

I shake my head. "Not today." I shift on the bed, looking to Captain's empty one. I take a deep breath.

"So... how are you, I mean who are you gonna talk to first?"

My brows pull in, and I squint to her.

She studies me and slowly her head pulls back. "Raven, tell me you're gonna..."

"Gonna what?"

"End this."

My head jerks back. "End what?" Right as I say it, a bitter laugh leaves me, and I stand. "Victoria, don't." I warn.

"You don't." She stands with me, facing me from the other side of the bed. "This changes everything."

"It changes nothing!" I shout instantly.

She jolts back. "You don't have to do this, Raven."

"I already did."

"But—"

"But *nothing*! I married him, Vee. I *married* Captain."

"Oh, come on, Raven," she hisses, stepping around the bed. "You don't give a shit about marriage!" She throws her hand out. "Don't stand there and pretend you do."

"You're right!" I snap back, getting in her face. "I don't give a fuck about the word. That's all it is to me, a fucking word. I have *no idea* what it means, no clue what I'm suddenly supposed to be with the title of *wife*, it's not like I had a role model." I push even closer to her, my chest bumping hers, my jaw muscles clenching. "So, you're right, Vee, I don't give a *shit* about marriage, but I give a shit ton about him."

"I'm not questioning how much you care about him."

"He gave up his future for mine, then almost gave his life, *for mine*," I snap. "Did we find out things I wish we'd have learned of earlier? No fucking duh, but we didn't, and I made him a promise. I'm keeping it." I step back, keeping my eyes on hers. "This is where we are. Period."

Her eyes soften. "You made a choice when the alternative was something you couldn't live with; he did the same thing. He'd understand."

I swallow, shouldering past her, but she grips my elbow, spinning me back around.

I yank free from her hand, pushing her as hard as I can in the chest.

She flies back, slamming against the bed tray and knocking all the shit on it to the floor.

The loud crash has one of the boys yanking on the locked door handle.

The banging follows, shouts from all of them after that.

I glare. "Are you saying this just so *you* can have him?"

"I'm saying it because it's the truth and you know it." She glares back.

I get in her face, fighting to hold back the moisture burning behind my eyelids. "What am I supposed to say to him," I hiss. "Hm? *How* do I tell him I want out?" I force past clenched teeth, my entire body shaking. "That I *need* out. That I never should have fucking agreed to this, ever. That we were all wrong and we should have fought from the beginning? That I can't be his wife because I will never be his and I don't want to be?"

She swallows, but her eyes only sharpen more and she pushes off her elbows, standing before me, my hands shooting out to grip her wrist when she lifts it.

Her palm opens, letting me know she wasn't trying for anything.

"You tell him just like that, Raven," she says strongly. "Word for fucking word. He needs you to say it."

He needs words...

My jaw starts to tremble, so I clamp it shut to stop it.

Keys clank in the hall, and the door flies open, too many footsteps to count shuffling in, each one halting at the entrance.

"You can do this," she whispers, eyes firm.

"What if I told you I was afraid?" I force out in a shaky whisper.

She licks her lips, her eyes moving over my shoulder. "I'd say you're human after all."

Mine tighten with my grip before I shove her away.

"Bass," I rasp, knowing he's in here without looking.

One set of footsteps grow closer.

"Victoria could use a walk, see her out?"

Her eyes slide between mine, unsure.

Bass takes a step closer, but Victoria's head snaps his way.

"Touch me and I'll crush your nuts." she snaps, she shoulders past me, not looking back as she steps out.

I stand there facing the wall opposite of them as long as they allow, only turning around when my name is called.

With each pair of eyes met, heaviness falls on my shoulders to the point I have to sit.

I look to Captain, who stands there in his gown, eyes slowly shifting from the floor to me, but then I notice the pressure with which he's gripping the rolling IV machine and motion for his bed.

A frown hits his brows and he stands taller as if he has to prove his strength.

He doesn't.

"Sit down, Captain. You've been standing a long time."

"I'm good," he assures me, then looks me over. "I could use some of my own fucking clothes, too, though."

I nod. "Maybell brought something for all of us," I pause. "Or for us three..." My eyes fly to Maddoc's, and the move alone almost crushes me on the spot.

His hands open and close at his sides, and he can't keep eye contact. His deep, sharp inhales and exhales causing a sting in my own chest.

"Because I wasn't here," he growls at himself, his head falling back. He takes a quick glance at me down his nose but then squeezes his eyes shut and spins around where he stands. I stare at the back of him as his hand comes up to cover his mouth.

He feels guilty, like this is all his fault.

"Royce," Cap says slowly, almost unsure. "Help me out?"

"I can help you," I rush out, the slight croak in my voice giving away the panic flaring in my gut.

My eyes land on Maddoc's back, and sure as shit, his head falls, his hands coming up to cross behind his neck.

Royce grabs the shit from Captain's bag before making his way to me.

He drops in front of me on the bed, his eyes tight, lips pinched flat. "I'm so mad at you, RaeRae," he whispers, shaking his head. "I should have been with you for all that shit. Not Bass fucking Bishop. Me. Someone who loves you, someone who could have held you, helped you, fuck I don't know..." His voice trails off. "Something."

I lean forward gently touching my forehead to his, ignoring the sting from the bruising there. "You did," I whisper, and his eyes lift to mine, our foreheads still touching. "If it wasn't you who walked in the bathroom when I was talking to Maybell, I would have broke. Nobody would have done in that moment but you. You didn't push me, didn't ask me any questions, you were just there, which is exactly what I needed."

He swallows. "Yeah?"

"Yeah." I nod against him.

"Am I gonna hurt you if I hug you right now?"

A laugh spits from me and I shake my head no even though, yeah, it probably will.

He knows that, too, so he's gentle in his hold. Before he pulls away, he whispers in my ear, "Talk to him, baby girl. If he didn't break when he left, he sure as fuck did after that conversation."

I grip him tighter, not wanting to let him go, but his fingers glide to mine inconspicuously and he pries them open, holding my eyes as he steps back and stands, only breaking contact when he spins to Captain.

Captain, who's looking right at me. He gives me an encouraging smile, but guilt fogs his features just the same.

I give a slow shake of my head, and the corner of his mouth tips the slightest bit.

"Come on, Cap." Royce lays a hand on his shoulder.

"Maybe I can get that nurse of yours to give your sponge bath to me instead."

"She's like fifty," Cap says.

"Cougars love me."

With a small laugh, the two of them walk out, leaving Maddoc and me alone for the first time in weeks.

Chapter 35

MADDOC

THE DOOR CLOSES WITH AN EASY CLICK, BUT IT REBOUNDS OFF my ears like a hard hit to tin.

I have never wanted my brothers to get lost so bad in my life. Problem is, I never wanted them to keep their feet planted right where they were so fucking bad either, now here we are, alone.

My baby and me.

Only she's not mine anymore, or at least that's what we have to pretend, even now when it's nothing but the air in her lungs filling mine.

Her mom held a gun to her head, loaded and cocked back, ready to shoot her. I could have lost her for real. Completely.

Knowing this makes me realize, even if I have to stand back, watch her fall in love with my brother like she loves me, I will. Happily, if it means she's still here, still in sight where I can protect her.

Captain may be strong but there is no doubt in my fucking mind, nobody can protect her like me. Nobody.

I stay, I can steal what should be mine – her touch. I can brush her hand with my fingers when I walk by, claim it was an accident or grab her arm to get her attention. Anything to feel the heat of her skin on mine, if even for only a second and as innocent as that.

Only it won't be innocent.

Every time I'll wish her stormy eyes would move to mine with purpose, need. Want.

She killed her mom.

She banished Perkins.

She burned the Graven Estate to the ground.

She found out her only friend had – has – more secrets than we do.

She found out who raped her when she was younger – my own fucking blood.

Family runs deeper than blood.

Just when she probably felt things were coming together, Leo and Vienna come out of the woodwork, ready to tear her apart, hand her over like a dirty prize.

I did this.

All of it.

I jerk when her hand touches my shoulder blade, every muscle in my body tensing, but only for a moment, because in the next, her other one meets my bicep. Her little fingers wrapping around it the best they can, and it's over.

My knees give, and I slam against the floor, welcoming the sting that shoots up my thighs. My head falls to my chest, my fists to the floor.

Her sharp, shattered inhale has the cords in my neck tightening, and I hate myself a little more.

After a few seconds, her sock covered feet come into view, followed by her knees as she plants herself right in front of me.

She sits back on her feet, and when her hand lifts, I squeeze my eyes shut.

Her soft fingers shake against my cheek and I hold my breath, swallowing the little air I have in me. Heat covers my cold face as her palms meet my jaw, her hand spanning out until the tips of her pointer fingers are positioned behind my ears, the others caging in my neck.

She lifts my head, the soft shuffle letting me know she's scooting closer.

It takes her a minute, but then she speaks. "Open your eyes, Big Man."

Her breath wafts over my face, and I flatten my lips to keep the feel of her off me.

Fuck.

"B—" she cuts herself off, and her shuddered inhale matches mine. "Maddoc, please," she whispers. "Open."

My hands fly up to grip her wrist and she freezes, her fingers lifting from my skin, but I slide my hands up her wrists, covering the backs of hers with my own, and push them back down, leaving mine where they are and finally she relaxes again.

My eyes snap open, and instantly hers fall.

"Nuh-uh, baby," I whisper. "That's not fair."

"Fair..." she whispers, a sad chuckle leaving her, and finally her eyes come.

Both our grips strengthen at the same time, hers on me and mine on her. It's instinctual, to hold on tighter, to subconsciously fight for contact we want but can't have.

"Royce found you," she rasps. "Where'd you go?"

"For a ride." I bite at the inside of my cheek, my eyes moving between hers.

"A ride..." She trails off, a shuttered breath leaving her as she pulls her lips between her teeth.

She knows.

"When I left the school, I ditched my phone and GPS. Went straight to the tracks."

Her jaw begins to tremble.

"Hopped on the first train to pass, got off when it stopped. Did it over again the next day."

Her head lowers, and she blows out a long breath.

She understands, knows exactly why I chose to ride around on steel tracks.

I needed to feel you, baby, and that was the only time I came close.

"I'm sorry," I whisper, my nostrils flaring as hers grow red. "This is on me, all of it." Everything I just convinced myself of goes out the fucking window, and the words fly from me. "I never should have agreed to this. I *never* should have let him have you."

"Stop."

"You can't be anyone else's when you're already mine, Raven. And you are. Mine."

"Maddoc..." she croaks, and when her eyes fall so do her tears.

"I'm not asking you to hurt him," I whisper as I slide closer, our knees now touching. "But, baby... I want you."

"I'm pregnant."

Her words are a rushed, harsh exhale, and my hands fly from her so fast she flinches.

I fall back on my heels, only to tumble to my ass.

I stagger to my feet, falling over once more, but I catch myself on the edge of the bed, only to stumble against the cabinets near the door. I tug it open and fall into the hall.

"Maddoc, wait!" she shouts, but the door closes me off from her.

My head slams against the wall and my cheeks start to shake.

I bite into my gums, until blood coats every inch of my

mouth, slipping onto my lips. I squeeze my eyes shut, anger boiling as moisture invades the corners of my eyes.

Slow, heavy footsteps echo down the hall and I know they're coming, but I have nothing in me to shake off this feeling, whatever the fuck it is.

I have nothing in me, but I'm not numb. Every inch of me aches, every fucking muscle is ready to tear, stretched to its max, and the tethers to my fucking heart are right there with it. I'd swear there was a hand inside my chest, squeezing, pulling, ripping it from my body if I didn't know better.

"Madman?" Royce urges.

"M-m." I shake my head. "No." I scrunch my face up and push off the wall, blindly punching the one across from me before opening my eyes and storming down the hall.

I go straight for the elevator.

Right before the doors close, a hand slides in, forcing them to open again and Victoria stands glaring at me.

"Get the fuck away from me," I growl, blood falling from my mouth.

She steps inside, pushing the close door button only to pull the emergency handle the second we start moving.

She turns, her brown eyes hard and focused on me. "Don't talk. Listen."

Raven

I'M STILL STARING AT THE DOOR, TEARS FALLING DOWN MY FACE when it opens, but it's not the boys like I thought it'd be. It's Rolland.

He's slow in his steps, slipping his jacket off as he grows

closer, setting it on the bed as he passes by. He grips the thigh of his slacks, tugging them up as he leans down in front of me.

His eyes are grave, earnest, and just as green as his son's, it's hard to look, harder to look away. His hand reaches out to grip my forearm, slowly, as if I might jerk away, but something has me leaning in. My face drops to my hands and I let them fall to his shoulder.

"What have I done, Raven?" he whispers. "Did I destroy my family?"

I shake my head against him. "This is beyond you. This goes back, way before you and everything after hit your blind spots hard."

"What blind spots?"

"Your boys," I rasp, taking a chance on what must be true. "Her."

He tenses but only slightly. "I did love your mother, Raven."

"Of course you did. She was a lone apple in a starved kingdom." I sniffle. "Full of delayed poison. Like a fucking extended-release pill, hits you slowly and over time. Just as soon as it's almost gone, when she's finally out of your head, boom. Another blow burns in your veins."

"I was just a boy, she was the first girl I cared for, so even though I couldn't stand her later, I couldn't stop trying to protect her in some way over the years."

I nod, looking to him. "I ruined your family, not you."

He shakes his head, eyes intent. "No."

"You sound so sure."

"Because I am. You're strong."

"Look at me." I flop my hands out. "Do I look strong to you?"

"Considering it all, yes. You do."

I roll my eyes. "You're so far out of the loop right now, Rols, you have no idea."

His lip tips and a sad laugh leaves him. "Man, haven't heard you call me that in a long time, black bird."

I scoff a laugh, looking away. I run my hands over my hair, letting them fall to my lap. "Things can't go on like they have been here. These people, they're here for a reason. The families in this town, the kids at the school, they want the future this place promises. The best of both worlds."

He nods, looking to the door and back. "It really is, the grit and the glamour. Balls at seven, brawls at eleven," he jokes, earning a small laugh from me, but it dies quick.

"I could do without the balls you speak of," I tease, making him laugh.

"But for real, though, they deserve it." My eyes slide between his. "I know nothing other than no one should fear without reason and no one should hurt without fault."

"I'm with you, Raven. Whatever you need, whatever you wish for. If you let me." He holds my eyes. "I will stand with you."

I wipe my face, looking away, thinking a moment before asking. "Do the families meet regularly?"

"Once a month, unless we call for something sooner," he tells me. "I can have them here by end of day if need be."

"No," I say. "I want to catch everyone off guard."

"Then it'll be six days from now."

I nod. "Call that designer chick back." I look to him. "The one redoing the room across from Captain's for Zoey. Have her come, today. Now. Whatever they talked about, her and Cap, tell her to make it happen and more."

He jerks his head. "Done."

"And uh." I lick my lips, biting into my bottom one before letting it free. I push to my feet, staring down at him. "I'm gonna need a nursery. I'll pay for it, but I don't know what, um..."

His face falls, his eyes softening as he pushes to his feet

before me. He reaches out, ready to grip my hand but decides against it. "We'll make sure to get everything you'll need." He swallows, hesitating. "When should I be sure it's ready by?"

"Go, Rolland," I whisper.

He nods and moves for the door, but pauses when I say, "Purple."

Confused, he looks to me.

"For Zoey." I think back to her basketball and the playhouse, the flowers lining the entry. "I think it's her favorite color."

He nods, pushing the door open but I hold him back once more.

"Why did they let you come in here?"

He considers what to share a moment before he sighs. "Maddoc didn't look so hot when he came out, stormed off. They followed, but Victoria locked herself in the elevator shaft with him."

My features drop. "What?"

"I imagine they're trying to get it moving." He shrugs. "Nothing they'll be able to do until the flip is switched from the inside."

I turn away, biting on the edge of the cotton cuffs of the sweatshirt. Even if Bass told them everything, like I asked him to, he couldn't have added in the final piece.

The potential silver bullet, but we're too far gone for new weapons.

Kings have been named; kingdoms set.

But it all comes down to the power of the queen, doesn't it?

What about the power of two?

Chapter 36

MADDOC

I'M AT A FUCKING LOSS.

No clue what to think. No clue what to believe or what move is right if a right move exists at all. I'm fucked in my head and see no way out. It's been three days of silence from everyone all around. Nobody speaks to one another. The only words shared are when someone announces they're going for a walk or stepping out for a call or some bullshit like that.

I came outside today as soon as I heard Raven puking in the bathroom in the hall. Now, hours have passed, another sun gone, and I'm still sitting here alone against a tree at the edge of the hospital, away from all the windows.

Away from her.

Of course, the second I fucking think it, Bass Bishop drops down beside me, resting his arms on his knees as he lights a cigarette.

I glare at his profile a minute before saying what I should have the second he told me all he's done for her. "Thank you."

He takes his time, pulling in a long drag before blowing it out, then slowly slides his eyes my way. "For what, man? Letting your brother get shot, twice? For letting a gun get shoved in Raven's face, forcing her to kill her own mom when one, I should have been there to prevent all of it, or two, been there soon enough to be the one who drove that knife through Ravina's side so Raven didn't have to?"

I shift my glower to the green strip of grass ahead of me.

"How about for not seeing Leo and Vienna coming? Or for letting Raven take off in the Graven house for too long, and having to drag her ass out with the help of Gio while she kicked and screamed, trying to convince a Graven to live instead of die?"

"Stop."

He scoffs, looking away. "Then don't fucking thank me, man."

After a second, I ask him, "Where's the body?"

"Got it to the crematory, quietly. They've got it ready and waiting in case she wants to bury or burn her. And she will."

"She wig out?" I ask him.

Bass shakes his head, looking to the grass. "Nah, man. She held it all in, hid everything like the soldier she is. Her first crack, Royce was there for, thank fuck. She's holdin' on, but not by much at this point. She doesn't know what to do. Her moves were easier before, helped all of you. She's having to think now, and we both know that's not the way she works, so she's lost. She wants you, man, but she has guilt, a sense of debt."

"Cap would never hold anything over her head."

"Nope. He wouldn't. But she thinks he gave up everything for her, and you? You plain gave up. What's she supposed to do with that?"

I run my hands down my face, dropping my head against the tree.

"Fucked up shit, yeah?" He takes another drag, speaking with a held breath. "I'd've told you to fuck off and walk if I thought for a second you'd leave her after you put me on her tail."

He meets my glare. "Yeah, well some shit happened after that, asshole."

"Oh, I know. She tried to do what she thought was best for you. Handled things quietly, out of your faces." He swings his head toward me. "Every fucking body here knows she's never been good at decisions, but when she moves, make no fucking mistake, she moves with you in mind."

"Yeah?" I snap. "Every move she makes, huh?" I mock.

He eyes me a long moment before looking away. He flicks his cigarette before jumping to his feet. He stares at the hospital building behind us.

"Donley mentioned a video when we were there, proof of something." His eyes come back to mine.

Perceptive asshole.

He pushes from the ground, offering me a hand so I let him pull me up.

I eye him. "I'd bet she won't be going anywhere for a while."

He shakes his head, already knowing. "Then neither am I, man. And heads up, your brother's coming."

I nod, looking behind him when Royce steps around the small walkway, headed right for me.

Royce makes sure to knock his shoulder into Bishop's as hard as fucking possible, but Bishop ignores him and makes his way back to Raven and the others.

"I'm tired of the silence. How is it I've been here and don't know shit? Tell me what the fuck's goin' on?" Royce demands, crossing his arms angrily.

"She's pregnant."

His brows jump, not at all expecting that. He gapes at me,

and the longer he stares, the more it sets in. Tension lines his forehead.

He steps forward, eyes hard, but he wraps his arms around me in a hard pat.

An apology. Pity maybe, but I take it, hugging him back.

He doesn't say anything, but what could he say? It's been two fucking months she's been married to my brother.

Were we suppose to prepare for this shit?

"I've been needing to get fucked up and fucked off for a good minute, so how's about a drink, brother?"

"How 'bout a few?"

He scoffs, stepping back and we had for his SUV.

He pulls his phone out, putting it up to his ear. "Mac money, find me a honey," he jokes into the line. "I need a solid distraction and Maddoc needs to be put on his ass. Party pad in twenty."

With that, we leave the hospital, ready to forget for a little while.

Let's hope this time it works.

Royce's twenty minutes turned into an hour. We took a detour home so he could change, but I couldn't even drag myself from the SUV.

It's not until we get there, we remember it was being gutted and redone.

The spill-proof leather sofas we had against the walls are gone, replaced with larger, softer ones. The black curtains are now a light blue to match the fucking rug laying on the floor and the fake flowers sitting on the new, white kitchen table.

There's a small dollhouse against the west wall, a tea set alongside it, right where the beer pong table used to be.

"Maybe we should—"

"No," I cut Royce off, spinning back to look out the door when the crunch of tires against gravel alerts us Mac's here with a few more from the crew.

He steps out first, walking straight for us while they slowly hit the trunk of his car.

He moves in for an easy fist bump that I meet, not acknowledge my being gone but nods his head as if to say he's glad I'm back.

"Figured we'd start small, but I got more on wait if you're looking for a louder night." He glances from his carload to the two others who just pulled up behind him.

"Nah, this is good." Royce nods, eyes scanning around.

Mac pulls a fresh bottle of Crown from his back pocket and holds it out for me. "This is all you, my man."

I don't hesitate, but crack it open, downing a quarter of the fifth in one go.

Mac clasps my shoulder before moving toward the group with bags in their hands. "Beer in the fridge, snacks on the table. Stay outta the rooms unless a Bray invites you to one."

Music blasts from inside the house and I spin to find Royce plugged in his phone.

He gives a dry grin, shouting, "The system may be gone, but they didn't tear down the walls, speakers are still embedded."

With a nod, I take another swig, stepping to the side as the carloads file in.

Chloe pauses in front of me, eyeing me from head to toe. "Looking rough, Brayshaw."

"Lookin' good, Carpo."

Her lip twitches and she shakes her head. "Yikes," she teases. "You're really in bad shape if you're complimenting me. Take it easy on the whiskey, huh?"

With a glare, I down the rest of the bottle, tossing it to the side without looking. "What whiskey?"

She frowns. "Suit yourself, but from the looks of it." She glances toward Royce who tosses back two shots of something dark, chasing them with a fresh popped Pacifico.

"There won't be anyone to sweep your ass off the floor tonight."

I kick off the wall, leaving her standing there to join Royce in the kitchen.

Within minutes, I'm feeling good, listening to updates Mac gives about the school. Laughing at nothing, swaying to the music from my seat.

A while later, Royce stumbles into the living room and starts dancing with a couple girls, leaving the spot beside me open for anyone to take.

And a dark-haired blur is quick too.

She's subtle, I'll give her that as she shifts closer, but the second her hand touches my arm, it's snatched up by another.

She's spun around, and tossed against the wall with a hard thud, gaining the attention of several people in the room.

Mac looks from me to the girl, but I only move my eyes.

"Get the fuck outta here before I put you through this window."

"Who the hell are you?"

"Gatekeeper, bitch."

Victoria.

I roll my eyes, pushing to my feet, but stumble over them, and fall against the wall.

With a light growl, she slips under my arms, snapping at someone, "A little help, here?"

Next thing, I know Mac is under my other arm.

My body's moving, but I can't feel my legs and everything in front of me is fuzzy. Only if I blink real fucking hard, can I see.

I slump, but then I'm jostled again, and we keep forward.

Then the song changes on the system, my spine straightens, my feet planting firmly into the ugly ass carpet.

The stupid fucking song she was listening to in the hall that day comes on, and I jerk around, reaching for the phone. I grip it right as the chorus hits and starts fucking screaming about not wanting to live for nothing, but that's exactly what this life is for me now.

Nothing.

What purpose can I serve without her? Who am I without her?

No fucking one.

A burst of drunken strength hits, and I tear it from the wall, sending a loud screech through the room, before I spin and chuck it at the TV, leaving a gaping hole in the center of it, before tearing the TV from its mounts completely.

People gasp and fly out the door, but I don't give a fuck.

I grab the empty beer bottles lining the fireplace and chuck them at the walls, reveling in the crashing sound that follows. Somehow, I manage to lift the coffee table that was pushed against the side wall and slam it against the stupid fucking kiddie tea set, ready and set for three.

Him and her. Mine.

She's mine.

I don't know how I get there, but next thing I know I'm on my knees in the grass out front, not an ounce of strength left. A scream echoes in the trees around me – my voice.

I lay out, looking up at the stars, but they quickly become nothing but a blur before everything goes black.

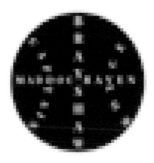

FUCKING BIRDS.

Their piercing chirps are enough to send my head kicking, and my eyes begin to peel open. I blink a few times, freezing when I turn my head, and find Raven sleeping on the bare grass beside me.

My chest starts to ache instantly, my heart pounding a hundred times harder than my head ever could, even after a fifth of whiskey to the dome.

I wanna move to my side, to stare at her better, reach out to see if I'm trippin' on more than liquor, but I don't dare move and chance waking her. If she wakes, she might leave.

She was right, so fucking right. Love made me weak, but only for her.

I don't want to let him keep you, baby.

My eyes fly to hers right as a tear rolls over the hump of her nose.

She pulls her lips in and more come.

"Why you here?" I rasp.

"You asked me to be," she whispers back.

I frown and finally her eyes open, meeting mine.

They're bloodshot from lack of sleep, meek and flightless – not Raven.

"I asked you to come to me?"

She nods.

"And you did?"

"Always will."

"What if I asked you to leave him?" I study her. "Would you?"

"Am I sick if I say yes?" she whispers back instantly.

My eyes slam shut.

Fuck.

"You were hoping for a different answer."

"I don't know, Raven. I don't know anything anymore."

She's quiet a moment before she says, "You wouldn't do it, would you? You wouldn't ask me to?"

I force my eyes back to hers, and the weight of a ton of bricks settle over me. She stares, completely vulnerable, eyes bare in every way and locked on mine.

Pleading without words.

"Stop, Raven," I rasp, pushing myself into a sitting position, taking a second to shake off the dizziness that follows.

"Stop what?"

"Stop looking at me like that."

"Like what?"

I shake my head, looking everywhere but at her. "You know like what," I whisper. "I'm not strong enough to say no to you."

"Maybe I don't want you to be."

"That's not fair."

"None of this is fucking fair!" She shoots to a sitting position.

"You don't have to do this," I mumble. "I already lost, but—"

"Lost?" Angry, her eyes slice to mine as she speaks through clenched teeth. "What did *you* lose here, huh?" she spits, shoving at me angrily. "You not only cut me at the fucking ankles, you left me there to bleed, too," she rumbles. "*You* gave *me* an ultimatum that I didn't even have to think on. Choose him, save your family – the only family I have ever known – fucking done, Maddoc!" she shouts. "It's not my fault you pussed out and ran off like a little bitch at the first fucking sting!"

"First sting?" I gape at her. "Are you for real right now?" I push even closer. "You think standing there, asking you to be with my brother, that giving you away when all I've said was I'd never, that you were mine no matter what, didn't fucking burn me, Raven? Because it did. I'd have welcomed a knife to the fucking side over that, over any of this, any day, all fucking day."

"Yeah well, my mother got one in hers instead!" she shouts, dropping her arms to her side and looking off. She pulls her lips between her teeth a moment before her head snaps my way.

"I legitimately think I'm dying inside, Maddoc, and it's like every second of every day I grow closer to emptiness. I look at him and guilt consumes me. I think of you and pain sends me fucking reeling. I look in the mirror and pure *hatred* stares back. I'm weak, I'm tired, I'm—"

"Pregnant," I cut her off with a sharp tone. I snap my head toward her, and she frowns. "You. Are. Pregnant."

"I didn't do this on purpose." Her brows meet at the center. "You think I know what to do with a kid, because I don't. Or that I wanted one, because that would be a no, too. I've never even held a baby before. This was an accident," she grates. "I wasn't even supposed to be able to—"

A laugh bubbles out of me, but there isn't an ounce of humor in it. I jump to my feet, ignoring the pounding of my head.

"Is this supposed to make it better, Raven? The story of how you *accidentally* got pregnant, and it wasn't part of the fucking newlywed plan?" I shake my head, glaring at her. "You two must have been real fucking busy if I fucked you, *for months*, skin to fucking skin, over and over again, and you didn't have so much as a damn scare, and here you are, married to him for what? A few days before he was in a coma and boom, baby fucking Captain is on the way?"

Her head jerks back.

"Or maybe you were on birth control when we were together, and stopped once you were a married fucking female, yeah?"

Her eyes fall to the grass, and slowly she pushes to her feet.

When they come back to mine, she blinks several times as she backs away. "Maddoc..." she whispers all staggered like, shaking her head slowly. "Wow."

Her shoulders fall, and she looks away. Her lips start to tremble, but then as if she's resigned herself to her thoughts, she stands taller, wipes her hands down her sweats and steps around me, only to freeze once she's at my back.

"You've got it all figured out, huh, Big Man."

"Sorry you couldn't hide it from me like your mother hid you from the brothers she destroyed. Like mother like daughter, huh?"

Her chocked laugh serves as a bullet to the heart. "*Wow.*"

Neither of us turn around, and not a word's spoken after that.

She walks away, a car door opening and closing as soon as her footsteps stop.

The front door creaks, and my eyes move toward the porch.

Bass steps out, glaring at me as he passes, and not a minute later, the car peels out.

Right as my head hangs, another set of feet slide into view.

"You're a fucking idiot, you know that."

My head snaps up, eyes wide when I find Captain standing there, a hard glare etched across his face.

"Open your eyes, Maddoc."

"My eyes are open, Cap." I throw my hands out. "I'm accepting what is."

"By forgetting who we are," he growls.

"What does that even mean, brother?"

"If you have to ask, maybe this is for the best." He steps toward me, Royce at his back. "I asked you to trust me. You said you did."

"Guess I didn't think you'd be so ready and willing, not to mention quick, but maybe I was blind, brother. Maybe I saw

317

this coming all along. This why you wouldn't kiss her at the cabin? Afraid you couldn't let go once you had a taste?"

His right hook slams across my face, and my head snaps to the side, blood flying from my lip, but I don't even wince.

I know that hurt him more than me, he wasn't even supposed to leave the hospital yet.

He bumps past me, using the same shoulder he was shot in without so much as a grimace leaving him.

Royce stops in front of me in a flash. "I should knock your fucking teeth out," he forces past clenched teeth, but then his eyes slope and he looks off.

"Go for it, brother." I spit blood on the ground, but it lands on my shoes instead. "Bet they're nice and loose for you now."

His jaw ticks and he glares after Captain, but hisses to me, "Why agree to come back if you planned to forget everything we stand for?"

With that, he walks away, the roar of an engine and the dust from smoked tires engulfing me in the next second.

I hang my head in my hands and plant my ass on the porch steps.

"You know," comes from behind me, and I hang my head. "I used to think you were the smart one."

I groan, extending my legs and glance over my shoulder at her. "Why you still here?"

She shrugs, pushing off the frame. "Mac likes to pretend he's not mine when the sun hits, so we do this little dance. He takes off when he thinks I'm sleeping, and I pretend I am so he gets his clean escape."

My brows raise, doubting her. "You and Mac?"

She nods, dropping beside me. "Trust me. *No one* is more shocked than me. He's so far from my type, or so I thought."

I shake my head. "What do you want, Chloe? I'm not in the mood."

"No, you're just having a pity party for one."

I glare at her but she only stares.

"You know Raven has never met my dad," she says. "Weird right, him being head of security, you'd think she'd have been introduced to him long ago."

"Chloe," I grate, sliding my eyes to hers.

"Couple weeks ago, Daddy was dusting off his old black suit," she says. "The one he wore at our first communion. Remember that?"

"That was a spectacle."

She nods, wrapping her arms around her legs. "Yep. All to trap the bad guys, another day in the land of Brayshaw, right?"

"If you have a point, find it. I'm not in the fuckin' mood."

Her eyes shift between mine a moment and then she seems to ignore me. "He asked me to fix his tie, I asked him why he was wearing it and he said something interesting..." She trails off.

My eyes narrow.

"He said '*almost, honey, almost.*'"

I glare at her, pushing to my feet. "I don't have time for this shit."

"Know what he said when I asked him if he was aware Rolland was released from prison? '*Almost, honey, almost.*'"

I spin around to face her, and she pushes to her feet.

"And when Raven first got here, and I asked him why I couldn't get rid of her, why you guys flocked to her?" Her brows lift as her lips purse. "'*Almost, honey, almost.*' Every time something revolves around Brayshaw and he doesn't want to or can't share it's the same line."

I step toward her. "Chloe..."

"He's really holding on to the whole 'not until I graduate' thing."

"*Chloe.*"

She eyes me. "The very next day, Collins Graven sneaks in the student body office, locks himself and Leo inside and does what? Rocks our Brayshaw High world." She lifts a knowing brow and pushes past me. "Strange, right?"

I whip around as she opens her door.

She stands there, leaning over the edge of her door frame. "You could use a shower. I have plenty of those. Daddy's home today, too, but only for a little while. Guess there's some sort of... meeting happening today. Called by a Graven, no less." She lifts a brow, pushes a button and the top to her convertible rolls down. She steps in, standing above the window. "What do you say, Brayshaw? You coming or not?"

I slide in the passenger seat, but before we can pull away, Royce is whipping in behind us, blocking our exit.

Captain throws his door open and jumps out, storming toward me.

He bends, getting in my face, anger radiating off every inch of him to the point his entire body is shaking.

"Never in my fucking *life*, would I turn my back on you. Never would I take from you, or step on your toes, or do any damn thing that would destroy who we are and the bonds we have. You're my fucking brother, Maddoc. My *brother*."

Captain clenches his teeth, plants his hands on the side of the Corvette and brings his eyes level with mine.

"I never. Fucking. Touched her." He swallows, pushing off the car and walking backward. "Not fucking once."

Chapter 37

Raven

I spot his reflection in the window before I hear a sound, and my eyes fly to his.

"What are you thinking about?"

"How I never should have punched Victoria the day my mom showed that first time."

Captain drops onto the free swing to my right, staring at me in the long slider at the back of the girls' Bray house.

"If I hadn't, I never would have moved into the house and put everyone on high alert."

"It wouldn't have changed anything, Raven," he speaks quietly. "This was all meant to happen."

I shake my head, looking to him. "All of it?"

He eyes me a minute, before looking away again. "I knew Donley wouldn't turn down the idea of having a power couple who loved each other over Collins and a forced bride, so I put an impossible decision down, forced both your hands. Ultimately, this is all my fault."

"I agreed, too, Cap."

"But you didn't." He meets my stare. "You said no. You were braver than we were, stronger than we were when it mattered, and in front of everyone. In a room full of powerful men you'd never seen before, you said no."

"And then I caved."

He gives a sad scoff, shaking his head. "You didn't cave, Raven," he whispers with a scowl. "Maddoc told me what he did, how even after he talked to you, you wanted to say no."

"I should have held my ground."

"You did the most selfless thing any of us will ever witness, because you love him that much."

I glare at the dirt road behind us. "I tried to tell him love is for the weak."

"I lied to you," he rushes out.

I frown, not quite understanding, but it doesn't matter. "I trust you, Captain."

"I know you do, but that doesn't make this right." He shakes his head, a heavy sigh leaving him. "I love you, you know that, just like you know it's not the way Maddoc does," he stresses. "But I asked you and Maddoc both to trust me for a reason."

His eyes move between mine. "I had to make sure my family was safe, and that includes you, so I did what I could to make sure that happened, but in the back of my mind, this was always temporary until we found another way."

I shift my feet in the dirt so the swing is facing him better. "Temporary."

"I knew everyone was watching. Brayshaw High would believe it easy enough, but I knew Donley wouldn't. He had to see the struggles, the slow growth and solo decisions on our part."

"The bud of a real relationship."

"Exactly."

I eye him.

"I let you believe this was real."

"You don't have to do this." I shake my head and his jaw tightens. "I've been with you every day, Captain. I saw you struggle with what we were doing, felt it just the same. You don't have to justify this. You say you lied, well we both did. We lied to our damn selves, pretending we could ever be anything different considering. Neither of us wanted this to happen. I mean, that's not even a question worth asking, but it did. Either way, Cap. We both knew the truth behind the mirror. I could never be yours for real, just like you could never be mine."

His eyes pull, the muscles in his neck flexing against his skin. "What happened to you not dragging things out of me?" he teases lightly.

I squish my lips to the side in a halfhearted grin before I grow somber. "I would have never hurt you, though, Packman. You know that, right?"

"Not on purpose, you wouldn't have," he replies, and my gut clenches. "Not that you had the power to in the way that you mean, but I could never risk it possibly getting there, if it even could. That's what my *just in case* was for."

"Just in case?" I frown.

He nods, a softness to his voice that gives him away. "Yeah, Raven. My just in case."

I grip the metal chains tighter, cutting my eyes away. "You heard us."

"Why didn't you tell me?" he whispers.

I shake my head, looking to the sky. "How the hell was I supposed to admit I never wanted to be a mother when I'd *just* promised to be your wife." My eyes hit his and his features soften instantly.

He stands, pulling me off the swing with him.

He tilts my head up, looking straight in the eye. "Zoey?"

I nod, gripping his fingers with mine. "She deserves better than I could ever give her."

His jaw flexes and he smiles tightly. "You'd be surprised how easy she is to love. You wouldn't even have to try. I have no doubt you will love her with all you are and for all she is," he says quietly before adding. "Just like she'll love you, and just like you'll love your own baby when he or she gets here."

"I fucked up, Cap. I told him and when he looked at me like I was a twisted bitch, I just... closed my mouth, let him tear himself apart on the inside." A harsh huff leaves me. "I let him think it was yours."

"And he got his ass punched in the jaw for suggesting it."

I can't help it, a laugh bubbles out of me and I drop my forehead to Cap's chest.

Wait.

I pull away. "He knows?"

"He knows. Only one move to make now."

"Run?" I joke and this time Captain laughs, and damn if it doesn't feel good to hear it. "How is he not standing here right now?"

"You think he has any fuckin' clue what to say to you?"

My shoulders fall. "What the hell do we do, Cap?"

"Since when do you stop and think, Raven?"

My eyes move to his, narrowing. "If I fly off the fucking rocker, Cap, I'm busting balls the entire way down."

"Good thing we wear cups."

I push closer. "Tell me now if there is even the slightest concern over Zoey."

"No one will ever touch my daughter and anyone who threatens to..."

I nod, fire creeping into my soul.

Cap's forehead tightens as he gives me a hard look. "Donley called a meeting today."

"Why would he do that? They meet in two days."

"Someone told him I was shot and in the hospital. Coma."

"Well, you're not."

"But he doesn't know that."

I eye him. "*You* leaked this?"

"I had help."

"Help?"

He nods. "He's been fishing since you ran him off anyway. This way he thinks I'm still out of it, giving him the advantage."

"Advantage to what exactly?"

"We agreed to be Graven, you told him we got married. If I'm out of commission, who does that leave in lead of this town?"

"Me," I snap instantly.

Captain chuckles, shaking his head. "In your mind, yeah. We're talking Donley and the rest of the *men* on that council."

My brows pull in. "Him."

"Exactly."

"How much time do we have?"

Cap eyes me. "Couple hours."

I step away, taking a deep breath. "I'm gonna need a shower. And Chloe."

"Chloe," he deadpans.

I shrug my shoulders. "Can't be a queen in Kmart clothes."

Captain's smile is tender as he reaches out, placing his palms on my face. "You could be queen in trash bags and no one would dare question you."

A full shot of air fills my lungs for the first time in weeks and I stand tall, nodding.

"Thanks, Cap, but let's catch them all off guard in every way we can. Your dad said this place is the best of both worlds, grit and glamour. Let's give it to them. Question is, are we walking in as husband and wife?"

"We walk in as Brayshaw."

My smirk is instant. "Damn straight we do."

The squeak of the slider door draws our attention, and Victoria steps from the back of the Bray house, her bag slung over her shoulder.

She eyes us a moment before I wave her over, meeting her halfway.

She stares, and when I reach for the borrowed duffle, she rolls her eyes with a slight tip of her lips. "Last thing you need is to carry this beast."

"I'm not a fucking flower. I can carry a bag."

"You wanna know what I told him?" she suddenly offers, referring to hers and Maddoc's conversation.

"I told you I trust you. Get it through your head already."

She shakes her head, faux disappointment on her face. "Again, with that dirty little word."

I shove her and she laughs lightly. "Go, I'll be there by the time you're out of the shower." Her eyes fly over my shoulder to Captain.

I eye her, backing away. "All right."

I turn to Cap, who brings his eyes to mine.

"I'll call them, we'll be ready," he assures me.

"Cap..."

He'd walk away if he felt like it, but I can always make her leave, so he doesn't have to.

He shakes his head. "I'm good, girl. Go."

"Do you like her?"

His eyes cut to mine, narrowing.

"I mean, I know I'm your wife and all, but you can tell me," I joke.

With a chuckle, he gently nudges me away, so I go without another word.

I walk back the way I came, down the dirt road I used to stare at, wondering where it could possibly lead, and into the house I never imagined I'd be a part of, the home I haven't set foot in in weeks.

Rolland jumps from the barstool the second I enter, rushing for me. "Raven."

"We're ready to end this. Are you with us?"

He looks behind me, a frown pulling at his brows when the door doesn't open behind me.

"They'll be here. All of them."

He nods. "And I'll be with you, too."

"I need a shower."

He understands what I'm asking, I told him to take my room and make it Zoey's after all, so I'm not sure I have a right to walk up those stairs.

He holds a hand out, leading me the opposite way of the house, back behind the pool table and down the hall where the gym once sat, his office not far from it.

I enter, finding a brand-new bed, a California king with a large, dark grey headboard that almost meets the ceiling, plush pillows covered in royal purple lay atop of a stark white comforter. A matching grey dresser sits across from it, a rocking chair with cushions the same color perched beneath the window.

Something catches my eye on the nightstand beside it, so I head that way, finding a small double frame.

With shaky hands, I pick it up.

My sonogram cased behind the delicate glass, my mother's right beside it.

I bite into my cheek.

"I thought the purple would work well for you, too," he admits quietly, having noticed the color of the writing on my mother's image.

I set it back down, turning to meet his eyes.

He walks over to the closet, pulling it open. My clothes hang on one side, while the other holds nothing.

"This is mine? You did this for me?"

"This is your home, Raven, more so than anyone else's. This is where you will live, Graven be damned," he says, leaving no room for query. Strong, final.

My eyes move back to the closet, and Rolland steps into my view, blocking the emptiness.

He gives a slight smile. "I thought I'd leave this side open, just in case."

My jaw muscles tighten, and I glance around once more.

There's a flashlight on the nightstand, see-through purple curtains draped over the window, the sun shining through them perfectly. I slip my fingers through the sheer material, running them across the windowsill – it's lower than the one in the room upstairs. My fingers pause when they meet a groove in the wood and I step closer.

I need some R and R, is carved directly into the white paint.

My eyes pull in when I notice the grading at the edge of it, and I slip my knife from my pocket, flicking it open.

I run my fingers over the middle of the blade, then look to the window again.

My eyes snap to Rolland, who smiles meekly.

My mind takes me back to the night he gave it to me, and the careful words spoken.

"The words inscribed are true. You don't have to accept your life just because you were born into it. Family is a choice, Raven. Not a burden of birth. It's up to you to find the feeling and remember, never settle for less than what you want."

With a frown in place, I plant my feet directly in front of his.

Never settle.

He wanted me to fight back?

It's on the tip of my tongue to ask about that day in my trailer. To ask how he knows all these little things about me, about the knife, and the room, and the meaning of the words my mom carved here, but I don't.

For the first time he reads me right, that or I dropped the shield enough for him to see. He offers a tight nod. "You're welcome, Raven. It is the very least I could do."

With that, he walks away, and I stand there a moment, thankful for the first time, for the fucked-up path that led me right here.

WHEN I STEP FROM THE SHOWER, VICTORIA IS PERCHED AT THE head of my bed, glaring across the room. I step farther in, finding Chloe hanging dress after dress across some sort of changing contraption, something you see in the small Chinese restaurants in Stockton – a three-piece wood-like shield of sort that the owner's kids would hang out behind.

Chloe's eyes snap to mine, lighting up. She claps. "Okay, show me my canvas."

My hand pulls back and I look to Victoria who rolls her eyes, popping a grape in her mouth. "She wants you to strip down for her."

"You're lucky I took underwear and a bra in there with me." I toss the towel on the bed and she shrieks, rushing to pick it up.

She glares at me. "Do you have any idea how much a duvet like this costs?" She runs her pink painted nails across the bed.

"No, Chloe, I don't, and you're getting on my nerves already." I cross my arms.

She ignores that, instead saying, "Think of how much you spent on *all* of your punk-chic, J-lo from the 90s clothes, or whatever you consider them—"

"Ghetto," I offer with a grin. "You can say it."

"And add the price of a Ford Focus to that."

My wide eyes snap to Victoria's right as she meets mine, and she freezes, looking from her boots to the blanket, or *duvet* as Chloe called it.

Slowly, she kicks them off, making me laugh, while Chloe makes a show of hanging my towel on a small hook just inside the bathroom door.

She spins back with an exasperated sigh, but as her eyes travel over me, they slowly lose their confident, queen bee gleam, and her lips flatten.

Victoria clears her throat and looks away, while Chloe's stare snaps to mine.

"I'm sorry," she breathes, shaking her head.

"For what? You didn't cause any of this." I hold my arms out, letting my hands smack against my thighs when they fall.

"If anyone touched me like that, Daddy would strangle them with his bare hands, and it keeps happening to you. How are they still alive?"

"You think they should run around killing everyone who touches me?"

"People come here for a reason, Raven. They disappear for less."

"People also do stupid things for stupid reasons." I shrug, walking toward one of the dresses that catches my eye. I reach out, running my hands over the black rhinestone material trailing the bottom. "Most of them are driven by something else, rarely is it ever a solo thought people run on."

"And that permits harm without retaliation?" she quips.

"No." I shake my head, tugging the dress from its hanger, ignoring the gasp from Chloe when I do so. I fold it over my arms and turn to her. "But where there're questions to be asked, there're answers to be found."

Her brows lift, and she scrunches her lips. "I don't get it."

"Vienna wanted security, who offered it to her? Leo wanted to feel important in a world where he was nothing, who was going to give it to him? My mother wanted revenge, who hurt her so bad she felt she needed it? Collins was searching for his identity, who stole it from him? A girl was sold to a pedophile, by who?"

Chloe's temples crinkle as she lowers herself onto my bed.

"A rich, mean girl who took pleasure in making people feel worthless and small, changes her tune, why?"

Chloe's shoulders settle as a smile takes over her lips. She shakes her head, and it only widens, her perfect teeth gleaming at me. She glances to Victoria, who stares at me with reverent eyes, and Chloe's fly back to mine.

"Man." She looks me up and down, leaning forward. "I never stood a chance against you. This town won't know what hit them."

I unfold the dress, holding it up to get another look only for Chloe to reach out and take it from me.

She shakes her head, setting it aside. "There is no way any of these will do. They're not... you."

My brows jump.

"Give me a minute, I've got this."

So, I do, and just over an hour later, the three of us are meeting Rolland in the entryway.

His back greets us first. A sliver of white from his dress shirt peeking out of the navy-blue suit he's wearing, Maybell beside him.

Our footsteps aren't quiet, so his head turns, and a grin splits his mouth, and Maybell follows.

"Damn," Chloe whispers. "No wonder Daddy won't let me sit in on meetings yet. I'd be all over that."

"Shut up, Chloe," I snap quietly.

"I thought you were hoing it up with Mac?" Victoria throws back.

Chloe mews. "Yeah, but if I wasn't..." She trails off, rushing the last few steps to Rolland.

"Mr. Brayshaw, great to see you. Ms. Maybell, a pleasure."

"Ms. Carpo." Rolland nods. "Thank you for helping on short notice."

Maybell, though, she scoffs and looks to me, making me hide my grin.

She smiles, then steps aside.

"How do you feel, Raven?" he asks.

I nod, running my hand over the tips of my hair.

I cut a quick glance a Chloe. "Like myself."

"Also known as angry and unladylike." Chloe tilts her head. "But she went from hobo to hopeful so it's a win."

Victoria scoffs while Rolland gives a small chuckle.

"Right," he says, but quickly grows serious. "Are you ready for this?"

"Is it cliché if I say I was born ready?" I stand tall.

"I'd say it's quite fitting." He nods, a hint of a grin on his face. "Is there anything you want to go over beforehand? Anything I should know first?"

"What if I told you I was winging it?"

A chuckle flies from him and his eyes widen slightly. "Well then, I'd say I expected as much."

Suddenly, the door is thrown open, and Royce jerks to a stop.

"Hoo, hooo, baby *girl*!" Royce's head pulls back slightly, as he bites his lip. "Just... yes." He slaps his chest dramatically.

I roll my eyes, reaching for the handle but he swiftly steps in, slamming it behind him.

"I told you to stay outside!" Chloe snaps.

My glare flies to her, but Royce speaks before I can.

"Sorry, wannabe Raven, but I'll hang my dick to dry the day I listen to you, now back to the important stuff." Royce steps in front of me, eyeing me up and down before hitting my grey eyes with his deep brown ones. "You done, done it, RaeRae."

"Done what?"

"Morphed into the perfect Jill to my *Jack*."

"Oh my god," Victoria grumbles behind me.

I start busting up laughing, though, and Royce laughs with me. He's kidding, but maybe I'm the only one who gets it, and honestly, I like it like that.

He grins, stepping in to hug me, whispering, "I dig it, RaeRae. It's you."

"Son, if you don't go, they're all gonna come in and we'll never get out."

"Oh, I know." Royce steps back with a grin, smoothing his hands down the black dress shirt he's wearing. "But I'm the troublemaker, never listen to shit. Gotta keep up the rep." He shrugs, grins, and runs back out the door.

With a shake of her head and wide, confused eyes, Chloe reaches for the handle, but yelps when Royce shoves his head back in quickly.

"Might wanna wait like three minutes before you come out. These fuckers are slow to slide in." His eyes move to Chloe playfully. "I'm in quick but stay long, and I'm not just talkin' time, I'd say ask VicVee over there but she's being stingy."

"For fuck's sake," Victoria mumbles, burying her face in her hands.

"Wow." Chloe purses her lips.

Royce winks.

"Jesus."

The three of us look to Rolland who tries to hide his blush with a frown, making us laugh.

I slap my hand on his shoulder and his eyes slide to mine. "Get used to it. It literally only gets worse."

"And yet you're smiling as you say it." He tilts his head slightly.

I clear my throat and look to Royce who reaches out to squeeze my hand.

He's acting like himself today, smiling, teasing. It's a good thing.

"Why is everyone just laughing and joking and carrying on like normal?" Chloe asks. "Are you not walking into a pack of ruthless beings?"

"We are." I look to her. "But we have wolves." I grin at Royce, holding my hand out for Victoria.

She slaps her palm in mine, a smile pulling at her lips. "And a Raven."

Royce's eyes widen, snapping to Maybell.

Curiously, mine slide between them, catching the small wink she gives.

Royce sighs, giving a small nod, his eyes brightening before us all as he barely whispers, "And so, the Raven led her wolves..." His smile is slow. "It all makes sense now. There was no other ending after the way it started."

My confusion can't be missed, but Royce only offers a wink, slams the door and it's just the five of us.

"I so don't get this family and their riddles sometimes." Chloe shakes her head and tugs the door open.

Like fuel to the flame, Maddoc's stare burns into mine.

With the car door open, one foot already in, he freezes.

Tension radiates off him, hitting me like a shockwave.

Before either of us can move, Captain blocks him from my view. Royce meets his back, Mac a few feet back, while Bass leans against the bumper, taking it all in.

"What the hell are they doing?" Victoria asks, not quite yet on our wavelength, if she ever gets there.

Chloe sighs, smirking at the scene as if she knows. "Taming the beast."

"Nah, they know better than that."

I don't want him tame.

I like him wild.

I need him defiant.

I love him limitless.

Both their heads snap toward me, but I don't look away.

The shift in their stances, the change in their energy. The flick of the fire as it sets beneath their bones.

The hairs on the back of my neck stand up.

A slow grin splits my lips as I step farther out on the porch, a calm settling over me.

There they are.

My boys.

Chapter 38

MADDOC

CAPTAIN BLOCKS MY VIEW AS ROYCE SHIFTS BEHIND ME, AND MY brows snap together.

She's not fifteen feet away. It would take less than ten seconds to reach her.

They really think they could keep me from her if I went for it?

I've been forcing my feet still all afternoon. Never have I ever possessed so much restraint in my life, and I'm about to say fuck it, fuck them, fuck everyone until I get what I want straight from my baby's lips.

Slowly, I put my foot back on the ground, spinning to face my brothers, both who step closer, but the anger slowly washes from both their faces. Simultaneously, they look to the town car waiting for the girls and our dad, then back to me.

Tell me you feel it, brother.

"Not right," Royce voices first, scratching the back of his head.

"No," Cap adds with a slight nod. "Three legs are sturdy."

I eye him, standing taller. "But four's solid."

One step out of time and without even realizing it, our circle becomes a solid line.

All our eyes lock on her.

A slow grin splits her lips as she steps farther out on the porch, and her chest rises, creating a chain reaction across us.

There she is.

My baby.

With her head held as high as ever, Raven passes the town car moving right for us, and finally, I let my eyes leave hers.

I was with Chloe, waiting to talk to her dad, when she got the call from ours, and I was the farthest fucking thing from down with Raven's choice on the revamp.

She doesn't need to change how she looks, not for anyone, no matter the fucking reason, but looking at her now, my chest walls tighten. Never has she looked more like *my Raven*.

Angry and unwavering, sass and strength.

Her long black hair shines like silk, sleek straight and flat down her back. The white long-sleeved top fits her like a glove and runs all the way up, wrapping around her throat, a silver necklace hanging from around it. The black leather skirt comes up high, stopping just below her ribs and hides her shirt beneath it.

My eyes lock on the smoothness of the leather there, and I search for sight of her truth beneath it.

When she plants her left foot a space away from her right, my eyes drop to her shoes. Black boots, not unlike the ones she already owns, they cuff her at the ankles, the laces left untied, but they're new and give some added height.

I must have stepped forward because when my eyes lift, they're not far from her lips.

Full and soft as always, but colored red. A bright, vibrant red you could spot a mile away. When they part, my eyes snap to hers.

Dark, thick, black liner fans across her eyelids, making the gray shine almost silver.

The last thing I want to do right now is leave here. I need to talk to her, fight with her, something, but the fire in her eyes isn't gonna settle. It won't go away, and it shouldn't.

She wants to push. We'll be the driving force behind her.

She wants to lead. Where she goes, we'll follow.

She wants her reign. We'll make sure she gets it.

Always.

She blinks, bringing me back to focus.

Cap steps forward and her eyes do nothing more than shift to his, but damn if a knot doesn't form in my gut.

"It was stupid to think this could go any different," she says, shaking her head, her eyes sliding back to mine. "I don't *want* it to go any different. All bullshit aside, nothing makes sense when it's not the four of us."

Her eyes focus on his, mine, then Royce's, then move back to Cap.

Bass walks around the back right then, understanding her just as much as I knew he could. He dangles the keys over her shoulders, and her hand lifts, her fingers wrapping around the cool metal without looking.

She extends her arm, letting the keychain hang from her finger.

With a slow smirk, Cap opens his hand, allowing her to drop them in his palm.

His eyes meet Royce's who stands tall, a matching smirk in place.

Cap steps around the side and Royce slides in the passenger seat.

Raven's eyes hit mine and she steps closer, my pulse kicking harder with every move she makes, but she doesn't touch me like I need her to. She slips right past and into the SUV.

When she turns to me, there's a slight tip to her lips, but it's only my eyes and hers now, and hers are screaming so much more. Anger and apology, determination.

She sees it, my resolve slippin', and quickly shakes her head. "Soon, Big Man." Her words start soft but end strong. "Get in the car. Now."

I slide in beside her.

We don't wait to make sure the others are in and ready but get straight on the road. Royce blares some music, and everyone concentrates on their own thoughts, mine being Raven.

My eyes travel over her legs and thighs, moving up from there, pausing on her face. Her eyes are focused, laser-sharp and locked on the edge of the window. Her breathing is calm, body relaxed. She's in her fucking zone and nothing is getting in her way.

Since she got here, we've constantly tried to take charge, make the final decisions and demand to be let in on her next move before it was made.

Not today.

Today, we're her back up, her armor. Any move she makes, we'll match ten fucking fold. We underestimated her once and quickly learned how wrong the move was. Never again.

She's brave, bold. Beautiful. Fearless and capable. She's the fiercest fucking thing this town has ever seen, and *exactly* what it needed. What we needed.

What I need.

We're pulling up at the building too fucking quick and unease swims in my gut. The last thing I want to do is allow her to walk into fire, but Raven asks for no permission. All we can do is stand beside her, have her back.

She's out of the car before the engine is off and we fly out with her.

She spins, her eyes on the others pulling in right behind us.

Bass, Victoria, and our dad step out.

"I thought Mac was coming?" Raven asks, suspicious.

Victoria's eyes slide to Captain before moving back. "He'll be here, dropping off Chloe on the way."

Raven spins on her heels and without a word spoken, the security at the door, steps aside.

She walks straight through, leading us – me at her back, Cap and Royce beside me, our dad, Bishop, and Victoria behind us.

"Donley," she calls sweetly before our feet even hit the floor, and all heads jerk our way.

He starts to shoot to his feet, but calms himself, sitting back instead. "Raven." His eyes move to me at her back and narrow before shifting to Captain. "Captain, good to see you, son."

"I'm not your son."

His face grows taut. "I was informed you were injured, I came here to relay the message, let them know we still stood strong and that I was here if needed."

The men in this room are smart, and questioning eyes began to roam, but Raven doesn't give them time to decide what to ask.

"My name is Raven Brayshaw."

Eyes narrow, some lean closer in their seats, Royce and Cap stare unsure and Rolland's lips tighten. Everyone knows who she is, but curiosity keeps their mouths closed and eyes intent.

"Like Captain, my choice was taken from me."

Donley frowns, trying to gauge her. 'Course he's not smart enough to stay quiet.

"No one is questioning your status, Raven. We are aware, and I made sure all assets you were due have been signed over."

"They have," she agrees. "Financially."

Our dad's stance widens.

Donley's eyes narrow. "What does that mean, exactly?"

341

"It means you're sitting in a seat that doesn't belong to you."

"This seat," he counters. "As per our agreement, belongs to a Graven. *I* am Graven."

"And I'm not?" she shoots back instantly.

He balks. "Not until you give me that video you're not."

Cap and I share a subtle look.

"Tell me, Donley, did she scream?"

His eyes flash with what I interpret as understanding, his grip tightening on the red suede.

"What is this?" the head of the Greyson family asks lowly.

Raven ignores the guy, speaking directly to Donley again. "Get out of the chair, Graven."

"That chair belongs to the head of—"

"And I'm the head of two," she cuts Romero Hacienda off. "That's more than any of you can say."

They glare but don't argue.

Her eyes go back to Donley, but she speaks to the others. "Nineteen years ago, my mother was promised to Felix Graven, but they never made it to their wedding. Donley Graven—"

Suddenly, Donley, jolts from the seat, flying at her only to be caught behind the thigh by our dad.

Every person in the room is on their feet in seconds, watching as Donley falls to his knees.

It takes everything in me to stay planted where I am, but Raven doesn't so much as flinch through the entire thing.

"I see you haven't changed. Nineteen years later and you still think you're allowed to put your hands on a female?"

He attempts to get up, but when we all take a step closer, he thinks better of it.

"You have no idea what you're doing," he growls, his chin lifted. "There is still time for you to walk away. Give me the video I asked you for, let Captain sit, and we forget all about this."

"And give you a victory you've waited years for? I don't think so, and there is no fucking video." His eyes slim in anger, but he had to of figured as much. "So, you can threaten me all you want, Donley, but I have no soft spots for you to prey on."

"Sweet Brayshaw princess," he spits. "You *have* a weakness. *They* are your weakness."

She gets in his face, her teeth bared for all to see. Her eyes cut to mine briefly before she growls, "They don't make me weak, Graven. They make me unstoppable."

In one swift motion, she pulls her knife from her skirt, flips it open and holds it backward, under his neck.

"And I'm no princess," she leans in, whispering. "I'm a fucking queen of your own making, this is my kingdom, and you have no place in it. You wanna play medieval times, old man? I'm game. You disrespect the king, you get hung, but doing as little as putting your eyes on the queen without permission? Lose your hands, then your feet, right before you're beheaded for all to see. Or maybe we're talking the Romans. I could throw you in the ring, let you battle for your life against my strongest man. You tell me, Graven? What era we playin' tonight with arranged marriages and family debts owed?"

He pushes against her, so her left arm comes around to add power to the blade and a small drop of blood rolls down his Adam's apple.

"You know this is where she held the gun," she whispers suddenly, and my eyes fly to Cap then back. "Just like this." She tucks her hand up more, the blade disappearing under his chin. "Cocked it back, ready to take me to the grave with her. Wanna know what she said to me?" She doesn't let him speak. "She said 'he doesn't get to have you.'"

He tries to bait her, asking, "Where is your mother, Raven?"

Her jaw starts to shake, eyes narrowing. "My weakness," she whispers and his eyes damn near fucking sparkle.

She slides the knife against him, not even a centimeter, but his nostrils flare as the blade cuts a little more.

"You're a cunning piece of shit," she rasps. "You didn't need the blood from her, but you showed up on her doorstep anyway, didn't you? Shared the news, finally a Graven and a Brayshaw. You knew she'd come, and you bet on me. You knew I'd protect him at all costs. Risky move, Graven, but knowledge is dangerous, right? You needed to eliminate the last and final threat that could fuck you from what you believed you deserve."

"*Where* is your mother, Raven?" he repeats with a sneer. He knows he's a goner, nothing left to do but try to tear at her.

But he doesn't know Raven like he thinks he does.

"Same place she's been since the day you raped her." Donley's face turns red with anger. "In Hell. If only you could see past the meat between a man's legs, hm? Then we'd have been yours to mold. Bet we could have landed us a Brayshaw so easy, too," she taunts.

We?

My muscles constrict, and I flex my fingers at my side.

Donley frowns at her, causing Raven's smirk to grow.

She swiftly steps back, and my dad shifts closer to Donley.

Raven flips the blade in the air, catching the sharp metal in her palm and Royce takes a step forward, but my hand flies out and he halts his movement, glaring at me.

I frown, watching.

She glances behind her, half spinning and holds her arm out, her eyes flying to Victoria.

Victoria tenses, but the longer she stares into Raven's eyes, the more she eases. She steps forward, wrapping her hand around the silver handle, around the words of Brayshaw.

Raven gives a hard nod, and Victoria yanks it back, blood spilling from Raven's closed palm to the floor.

Captain's eyes fly to mine, tension lining his brow, but I give a small shake of my head.

Let her be.

Victoria looks from the blood to Raven, to Donley, and then steps closer. Without hesitation, Victoria palm seals around the bloody blade, and she yanks the handle back. Her hand falls to her side, Raven's bloody one slipping into it.

They step closer.

Raven pulls her hand from Victoria's, slapping it against Donley's face, and dragging it across his jaw. When the base of her palm meets his chin, she shoves his head back, forcing his ass to meet his feet.

Donley tries to swallow, but coughs, making a dark chuckle leave Raven.

She smiles wickedly. "Does our blood sicken you, *father*? Is it not thick enough, not dirty enough? Or maybe it's too dirty for the man who traded one daughter for information on the other?"

What. The. Fuck.

All three of our eyes fly across each other's, landing on our dad who frowns.

He had no clue.

I look to Raven and Victoria, both standing in front of Donley, both bleeding before him.

Sisters.

"I was never supposed to live, was I? You ordered an abortion, but my mom saw an opportunity. She'd taunt you every day and from *miles* away. She knew she'd be in the back of your mind, hiding in your darkest corner where your fear lies, just like you were in hers." She laughs again, but it cuts off sharply, her eyes flying to my dad.

"Mero Malcari, the man you gave your other daughter to,

rapcd me when I was twelve years old," she says monotone, her eyes sliding to Victoria. I can't see Victoria's face from here, but Raven's eyes tighten, and she looks away, swallowing whatever was on her tongue.

"My mother paid him, asked him to make sure what happened to her couldn't happen to me. I was the spawn of her very own devil, and Satan forbid, I'd ever carry my own."

Donley glares, his lip beginning to curl.

"She knew we'd get to this point, and she wanted me useless to you, to make sure you could never have a true, blood born, Graven *boy*, because *girls are of no use to you.* But guess what, *dear father*," she forces past clenched teeth. "She f—"

"Raven!" I boom, stepping forward and my brothers step with me.

Her mouth clamps shut, her eyes flying to mine.

No, baby.

The grey grows icy cold, her brows dropping so low her eyelids are hidden beneath them. Finally, she blinks, turning back to him.

"You're a piece of shit," she rasps. "And you're leaving here with nothing. If you'd rather die, let your eyes touch my boys and your wish will be granted without so much as a second's hesitation, I swear it. You're done, Donley, and so is your name."

Raven looks across the heads of the other families, all who stare at her, a little in awe, a little unsure and shocked, but one thing they show is respect.

Her eyes fly to Trick Rivera when he stands, walking toward her with Alec at his back. "Get him out of here," he says over his shoulder.

Both Alec and Bishop pull Donley to his feet, not letting up when he jerks in their holds.

He yells, argues back, but he's ignored, his voice cutting off completely once they've shoved him in the cellar room, closing the door behind him.

Trick nods his head and holds his arm out for Raven to take, but her head snaps toward me before she moves a muscle.

Fuck me if it doesn't settle my fucking soul.

I dip my chin, so she slips her hand through the bend of his elbow, letting him guide her to the fifth and final chair in the room.

Raven takes a deep breath, eyeing the seat with contempt.

"Mr. Hacienda," she calls, slowly facing the others.

My eyes meet my dad's a moment.

Romero Hacienda's eyes narrow and he sits forward in his seat.

"Do you represent your family or your town?"

He glares. "We are one in the same, do not question me."

She ignores him. "And the rest of you, you'd all say the same, yeah?"

They study her, but don't speak.

Raven's bloody hand trails over the empty seat, and she slowly steps around it. Standing behind, where the seconds in command stand.

She looks to Alec, back in his place at the end, behind Trick's chair, Trick who is still standing. She meets his eyes. "Do you trust Alec with your life?"

"My family's, my town's," he answers instantly.

"Would you give him your seat today?"

"Without thought."

She nods, looking to the others, all who nod in agreement.

Her eyes fly to Bass who jerks his chin moving to the security at the edge of the room.

They disappear down the hall.

Raven licks her lips, dropping her palms on the edge of the chair, and her eyes fly to mine.

Mine tighten, but hers never waver. They stay just as strong, just as clear and sure.

My feet carry me to her.

"Sit," she demands in a whisper.

My head starts to pull away, to look to my brothers, to Captain who gave it all for her, but her eyes slim.

Trust her.

Everyone looks when Bass returns with several guards, all carrying a chair if not two in their hands.

They place one between each of the others, laying a few extras near the edges, creating a large U-shape before returning to their posts.

Raven looks to the men behind their guides, to Alec, and once they get the approval of their leaders, they move, taking the seats laid out for them.

Her eyes find my brothers, softening. "Sit," she whispers.

Captain and Royce are slow in their steps, stopping right beside me.

Our minds work the same, our thoughts matching.

It's Captain who steps closer, reaching for her hand.

Steadily she gives it to him, allowing him to lead her around the front.

"We will," he whispers. "But not today. Sit."

Her lips press together to fight her smile.

She sits, leans back and crosses her legs. "You have one man you trust with your worlds; I have three. This chair belongs to Brayshaw." Her eyes meet my dad's a moment before moving back to the others. "And anyone we should trust to sit in it."

Raven looks to Victoria, who gives a small smile, but takes a step back, letting her know she's not ready should Raven believe she is. Our dad shifts to stand beside her.

"Rolland." The Greyson leader eyes him.

"I was once what was right for this town, but times have

changed. Should I even deserve a seat, I won't be taking it," he admits, his chest rising with his decision.

"So, it's settled." Hacienda claps, sitting back. "The council is full." He looks to Raven. "Welcome home, Mrs. Brayshaw," he says and my gut clenches.

"Yeah," Captain rasps, stepping forward again. His eyes move to mine, then Raven's. "About that."

Chapter 39

Raven

Captain's sheepish look has me holding my breath.

What the fuck else is—

My thought stops when Mac walks through the door, the reverend from mine and Captain's midnight wedding right behind them.

"James?" Rolland worries, stepping forward. "What happened?"

"Mr. Carpo?" someone says from behind me.

He holds his hands up, a sympathetic smile pointed at me.

Carpo.

"Are you fucking kidding me?" I push to my feet.

"This isn't a place to bring your town problems," Mr. Henshaw says.

"Their arrival holds purpose," Captain tells them, but his tension-filled eyes hold mine. "Raven."

I look back to *James*, allowing myself to be a judgmental bitch as I take in the tattoos that cover his arms – the ones his

351

black fucking robe covered the night I met him – and the slight ruffle at his belt and boot, a tell-tale sign of his weapons.

I scoff, looking to Captain.

Captain's shoulders sag, his eyes sloped around the edges.

"Your *just in case?*"

He nods, giving a half smile.

"What's goin' on?" Royce asks, glancing around.

"She's mine." Maddoc glares. "He made sure she stayed that way."

"So, you're *not* married?" Royce's eyes widen.

"No, man," Cap clears it up. "We're not."

My chest tightens, and I lick my lips. "You're Chloe's dad?" I look to James.

"I am." He answers as if he was waiting for this moment, almost as if he needs it.

"So, you're head of Brayshaw security?"

"Yes."

"And you lied." I frown, shaking my head. "Straight to the face of one?"

"I did," he admits with zero hesitation but complete sadness. "Which is why I will be leaving my position."

Captain and Rolland both jolt forward. "James, no."

But he holds his hands up again, focused on me.

"Serving Brayshaw has been a true honor, and the things they have done for my family will never be forgotten, but the Bray in me is telling me it's time I become a member of our community rather than the monitor of it."

I flex the muscles of my jaw, glancing to Rolland briefly.

"This is my doing," Captain interrupts. "You were helping us. You helped *protect* the granddaughter of the man who first brought your family in."

James shakes his head. "The very moment I even paused to hear you out, Captain, I knew it was my time to step back." He turns to me. "At the same time, I also knew I had to do it, for you, and in the name of Brayshaw. You deserved more than what you were getting, you deserved to love freely, something they stole from your mother, and I had to do all I could to try and help.

"However, loyalty is loyalty, and trust ..."

"Must be earned."

He nods. "We met on a lie, Ms. Brayshaw. In my line of work, there is no coming back from that, and I cannot be what is needed without it."

I bite into my cheek, staring at the stranger in front of me. I don't know why, but want to tell him we could try, to ask him to stay and remind him of all the trust he does have here, but the resolve in his eyes begs me not to say a word. This is hard for him, but he's confident in his decision.

I nod, and he grins, reaching out his hand as if to ask for mine.

I allow it.

"Thank you for accepting." he says, a deep breath leaving him.

"James," Rolland starts. "You're sure?"

He reaches out, gripping Rolland's shoulder. "When I took over for my father, he told me one decision is all it took for him to know it was time to pass it over. It's time, Rolland."

"Your dad was head security?" I ask.

"He was."

"And it went to you?"

James inhales deeply. "It did."

"Chloe won't be gaining your position."

A chuckle leaves him, and his eyes widen. "Trust me, I know. Maybe, in time, you'll come to believe in her," he says, hopefully. "She's got a lot of work to do before then."

Rolland motions for the door. "We should step out, they have more to discuss before they can leave."

The three of them walk out, leaving the five of us in here.

"Raven," Greyson says slowly. "I understand a lot has happened here, and I am truly sorry for everything Donley put you and your family, your people through, however..." He trails off.

I square my shoulders, shifting to face him better. "I don't need lead up. Say what needs to be said."

The man nods. "A new lead does not overpower an old debt. A contract was drawn, a deal made and accepted from two families. We don't have a lot of rules, but the few we do come with no exceptions."

"Are you not hearing me?" My head pulls back. "Did you miss everything that happened between that asshole and me? He *raped* Ravina Brayshaw, the woman he was bringing into his family, and I'm the product of that – a Graven and a Brayshaw. Am I not them getting what was promised?" I shout.

"I realize the situation is complicated and I acknowledge what he did was sickening. He *will* be dealt with; I can promise you this. Everything he has will be turned over to you, as you demanded – being the heir to the Graven estate and its assets allows that."

"I give a fuck about his money!"

"I understand that, but the fact remains." He sits back, looking across the others for back up.

I look to Trick who flattens his lips.

Fuck.

"Aside from everything, Raven," he whispers. "What he's saying is true. Your mother ran. Was she hurt? Yes. Would I stop my daughter if the same happened? Never. Did they gain you, yes, but—"

"But the Gravens never got their wife."

He nods.

My eyes meet Captain's.

Zoey.

He winks, his gaze flying over my shoulder and holding.

The shuffle of Victoria's shoes has me spinning around, staring as she pulls a small grip of rolled white papers from the inner pocket of the leather jacket she borrowed. She steps up, handing it over to me.

"What are you doing?"

"You asked me to help you, this is me helping you."

"I asked you to stand with me."

"You don't even know what it is."

"So, tell me."

"It's the contract."

I frown, snatching it from her extended hand only to toss it to the floor.

"You kinda need to read that."

"I kinda wanna knock you out."

She chuckles, but quickly cuts it off, clears her throat and stands tall. Her brown eyes move between mine. "The contract is real, solid. There's no getting out of it. Every single loophole if one would ever work in this situation was tied up. The Gravens *are owed* a Brayshaw."

My nostrils flare, pressure forming between my eyes. "And you just had to restate the obvious?"

She steps closer. "Raven." Her brows lift slowly. "They're owed a *Brayshaw,*" she stresses.

My fingers fly to my temples as I attempt to make sense of it all.

Cap's hand on my arm has me glancing over my shoulder. "There's nothing in there about taking the Graven name," he whispers. "Nor does it say a damn word about a female."

Trick walks over, grabbing the papers from the floor. His eyes skim the highlighted area and he passes it down the row.

"A Brayshaw," I whisper, and it hits.

My hand flies to my ribs with a gasp, and I whip around, and our eyes crash into one another's.

He steps toward me, but I step back.

"I've taken over Graven and the Brayshaw lead was passed to me." I look to the men, needing complete assurance. "Two families had to agree, but I'm both. I get the final say. I get to offer *and* take what I want."

"Sounds fair to me," Alec speaks for the first time and all eyes fly to his.

Slowly, the other members nod in agreement.

"If a Brayshaw weds a Graven, legitimately this time, the contract will be considered fulfilled."

My eyes snap to Maddoc. "I'm gonna need you to marry me, Big Man."

His jaw flexes. "For them?"

My eyes soften, and I step toward him, tilting my head back to look at him better. "I don't give a damn about a contract or making people happy, but I want to be everything my name says I should be, and I want my family safe at all cost," I say, and his eyes harden. "But at the end of the day, if there's only one thing I can pull off, then I want it to be keeping you."

His eyes narrow with his heavy inhale.

"So, what do you say, Big Man? You game?"

Chapter 40

RAVEN

I SHIFT, LOOKING INTO THE MIRROR AS I GRIP THE NECKLACE the boys gave me last night – the bullet that hit Captain, melted down, reshaped and engraved.

A basketball, our names serving as the threads that create the shape.

The line across the center – Brayshaw. Mine and Maddoc's on the strip across the center. Captain's is the curved on the left, Royce's on the right.

Four tethers, laced together, just like Maddoc's tattoo. A representation of us all.

My family.

I look to my eyes, half smiling at the girl who stares back. A girl I never really thought I could like, and for the first time ever, I see *me*. Who I am on the inside. Who I want to be.

I see a Brayshaw.

And I'm about to marry one for real.

357

I inhale deeply, my hand coming down to cover my stomach as I spin around. "I think I'm gonna be sick."

"It's called you're pregnant. If you don't like it, use condoms after this one."

Both mine and Victoria's glare flies to Chloe, her head popping up to meet my stare at the same time.

"Sorry," she forces out slowly. "It's too natural to—"

"Be a bitch?" Victoria supplies.

Chloe crosses her arms, her head tugging back. "Better than being fake."

"Are you calling me fake?" Victoria jumps to her feet.

"Seems fitting."

"Why are you even here?" Victoria snaps back. "You weren't invited."

"What, worried Raven might start to like me, gain a new friend and leave you behind?"

"Bitch—"

"Okay!" I shout, turning to Chloe with a glare. "Will you just... go outside with the boys or something?"

Chloe throws her hands up, tossing the hairbrush to the couch as she exits the room.

I wait until the door slams closed behind her to drop onto the sofa. "Why did we have to do this? Why not the same shit me and Cap did – small ass room with nobody around but the two of us – only with a real reverend, or minister or what the fuck ever you call them."

"Everything you just said is exactly why you have to do this." Victoria looks at me like I'm crazy.

I glare at her.

"Dude, you married his brother."

"Obviously not, asshole," I snap, dropping my head back on the cushion as panic stirs in my gut. "I can't do this."

"You want out?"

"Fuckin' funny, Vee," I rasp.

"Look." Victoria scoots to the edge of the couch. "The only people here are the people you care about – and Chloe." She glares making me laugh.

"I don't really care about Mac either," I try and joke.

"Well, other than them." She chuckles. "Who I'm *pretty sure* invited themselves so they could party with us tonight. It's us, the boys, and that's it. Maddoc is already making this easy. No dresses, no suits, just us. Chill the fuck out and look out the window at the guy you almost lost. All you're doing today is making sure you never do. That's it."

"We're eighteen-year-olds who will have to go to summer school just to graduate now, and we're having a fucking kid and getting married? Vee, I haven't even got to talk to him yet. I thought I was married to his brother less than a day ago, now here we are."

She eyes me, shaking her head. "Does any of that matter?"

"Shouldn't it?"

"No. You said yourself, you don't care about the word. It means nothing to you, but *he* means *everything* to you. This whole husband and wife thing that might be for the sake of some stupid contract today, but in the morning, when you wake up beside him it could mean something more." She jumps to her feet, holding a hand out, so I slap mine into it. She yanks me up, our eyes meeting. "Tonight, he'll officially be yours, Raven."

"He already is," I say, squeezing my eyes closed.

"So, what's the issue? Why are we standing here when we could be making s'mores by the fire already?"

I scoff and shove her away with a smirk. "You're trippin' if you think you'll be seeing me tonight, Vee." I take the stairs down two at a time, turning to look up at her smiling from the top. "Straight trippin'."

She jogs down, following me into the room. "Should I tease

you for wearing a dress even though he said you didn't have to?"

"If you wanna get punched, go for it."

She laughs, nudging me out the door.

Maddoc

"Fuck's she taking so long for?" Royce looks at his watch then back at me.

I frown. "You good, man?"

"Are you?" His eyes widen as his brows lift. "I mean, fuck, bro. You're about to get married and your punk ass is standing there all fuckin' calm and shit."

Cap chuckles beside him and the corner of my mouth lifts.

"Why you laughin'?" Royce shoves at Cap playfully. "Now you can't run around here pretending you don't have a Victoria-sized stick up your ass."

Cap's eyes narrow, but when I lift a brow at him, his features smooth and he pops a shoulder. I don't miss the subtle tip of his lips either.

"Man, we look too good to be standing in the woods right now." Royce runs a hand down his suit jacket. Grinning at himself.

"Won't she be pissed when she sees you guys in suits when you told her she could wear her jeans?" Mac teases. "Every girl I know would flip if she showed up anywhere underdressed."

The three of us grin, and Mac looks at us confused.

Royce grips his shoulders, shaking him lightly. "That's right, my man. Any other girl would flip. Raven ain't any other girl. She speaks Brayshaw." Royce looks to me. "She speaks Maddoc." He grins lightly. "She knows what he really wants."

Chloe only shakes her head, pouting in the seat she took when she came storming from the cabin.

The reverend makes his way toward us, so Cap slips the flask we were passing around in his inside jacket pocket.

"Gentlemen." He nods his head with a smile. "Are we ready?"

"Is she?" Royce asks, making us laugh.

The man turns to him. "She is son." He looks between Captain and Royce. "And she's asking for you both."

My brows snap together and look up the small incline, finding Victoria making her way down, her eyes on the ground.

I take a half a step forward only for the official to slide in front of me with his hands up.

"Please." He smiles. "Stay."

The boys jog up the hill without a word, both their eyes on Victoria as they pass her, but she doesn't look up until she's almost to me.

She nods, the corner of her mouth lifted as her eyes scan over me. "She was right." She looks to me. "Nice suit."

"Nice outfit."

She shrugs, and steps to the side. "Not supposed to be the one in white, but it's what the queen ordered, literally," she jokes, running her hands over the satin top while she glares at the white skinny jeans. "How you guys got all this shit here overnight, I'll never understand."

"Get used to it."

Her eyes find mine.

"It wasn't only our lives that changed yesterday. Yours did too."

She licks her lips, looking away in thought.

A moment later, Royce steps around the corner.

He points at me, slips his shades on, then gives me his back. Cap steps around next, pausing right beside him.

Royce holds a hand out.

It's her fingers I see first, slipping into my brother's. Then her wrist, but Cap slips to the left, blocking the rest of her.

I tilt my head, my eyes narrowing but it doesn't help.

Right when I'm about to push forward, go get her my damn self, Cap moves aside, and there she fucking is.

My girl.

Black leather jacket unzipped, laying over a lacy, white dress that allows her skin tone to peep through, and cuts off at the knee. It's tight, shaped to her hips and fucking perfect for her. Simple, easy, but damn if she doesn't bring it to life.

Her hair is curled and down, laying all around her, a deep part in the center, and she's got those red lips again, her black boots covering her feet.

Fucking perfect.

I force my eyes left, scanning across the three.

A solid, tight line. My brothers both hold a hand of hers, leading her right where she belongs.

Right to me.

My baby, or more, my *babies.*

We're having a fucking baby.

If someone had asked me months ago if I wanted a kid, I'd have laughed in their face. My answer would have been a thoughtless, easy, never.

But now, knowing Raven has a part of me inside her, that the two of us will be linked on a deeper level, a level no one else will ever reach, no matter how hard they might try, I'm desperate for it.

Desperate for our little one.

And I'll kill anyone who dares to threaten our future.

Our family.

My body grows warm, a calm spreading through me I haven't felt in weeks, a purpose I've never known crawling up my muscles and settling into my bones.

My feet carry me to them, and the closer I get, the higher the corner of her lips rise.

I stop right in front of her, my hands landing on her hips, and I lower my forehead to hers.

Slowly, my brothers release her hands, patting my back as they walk by and Raven's palms slide up my chest, fisting my jacket at the collar.

Her choppy breaths fan across my lips and I fight the urge to drop mine to hers.

Not yet.

"I don't think this is how it's supposed to go," she whispers. "I'm pretty sure I was supposed to walk to you."

"Yeah, well, we don't do things the right way, baby. We do it our way." My hands move up her ribs, under her jacket and squeeze. "And our way is how I like it."

She nods against me. "Me, too."

"You ready, baby?" I whisper. "Ready to belong to me?"

She pulls back, looking up at me. "Come on, Big Man," she murmurs. "You know better than that." She lets me go, stepping back and around me, so I slowly spin to keep facing her.

She walks backward, toward my brothers, toward her sister, and the reverend.

She smiles, holding her hands out, speaking for all of us to hear. "I've always belonged to you. Let's make it official."

I lick my lips, clenching my teeth together to keep myself in check when moisture threatens to surface in my eyes.

It's been a helluva year, I'm ready for a helluva future.

I follow, stepping right beside her, pulling her into me as the reverend begins to speak, but I don't catch a damn word.

I hear nothing but the pounding of my heart against hers.

Proving further we're one in the same, Raven's fingers plant themselves directly over my left pec, and she closes her eyes.

I hold her tighter.

Mine. Forever mine.

Chapter 41

RAVEN

"Kinda morbid, isn't it?"

I look to Collins. "What?"

"You got married ten feet from here less than two hours ago, and here we are pouring our mothers' ashes in a creek."

I glance from the fancy marble ern in his hand to the wooden box the morgue gave me that holds my mother's remains. I open it, unseal the plastic bag on the inside and dump it all out in one shot. "Yeah, I guess it is."

I sigh, staring at the small bubbles in the water as the steady flow creeps over the small rocks beneath the bridge.

Rolland told me she liked it here, that they would sit out on the balcony of the Bray cabin and listen to the water run.

There's no comfort in the words he gives and bringing what was left of her here, pouring them into the water, it means little to me. I can't forget eighteen years of what she was, but I could at least leave her in a place that wasn't tainted. I can't say if she deserves it, but I know all about getting things you don't deserve.

"I've gotta admit." I cut my eyes to him. "Out of all the

365

things that surprised the hell out of me the last few months, this right here takes the cake."

Collins gives a light laugh, looking out at the water as he slowly pours his mother's ashes out.

"I tried to get her to live," I admit after a minute. "Your mom wouldn't hear me."

He nods. "Yeah, she uh... she wasn't really alive as it was." He looks off. "I lost her to depression a long time ago. She had to be a cold statue around Donley so much, I think she forgot who she even was. Me following his orders later didn't exactly help her heal either."

"We're orphans."

"Can you be an orphan if you're over eighteen?"

I shrug.

After a minute, he pushes off the railing and faces the opposite end of the creek.

"It's a little pathetic to admit, but I feel free for the first time, I get to make my own choices for once."

"What do you even want, Collins?"

He hesitates a minute before nodding and meeting my eyes. "To leave this place, start over somewhere new."

"You can't run from who you are, I learned that the hard way."

"But who am I, Raven?" he asks, hopelessness in his tone that has me looking away.

"Where will you go?"

"Anywhere," he admits. He sticks his hands in his pockets, holding up a pair of keys. "To the cabin and the house."

"You might come back."

He shakes his head. "I won't, and besides that, they're yours. Not mine. So is the money in my trust fund."

"No." I shake my head. "Your parents went through a lot, and all they got for it was you and money. It's yours, Collins. You'll take it."

He stares at me a minute before a slow smirk finds his lips. "Man." He smiles. "Raven Carver, an honest to God, unicorn."

A light laugh leaves me, and I head back for the cabins, but he doesn't budge.

I meet his eyes once more.

"I'm going to say goodbye, quietly, and then I'm going to leave just as quiet."

I nod.

"Good luck, Raven," he says earnestly. "And thank you. You didn't have to save her corpse or tell me what happened or anything you've done along the way. You really didn't have to allow me to come here today for this."

"Last thing I wanted was to see you on my wedding day," I say teasingly, even though we both know it's true. "But I wanted it done."

He nods, understanding. I think he wanted it finished too.

"I hope this place brings you everything you need," he tells me.

My eyes slide to the balcony behind us and the man standing at the foot of it, watching. "It already has."

Maddoc's eyes keep mine as he makes his way down the stairs, so I wait right here, allowing him to come to me like he wants.

He steps against me, his eyes full of so many things, none that have to be said out loud, at least not yet.

Maddoc looks over my shoulders. "You helped Captain leak the information to Donley about him being shot. That leads to the meeting being called and all of us standing here after."

"It was the least I could do," Collins responds.

"You didn't have to do anything. The Graven I knew you to be wouldn't have considered helping us in any way."

I grin against Maddoc's chest. That's the closest to a thank you he'll ever give Collins.

Good job, Big Man.

"For what it's worth, I'm sorry for all the shit I did. I'm leaving, you won't hear a sound from me ever again."

Maddoc's muscles tense a moment, and then he says, "It's not worth shit, but knowing you'll be far away from her helps."

A light laugh leaves Collins, and I look up to Maddoc right as his eyes come down to me.

Without another word spoken, Maddoc leads me up the small hill, and toward the front of the cabin.

His arms wrap around me and he buries his head in my neck, breathing me in, his deep exhale the most calming thing I've ever felt.

The creak of the old wooden deck has him slowly pulling away, and spinning to stand at my back, his arms still locked around me, palms flat against my stomach.

Cap, Royce, and Victoria step from the cabin, while Mac, Chloe, and Bass walk up from where they just set up some chairs for our fire tomorrow morning – they don't get us tonight.

"You were stressin' out," Victoria teases.

"Fuck off." I flip her off, not letting my smile free. "But for real though, how do normal people not jump off cliffs on a daily basis?"

Everyone chuckles.

"It's called nerves, Raven," Chloe says. "And *normal people* have been getting them since they learned to walk, so we're well versed in how to handle them."

"Please." Victoria rolls her eyes. "Everyone knows you pop a Xanax before all your routines."

"Excuse me, but I—"

"I think we're ready to turn in," Mac interrupts the two, stepping forward to give everyone one of their bro shakes.

He smiles when he gets to us. "Congrats, guys. Thanks for lettin' me be here."

"Yeah, man," Maddoc says. "Thanks for giving us your cabin for the night."

"Of course." Mac grins. "We've got Chloe's."

Chloe winks and the two walk off, climbing into Mac's Jeep.

"I'm going in too, I need to get off my fucking feet, call Zoey before she goes to bed," Cap announces before he steps forward with a soft smile.

I nod and am about to move forward to hug him, but Maddoc's grip on me tightens, so I stay planted.

He steps to me, kisses my temple then clamps a hand on his brother's shoulder before walking to the door, but he only stands there with the handle in his grip, eyes on Victoria.

"What?" she asks.

His eyes narrow, but I'm not sure it's enough for her to notice. "You planning on coming in, or you waiting for an invite to the party?"

She looks around, confused. "What party?"

Royce chuckles, glancing to Mac who nods to him and turns back to us with a grin. "Sorry, VicVee. This is a party for three. I'm going to play with the wannabe princess and her *Mac* daddy." He waggles his brows, slaps Maddoc's back and rushes off.

We stare as he lifts a wide-eyed Chloe from the passenger seat, slides in then spins her, placing her on his lap in a straddling position.

Her head snaps to Mac, obviously unaware of the third-party member, but when Mac leans over, kissing her as he revs the engine, she settles in.

"Wow," Victoria deadpans.

"Yeah," I sigh with a grin. "No shame."

Madduc's silent chuckle shakes against my back and Vee sighs.

"I... guess I better go in before he locks me out," she mumbles where Cap can't hear.

"I bolted all the bedroom doors, so you have to either sleep in Cap's bed or on the couch."

Cap shakes his head while Victoria's glare flies to mine.

"I'm kidding." I laugh. "Last room on the right is for you. You have your own bathroom and everything, so you don't even have to come out until morning if you don't want."

She nods, walking for the door and slipping past Captain, leaving me and Maddoc alone.

He inhales deeply, dropping his cheek to mine. "You're in so much trouble," he rasps. "So much trouble, but it's gonna have to wait, because it's been too long since I had you. So, baby, turn around and jump on me. Let me take you to bed."

I spin in his arms, my eyes flying to his, my breath hitching at the desire in his.

We haven't touched more than we did five seconds ago in weeks, and when the reverend said you may kiss the bride, he turned me around, blocked me from view and barely grazed his breath across my mouth, so technically, we haven't even sealed our marriage yet.

He's holding it in, waiting to get me alone so he can take.

The thing about Big Man, about *my* man, though, is he takes just as much as he gives, and it just so happens I want it all.

I jump, wrapping my legs around him with ease.

His hands come down, sliding under my ass cheeks and he starts walking forward.

Not once does he take his eyes off mine, walking me blindly to the cabin a few spaces over and through the door, but he doesn't even attempt a bedroom.

He spins so fast, leaving the door hanging wide open and plants my back against the wall.

His hips cage me in, so his hands are free, and both trail slowly up my ribs and chest, until his thumbs meet my lips.

He glares at my mouth, angry lines forming between his brows, and his body moves closer, no space for air left between us. His head lowers and tilts, but when he's a hair's space away, his eyes flash to mine.

"You're mine."

"Yeah, Big Man. I am."

"Show me."

I don't hesitate.

I drop my lips to his, and he pushes back just as hard, just as punishing.

His hands slide up my thighs, taking my dress with them, until he can slide his fingers under the strap of my thong. He grips my ass tight, grinding me against him.

My hands fist his hair and I tug. Suddenly my back is off the wall and we're moving.

In the next second, I'm dropped on to the fresh sheets he had put on the bed.

He doesn't wait, climbing between my legs in the same second.

His tie brushes against my throat, so I yank.

He growls but does as he's directed and gives his mouth to me.

Blindly, I tug at his clothes as he does mine, and somehow, I'm completely naked while I've only managed to kick his shoes off him and remove his jacket.

I shove on his chest, and with a growl he listens, standing before me.

I move to the edge of the bed, standing on the foot of the mattress so he has to look up at me.

His hands wrap around my ass, pinching as he follows my mouth, catching my bottom lip between his teeth.

His eyes are heated, open and barred with mine.

He runs his tongue across my lips as I work open the button of his shirt, my eyes move to his when I uncover the gold chain hanging from his neck, his key dangling from it.

I lift it, reading the inscription on the cooled metal.

Family runs deeper than blood.

"Your Brayshaw item." My eyes move to his. "You've never worn it like this. Why now?"

"I didn't understand it before, now I do." His hand comes up to cover mine. "This is my key to this world, to you, to our future." His grip tightens in promise. "Never again will a door stand in my way when you're on the other side of it."

"The key to the kingdom," I whisper.

"To our kingdom."

My body warms, and I nod, let go of the necklace and slip my fingers under the collar of his dress shirt. I slowly trail my hands across his skin, forcing the expensive material from his body.

My body. He's mine.

He holds my eyes hostage as I undo his belt next, and his slacks fall to his knees. He gives a little shake, helping them down and his boxers fall.

He slaps the back of my thighs, so I jump, wrapping my legs around his torso, and slowly, he lets my body slide down, until his dick is settled against my ass cheeks, pushing. Ready.

I pull my hips back and it slides up, right where I want it. My hold on his neck tightens, and I use that to lift, aligning him with my opening and he pushes in.

His eyes shift between mine, not missing a second as he fills me.

He drops to his knees, so my ass is on the edge of the bed, his dick inside me, and he uses his hold on my hips to roll me how he wants it, he's moving back and forth in slow, full motions.

After a moment though, his hand slides up my back until he's fisting my hair.

He tugs, tipping my head back and dropping his to my chest.

He kisses my breastbone and picks up speed.

My ankles lock behind his back and he groans, pushing off the floor and sliding me across the mattress so he can settle on top of me better.

He rolls his hips, pulling my nipple between his teeth.

"Mmm," a deep moan leaves me, and his mouth comes back to mine. Biting, nipping, sucking.

His elbows plant beside my head, and I feel him, twitching, growing impossibly harder, reaching impossibly deeper.

My body starts to shake, so he shifts us so he's sitting beneath me. He grips my shoulders, pushing me down, and I welcome every last bit of him.

His body shudders beneath me, taking my cum with it.

I clench around him as he twitches inside me.

We finish together, eyes open and locked on one another's.

We sit like that for a few minutes, catching our breaths, soaking up the skin to skin contact we've been desperate for.

He's slow to fall to his back, the pillows at the head of the bed allowing him to reach up and brush the hair that's fallen in my eyes behind me. His fingers run along my shoulders, causing a shiver to spread through me.

His smile is so soft, his eyes unblinking as his knuckles slide down my arm until he reaches my hand, my ring.

The ring the doctor gave me that day in the hospital, the one he pulled from Captain's pocket after surgery.

Turned out Maddoc bought it for me, but the day he found out we were married, he left it sitting on Cap's dash. Captain saved it for him, for us.

He knew.

He pulls the ring to his lips, kissing the tip of the crown, then the two diamonds beside it – a representation of us all.

"My queen," he whispers.

My heart hammers in my chest and my lips part.

I lock my finger around his and with shaky hands, move them to my stomach, flattening it against my skin. "Our prince."

His temples pinch and ever so slowly his eyes move to connect.

He stares for a long moment, then slowly places his left hand beside his right.

It's just a guess, but after everything, it feels right. A boy – both Graven and Brayshaw blood.

Maddoc gives a small nod, the corner of his mouth lifting as his fingers span out. "Our prince," he says, and his eyes come back to mine. "This is for real? Me and you, we did this?"

A small chuckle escapes me, and I nod, but it quickly turns into me shaking my head. "I don't know how to do this, Big Man. At all."

"Me either, baby," he admits, pushing into a sitting position so we're chest to chest, my legs now wrapped around his back. "But we're not alone. Cap will help us, Royce and Maybell, too. My dad maybe, if we let him. Either way, baby, we'll be good. We'll figure it out, together, 'cause it's me and you, baby."

He kisses me softly, but it quickly turns hungry and he tears away, dropping onto his back. He folds his hands behind his head, his eyes taunting and my favorite smirk in place. "Now." He licks his full lips. "Show me how good you can be."

I lean forward, biting into his bottom lip, allowing my teeth to scrape across the soft flesh until it tears free. "With pleasure, *husband.*"

Epilogue

MADDOC

We never made it down to the fire the morning after we got married at the Brayshaw cabin. We stayed there for the rest of the weekend, and then when Monday came and it was time to go back to school, we weren't ready.

We needed time, so time we took.

Captain headed straight home to see Zoey, and Royce went with him, but he called us a couple days later to let us know him and Mac were taking a drive up the coast and he'd be back soon. We knew it meant he was up to no good, but he deserved some fuck off time, so we left it alone. For now.

Me and Raven ended up in Stockton, in her old trailer park. After a day of going through the place, she decided there was nothing worth saving. One call to our contractor and eight hours later, Raven watched the only home she ever knew get dragged off the grounds.

She didn't bat a lash.

A few hours after that, she had a new modular home

brought in to take its spot, and then she signed it and the lot over to a woman she introduced me to at the nearby foodbank. The woman promised it would serve families in need, and Raven chose to believe her, and then she filled their shelves with a promise to keep it coming.

We sat back and watched as light poles were installed in the trailer park, then tested out the swings of the new jungle gym she picked out, the kids from the park right there with us.

After that, I took her to the beach.

She'd never been, and the weather was getting warmer so getting her to leave was hard, but we missed Royce and Captain, I know she's ready to see Victoria, too.

Splitting up like this wasn't something we liked to do, and the only reason we all agreed was because we promised to keep our tradition going. So, every night the four of us were apart, no matter where we were, we all took an hour to sit on Skype, had dinner together. It helped, but we're ready to be home, and they're tired of us being away.

On top of all of that, our town is ready for us.

Donley is gone, handled by the council members – I'll find out what that means for sure at the next meeting – and everyone is waiting for the new town leaders to take their place.

Raven sits up in her seat, letting go of my hand as we roll to a stop in front of the Brayshaw mansion.

Her face smooths out, her eyes shooting wide. "The flowers," she whispers.

"What?"

"Did he tell you?" she asks.

My brows snap together. "Tell me what, baby?"

She pushes open her door, stepping out of the SUV. Slowly she walks toward them, and then her eyes cut to the right, forcing mine to follow.

A playset.

"She's here," Raven whispers, a broken laugh leaving her.

Her eyes fly to mine, but then suddenly the door is thrown open and Royce runs out. With no warning, he lifts her, spinning her around and she laughs, hugging him back.

"Yo," I shout with a smile, walking toward them. "Easy on the merchandise."

Royce steps back, his eyes going wide when they fall to her tiny belly. It's hardly a bump, more a little pudge but on her frame, it's a noticeable change.

"You were only gone for a month."

"Apparently you start to grow the fourth month. Maddoc will have to carry me into summer school by the time the year is over."

Royce laughs then steps to me for a hug.

"Any chance you're gonna tell us why you took a quick trip out of town?"

"Told you. I got a heart to break, gotta get even. Had to set some things in motion." He grins, waggling his eyebrows. "Besides, I was only gone for a week. How much damage could I have possibly done?"

I smirk, shaking my head as he quickly moves back to the door. "Right."

Royce smiles wide. "Come on."

With tight eyes, we follow behind him.

Raven grows more and more apprehensive with each step taken, and my muscles begin to constrict.

When we reach the top of the stairs, she jolts to a complete stop.

But then Cap steps from the room across from his, his face lighting up. His eyes are clear, his body relaxed. There's a weightlessness to him I've never witnessed and it all clicks.

He comes to me first, and I nod, giving him a hug before moving aside.

He turns to Raven.

"Cap..."

He smiles, grabs her hand and nods his head, dragging her along, but when she reaches the door, she pulls away, slipping to the opposite side, facing me now.

I take a step forward so I can peek inside and a smile breaks free.

Blonde curls perfectly placed on the top of her head, little Zoey sits on the floor, a small, stuffed train in one hand, sippy cup in the other. Our dad sitting across from her with a stuffed animal of his own in his hand, and damn if it doesn't settle something inside me even more than my time away with Raven did.

My eyes roam around the room, taking in the white walls and the mural painted across them. Purple flowers, different shapes and sizes.

My stare slices to Raven's hair, and the fresh purple stripes she had put in while we were away.

Cap steps in the room which causes Zoey's head to snap our way, her little curls bouncing forward and hitting against her cheek.

She pushes to her feet and slowly walks toward us, pausing when she reaches Cap's leg and wrapping her little hand around it.

Our dad stands behind them.

"Can you say hi, Zoey."

Zoey hides one eye behind his pant leg, lifting her hand to wave, but then she spots Raven and her eyes light up. She runs to the door, stopping right in front of her.

"Hi!"

Raven swallows. "Hi," she breathes.

"I waited fuh you." Zoey smiles.

Raven's brows drop, but she smiles. "You did?" she asks quietly.

Zoey nods, spins on her heels and runs back in her room.

She grabs something from the little desk, hiding it behind her and runs back.

Raven looks to Captain with a small frown but slowly lowers to her knees, sitting back on her feet in front of Zoey.

Zoey smiles wide and brings a small crown from around her back, placing it on Raven's head.

It starts to slip, so Raven quickly catches it, holding it there. She smiles at Zoey.

Zoey reaches out and touches the purple of Raven's hair and Raven pulls her lips in.

"You know," Zoey says. "I like puple."

A small laugh leaves Raven. "Yeah." She nods. "I did know that Zoey."

Zoey smiles and runs back to Captain, who lifts her when she puts her arms up, and the two move farther in her room, Royce right behind them.

Raven, still on the floor, brings her eyes to me.

The crown slides down a little more but stays rooted in her hair.

I bend at the knees, running my fingers over the same strand of hair Zoey did.

She smirks, shrugging a shoulder. "A crooked crown is still a crown, right?"

A laugh flies from me and she stands, pulling me with her.

"Get in there. Play with your niece and your brothers," she whispers against my lips.

"What will you be doing?"

"Handling some business, then waiting for you in my new bed downstairs."

"Our bed."

She laughs and pushes me into the room. "Go."

I go with ease.

379

Raven

I MAKE MY WAY DOWN THE STAIRS AND OUT THE FRONT DOOR.

Victoria had said she wasn't comfortable officially moving in here without me, even though I'd secretly asked Rolland to also get a room ready for her, so she decided to stay at the girls' Bray house until I got back. I called as we were pulling in, but Maybell said she was in the shower, and she'd let her know to head this way when she got out.

I can't wait to do absolutely nothing other than kick back with everyone tonight, but first things first.

I smirk as Bass pulls up in the old school muscle car he scored after Leo smashed his other one in. "You thinking 'bout souping that baby up?"

"Eventually, yeah." He grins, leans against his car, and crosses one foot over the other.

I hold out an envelope, and slowly he takes it and tears it open.

His eyes fly to mine. "Fuck you doin', Rae?"

"You don't belong here, Bass."

He smacks the paper against his thigh.

"You're not a hands man, or security, or anything else that you could be here. You can never lead this place, but you don't belong behind anyone either."

"You banishing me, *Mrs. Brayshaw?*" he teases, but he can't hide the unease in his tone.

"If I have to get you to go, yeah."

He licks his lips, looks to the check again, then back to me. "This is *a lot* of money."

"It's every single cent of Donley Graven's money."

His brows jump.

"I talked to Victoria about it weeks ago, she wants none of

it. Left it in my hands, and I want it in yours," I tell him. "Take it, Bishop. Go, head over to Southern Cali, find a kingdom in need of a king, and become one. You've got it in you."

He looks out across the orchard, and after a moment, blows out a long hard breath. His eyes come back to mine and a slow smirk stretches across his lips.

"I think I know just the place."

"It's the rich bitch who only dates rich boys, right?"

He busts up laughing but doesn't answer, moving forward for a hug instead.

He pulls back just as quick, eyeing me. "Thank you, Raven."

"Get out of my town, Bishop," I tease, adding, "But come back if you ever need a Brayshaw at your back."

"How 'bout at my side?"

I wink, making him laugh.

He walks backward to his door, not taking his eyes off me. He smirks. "Later, Raven Carver."

"See ya, Bass Bishop."

With one more deep breath and one more look at the check, he slides in, backs out and then he's gone, and so is the weight of the blood money he took with him.

A heavy sigh leaves me and not a second later, Maddoc's chest hits my back. I smile, leaning my head against it.

"Couldn't stay away, Big Man?"

"Never."

I laugh, turning my head so he can meet my lips.

Heavy footsteps and loud laughter float from the door, and we turn just in time to see Royce run down the steps. Rolland walks out behind him, Zoey in his arms but he quickly puts her on her feet.

She runs to the edge of the porch, jumping into Royce's open arms. He sets her down and she turns toward Cap who softly tosses her a little basketball.

She catches it and off she runs.

Maddoc swiftly kisses my cheek, then jogs for his brothers.

Royce jumps on Cap's back playfully, making the other two laugh as he slips off, falling onto his ass, but jumps up just as quick.

They smile at each other, tethering their arms around one another's shoulders and off they go, following the little blonde who has no idea how deep they love her, and how far they'll go to protect her.

Rolland looks my way, a smile I've never seen from him taking over every inch of his face, and a heavy exhale leaves me as he turns and heads back in the house.

The crunch of gravel sounds behind me and I spin to find Maybell walking up, an ease on her face she doesn't usually show.

"You made it home."

I look to the house, nodding as I move my eyes back to hers. "I did."

She steps up, and her eyes grow thoughtful. She pulls a small journal from behind her, holding it close to her chest.

I look from it to her with a frown.

She holds it out, and slowly I take it.

"Your mother's," she whispers.

My chest grows tight with uncertainty.

"The last entry was the day she found out she was pregnant with you. I thought you might like to read it. Maybe the rest too," she whispers. "Get to know the real her."

"There's no such thing as the real someone, Maybell," I breathe. "There's only who we were and what we become."

"That's true, child. No matter." She nods her head at the notebook. "It belongs in your hands, not mine. You don't have to read it, but maybe one day you'll want to."

I swallow, nodding. "Yeah, maybe."

She smiles, steps in for a hug, then turns and heads back for the Bray house.

I look to the expensive leather, running my fingers across the impression on the cover, a deep crease forming between my brows.

Brayshaw Wolves...

My head snaps around, but Maybell is already to the treeline.

I look back to the item.

On the ride to the cabins, the night before the wedding, the boys told me about the story Maybell shared with Maddoc when he was young. A story about how a raven only mates once, finds a home and protects it all her life, leading her wolves along the way.

I made them Google the raven and the wolves, and it turned out it wasn't just some bedtime story spun with hidden meaning, it was true. It was nature working in weird ways.

It was inevitable.

According to them, Maybell believes my mother named me Raven on purpose, for this reason. To lead me home. To lead me to them.

I wouldn't go that far.

"Raven!"

I look to Captain when he calls my name, nodding when he waves me over.

He winks, turning his attention to the others.

My eyes move across each one and I pull in a lungful of air.

Three brothers, none related by blood, all by choice.

Smiling, happy, ready to take on the world.

And we will.

Together, we'll reign all of Brayshaw.

Epilogue

VICTORIA

THE KNUCKLE AGAINST THE DOOR FRAME HAS MY EYES POPPING open.

Maybell stands there, the frown on her face growing the farther into the room she steps. She taps the foot of my room-mate's bed. "Nira, why don't you take a walk?"

Nira looks from her to me, rolls her eyes and walks out.

Maybell scoffs as she drops beside me. "All these girls, they'll be the death of me."

"Yeah, but would you walk away if you could?"

"Oh, trust me, child." She grins. "I could go if I wanted, but to answer your question, no. I wouldn't." She's quiet a second before adding, "Would like to help care for the next generation, though, while I've still got it in me."

Next generation.

Right.

I swallow, looking to her.

"You put it off long enough, girl." Her eyes grow serious,

but there's still a softness in them I've only just discovered. "Go on, Tor. The sooner it happens, the sooner it's out."

"The sooner they send me packing."

"The *faster* they can forgive," she counters.

A humorless laugh escapes and I drop my head back to look at the ceiling. "Uh-huh, yeah." I force myself to my feet. "'Cause they're known to forgive outsiders."

"You're not an outsider."

"I'm not her, either." I look to Maybell. "I might not be *just* the blonde from the group home anymore, but I'm not her. They don't... they won't understand."

"She will," Maybell says. "And slowly, they'll follow."

"What if she doesn't?"

Maybell stands, stepping right in front of me. "Then you make her."

Make her. Uh-huh.

'Cause people are able to make her do things.

Yeah right.

With a deep breath, I step into the hall, out the front door and onto the dirt path that leads to the Brayshaw mansion.

The last few weeks, I've left for school earlier than necessary, and locked myself in the Bray house the second I get back, all to avoid the Brayshaws who I knew were home.

Mostly Captain.

Okay, only Captain. I didn't really care if I ran into Royce. Who knows, he might not even acknowledge me without one of them at his side, not that I had to worry about it. Neither of them has been to school since before Captain was shot.

So, I've reverted back to watching, hiding in plain sight, like before.

But Raven is home now, and she's very unlike Captain. Captain is subtle when he looks for me as he drives by, or at least that's what I like to think he's doing when his eyes scan the yard as he passes the girls' home. Raven, though, makes sure she sees me even if it means dragging my ass out the door herself.

My cheeks fill with air as I attempt to calm my nerves.

Out of everything – knowing who attacked Raven, being there when it happened, the truth about Donley, Ravina, and everything in between – this is where my real fear lies.

This is the part I've dreaded the most, them coming home.

It's not that I don't want to see her, because I do, but it's complicated.

"Standing in the shadows again?"

I yelp, spinning around with my hand at my chest.

My eyes shoot wide, my heartbeat erratic.

Captain.

He steps closer.

My spine straightens, and I move back until my shoulder blades meet a tree, allowing no room for an escape if I needed one.

"Hi," I manage to force out.

The corner of his mouth lifts slowly, his stare roaming across my face. "Hi. Why you hiding in my orchards?"

"Maybell told me Raven was home."

He nods, his face pinching in humor. "She tell you this today, or a week ago?"

"What?" I croak.

Captain chuckles, and then his chest pushes against mine. "You thought I didn't notice?" he whispers. "That I'd let you keep hiding in the shadows, watching?"

Shit.

Captain's eyes fall to my lips when my tongue sneaks out to wet them.

"You've been avoiding me," he says. "Why?"

"I haven't."

"You're lying."

"Captain," I whisper, quickly cutting off when he jerks closer, his lips now only a breath away from mine.

"You laid in my bed, touched me in your sleep," he rasps, the blue in his eyes darkening. "Dreamt out loud." A slow smirk appears. "That was my favorite part."

I swallow, my body growing lax against the tree.

I should push him away.

"This is the part where you tell me to kiss you, sleeping beauty."

I frown, my hands flying to his chest to shove, but my body betrays me, my hands not doing as I ask and instead pulling him closer.

His lips hit mine and I forget how wrong it is, my mouth opening when his tongue demands it. His teeth lightly scrape my bottom lip, forcing a low groan from him, and he pulls back before even getting started.

Captain chuckles, tilting his head to the side. "I knew it," he rasps.

"Knew what?"

"You want me," he says, drawing back, but only by an inch, and his knuckles skim down my neck. "Same way I want you." His eyes find mine again. "Say it."

Reality slams back into place and I tense.

What did I just do?

We've had a simmering attraction for weeks, months even. He's never said it, but I catch him staring, not that he tries to hide it. We've talked, but not about anything outside of what we've needed to. We've hung out, but never alone, except for the night Raven married Maddoc.

Neither of us could sleep, and we both ended up out on the balcony looking up at the stars. It was comfortable, the silence we sat in, so when he said he was going to watch a movie, I took that as an invitation and followed him to his room.

I did sleep in his bed.

I *didn't* realize I touched him, and while I have been known to talk in my sleep, he never mentioned it. Not that he had a chance.

Like he said, I'd been avoiding him, but not for the reasons he's thinking.

I swallow, shaking my head as I answer his question in a copout way.

"I hardly know you," I admit. "And you don't know me at all."

"But you want to know me, like I need to know you."

My skin heats at his words.

Like he needs...

"You won't like what you find."

"I like enough already, and I'm not asking you to tell me all your secrets, even though you already know about my biggest one."

Fuck.

"You've been out here every day, beauty. You've seen her, my daughter."

My jaw clenches tight and I consider lying for the hell of it, but he saw me, right?

I give a jerky nod.

"You want to meet her?"

My brows slam together, the hope in his eyes causing my stomach to grow tight.

He's gonna hate me.

"Come on." He steps back, while I remain frozen in place. "I was only supposed to be grabbing her ball from my car. Let's not make her come looking for me."

"Too. Fucking. late." Raven's chuckled words float from behind me and I tense. "We found you."

We? Oh no.

"Daddy!"

No, no, no.

389

Not like this.

Captain's eyes instantly cut behind me and he backs up even more, beaming at the little girl I know is just behind me.

He bends down, and as he does, two more sets of footsteps grow closer.

They're all here.

"Come here, Zo." He crooks his finger at her. "Come meet our friend."

My chest starts to ache, moisture building in my eyes and I force a deep breath.

I catch Raven's eyes a moment and she frowns at my demeanor.

She takes a half step toward me, but then Zoey bursts past her and her eyes follow the little blonde who throws herself against her daddy's chest. "Find you, find you!" She laughs.

Cap's smile bounces to me, but his eyes tighten at the sight. He keeps his grin on for Zoey, reluctantly pulling his eyes back to her.

"Zoey." He spins her around, and her eyes hit mine. "This is—"

Her eyes widen with her smile and she tugs free from him, running right for me.

I drop to my knees quickly and she wraps her little arms around my neck.

"Rora!"

I hug her back, my eyes rising to Cap as he pushes to his feet, in slow, methodical movements.

Royce and Maddoc step closer, while Raven stands frozen, eyes stuck on me.

Zoey pulls back, smiling at me. "I miss you, Rora!"

I swallow, forcing a smile, while tension threatens to knock me over. "I miss you, too, ZoZo."

She laughs and pulls away.

"Hey, Zoey Bear," Royce calls her. "Let's go get some ice cream, huh?"

"Ice cream!" she shouts and runs away, but not before pausing and running back to rub her nose across mine. "Eskimo kisses!"

I force the tears in my eyes to stay right where they are. "And butterfly hugs."

She laughs and runs away. "So much, Rora!"

So much, ZoZo.

Captain's jaw clenches and he takes a step back.

My hands lift and slowly, I push to stand, my eyes bouncing between the three.

Maddoc's glare is locked on me, while Raven continues to look from where Zoey ran off and back.

Cap though, he doesn't look away. His eyes turn to glaciers, the sharp edges of his jaw growing more profound as he drops his chin closer to his chest.

"I'm sorry," I whisper, looking between the two. "There was no right time to tell."

"My daughter knows who you are," Captain rumbles. "How?"

I look to Raven and back to him. "Maria," I whisper. "She's my mother."

Raven's brows snap together. "You knew?"

"I told you." My face contorts. "Discovering secrets was my purpose, remember?"

"How long," Captain snaps.

My eyes snap his way.

When I don't respond he pushes closer.

"How. Long. Have you known about her?" he forces past clenched teeth.

I swallow, admitting, "Long before you."

You'd think I slapped him. I'd go as far as to say he was

hoping for a different answer, that maybe there was one that wouldn't build a wall between us, not that an *us* existed.

"What does *so much* mean?" he asks, now completely detached, no emotion to be found, not even anger.

"Exactly what you think," I whisper. "It's... how she tells me she..." I trail off, unable to say it.

It's how she tells me she loves me.

She's the only person that ever has.

"I'm sorry," I tell them, my shoulders falling. "I don't know what else to say." I turn to Raven. "Don't hate me, please. I'll go, I won't bother you guys." My eyes cut to Captain and back to her. "But just... don't hate me."

"Go," Raven says, her eyes slicing to Captain. Something passes between them before she looks back to me. "And make it quick, Victoria."

With a slight nod and a heavy heart, I back away, unable to meet Captain's eyes. "I expected this, my bags are already packed," I admit. "I'll only be minutes."

I get a few feet before Captain says, "Well in that case, we'll send someone to get them."

My eyes cut over my shoulder, and I frown.

"You'll be moved in, in less than an hour," Raven tells me as she reaches for Maddoc's hand.

I spin to face them once more. "You want me to stay?"

She looks from Cap to me. "I'm telling you to."

Maddoc and Captain share a look, and then he and Raven walk away, leaving me and Captain alone.

"I'm sorry, Cap—"

"Don't," he cuts me off, stepping into my face, but I don't cower.

He looks ready to say something, but I couldn't guess as to what. His eyes give nothing. The second the ice within them starts to thaw he jerks away, stepping from the trees before turning to look at me once more.

"Welcome home, beauty." He spreads his arms out wide, the mansion taunting me in the distance behind him. "Might wanna sleep with one eye open."

My forehead tightens as my pulse spikes.

Does this make me the enemy?

The tautness of his eyes screams the answer is no, he doesn't want me to be.

Still, in the next moment, I consider running, disappearing, only the thought is gone as soon as it hits, because the cost of leaving this place is too high.

I'd lose everything I never had and always wanted.

I'd risk having the only people who'd ever made me feel like being myself was enough hating me forever. Allowing them to push me away when I've only just grown closer?

I don't fucking think so.

They pulled me from my hiding places, and I'm glad.

I'm tired of dark corners, tired of the background.

Tired of losing before I've even won.

Raven is my sister; this is my new home.

I'm ready to fight for everything that comes with it.

If I'm lucky, a blonde Brayshaw included.

Quick Note From The Author

Deep breath...and exhale!
Guuyss!!! We made it through!
Never in a million years did I imagine this world would take ours by storm. You guys have been so amazing, so down for this crew, it blows my mind! THANK YOU so much for coming back for more!
I am so so SO sad Maddoc and Raven's ride is over, but I leave them with a smile because their little life is only beginning! This isn't to say we won't see them again, but I can promise you this...their HEA is FOREVER!!
WHAT NOW???
Read **BE MY BRAYSHAW,** Captain's book, **TODAY**, and get even **MORE** of the gang!! Find it on Amazon today!

Want to be notified about future books of mine? Sign up for my Newsletter @ www.meaganbrandy.com

Stay Connected

Purchase EXCULSIVE Brayshaw merchandise here:
https://www.teepublic.com/user/meaganbrandy

Website https://geni.us/BMMBSITE
Newsletter https://geni.us/BMMBNL
Amazon https://geni.us/BMMBA
Instagram https://geni.us/BMMBIG
Facebook https://geni.us/BMMBFP
Twitter https://geni.us/BMMBT
Pinterest https://geni.us/BMMBP
Bookbub https://geni.us/BMMBB
Readers Group https://geni.us/BMMBFG
Goodreads https://geni.us/BMMBGR

More by Meagan Brandy

FAKE IT 'TIL YOU BREAK IT

Fake.

That's what we are.

That's what we agreed to be.

So why does it feel so real?

I thought it would have been harder, convincing everyone our school's star receiver was mine and mine alone, but I was wrong.

We played our parts so well that the lines between us began to blur until they disappeared completely.

The thing about pretending, though, someone's always better at it, and by the time I realized my mistake, there was no going back.

I fell for our lie.

And then everything fell apart.

It turned out he and I were never playing the same game.

He didn't have to break me to win.
But he did it anyway.

READ TODAY: https://geni.us/FITYBIBM

FUMBLED HEARTS:

He's the persistent playboy who refuses to walk away. I'm the impassive new girl with nothing left to give.
Things are about to get complicated...

After months of refusing, I finally agreed to make the move to Alrick Falls. My family thought it was best - that a new scene would be good for me—and I was sick of having the same conversation.
So here I am, and the plan is simple. Smile through each day and avoid her at all costs.
It's perfect.

Until the cocky quarterback comes into play.

The last thing I want is his crooked grin and dark brown eyes focused on me.
Yet here he is, constantly in my space, pushing me, daring me to care. Telling me what I think and feel, as if he knows.
He doesn't know anything. And I plan to keep it that way.

WRONG FOR ME:

They say to keep your enemies close, but 'they' never had to deal with the likes of Alec Daniels, the broody bad boy next door who loved to make my life a living nightmare...up until the day he disappeared.

See, Alec was a thief.

He stole my happy.
    My sanity.
    My first kiss.

I told myself I was glad the day he went away, and I'm reminded of why not five minutes after his sudden and unexpected return.

Now he stands before me with a heavy glare and hard body.
    But those greedy green eyes, they're darker than I remember, and brimming with a secret...

A secret I didn't discover until it was far too late.

Because this time, he didn't steal a simple kiss.
    This time... Alec Daniels stole my all.

Find these titles here: https://geni.us/BMMBSITE

Playlist

Curve – SoMo
Close To Me – Ellie Goulding
Burn It To The Ground – Nickelback
All Around Me – Flyleaf
Addicted – Saving Abel
Nightmare – Halsey
Alone – I Prevail
You Should See me in a Crown – Billie Eilish
Us – Carlie Hanson
My Demons – Starset
So Far Away – Staind
Queen – Loren Gray
Last Hurrah – Bebe Rexha
Take it All – Pop Evil
Crown – Samila Cabello
Hear Me Now – Bad Wolves
Castle – Halsey
You Made Me Do It – Tommee Profit
Cross Me – Ed Sheeran

Born For Greatness – Papa Roach
Him and I – G-Eazy, Halsey

Acknowledgments

First, my **family** for going on this journey with me! Without the support from home, I wouldn't be able to do what I love! To the man and our boys, you guys are the driving force behind me. Mom, Karen, Aunt Lisa, and everyone who reads even when it makes me never want to face you again (LOL). I love you for it!

Melissa Teo. My friend, PA, and all the other things. My bish. No words. Your help is endless. Your honesty invaluable. Your friendship irreplaceable. Thank you.

Ellie. Thank you to my editor for rocking this baby out and on an everchanging timeline! Thank you!

Danielle, my publicist! Thank you so very much for all your guidance and support! No matter the concern or question I may have, you are there with a solution or new step to be taken. I am so happy to have you on my team!

Serena and Veronica, my #teammeagan girls! You guys rock! Thank you for being by my side and helping make this process that much smoother! You're amazing.

STREET TEAM! OMG! You guys are insane! Beyond

supportive and always go the extra mile. I am so grateful you all jumped on this wild ride with me!

Stefanie and Kelli! Once again, we did it! Our Alpha/beta team is so solid, I can't imagine giving my roughest versions to anyone else! You girls understand my vision like no one else, and for that I am so grateful. Not everyone reads the same story, but you guys can somehow sense what I'm going for and don't stop until it get there! Thank you!

Sarah! I can't even! With 100% certainty I tell you that this series would not be what it is without you. Not even close. You took my words, felt them in your bones and forced me to give you more. Every. Single. Time. And holy crap did the push pay off! This first part of the Brayshaw series, Maddoc and Raven's story, went from a hard journey to an EPIC fudging ride, and you my *I'll never let you leave me* friend, are the reason behind that!

To my **review team**, I'm so thankful I can give you whatever my author heart requires and you're up for it! It means so much to have your support!

Monica! My writing partner! Girl, HOW DID WE PULL THIS OFF? Lol. Monica and I started out most recent books at the same time and on impossible deadlines, but we did it! Without her being at the same pace, and writing stages as me, I don't know if I would have made it happen on time! Let's do it again, girl!

Bloggers and Bookstagrammers, thank you for participating and helping spread the word! I hope you love the conclusion to Maddoc and Raven's story, and are here for more from the Brayshaw series!

And to **my readers,** holy crap!!! You guys are ride or die for this crew and I love it so much!! I never imagines you'd feel them like I do, but OMG guys! YOU SO DO! I hope you loved Reign of Brayshaw and trust me when I say there is still more to come!! I hope you're here for it!

About the Author

USA Today and Wall Street Journal bestselling author, Meagan Brandy, writes New Adult romance books with a twist. She's is a candy crazed, jukebox junkie who tends to speak in lyrics. Born and raised in California, she is a married mother of three crazy boys who keep her bouncing from one sports field to another, depending on the season, and she wouldn't have it any other way. Starbucks is her best friend and words are her sanity.

9 781088 029299